Fallen
KINGDOM

THE COMPLETE DUET

USA TODAY BESTSELLING AUTHOR
RACHEL LEIGH

PART I

HIS HOLLOW HEART

PROLOGUE

ELEVEN YEARS OLD

Bella

COLORS BOUNCE off the walls in a prism, as the light catches the crystal suncatcher hanging in the window. I blink a couple of times, adjusting my eyes to the brightness. Rolling over to my side, I see the empty bed next to me. I sit up abruptly and notice all of the beds are empty. Each one made perfectly. An old comforter tucked around every corner of the twin-size mattresses. One flat pillow lying centered at the top of each bed.

The sudden realization that today is *the day* has me flinging off my blanket. My bare feet hit the old wooden floorboards that creak as I hurry over to my armoire closet.

Pulling down my pink poufy dress—my only dress—I hold it out and cringe upon inspection. It'll have to do. Even if it has been worn so many times that the lace on the hem now hangs in stray strands. The white flowers now resemble more of a crescent moon, and the hole in the armpit reminds me not to raise my left hand today.

I often find myself gawking at Lucy, the neighbor girl, who is the same age as me. She always wears the most beautiful dresses. Rainbow colors, with sparkling gems sewn around the waistline. Cal always makes me feel better by saying, "*You don't want to be like those people. They wear their happiness on the outside, they don't feel it where it counts.*" But there is one dress Lucy wears often. It's baby pink with a floral lace overlay. She looks like a princess when she wears it, and every time she does, I watch her from across the yard and daydream that it's me. Living her life, hugging her parents. Cal thinks it's ridiculous, but there's not much that isn't ridiculous to him. Yet, he always has a way of helping me see the bigger picture. No matter what happens, I hope I never lose myself in *things.*

Cal told me that one day he was going to buy me all the dresses in the world, just to prove to me they don't hold my beauty.

After I'm all dressed and feeling content with my appearance, I brush my teeth in the shared bathroom and run my fingers through my cedar-brown curls, getting them stuck at the end and ripping through the matted mess.

Quiet baby steps lead me to the top of the staircase as I listen to see if they're here yet. The laughter of the other kids leads me to believe that I didn't miss them. If I had, it would be quiet. There would be tears. And, there is no way that Callum would have left, nor let them leave without waking me first. We made a pact, after all.

Part of our deal was that we'd do whatever it takes to stay together. If he is chosen and I'm not, he said he'd moon the visitors just so they didn't pick him and if that didn't work, he'd kick the guy in the balls. I told him I'd simply scream at the top of my lungs until they no longer wanted me. I mean, it's a solid plan. No one wants to adopt brats.

Callum and I came to The Webster House together four years ago. I was only seven years old; he was three years older. We've watched so many potential parents come and go during our time here, that we'd almost given up hope.

Only kids come to The Webster House—no babies. The youngest being Elizabeth, or Bibs as we call her. She's eight now, and I worry that she will still have many more years here. Everyone wants a baby or a toddler. Someone they can mold and hear their first words of "mom" or "dad." I'm not sure I could ever refer to another with that title. Especially since my only knowledge of a mom is someone who leaves you alone to raise yourself, so she can drink and do drugs, even at the tender age of four years old. Dads are just something I've read about as a fictional entity.

I often fantasize about having one. He would be tall, with dark hair, and muscular arms that he would sweep me up in as he plants kisses all over my rosy cheeks. He'd twirl me around in a brand-new baby pink dress as the bottom half catches the wind. I'd be his little girl.

Only, time is passing quickly. My days of being a little girl are numbered. So are the years I have left to build a solid relationship with new parents. Today is likely my last chance. Today, we welcome a family who is looking for a son and a daughter. I've heard through the cracks in the walls that they do not want babies or toddlers. They want older kids and they are ready and willing to provide them with a loving home.

Today is the day that Callum and I begin to live—really live. Public school, dances, sports, a life outside of these walls. I've always wanted to take piano lessons. I've learned a little by teaching myself on the old piano in the dining hall. It's missing a few keys, but it's better than nothing.

Tonight, we will celebrate the first day of the rest of our lives. Maybe even with blueberry pie—our favorite.

"Psst." I hear from down the hall.

I look left, and right, to be sure that the coast is clear. Callum and I have our own secret hiding space. We call it a secret, but everyone knows about it. They just know not to enter. Not only is there a big sign that reads "Keep Out OR ELSE" on the front of the knee-wall door, Callum also uses threats and punishment for all who enter.

Occasionally, we let Mark and Layla in, since they are the same age as us, but they've both proven to be tattle-tales and have shared some of the secrets meant to stay inside the small, squared space. For instance, when Callum broke Mr. Beckham's window last fall with a curveball. We made a pact that we'd take his wrongdoing to the grave. That was until Mrs. Webster told us that if no one comes forward then we had to spend the entire weekend in our rooms. Mark and Layla broke the pact. They never admitted it, but we knew.

"What are you doing?" I drag my eyes up and down the hall to be sure no one is out here. When I'm sure the coast is clear, I duck my head and enter the crawl space. "I thought our parents were on their way."

That's what we call them. *Our parents.* Because, we just know that they will choose us. We've had this planned ever since we learned of their visit over a month ago.

Callum sweeps the air with his hand and walks over to the petite dormer window. He presses his palms against the wall on each side. "They're late."

I can immediately tell by his tone that he's upset.

"They're still coming, though, right?" I walk to his side, taking notice of his gray slacks that are far too short. His long-sleeved button-up shirt is tucked only in the front and missing a middle button. A pain stabs at my chest. "Cal, tell me they're coming."

He shrugs his shoulders, then kicks at the wall. Hard, loud, and frightening. I wince at the sudden shock of his outrage. Most of the kids here are scared of Callum. He's a bit rough around the edges. I've seen his heart, though. He has one in there; he just doesn't share it with the world. In a way, it makes me feel privileged. Everyone else gets bitterness and a sour attitude; I get the sweet stuff.

In one swift motion, Callum spins around. "Bella," he grips my shoulders, "promise me, again. Promise me that you will never leave me."

My body tenses under his aggressive hold. My heart's racing, palm's sweating. Something is wrong. "Cal, what's this about? What happened?"

At first, Callum was like the big brother I never had. The older we get, though, the more grateful I am that he *isn't* my brother. The last couple of months I've seen him in a different light. When he walks into a room, butterflies free-fly through my stomach and my heart rate excels. I continuously shake off the notion that I could possibly have a crush on my best friend, because this is the same boy who has slept in my bed countless nights due to his recurring nightmares. We're friends. Nothing more. Nothing less.

It's also the same boy who beat up Mr. Beckham's preppy fourteen-year-old son, Trent, because he lifted my skirt once. He literally beat him to a pulp. Blood painted the Beckhams' well-manicured lawn a dark shade of red.

"I just need to hear you say it. Tell me I'll always have you." He pulls me into his chest, wrapping his arms around my head in a gentle, yet abrasive hold. Our hearts beat in sync. Rapid and unruly. Shattered pieces meant to mend together. But, I can feel him slipping away, even as he holds me so tightly.

"What did you do?" I know this can't be good. Callum is always getting in trouble, and if he did something to mess this day up, so help me...I can't even think about it.

Everything is fine. We're minutes away from our new life.

"I screwed up. I really screwed up this time." He pulls away and looks me in the eye. "I've always got you, right?" The desperation in his voice slices through my happiness. An uncertainty for our future. The burden of a decision that decides our fate.

The slamming of a car door has us both back at the window. "They're here." His eyes close, then open slowly. "I'm gonna need that promise now, Bella."

I don't even think. I just feed him the words that he craves. "I promise, Cal. Until kingdom come. It's you and me. Always."

1

TWELVE YEARS LATER

Bella

WITH THE LIFE I know behind me, I look over my shoulder, and my heart splinters in two. A large sign stares back at me, *Thank you for riding with Falcon Ferry*. It slowly disappears into the abyss as the ferry leaves the dock.

Destination: Elizabeth Islands

My hand rests on my luggage bag. One bag with everything I should need for the next six months. A single tear drops down my cheek when I pull the image from memory of Mom and Dad waving goodbye from the driveway hours ago. I brush the dampness away with the back of my hand and swallow hard, anxiety overwhelming me.

I've never even left the state without them. When it came time to choose a school, my heart longed to accept the offer in the Piano Department at Juilliard, but the miles between here and there seemed too long. Not to mention, I couldn't afford it. There was a scholarship, if I really wanted to go, but how could I when I had so much lost time with my family to make up for? So, I decided on an interior design degree at a local university. Yet, here I am—leaving. Six months secluded from civilization.

My parents are empty nesters now. Mark is away at law school in New York, and I doubt he'll ever move back to our hometown in Rhode Island.

This temporary move is a good thing, I keep reminding myself. I never would have imagined that I would be leaving our small town and moving eight hours away. But, this is an offer that anyone in their right mind would take. I don't claim to always be in the right mindset, but that's exactly what I did. I jumped on it.

With little time to prepare, I didn't even make a list of everything I needed to bring. Just threw some clothes into a suitcase and left the next morning. Normally I would have sat on it for days, weeks maybe. I have no idea why the president of Ellis Empire would want little old me working on the design of one of his exclusive hotels, but he does. So here I am, starting a new chapter in my life, one I never even knew I wanted, but one I can't wait to begin.

A phone call interrupts Selena Gomez's voice through the speakers of my earbuds. I take the call with a chuckle, "I haven't even hit the interstate."

"Just turn around, babe. It's not too late to change your mind."

Taking a deep breath, I say what needs to be said, "This is going to be good—for both of us. I promise."

I've been with the same guy, on and off, for the last three years. We've hit so many bumps in the road that I barely even notice them anymore. We've come to the point in our lives where I think we are headed in separate directions, and I'm not sure that what we have is strong enough to survive the pull. He proposed last week, and I still haven't given him an answer, even if deep down, I know what it will be.

"When you get tired of this job, come home. I've told you, you don't need to work. Let me take care of you."

Holding my breath, I count to five in my head. *One. Two. Three. Four. Five.* "We've been over this, Trent. I need my independence. I have to go, we're hitting rough waters. Talk soon." I end the call and blow out an exasperated breath.

I'm leaving a lot behind, but if things go as planned, I'll be finding something even better—myself. My own identity. With zero connections on the island, my past doesn't have to follow me.

"Excuse me, miss?"

My eyes flutter open as someone shakes my shoulder. Smacking my lips together, I hope I wasn't drooling. I pull out my earbuds and set them in my lap, then look up at the big burly guy in front of me. "I'm sorry, what?"

He doesn't even smile, just stands there with a scorned look on his face. "We've docked. You may exit the boat now."

"Wow. That was fast." I drop my earbuds into my purse, along with my phone, and grab the handle of my suitcase. "Thank you very much." I smile politely at the asshole.

Dragging my suitcase behind me while Mr. Grumpy watches, I make my way down the ramp.

Surprisingly, there aren't many people. I've got no idea where I'm going from here, but I was told there'd be a gentleman waiting to transport me to the hotel where I'll be staying.

My eyes sweep the small crowd and I spot him. A tall, lanky man holding a white piece of paper that reads Isabella Jenkins. Seeing it makes this feel all the more official.

Here we go. I'm off to an island in the middle of nowhere with choppy cell service, no car, and strangers as co-workers. It's intimidating as hell, being the new girl at any job, but this isn't just any job. It's *the* job.

I approach the man with heightened nerves. There's still time to back out, but if I take this boat ride, it's pretty much written in stone. Sure, I can leave if I want. But, that would make me a quitter and I'm not known to quit.

He lifts his chin from me, then looks down at the sign with questioning eyes. I give him a nod and he smiles. Breathing out a sigh of relief that he's not as much of a browbeat as the guy on the boat, I greet him. "You must be my ride out of here."

"And you must be Isabella?"

"That would be me."

"I'm Jeffery, and I'll be your escort. Here," he takes the handle of my suitcase, "allow me."

"Thank you," I tell him as I walk next to him, down the waterfront sidewalk.

Jeffery looks at me and quirks a brow. "Are you excited about your stay at Cori Cove?"

"Nervous is a better word. It's a big change."

"I can imagine. Working for Mr. Ellis does sound quite nerve-wracking."

Gee. Thanks for the encouragement. "You don't work for him, then?"

"Not quite. Mr. Ellis doesn't get many guests on his island, but when he does, I escort them from the docks. I'm not on his payroll, though."

"Interesting." Now I'm curious how many people will be working at the hotel. Jeffery refers to them as guests, but the hotel isn't set to open until next year. From my understanding, there's a lot to be done. Positioned all over the world, Ellis Empire is known for their gorgeous castle-like hotel chain.

Mr. Ellis, who is a billionaire, purchases these very old castles—most of which are on private islands—completely guts them and turns them into these magical kingdoms. A one-night stay at one of his hotels is said to cost around two-thousand dollars, depending on the location.

Jeffrey waves his hand, gesturing me toward a tiny little boat that actually resembles more of a raft with a motor. "After you, Ms. Isabella."

I hesitate, unsure if I'm ready to risk my life. "Is this...safe?"

Jeffrey laughs at my hesitancy. "Of course it is. I've been doing this for twenty years. You're in good hands, dear."

His warm smile calms my nerves slightly as I take his hand and allow him to help me step into the boat. With only three seats, it's quite small. I suppose something larger isn't needed, since it's just me taking this trip.

"How long is the ride?" I ask him, hoping that it's not too far.

"A short ten minutes."

Okay. I can do ten minutes.

I've never been a fan of water. Don't care much for swimming. Went on a boat once with my parents and Mark and threw up all over the side of it. I prefer that my feet stay on solid ground, especially since I'm somewhat of a ditz and tend to do myself more harm than good.

Jeffrey looks over his shoulder. "Ready?"

Biting hard on my bottom lip, I nod as the motor purrs to life.

What starts off as a slow tug, quickly turns into us skating over the water at full speed. It looks as if we're driving straight into the fire glow of the sunset. My hair catches in the wind as I hold tightly to my suitcase. My heart is settling in my stomach, but the breathtaking view calms me slightly.

A few minutes pass and we start to slow down. I look past Jeffery at the immaculate structure in front of us. "Is this where we're going?"

Jeffery looks over his shoulder with a crooked smile. "Welcome to Cori Cove, Ms. Jenkins. One hundred private acres surrounded by water with a castle sitting as the heart of the island. Also known as your home for the next six months, or longer, if you decide to never leave."

"Oh, I doubt I'll stay forever. Though, I might not mind this short escape from civilization."

2

WE COME to a stop at a long dock that stretches out over the water. There's a small tin boat without paddles, but that seems to be the only way off the island, aside from public transport. Jeffrey steps onto the dock and offers me his hand.

I smile warmly. "Well, thank you for the ride." Jeffery is a stranger that I've known all of thirty minutes, and I can't help but feel like he's my last encounter with another person, outside of Cori Cove, for a very long time.

"Up the dock, follow the steppingstones and you'll see the main doors. Mr. Ellis is expecting you." Jeffery checks me with a smile. "See you in six months, Ms. Isabella."

I just stand there. Watching as he pulls away. The little orange boat becomes nothing more than a speck in the wide-open water. Once it's faded from view, I turn around and look up at the castle staring back at me.

Made of stone and ashlar over a century ago, the castle stands tall and fierce. Likely weathered by storms and neglect, its wear only adds to its beauty. The turret on the very top of the ʿcastle catches my eye and I can only imagine how gorgeous the view is from up there.

From what I've read about the monumental castle of Cori Cove, it hasn't been inhabited by people for over forty years. Passed down from generation to generation by an English family, the Bromleys, I believe. The last owner opted to forgo the legacy and sold it—to Mr. Ellis, I assume.

The sun is dipping low in the clouds and there's only minutes of daylight left. I get a grip on my suitcase handle and begin walking down the dock. Each step has me feeling all the more permanently affixed to this place.

It's only six months. It is not a life sentence.

I've never been bold. Never taken risks or chances. I've got no idea what to expect as I walk at a leisurely pace toward the front of the structure. There is not much information regarding the Ellis family online. All I know is that the former Mr. Ellis passed away around seven or eight years ago and his son has taken over the business. I'm imagining a burly man with a beard and a 'better than thou' attitude, though, who am I to speculate? This man doesn't know a thing about me outside of my resume filed with the job search company I desperately sought out. Waiting tables at the local diner can only take someone so far and there isn't much demand for an interior designer in Hickory Knoll. So, here I am.

The scent of wet cement fills my senses as I walk up the steppingstones. Each one is half-buried in the dirt while the other half is covered in lime green moss. There's some sort of engraved design on them, but I wouldn't be able to make it out even if I dug them up.

I do take note of the two-lined engraving on a slab of cement sitting on two knee-high pillars.

Welcome to Cori Cove.

Where secrets hide and desires lurk.

That's an odd welcome sign.

When the stones end, I step onto the broken cobble-stone beneath a granite arch. From here, I'm able to see the front entrance. Two very wide double doors with paint chipping away. It seems there's a lot of work to do, starting with the entryway. I envision antique wooden doors with black, wrought-iron, U-shaped handles. Fresh steppingstones and a new sign out front. That one is just creepy. *Secrets and desires?* Guests would assume they're walking into a swingers' resort.

Swallowing hard, I reach for the handle on the door, but to my surprise, it's already opening. "Good evening, Ms. Jenkins. We've been expecting you." From the other side of the door, an older gentleman greets me with a thick Boston accent. He's wearing a black butler's suit with one hand behind his back and the other on the door. His fluffy white beard is peppered with streaks of black and his blue eyes are soft and inviting.

"Hello. And thank you. I'm happy to be here." It's partially true. I am excited for the job. As long as this unsettling feeling diminishes quickly, I'll be fine.

I step inside as he holds the door open. As I'm looking around at the very large open space, the door closes with a thud, startling me.

The butler takes my suitcase and motions for me to follow him. "Right this way. Mr. Ellis is expecting you."

Gripping the strap of my purse, I follow behind him.

It's apparent the hotel still at the construction point. It's damp and that smell of wet cement returns. Straight in front of me is stone-arcading supported by columns. It's completely open to the outside, allowing anything or anyone to come in and out. It looks as if it leads to the backside of the property. There's a puddle to the left and I look up to see an actual hole chiseled in the concrete ceiling. I guess the settlers didn't believe in drywall or boards back then.

The walls are completely bare, with only a clay-like color that actually resembles clay. No paintings, no decorative hangings. Not even a glamorous chandelier. I hope this place at least has electricity and running water.

Following behind the butler, we round a few corners and stop at an elevator. To my surprise, it's not old, nor stone. It looks like it was just put in. With two very wide stainless-steel doors. We step inside and it smells like fresh paint and fresh wood.

I watch as my guide presses the number eight on the panel, which appears to be the top floor.

When we come to a stop, the doors slide open and I follow his lead. The hallway is dim, lined with lanterns hanging from the cement wall. All lit with dancing flames.

I look around and it's like we've stepped into an entirely different castle. The floors are clean, without a crack to be seen. The walls are coated with a layer of glossy epoxy and that smell...it's weirdly familiar—lemongrass and a hint of mint—it smells like the home I lived in as a child.

Unease swarms in my belly. A blast from the past. A lifetime of memories hit me at once.

Me. Him. Us. Then and now. What we were and what we're not. What we'll never be.

It doesn't happen often, but every now and then, Cal gets into my head and reminds me of the choices I've made. I tried to find him a couple times but never had any luck. For years, I wondered what his life had become. Did he get out? Find a family? Is he married with kids? Is he even alive?

With my mind wandering back to another time, I don't even realize that the butler has opened the door to a room. He stands there with his hand pressed to it. "Ms. Jenkins? Is everything okay?"

I snap out of my thoughts and acknowledge him, "Yes. I'm sorry."

"As I said, this will be your room."

I take a step forward, and gasp when I see the beauty behind the door. "This? Is mine?" I look at him for assurance, because it's far too spectacular. This isn't just a measly hotel room. It's a room built for a queen, or at the very least, a princess. French doors that lead to a private balcony made of the original stone structure.

Bright, white paint covers the stone walls. A king-size bed sits in the center of the room with a large baby pink canopy overtop. The white lace that lines it dips into small V's and every centimeter of fabric is precisely cut. The canopy alone must have cost a fortune. The bedding matches in color, dressed in a soft satin.

There's a large vanity with a stool and a matching white dresser on the opposite wall. A large, white, wooden jewelry box catches my eye. As we pass by, I lift the top and a ballerina pops out. A tune begins playing and I shut it quickly because of the familiar sound.

The butler steals my attention as he lugs my suitcase across the hardwood floor.

I follow behind him as he walks toward, what I take to be, a walk-in closet.

"This is all yours, Ms. Jenkins."

I'm staring into a room that is big enough to be a bedroom. But that's not what takes me by surprise. It's the dozens of ball gowns. Every shade imaginable. On another wall are shoes—heels, flats, pumps, sandals. I grab a pair and hold them up—even tennis shoes?

"There must be some mistake. Why would all of this be in my room? I'm just a measly interior designer."

"Mr. Ellis makes no mistakes." He sets my suitcase upright and leaves the closet.

I set the shoes down and walk briskly behind him. "Excuse me, what did you say your name was?" I grab his arm and go to spin him to face me as confusion washes through me.

"Peter. Peter Blake."

I drop my hand and bite my bottom lip, trying to understand what all this means. My thumb shoots over my shoulder. "Are those his wife's clothes?"

"Mr. Ellis is not married," he says point-blankly.

"Daughter?"

"No kids."

"Hmm. Okay. Could you please take me to him? I just feel as if he's mistaken about my stay here." The assistant I spoke with was very specific about my duties. This is a job, not a vacation.

Peter folds his hands in front of him and nods, very properly at that. "Of course."

As we continue down the hall, it begins to feel more and more like we're in a finished home. There's an open sitting room that's decorated immaculately. All-white furniture, a gray shag rug in front of the larger couch. Fresh flowers in a vase sitting on top of... I stop walking, gawking at the grand piano in the room. It's beautiful. Hand-carved wood, stained in a cherry finish.

"Ms. Jenkins?" Peter quips.

Right. I peel my eyes off the piano and scurry down the hall behind him.

A new smell invades my senses—garlic. "Is there a kitchen on this floor?"

"The kitchen is on the first floor, not to be mistaken with the main entrance on the ground floor. Dinner is being served shortly."

"Do you stay on this floor?" I feel redundant asking so many questions, but this is nothing like I'd imagined.

"The live-in staff stays on the sixth floor."

Isn't that what I am, though? Live-in staff?

At the risk of driving this man crazy with all my questions, I offer some light humor. "I suppose your room wasn't equipped with enough dresses to attend a lifetime of balls?"

He doesn't respond as he continues on his path. Guess he doesn't do humor.

Peter stops in front of another door at the very end of the hall. "Here we are."

He just stands there, looking as if I'm expected to open the door and shout, *"I'm here."*

Finally, he taps his knuckles to it.

"Come in," a gruff voice trails through the sliver of an opening between the floor and the door. The vibration of his voice climbs through me and leaves me feeling anxious to put a face to the sound.

Peter turns the knob and pushes the door open. Cautiously, I step around him and look inside. A door at the end of the room closes and Mr. Ellis is nowhere in sight.

My eyes skim the room. There's a very dark feel to it. A large desk is placed in front of a wall-sized window. Above it is elegant stained glass with the design of a tree and fallen leaves. The roots are the focal point of the artwork. Spread along the entire bottom, ending where the glass meets the window beneath it.

There's an antique artifact sitting on a tall, black pedestal of a naked woman with her hand on her chest that looks like it was made from limestone. Beside it is a large black couch that looks like it's never been sat on. Then, there's a square, glass table with a chessboard on top of it. The walls are white, aside from an accent wall that is black and displays a large, vintage-looking clock. It smells like black currant and spice and it's most definitely a man's office.

My body jolts when the door closes and I realize Peter has left. My legs begin to feel weak and wobbly as I stand here alone.

"Hello," I call out, looking toward the other closed doors in the room.

"Have a seat. I'll be out in a minute."

That voice again. It's masculine and stern. Sexy and mysterious.

I walk over to the desk and take a seat in the leather chair in front of it, opposite the chair I presume to be his. It looks more like a throne made for a king. There are chess pieces jutting from the back corners. All black, leather, with snake heads on the ends of the arms. It's actually pretty creepy.

The door that Peter just walked out of opens back up, causing me to look over my shoulder. A man walks in. He's not dressed in business attire. Instead, he appears sharp in a pair of beige shorts and a tucked-in polo shirt with a Manila folder placed under his arm. Slicked-back, blond hair, gorgeous blue eyes, and a muscular build.

"You must be Bella," he says chipperly as he joins my side. He extends his hand and I return the gesture.

He's the first to call me, Bella. While that's what everyone I'm close with calls me, my legal name is Isabella. "I am. You must be Mr. Ellis."

"Oh no," he chuckles, "I'm Byron Davis, his attorney."

My brows shoot to my forehead. "Attorney?"

"That's right. Mr. Ellis is tied up on a business call at the moment, so we're taking this time to finalize contracts."

"Oh, right." I nod. When I got the call for the job from Mr. Ellis's assistant, she mentioned paperwork and contracts.

Opening the folder, Byron shuffles through some documents and pulls out a small stack. "Go ahead and have a seat. This shouldn't take long."

Once he finds a pen, he hands it to me and points to an X on the paper. "You're welcome to read through them if you'd like."

I've never been one to read through legal documents and it hasn't bit me in the ass yet. I'm getting a job. I'm staying on the job site. And I'm getting paid more than I would ever ask for. I press the pen to the paper and sign my name. He flips a page and I sign again, and again, and again.

"That should be all. I'm excited to see what you and Mr. Ellis do with the place. You'll see me around from time to time."

"Thank you," I say to him. He tips his chin and turns to leave the room.

As one door shuts, another opens. I look over my shoulder, and that's when I see him.

At least, I think it's him.

3

Staring back at me is a gorgeous statue of a man, standing at least six-foot-three. Black, disheveled hair. Skin that doesn't look like it's seen sun in years. Eyes so dark they're almost black. He's wearing a black suit, tailored to fit him perfectly. There's a bit of scruff on his face, but it only adds to his appeal.

A strange feeling washes over me. There is something oddly familiar about him. *Have I met this guy before?*

"Hello, Bella," he says, standing afar and taking me in while I do the same. Those two words are like music singing to my soul. I can't pinpoint exactly what it is, but I feel like I've known him for years.

I should get up. Greet him properly. Though, I don't move as he comes closer. His eyes boring into mine, as if they're searching for something.

Swallowing hard, I take in a deep breath to try and steady my racing heart. "It's nice to meet you." I finally stand. Stepping around the chair, I meet him face to face.

"This is a beautiful place." Breaking the gaze I hold on

him, I give the room a lazy sweep. Looking into those eyes is dangerous. They have the ability to turn off all logical thinking, while paralyzing my whole body.

With his feet planted firmly to the floor beneath him, he folds his hands in front of him. "It will be."

His voice, again, sends a rapid-fire of electricity through me.

It's apparent he's a straight-to-the-point man and doesn't mind that he's making me feel highly intimidated at this moment.

Tension sizzles between us as we stand there silently. Even if I was standing here completely naked, I'd still feel the same level of exposure I'm feeling right now.

Say something, Bella.

I go with the first thing that comes to my mind. "I met your attorney and signed the contracts."

He gives a subtle nod, keeping the same blank expression on his face. Not even a tug at his lips.

"Okay," I drop my shoulders, "I'll just see myself to my room and we can get started in the morning?"

Nothing. Not a hint of a smile, nor a frown. This man is completely zombified, and even if he is freakishly handsome, it's sort of creeping me out.

I press my lips together firmly and walk to the door.

"You've changed."

His words catch me by surprise. I turn around to face where he stands. Puzzled, I question his statement. "I've changed?"

"Your eyes." He takes a step closer, examining me all over again. Each step has my heart sinking deeper into the pit of my stomach. "They once spoke to me. I could read your thoughts with just a look."

That strange feeling washes over me again. *No.*

It can't be.

I push away the bizarre thought. Tilting my head, I look into his eyes, probing for the reason behind the familiarity. It's uncanny. But I refuse to believe that the man in front of me is Callum.

Concentrating on his face, I dig deeper. Dark brown orbs that wear a lifetime of pain. I see loneliness. I see hate for the world he's forced to live in. I see him— Callum. Fourteen years old, standing at the dormer window in the attic. The same eyes that looked back at me as I drove away. His stare shot through me with more force than a silver bullet. Much like this moment.

He comes closer, eating the foot of space between us. Looking down on me, his warm breath clouds my logic. "We meet again, Bella." The way my name rolls off his tongue makes me dizzy.

"Oh my God!" My hands clap to my mouth. I'm speechless. It really is him. In an instant, I throw myself into his arms while he remains impervious. His arms are draped at his sides, his expression still as serious as ever. "I can't believe it's really you." I can't think straight. The words I'm choking on as they come out of my mouth are barely audible. I pull back, looking up at him. "How? How did this happen?"

His eyes bore into mine, though, they're different. Everything about him is different. What once was a tall and lanky boy with glasses and in desperate need of a haircut, now stands before me as a muscular grown man with facial hair and a jawline that could chisel glass.

"Fate," he finally says. One simple word that speaks a thousand different volumes.

"Fate?" Am I naive to think that fate brought us back together?

I'm sure Cal can see the rapid beating of my heart as we stand mere inches apart. Yet, he fosters the same hard glare he's had since the second I looked at him. Proof that fate did not bring us back together. He orchestrated this. He brought me here.

"You've had a long day of travel. The cook has brought dinner to your room. Go eat and get some sleep. We'll talk tomorrow.

"But, I—"

"Tomorrow," he says sternly.

I nod in response. Hesitantly, I take a few steps back and turn around to leave.

When I reach the door, I glance over my shoulder. Cal has given me his back as he fidgets with his phone.

Tomorrow.

4

"SMILE, Callum. This is a good day. You finally get a home," Mrs. Webster says as I sit nervously on the porch, waiting for my new parents to pick me up.

I haven't smiled in almost a year and I'm not sure that look is possible at this point. I'm not upset that I'm finally getting out of this hellhole, but I hate people, especially ones that know my misfortunes. I've been pitied for far too long and I'm ready to take the world by the horns and ride out of this bitch on my own. I don't need anyone.

A vehicle comes down the gravel driveway and it's not what I expected at all. The sun bounces off the fresh coat of wax on the shiny black car, blinding me. I turn my head, squinting my eyes while still trying to look. It's most definitely a Mercedes, though I'm not able to make out what kind. Maybach, maybe? I might be washed-up goods, but I know cars. In fact, reading a book every day for five years has made me exceptionally smart, even if I don't apply my knowledge to my schoolwork.

"Here we go." Mrs. Webster grabs my dingy black bag that

holds the only things I need. My writing book, my memory box, and a clean pair of underwear.

I run my fingers over my bald head, remembering that I have no hair left. Bibs thought it would be a good idea to freshen me up with a haircut before leaving, and she royally fucked up so Mrs. Webster had to shave it all off. I look like Mr. Clean, waiting for a flood in these pants, and I wouldn't be surprised if the car turns back around and leaves us standing here in dust. Who the hell would want me? Especially someone who drives a car that nice.

An elderly man steps out of the back seat and I'm confused as fuck. He's old enough to be my great-grandfather. Why would he want a rebellious teenage boy living in his house?

This process was a bit different for me. Most of the kids meet their adoptive parents before pickup, but not me. It wouldn't surprise me if Mrs. Webster sold me just to get me out of her damn house. Not that I care. At least I'm getting out.

"Hello there," the gentleman says. He offers a hand, but I just look at it, then slide my eyes up to his. They're warm and welcoming behind his glasses.

"Aren't you a little old to be adopting a kid?"

The man chuckles, and Mrs. Webster swats my arm. "Forgive him. He's a jokester."

"It wasn't a joke."

"I'm Peter," the man says, trying again with the hand.

Instead of giving it a shake, I bump my fist to his hand. "Callum. But you can call me, Cal." I snatch my bag away from Mrs. Webster. "Let's get the hell outta here."

Mrs. Webster grabs my attention as I walk away. "Callum?"

I turn around and give her one last look. "Take care of yourself."

And then it happens—I smile. "I plan to."

When you enter the world alone, you have to take care of yourself. No one else is gonna do it for you.

My body shoots up in the bed as I pant, trying to catch my breath. I look behind me at the sweat spot on the black, satin pillowcase.

I prepared myself for the possibility that the nightmares would get worse, but in reality, nothing can prepare either of us for what's to come.

5

I SHOULD HAVE DUG DEEPER. Asked him how he found me and why he brought me here. It certainly wasn't for my expertise in interior design.

God, I'm such an idiot. Here I thought that this successful man saw my portfolio and was impressed with my skills and actually wanted me to work on the scheme of his hotel. I thought this was my big break. Freedom from the chains that hold me down. My guilt-free escape from a small town where you only grow as big as your parents.

Unless? Unless Cal was searching for a designer and just happened to come across my info at the job agency and he was impressed, only to learn that I was a blast from his past. Maybe he wants to rebuild the friendship we once had. Or maybe he wants more.

He's a godly form of man, that's for sure. I'm not sure I've ever even talked to a guy as sexy as him. I've always been a pretty forthright person, but Cal stole my breath away and left me unable to comprehend a sentence, and that was before I realized it was him.

My best friend grew up fucking hot as hell, and filthy fucking rich.

Stop thinking, Bella.

A beam of light casts through the glass doors that lead to the balcony, reminding me that it's now morning and I haven't slept. I'd credit it to being in a ginormous castle that's been desolate for forty years, but that doesn't even faze me.

It's him. The way he looked at me like I was a stranger who came on his property uninvited. He barely spoke, yet when he did, goosebumps danced across my skin.

Tugging the comforter aggressively, I curl into a ball on my side. My eyes wide open as I stare into the closet. He bought me dresses. Cal knew how much I loved them, and he bought them just for me. Why?

I know that I never forgot about him, but I was certain he'd forgotten about me. We spent four short years together at The Webster House. Four years compared to the twenty-six of his life. So why now? Why me?

Tossing back and forth, I try to drown out the pounding at the door, hoping for just an hour of sleep. When it continues, I drag myself out of the bed and pull on my robe that's lying on the footboard.

When the knocks become more forceful, I pick up my pace as I make my way across the room. "Coming," I holler. Turning the crystal knob of the Victorian door handle, I pull it open. "Peter. Good morning."

Peter graciously folds his hands together in front of

him. "Good morning, Ms. Jenkins. Mr. Ellis has requested your presence in the dining room."

"Really?" I rub a fist into my tired eyes. "What time is it?"

"Six a.m."

I nod. "Six a.m.? Okay. Please tell him I'll be there shortly."

Why are we up this early? Surely, this won't be the normal business hours?

Everyone is so formal here and I can't help but feel inferior. I'm not fancy, proper, or even well-mannered. I use informal words and have the mouth of a sailor.

Peter leaves and I close the door behind him. I could really use a shower, but I don't want to keep Cal waiting. Besides, more than anything, I need answers.

I quickly throw myself together with my hair twisted into a bun on the top of my head. I opt for a black skirt and a cream-colored, knitted sweater. Hopefully it's appropriate for the occasion. Then again, it's six o'clock in the morning, so Cal shouldn't expect much from me.

I make my way down the hall. I remember passing a dining room on the way in, so hopefully I'm able to find it on my own.

There's a chill in the air this morning, but I'm not sure if it's due to the weather, or the ghost of my past lingering around me.

Two minutes later, I find myself looking into a large sitting room. The one that has the piano. It's been at least five years since I've even played. There was a time my fingers danced across the keys for hours a day. Cal would sit beside me while he wrote stories in his notebook and most of the time, we never spoke, we just enjoyed each other's company.

Once I left The Webster House, I took lessons for a couple years. Even played in a musical during freshman year, but I was never a fan of the attention. Slowly, the passion fizzled out and was replaced by school and friends.

Tiny hairs on my neck prick when someone comes up behind me. Not just anyone. It's Cal. I can feel him standing there. Stray strands of hair hit my face with each exhale he makes. "Do you like it?"

I don't turn around as I gaze into the room. "It's beautiful."

"Steinway 1942. When I got her, she was pretty dinged-up. A few coats of lacquer and she's as good as new."

My jaw drops open and I turn around to face Cal, not realizing he's so close. Our noses almost collide and I take a few steps back. "Is it… Did you—"

Cal nods, knowing exactly what I was going to ask. It's the same piano I used to play as a kid.

"When The Webster House was shut down by the county, everything was auctioned off. I was able to get a few priceless things out of that mess."

I knew Mrs. Webster was convicted of sex trafficking about five years after I left. Apparently, the older girls were forced to "work" on the weekends. I only knew of one girl who was placed there at the time and my heart broke for sweet Bibs.

I look up at Cal, tears threatening to break free. "I wish I could have done something to help those girls."

Had I stayed, maybe I could have protected them. Bibs was eventually placed in another home until she was old enough to leave two years ago. I reached out to her last year. She's having a hard time with life but getting by. I promised her we'd keep in touch, but time sort of got away from me.

Cal holds his stare on me. "Maybe you could have." He steps around me and walks into the room, hands in the pockets of his black dress pants. "But you chose to leave and now you have to live with that choice."

He's right. I did make the choice to leave. A few steps forward bring me into the room. There's a large window that overlooks the mountains on the island. "You would have done the same thing." He can lie and tell me he wouldn't have, but he'd have left too.

His fingers trail featherlike over the closed lid of the piano as he walks around it. Finally stopping, facing my direction. "That's where you're wrong, Bella. I made a promise and I keep my promises."

One hand still in his pocket, he waits for a reaction from me. But I don't even know what to say. I decide to go with the response he's likely waiting for. "I'm sorry, Cal."

"It's Callum. No one calls me Cal." No smile that tells me he's fucking with me. No wink, no flutter of his lashes.

What happened to the boy I used to know?

"But, I've always called you Cal."

"You called your friend Cal. I am not your friend."

Like a knife straight to the heart, my hands fly to my chest as I try to catch my breath. "Are you angry with me?" Chances are he'll lie and say he's not, but he's distant and cold. It's apparent he's harboring some bitterness toward me.

As he should. No matter how I feel about the choice I made and no matter what my reasoning was, he'll never understand because he didn't have to make the choice. I did. I was the one in that position because Cal was reckless and troublesome. If I'd left it up to him, we'd have been in that home until we were eighteen years old. I would have been sold to the highest bidder on the weekends. Not him.

"How can I be angry with someone I don't even know?" He stalks toward me and when I think he's going to stop and elaborate, he keeps going. Leaving me standing in the room alone.

I pivot around and watch him walk away, but not before hollering at him over his shoulder. "You got a good life, Cal. Look at all this." My arms wave around the room. He doesn't even acknowledge me. Just keeps walking until he disappears down the hall and into a room I take to be the dining room.

He *did* get a good life. Cal has anything anyone could ever dream of. If anything, he was better off without me.

My black flats traipse across the floor as I walk briskly down the hall. Following the same path that Cal did, I find him taking a seat at the head of the twelve-foot, oblong table. The room looks like something out of a magazine. There's an entire row of windows with stained-glass panels. A large crystal chandelier hangs from the ceiling. A dozen cream-cushioned chairs organized perfectly around the table.

I stop in the doorway, cross my arms over my chest, and lean against the doorframe. "What did you mean when you said you don't know me?"

Cal jabs his fork into a perfect triangular piece of pancake and stuffs it into his mouth, watching me intently as he chews. "Sit down. You need to eat."

Taking a stance, my feet stay planted. "I'm not sitting anywhere until you tell me what you meant."

"Suit yourself. Your hunger only hurts you, Bella."

"My name is Isabella. Only my friends call me Bella, and if I remember correctly, you're not my friend."

The corner of his lip tugs up as he looks down at his plate and bites back a smile. Maybe he's human, after all.

He may be human, but he's still stubborn as an ox. Against my better judgment, I walk into the room, my eyes glued to him as I lift the lid on the tin platter and grab a pancake with my hand.

Cal looks from me to the tongs sitting beside it and I, ever so gracefully, drop the pancake onto a plate with a smirk. Lathering it up nicely with syrup, I scoop some scrambled eggs and a few pieces of bacon, then sit down about four chairs away from him.

As much as I'd like to return his stubbornness, this food smells damn good.

Once I've taken a couple bites and my hunger begins to subside, I try again. "Why do you feel like you don't know me?"

Cal pats around his mouth with a cloth napkin, then sets it back in his lap.

"Should I know you?" He sticks another bite of pancake into his mouth.

"Well, yeah. It's me, Cal. We spent every waking minute of the day together for four whole years. For the longest time, you knew me better than anyone."

It's true. Cal knows my dreams, my secrets, the lies I've told. He's heard the stories of my harrowing childhood. And, I know his. Cal has always been quiet, but he let me in and, in some ways, it made me feel special.

Granted, it's been twelve years, but to say he doesn't even know me is crazy. We weren't just friends who shared the same house. We were so much more than that.

"Four years that meant nothing." He drops his fork on the plate and pushes it away from him.

"What are you talking about? It meant everything. Just because I left, doesn't mean I didn't care about you."

"Well, thanks for clearing the air, Bella. Everything is fine now." His chair slides back abruptly as he gets to his feet and attempts to leave.

Oh no, he doesn't.

I jump up, almost tipping my chair over. With syrup still on my lips, I round the table and step in front of him. "You're not walking away again. Not until you tell me why I'm here. How did you find me? If you're so angry with me, why not just let me live my life as if…"

"As if what, Bella?" He steps into the space between us. "As if I didn't exist?"

"No," my head shakes, "that's not what I meant." My shoulders drop in defeat. "I just want answers. Yesterday I thought I was meeting an older man with a beer gut who fell into money. Thought I'd be fixing up a hotel and making my own money. Then I come here and find this extravagant room made up for me with ball gowns, shoes, and the piano. This wasn't a coincidence, was it?"

"Well, you got one thing right. I do have money. Lots of it. But, I certainly don't have a beer gut and most definitely didn't fall into it. It was earned. I bled for everything I own." His lip curls, brows dipped into a tight V. "In response to your previous statement, just because it looks like a good life, doesn't mean it is. The light you see on the outside only shines because of years of darkness on the inside."

His chest is heaving by the time he finishes. I can tell I've hit a nerve and dammit, I don't want to. I just want to make things right. No matter what he thinks, I do care about him. Probably more than he will ever know.

"You're right. Perception is everything. Maybe it's time you consider the fact that I left because I wanted to avoid the darkness. Why does that make me such a bad person?"

"I never said you were a bad person. You wouldn't be here if I thought you were."

My breath hitches as I search for the answer to the question that's been lingering since last night. "Why am I here?"

"To work. For me." Cal's cold fingers brush my cheek before tucking a stray strand of hair behind my ear. "Now eat."

"What happened in the last twelve years that made you this way? Why are you so bitter?"

Cal drops his hands to his sides and bares his teeth as he speaks, "If you even have to ask that question, then you're more of an idiot than I thought you were."

"Oh, so now I'm an idiot?"

His eyebrows elevate, the tension between us coiling with each breath. "You really don't get it, do you?"

I do get it, but no matter how I explain my reasoning, I know it'll never be good enough. "I messed up, Cal." My chest rises and falls quickly as I confess my own sins. "I was scared that you'd just keep getting in trouble and we'd be stuck there forever. I had no time to think about it, so I reacted."

"Without even a goodbye? Was I that insignificant to you?"

"It would have been too painful. I was worried I'd change my mind. You were the only person in the entire world who ever gave a damn about me and no explanation at the moment felt fitting. So, I just left."

I never even packed my things, just grabbed the photo of my mom and wore the stringy dress I'd put on that morning. There was nothing in that house I wanted to take with me—except Cal, but that was impossible.

"Then maybe you should try and see things from where I'm standing. Because you were the only person in the entire world who ever gave a damn about me, and you left me. You may not have been the one to deal me this shitty hand called life, but you stretched that hole inside of me and because of it, I entered a new world of suffering. A world that you now get to live in."

A tear falls from the corner of my eye, and I sweep it away. "So, what? You want to own me? That's impossible. You can't just keep me here."

Cal's breathing becomes heavy, his eyes glowering at me. "Want to?" he grinds out. "I already do own you." Two

41

hands grab me by both arms and slam my back against the wall, stealing my breath. "You see, this was no accident, Bella. I brought you here and I *will* keep you here."

For the first time ever, I'm scared of Cal. Like really fucking scared. "Why do you want to hurt me?" I choke in an outbreath.

"Because you hurt me." His gaze dips downward and he lets out a low grumble. "For the past twelve years, I've wondered what you look like, what you smell like, what makes you smile, and most importantly, what it feels like to be inside of you. Your tight walls clenched around my cock."

Bile rises up my throat, and I swallow it down. "Please move."

His eyes ride back up to mine as he positions his hand between my legs, trailing his fingers up my inner thigh under my skirt. "Tell me, Bella, have you been fucked in the last twelve years?"

I don't answer when he blows out a menacing laugh. "Of course you have. You're what, twenty-three now? A body like this doesn't go untouched for that long."

Without denying or confirming his assumption, I roll my eyes and look away from him.

Cupping my crotch, he presses his fingers against my entrance through the fabric of my panties. "Please, Cal. Don't do this." Tears fall carelessly down my cheeks and I swallow hard.

Warm lips graze the shell of my ear. "You want me to stop?"

I nod repeatedly in response.

His head comes back up and he looks at me while I continue to cry silently. "Then why are you so wet?"

My heart begins racing as tingles trickle through my entire body. Pressure builds inside of me and it's burning hot. I'm disgusted with myself for being partially turned on by his forward behavior. "I...I'm not."

Cal pushes my panties to the side and begins rubbing circles feverishly at my entrance. His eyes skate down to my mouth and he leans forward, darting his tongue out and licking a tear off my lips. I'm completely caught off guard when his mouth collides with mine. I squirm and try to pull back, but it does no good. I might as well be shackled in chains and handcuffed to this wall.

The taste of syrup and salty tears seeps into my mouth when his tongue enters. "Mmm," he hums, "You taste better than I ever could have imagined.

"Stop," I whimper into his mouth. "Just stop."

He finally pulls back, looking at me, and it's like he's had an epiphany of some sort. His eyes are suddenly full of awareness, and perhaps, guilt. He drops his hand from beneath my panties and they fall back in place. He goes to speak, but says nothing, before turning around and storming out of the room.

6

MY FEET DON'T STOP MOVING as I slam my bedroom door shut behind me. Pacing the length of the room, up and down, back and forth.

Stop. Just stop.

Those words were deafening. A wake-up call and a slap in the face at the same time. What the hell am I doing? I need to get some control over myself before I completely lose my mind and hurt us both in the process.

I should go downstairs, relieve some stress and clear my head.

No.

I'm done with that. I made a promise to myself that it would end the minute she came to the island.

Sweat gathers at my hairline, even though it's only sixty degrees in this room. Always sixty degrees. Never more, never less.

"Fuck," I bellow, gripping the sides of my head and tugging at my hair. My fingers dig deeper, nails scraping my scalp as memories of the past flood my mind.

"My name is Callum," I shout loudly at the crazy bitch standing in front of me.

"No, honey. You're just confused." She brushes my hair back with warm fingers. Her eyes are lit up like she really believes I'm her dead son standing in front of her. "Now, go eat your breakfast, so Peter can bring you to school."

My voice rises as I do everything Vincent forbids me to do. "I don't go to school. Wanna know why? Because you crazy people don't let me. You keep me locked in this house, pretending I'm someone I'm not, just so you don't have to face the truth."

Her hand presses flat against my forehead. "Are you sick, Caden?" Her eyes dart to my open bedroom door and she hollers, "Vincent. Come in here, please."

Vincent is my adoptive dad, and standing in front of me is my adoptive mother, who is three crayons short of a full box. I know exactly what the rules are. I also know what's coming from breaking them, but I hate this. Pretending to be someone I'm not, just so this lady can keep living in a fantasy world.

For the most part, I do as I'm told, but every now and then, I get fed up and this is one of those moments.

My heart rate excels as Vincent's footsteps come closer down the hall.

"Daddy will take you to the doctor and we'll make you all better, Caden."

Slapping her hand away from me, I scream, "I'm not Caden!"

That's all it takes for me to be gripped by the back of my shirt and anchored off the ground. Delilah continues to ramble nonsense to Vincent about how she thinks I'm sick and have a fever, but neither of us pay any attention as I'm being carried out of the room.

"I didn't mean to—"

"Shut your damn mouth," Vincent growls, taking me down the hall. The collar of my shirt digs into the skin of my neck and I can feel my throat restricting. He stops outside my bedroom door and messes with the thermostat.

"No. Please. Not that. I'll do anything. I'll tell her I'm Caden. I'll let her read me a story. Just please, don't do that."

Vincent kicks the door open and tosses me inside. My body comes to a rolling stop in front of my bed and I sit up quickly as I watch his shiny black boots coming toward me. "I'm sorry," I cry out, "it was a mistake."

I keep scooting, trying to bide as much time as I can, although my punishment is inevitable. I open my mouth to speak, but nothing comes out as the back of Vincent's hand pierces my cheek. The sting lingers, but it's quickly replaced by the pain in my stomach as the point of his shoe meets my side.

"If you wanna be Callum, you can go back to that shack of orphans you came from. In this house, you will be Caden."

"Stop. Just stop," I beg of him.

The kicks continue, targeting every part of my body as the air in the room thickens to the point of suffocation.

Once I'm unable to move, or speak, Vincent finally leaves.

The door closes and each lock on the outside echoes through my body.

An hour or more passes and I'm finally able to push myself off the floor and strip out of my clothes. The temperature continues to rise until I'm vomiting on my own legs. It's at least one hundred and twenty degrees at this point, and I'm barely able to keep my eyes open.

So I shut them, drifting away to another lifetime. One I

created just for myself. A castle on a private island where no one can touch me. Maybe she'll join me. Maybe I'll make her.

Delilah took her life the night before my eighteenth birthday. I think part of her knew I wasn't Caden. It was just easier to pretend I was. After all, that's the only reason Vincent adopted me—because I was a loser with nothing but a name, and the spitting image of his offspring. The next day, when I turned eighteen, everything changed.

I never knew Caden, but I knew everything about him. I lived his life, took over his room, and was given his name—not legally, though. Apparently, he died only months before the Ellises took me in. Delilah was always crazy, but the death of her son pushed her over the edge. She refused to accept he was gone, and Vincent refused to let her. So I played the part of the dutiful son, just biding my time until I could make Vincent pay.

And pay he did.

7

Last night I had assumed it was only me, Cal, Peter, and Cal's attorney on the island. Now it's been confirmed that there's a Michelin star chef, a housekeeper, and a couple security guards.

I haven't spoken to Cal since he assaulted me at breakfast, so I've taken it upon myself to get familiar with the property, even though the job feels moot at this point.

Peter is showing me to the back yard while I take notes on a clipboard. It's an open exit with no wall covering or doors. There's another arch positioned overtop where the cement continues. A round glass table and a couple wrought-iron chairs sit around it.

We step outside and I draw in a deep breath of fresh air. "This is gorgeous," I say to Peter as he walks beside me. "Could use a little upkeep, but there is so much potential back here.

"Little is too weak of a word. I'd say massive is more fitting."

I chuckle. "Okay. Massive.

"I envision a wet bar made of stone with pillars that extend up to an overhead canopy."

There's a curtain wall in the distance that looks like it goes beyond the length of the castle. To the right, I see a wooden bridge that doesn't seem stable enough to hold a small child, let alone an adult. I walk closer to see what's beneath it, and it looks like it's a man-made pond, though it's very small and only runs under the bridge. It's very pretty, though, and I can only imagine what it could become.

I continue to babble as we walk. "A separate garden area with wildflowers and fountains. Maybe a pond with goldfish. All of this with the breathtaking view of the mountains that rim the backside of the island. The possibilities are endless."

A gust of wind sends chills down my spine. Peter had mentioned a storm heading for the island, which had me a little nervous, until I remembered that this place has weathered storms for over a century and it's still standing tall.

Looking up at the sky, I take it all in. For a brief moment, I feel at ease. That is, until I level my eyes and see Cal standing five feet in front of me.

"Lunch is ready," he deadpans.

I don't even humor him with a response. Tilting my head, I look back up at the sky where a flock of birds flap hurriedly, likely fleeing the storm that's coming.

"Peter," Cal says, "please see Ms. Jenkins to the dining room."

Peter acknowledges him with a nod.

Once Cal is gone, I look at Peter. "You don't have to

escort me. I can find my way." It's obvious Cal is angry with me. Hell, he might even hate me. After the way he fondled me, I should hate him.

Maybe my coming here is some sort of revenge scheme he's cooked up. After the tension during breakfast, I'm not sure that I'm ready to have a quiet meal with Cal again, at least not yet.

"Boss's orders. Besides, it will be my pleasure."

"I'm actually not very hungry." It's a lie. I didn't eat much at breakfast and I'm actually starving.

Peter shrugs a shoulder. "Mr. Ellis makes the rules. I only follow them."

Once I finish up my walk through the yard, or what will eventually be a yard, we head back inside. Peter follows behind me, hot on my trail. Instead of going to the dining hall, I go straight to the first floor where the kitchen is to get a plate of food directly from the chef.

"Ms. Jenkins, I do think you should have lunch with Mr. Ellis. You wouldn't want to anger him on your first full day."

"Oh, I think I've already angered Mr. Ellis." I smirk as I pull open the stainless steel door to the kitchen.

Just as I'm about to step inside, in my periphery, I see Cal coming out. Ignoring him completely, I go into the kitchen. Peter hangs back and I can hear his chatter from outside the door. "I tried but she's a mulish one, that girl."

"That she is," Cal hisses, jerking the door open. I step to the side, hoping to hide from him like a child, but it does no good.

Cal grabs me by the arm hastily. "Hey! What are you doing?" I attempt to jerk my arm away, but his grip tightens as he walks me out the door. "Let me go." I jerk again to no avail.

"You are here on a contract and that contract states that your living quarters are upstairs. Your lunch is waiting." He gives my arm an aggravated shove and heads toward the elevator.

My arms cross over my chest and I scowl at his backside. "And what if I don't?"

Cal eats back up the space he just took and gets right in my face. "Then you're breaching your contract. Do I need to tell you what happens when a contract is breached?"

I swallow hard. He's dead serious right now.

"Cal?" I say his name in question. "Why are you doing this?"

I'm upset that he's behaving this way, but more than anything, it hurts.

He doesn't respond, just breathes fire into me as he clenches his jaw.

"I can't live like this for six months. If you expect me to work for you and abide by *your rules*," I air quote, "then I want answers."

He's silent for a moment before he exhales a drawn-out breath. "We can discuss the terms of your contract if you have lunch with me."

My head shakes. "That's not enough."

"Fine. We will discuss the terms of your contract and I'll tell you why you're here."

With my head held high, I walk to the elevator and press the arrow going up.

At least he's giving me something.

I don't have to turn around to see if he's coming. Something tells me that Cal will be one step behind me for the next six months.

Hugging my chest, I position myself in the corner of the elevator and avoid eye contact. It's too painful to look at him this way. Never in my wildest dreams did I think Cal, of all people, would treat me as if I were menial.

The elevator stops and Cal gestures for me to go first. Silence descends down the hallway as we walk to the dining room. I take a seat in the same spot I sat in for breakfast, sinking down in the chair. Whatever is under those lids smells damn good but lifting it up and eating right now means eating my pride as well, and I'm not ready to do that.

Cal pulls out the chair at the head of the table, his eyes fettered to me. Two arms lie flat against the table and he blows out a breath. "What would you like to know, Bella?"

I hate the way he says my name. It sounds so formal. Everything about Cal is serious now and my heart hurts when I think about what he must have endured to become the man he is.

I decide to start with the most obvious question. "Why am I here?"

Being the finicky person he is, he doesn't answer my question right away. Picking up a glass of caramel-colored liquid, he gives it a swirl, ice clanking against the small glass. He takes a sip, darts his tongue out at his lips and I catch myself watching each precise movement that he makes.

His eyes lift, catching mine. There's a glint of a smirk on his lips and it infuriates me.

Finally, he sets his glass down and levels with me. "You're not an easy person to track down, even for a man of my stature. I always knew I'd find you. I just never expected it would take this long. If it weren't for your submission to the job agency, it may have taken me another twelve years."

"So you *were* looking for an interior designer?"

Cal spews a devilish laugh. "My family name has been refurbishing rags to riches for over a century. Vincent Ellis's great-great-grandfather started this empire and it's been passed down from generation to generation. We certainly weren't in need of a twenty-three-year-old girl with an undergraduate degree and zero experience."

Pins poke at my chest. A sensation that I wasn't expecting. I'm actually rendered speechless.

"Come on, Bella. You have to have known that we employ top-tier designers from all over the world."

Clearing my throat, I choke out, "I suppose you're right. I guess I was a fool to think that was real." I'm on the verge of tears but trying really hard to fight them off.

Cal pushes his chair back and comes over to where I'm sitting. Slouching down in front of me, his eyes smolder. "Cry, Bella. I can see you need to. Let me see those tears. Show me you're not the heartless bitch I take you to be."

I gasp at his words—completely caught off guard. "Excuse me?"

With knitted eyebrows, he watches me as if he's waiting for me to completely break down. Instead of giving him the emotion he wants, I push him back. "Screw you!"

He catches his fall, anger rippling through him. The shade of his eyes shifts from dark to crow black. Grabbing me by the wrist, he squeezes so hard I can feel the quickening of my pulse against his palm. "You wanna know why you're here, Bella? You're here because I caught you. My own little toy to pocket and keep. Running is no longer an option. The life you lived outside these walls is over. You're mine now and there isn't a damn thing you can do about it."

My bottom lip trembles. I've never been afraid of Cal before, but, at this moment, I've never feared anything more. "Why are you doing this?"

With flared nostrils, he sharpens his tone. "You did this."

His fingers are still wrapped tightly around my wrist, so much so that I can see the paleness in his knuckles. I pull back slightly, but he doesn't budge. No longer able to hold it back, tears fall from my eyes. Sliding down my cheeks and onto his cold, strained fingers. "I had no choice. You ruined everything that day by getting into trouble. In a split second, everything had changed and I had to make a choice."

His jaw clenches, lip curled. "And now you get to live with that choice."

My head shakes. "I want out of the contract. I'll go home and you can just forget about me."

"The same way you forgot about me?"

I'll never be able to make him understand, mostly, because I don't understand myself. I'm happy with the life

I was given, but it took years for the guilt of leaving him to subside. Oftentimes, I ask myself if I would make the same choice if I had the chance to do it over again. And I don't even know if I would. That right there is the reason why I can't justify my leaving him.

My chin hits my chest as the tears continue to drop. "I never forgot about you. I thought about you every second of every day that first year. As time went on, you slipped further and further away. But, I never forgot and I never stopped caring about you."

Cal places his thumb on my chin, tipping it up. "I can guarantee after your stay here, I will never slip your mind again." His thumb slides across my lip, catching a tear before he pries my mouth open and jams it between my lips. The saltiness of my own woes hits my taste buds. I don't even try to force his thumb out of my mouth as he watches his own movements. "As for the contract," he continues, eyes locked on my mouth, "there is no escaping it."

Turning my head, I pull back and his hand drops. "All contracts are expungable at a cost. How much is it? Double the salary?" I don't have that kind of money to buy back my freedom, but I'm beginning to think that I'd find a way to come up with it if it meant I could leave. Cal isn't just angry with me; he hates me. Mentally and emotionally, I can't live like this for six months.

"That's where you're wrong. I have the best attorney in the nation and he was very clear in the contract that there are no provisions that give you the right to end the contract. If you do, I have the right to sue." Cal pushes himself to his feet. His palms clamp down on the arms of the chair and he leans forward, invading my personal space. "It won't get that far, though, Bella. I've ensured you will be staying here. If you don't, your perfect little family will lose everything they own." Warm lips press to my forehead. "Welcome home."

"What does my family have to do with this?" I sniffle. "What have you done?"

"It's not about what I have done. It's what I could do." Cal leaves me sitting here, devastated in a mess of my own tears. That man's heart is as stone-cold as the foundation of this castle.

8

"Come on!" I hold my phone up, trying to get a signal. I've gone to every corner of my room and still nothing. I even went as far as dangling over the balcony and almost falling to my death. There's Wi-Fi in range, but it's protected and Peter played dumb when I asked him for the password. I could bite the bullet and ask Cal, but I doubt that will do any good. Besides, I'm in the middle of my own pity party and plan to avoid him for the next six months—as if that's possible.

It's apparent I'm not here to work. Cal calls himself my boss because those are the terms used in the contract, but the only thing he wants to micromanage is my emotions. If I had to guess, he wants me to feel like complete shit for leaving him. He's spent years dwelling on it and blames me for everything bad that has happened to him. Does he not realize that bad things happen to everyone? Even me?

The more I think about it, the more I believe Cal has been living in the darkness of his past for the last twelve years. Of course I feel bad for leaving like I did, but I was a kid. He's behaving as if I was an adult who made an adult decision. It's not fair.

Screw it. I'm getting that damn Wi-Fi password. With heavy steps, I cross the room and jerk the door open. I'm taken aback when I see Cal standing there. "Umm. Hi," I say, walking backward as he walks in, "can I help you?"

He doesn't respond, just looks around the room like it's his first time ever stepping foot in here. "I have to take a trip to Naushon this evening. I'll only be gone a couple hours. You'll have dinner in your room." He stops beside my bed and scoops up a pair of my clean panties. He holds them up as they dangle from his index finger, observes them, and drops them back down like they're contaminated.

I take long steps to his side and tuck my panties under the blanket of the unmade bed, pressing my hands against the comforter. "Why are you leaving?"

His head lifts and he looks me in the eye momentarily. "I have business to tend to." Glancing away, he takes in the rest of the room. "I'll send Paulina, the housekeeper, in to tidy up your room, but I expect you to be a little neater. We're not kids anymore, Bella."

A low grumble climbs up my throat. "That's a little hypocritical coming from someone who's still holding on to the past of their childhood." Tightening my upper lip, I step out the open doors onto the balcony. The grainy stone beneath me scrapes against my bare feet. My fingers wrap firmly around the stone banister as I look at the dark clouds rolling in. It's such a dreary day as it is, and now I've got my former best friend harping on my cleanliness, or lack thereof. He knows I've always been a bit of a slob.

Cal comes up behind me and my breath hitches when his hands plant on either side of mine. His chin is practically resting on my shoulder. "Maybe it's not the past I'm bitter about, maybe it's the present. Or both, perhaps."

His vocabulary has changed drastically. Like someone that just stepped out of a historical English novel. Cal never used words like 'perhaps.' He talked in slang such as 'gonna' or 'wanna' and now it's 'going to' or 'want to.' Everything about him has changed. He's gone from cold to ice. Angry with the world, to downright loathing it.

My eyes stay focused on the sky as if I'm speaking directly to the clouds. "You're the one who brought me here. If you don't like it, let me leave."

"Is that what you want?" His breath tickles the back of my neck as he speaks.

I'm not even sure how to answer that, so I go with the truth. "I'm not going to pretend this reunion has been a happy one. I always hoped I'd see you again, Cal, but I never could have imagined you'd treat me this way." I want to tell him how bad it hurts. Like a knife in the chest that twists and turns every time he talks down to me.

"You didn't answer my question. Do you want to leave the island?" Placid fingers sweep my hair to the side. Eyes shut, head tilting, as Cal's lips ghost the crease of my neck. Each breath sends chills riding down my body. My mind goes back to that foggy state it was in when I laid eyes on him less than twenty-four hours ago. Only this time, it's because I won't allow myself to think.

I'm not sure if I want to leave. Cal shouldn't be making

my body demand attention from years of neglect. The pulsating between my legs, the prick at my nipples. He certainly shouldn't be the reason for my dampened panties and the cause of me having to clench my thighs. He just showed up out of nowhere. A missing piece in my life that is trying to find a place to fit while tossing other pieces to the side.

Pushing the sleeve of my shirt down, Cal exposes my shoulder. My eyes open quickly when his lips graze the skin. "Answer me," he demands, in a no-nonsense tone.

"Yes. I want to leave," I say on a clipped exhale.

Cal's mouth leaves my shoulder and he pulls my shirt back up. "That's a shame. But, unfortunately, you signed a contract, and I don't barter with employees bound by their signed contracts."

I snap around, facing his bemused smile. "I want a copy of that contract."

Cal places his hands behind him. His shoulders drawn back. "Not a problem. I'll have Byron bring a copy tonight."

With slumped shoulders, I ask one of the many questions gnawing at me. "Am I really here to work, Cal?"

"Yes. I will take your opinions on the design of the rooms on floors two through five. I may use your ideas; I may ignore them."

"And the pay that was agreed on in the contract?"

"You'll be compensated, per the agreement."

Biting the corner of my lip, I find myself lost in so many thoughts. "For six months?"

"For as long as it takes." Cal grins at me as if he has a

plan already set in stone. My insides shiver when I think of what that plan might entail—me, as his plaything.

"Do you really plan on opening this up as a resort, or do you just plan on making this my own personal prison?"

"Someday, there will be guests." Grazing my cheek with the back of his hand, he licks his lips. "Make sure you eat your dinner tonight. The last thing I need to come home to is a hangry houseguest."

"Employee," I correct him. "I am not a houseguest."

"Tomayto, tomahto." His hand drops and he walks back inside my room.

"Cal, wait," I holler as I snatch my phone off the bed. He stops in the doorway, presses his hand to the frame, and looks at me with impatient eyes. I scroll to my Wi-Fi settings and hold it up as I walk toward him. "I have no service, but there's a signal in range. Could I have the password?"

His hand grips the door handle firmly. "No," he deadpans before slamming the door shut.

"Please," I shout, grabbing the handle and ripping the door back open.

I step into the hall where he's already halfway down. Jogging after him, I catch up and walk in step with him. "Please, Cal. I have a family. People who will worry about me if I don't stay in touch."

"Must be nice," he quips, continuing on his way.

Grabbing him by the bicep, I try to stop him, but he just keeps going, causing me to stumble over my own two feet. I hit the hard floor on my knees and begin sobbing where I sit. "Why are you doing this?" I scream so loudly that my words bounce off the cement walls. A lantern flickers beside me, then slowly fizzles out. "My fiancé knows where I'm at. He's planning to come here to visit at some point." My face drops into my hands and the tears keep falling.

It's partially true. I did tell Trent he could come for a visit. I was under the assumption I'd be staying in the hotel where I'd be working.

I'm completely caught off guard when Cal grabs me by the wrist and jerks me up. My wobbly legs give out as I fall into his arms. Fingers grip my chin relentlessly as he gets right in my face. "Then I'll fuck you and make him listen while you scream my name."

"Why are you doing this to me?" I whimper through heavy breaths.

"Because I lost you once and I will not lose you again."

"You can't seriously think you can just keep me here."

"You'd be surprised at what I *can* do." His eyes dance across my lips as my heart beats rapidly in my chest.

Even as he spews his threatening and hateful words at me, my traitorous body reacts. I blame fear for my life. Desperation to flee this place and never return. At this moment, I think I'd do just about anything to escape— even if it means giving all of myself to him.

When his eyes slide back up, I shake the thoughts away. Bile rising in my throat for even thinking that way. One more second in his close proximity and I just might vomit all over his shiny black shoes.

My chin is released, but we're still standing only inches apart. "When did you say yes?" Cal asks, his angry tone shifting to a more curious note.

"Say yes?"

"You referred to *him* as your fiancé. When did you accept his proposal?"

"Right before I left," I lie. I didn't say yes, but Cal doesn't know that. Maybe if he knows I'm spoken for, he'll drop this ridiculous idea of keeping me here as his prisoner.

Rigid cords tense along Cal's neck as he gnashes his teeth. "Why?" His voice rises to a near shout. "Why the fuck would you do that?" Shivers cascade down my body as he grabs me by both shoulders. "You're a damn fool, Bella."

Scowling back at him, I refuse to cower. "I've done perfectly fine living my life the way I see fit for the past twelve years." I attempt to walk around him, but his hold only strengthens. "I think I can make my own choices."

"Of all the guys," he tsks. "And you had to choose the one I hate the most in this world."

My eyes widen in surprise. *He knows.* I don't say anything else because whatever I do say will only make things worse. No part of me wants to hurt Cal, even if he is out for my blood as his revenge.

Cal turns around and looks down the hall, giving me his back. "I guess I should have seen it coming. You were always into shiny, pretty things. It's no surprise you'd marry into the uptight Beckham family."

"We were just kids then. Trent has changed. He's very smart and kind. He—"

"Shut up!" Cal spins back around, slapping a hand over my mouth, forbidding me to speak. "He's scum. A piece of shit on the bottom of my shoe."

Cal's fingers dig into the side of my cheek as he walks

me back up against the wall. My head rests between two lit lanterns, the only source of light in this dim hall. Sliding his hand down my waist, chasing the shudders, he keeps going until he's reaching low with his hand on my inner thigh. I tremble as his hand drifts up, cupping my crotch through the thin fabric of my leggings. Angry eyes stare back at me. Dark, empty eyes that bore into mine and chase away any logic.

Our noses brush as his fingers grate at my entrance through my pants. "Does Trent make your legs shake the way I do?"

"You're disgusting," I growl, turning my head to avoid looking at his fixed glare.

With one hand pressed firmly to the wall on the side of my head and the other groping me, Cal draws in a deep breath of the air between us. "Tell me, Bella, do you enjoy being fucked by the guy who tore us apart?"

My eyes bolt to him. "What are you talking about?"

"Oh, he never told you? What about that brother of yours? Did he ever once mention their seditious act all those years ago?"

"You're lying," I spit out. "You just want me to hate everyone but you. Well, guess what, Cal?" I enunciate his name with a smirk on my lips. "I love them and I hate you." The words just drip from my mouth, out of both anger and fear. The truth is, I'm not sure I could ever hate Cal. There's a reason he is the way he is. We've both had to work extra hard to find our place in this world and something tells me, Cal had to do overtime.

Cal moves his hand, and when I think this game of cat and mouse is done, he slides it down the waistband of my leggings. The muscles in my stomach clench and I take in a shaky breath. His dark eyes glisten with mischief. "Love. Hate. Is there really a difference?" His fingers slide up and down my sex, rubbing at my entrance, for just a second, before he removes his hand from my pants. "You say you hate me, but I think you're loving this just as much as I am." His fingers shove into my mouth, causing me to gasp. I squirm, trying to get away, but I'm forced to taste myself on him.

Finally, Cal backs up, freeing me from his clutches, so I use this opportunity to get as far away from him as possible.

Walking hurriedly down the hall, I go back to my room and slam the door shut. There are no locks, and I'm certain that was no accident.

Eyeballing my phone, I think hard. I have to find a way off this island.

9

Bella

I'VE PACED the length of this room at least a dozen times. My thumbnail is down to the skin since I've been chewing relentlessly on it. I'm slowly going crazy, that's all I can come up with. Playing out every scenario in my head, they all come back to me being stuck here. It's certainly crossed my mind to try and hide on Cal's boat when he leaves tonight, but it's easier said than done. For one, there are guards. I know of two, but there could be more. Chances are, those guards are here just for me.

The only option I can come up with is trying to get to the small boat I saw by the dock when I arrived yesterday. There were no paddles, but I'll use a damn broomstick if I have to. I vaguely remember passing by an island, just beside this one, that looked inhabited. It would take me twenty, maybe thirty minutes on a boat without a motor. All I know is if I stay here, Cal will hurt me more than he already has. He will tear me down, probably rape me, and possibly kill me. I've come to the realization that my friend is no longer inside of him. The

Cal I knew is gone, and I'm not sure if he's ever coming back.

Creeping down the hall, I listen intently for any sound that could mean someone is coming. Cal left a couple hours ago and said he'd be gone until dark. It's only five o'clock in the evening, so I have another hour, at least. I pass by Cal's room and curiosity gets the best of me, so I give the handle a turn, but it's locked. Of course it is.

Leaving everything behind except for my phone and the clothes on my back, I take the elevator down to the lower level.

The puddle I saw coming in has dried up to just a damp spot on the cement floor. I look up and see the hole has been filled and smoothed over. I wonder if Cal did that. I don't take him to be a carpenter or even a handyman. It's possible there are more people staying here than I thought.

There's a door off to the side I never noticed before. It's different from the other rooms in this place. This one has the old skeleton keyhole but also a modern-day password keypad.

Everything about this place is a mystery and I just need to get the hell out of here and off this island and never look back.

A gust of wind ripples over the backside of the castle. The overgrown bushes out back blow so heavily they practically cover the opening. Hugging myself, I head out the same way I came in. Pushing the large door open, I step out onto the cobblestone, looking out at the water in front of me. My eyes quickly dart to where the boat was and I breathe a sigh of relief when I see it's still there.

Hope washes over me. It's not going to be easy in these heavy winds, but it's either die trying or be at the mercy of a man who'd love nothing more than to shred me of any dignity I have left. Before the door closes behind me, I turn around and push it back open. Skimming the open area, I look for anything that can assist me in paddling.

"Yes!" I mumble. Long strides lead me in front of a couple strip boards perched against the wall beside the elevator. Dragging one behind me, I head down to the water.

I might not be physically fit, but I'm a survivor. I've proven that every day since I found my mom's corpse at the age of four. Addiction is an ugly thing and I'd love more than anything to erase those memories from my head. After two hours of staring at her in hopes of her waking up, I eventually realized she wouldn't. I kissed her forehead and ran to the neighbor's house. Twenty minutes later, I was put in the back of the car by a social worker and the adventures of foster life began.

I was in and out of so many homes that I lost count. Apparently, it's frowned upon when you're headstrong and speak what's on your mind. Slowly, I learned to keep my mouth shut. That's when I ended up at The Webster House.

The first time I saw Cal, it was like we instantly connected. Kindred spirits, soulmates—call it what you will, but it was special. My heart aches at what he's become. If I'd stayed with him, like I promised, maybe he wouldn't be so angry with the world.

Sucking it up, I swipe away the tears rolling down my cheeks. I drop the piece of lumber in the boat and it lands with a loud thud. The wind becomes turbulent as rain starts to fall. What starts as a light sprinkle quickly escalates into a full-on downpour. A thunderous boom shudders the ground beneath me at the same time a bolt of lightning lights up the sky.

In a matter of seconds, I went from bone dry to soaking wet. More rain comes as the wind picks up, pelting against my bare arms. I look down, trying to stop it from hitting my face.

"Why is this happening?" I cry out as another strike of lightning crackles through the clouds. Twisting and turning my head, I try to look out at the water, but it's a haze of cloudbursts and I can't see more than three feet in front of me.

I give the boat a push and when it doesn't even budge, I throw my full weight into it and push harder. "Come on, you damn thing." I try again, and it slowly begins to slip out of the muck it's lodged in.

Gripping the front of the boat, I crouch down and dig my bare toes into the moss and push with all my might. It slowly begins to slide out into the water, but with each inch that it is engulfed, the crazier this seems. I'm taking a rowboat out on the bay in the eye of a dangerous storm.

It's only a few minutes. I'll be able to dock at the closest island and call for help.

I'm knee-deep in the water beside the boat when I finally jump in. It rocks back and forth as I steady myself on the seat, wasting no time dipping the board in and paddling. I paddle to the left a few times then switch to the right, until I'm moving straight ahead, right into the torrent.

Rain pommels me, coating every inch of my water-logged skin while the boat begins to fill. I blink away the drops formed on my eyelashes, trying like hell to see clearly, but it's impossible.

I'm not sure that I've ever been so scared in my life, and I've been through some horrific stuff. I just need to go straight out of here and then to the right until I see the island. Hopefully, the rain will let up and I'll be able to see where I'm going.

It's okay. I'll be okay.

Just when I think I'm far enough to begin turning toward the east, I spot dim lights shining through the smog. My heart beats at warp speed when they begin coming closer, and closer. Steadily, I begin rowing backward. Left side, right side, over and over, as if the bright light blinding me is what's pushing me back onto shore. I pinch my eyes shut, but I don't stop rowing.

They're going to hit me. It's not Cal or the storm that will end my life. I'll be pushed into the water by this huge boat.

My life flashes before my eyes. But, it's him I see. The smile he wore the first time I saw him at the age of ten.

At eleven years old, when I saw the first tear that rolled down his cheek when Mrs. Webster told him that his birth parents were dead and never coming for him. He held it together around everyone else in the house, but when we were alone, the tears fell.

That time when he was twelve and got a bloody nose in the middle of the night and I was so worried that he was going to choke on his own blood and die. I didn't sleep at all that night as I held the cloth so his sleepy eyes could rest.

When he was thirteen I caught him staring at me with a new look in his eyes as I played his favorite song on the piano. It gave me butterflies and I never understood why —until now.

At fourteen years old, I never even told him goodbye.

And now, I'll never be able to make him understand. He'll never get a proper apology and I won't know what filled his heart with so much anger.

I can't tell him about my first kiss, or hear about his first dance. I won't know what year he graduated, or from where. All the little things that shaped us into who we are today are left unknown and all we have is the memories of our lives before meeting as kids.

My body goes into shock before reality can touch me.

I'm going to drown.

This is the end.

10

Callum

"DOCK US NOW!" I shout over the riotous downpour bombarding us. The boat catches in a gust of wind and sways us too far to the right. "Get it under control or I'll hire someone who knows how to drive a goddamn boat!"

Holding tightly to a limp Bella, I look down at her. She's pallid and unresponsive, but she has a pulse, so I know she's still alive. Her lips are slightly parted and each breath flares her sprinkled nostrils just a tad. She's always hated those freckles, while I'd always told her they were cute as shit. Now, I'm not so sure I like them. I'm not sure I like anything about her. Not her curls that no longer cover her entire head but just the very ends of her hair. Definitely not her pink, plump lips. And most certainly not the way she lies perfectly in my arms like her body was molded to fit with mine. No. I don't like any of it. In fact, I downright hate it.

Months before Bella arrived, I'd remind myself daily that all of this is an act of revenge. I will not fall under her spell. I refuse to be manipulated, just so she can pull the rug out from under me again and send me free-falling into twelve more years of hell. No. Falling for this girl is not an option. Everything I went through—everything I am—is because of her.

Another gust of wind whirls, sending strands of her hair over her face. I use my forearm to try and sweep them away from her mouth but fail horribly. Hail the size of marbles begins beating down on the boat, so I lean forward, using my body to shield hers.

I'm not sure why I do it, but I don't stop as I tug her closer. Her cheek presses firmly against my chest and I hold her like her life depends on it.

"I never took you to be a complete idiot, Bella," I say, looking down at her. Who the fuck goes out in a rowboat with a board as a paddle in the midst of a tropical storm?

We finally stop at the dock and Leo, the captain, begins tying the boat up. I don't even hesitate to cradle Bella in my arms as I stand. She's ice-cold and if she doesn't get warm immediately, hypothermia could set in.

"Anders," I say to my head security guard who rode along with us. "Page Joel and get him out here." Anders has been with me for a few years, but Joel has only been on my payroll for a short six months, and I should have known better than to trust the reference of a strip club bouncer.

Peter is waiting with an umbrella when my feet hit solid ground. He holds it over my head immediately and I scowl at him as water rolls down my face.

"I'm sorry, sir. We didn't—"

"Don't!" I reply sternly.

Joel comes walking amply down the beaten path, as if

we aren't all standing here in the rain waiting on his sorry ass.

Anders joins my side and I abruptly hand Bella to him. He catches her, cradling her in the same manner I was. "Take her to my sitting room and wrap her in a blanket. This won't take long." My eyes are held tightly to Joel's as he comes closer.

Peter hovers over me with an umbrella, and I swat it away. "Cover her. Not me."

I close the space between Joel and me, but before he can even come to a complete stop, I cock my fist back and plant it right between his eyes. He stumbles backward but doesn't fall, so I grab him by the head with both hands and lift my knee straight to his chin. Just as I release him, I look up and see Bella's watchful eyes. Her expression is blank, but she's just bore witness to the monster I've become—the monster *she* made me.

Joel lets out a low grumble but doesn't dare try and defend himself. "Get the fuck off my island." Giving him a push, he finally hits the ground and I walk past him.

Leo will be escorting him off the island. He's lucky he won't be getting dumped in the middle of the bay.

Blood runs down my hand, dripping to the ground as the rain washes it away. My feet move at a leisurely pace as I make no attempt to outrun the storm that's only strengthening with each passing minute. A little rain never hurt anyone. In fact, storms are one of the few things that make me feel alive anymore. There's nothing quite like the cleanse of a downpour while the sky opens up and shouts back at you. I've had my fair share of screaming matches with the atmosphere. It seems to hate me enough to keep me here no matter how many times I've tried to leave.

It was all for this—every beating from the world, every hurdle I've jumped—it all happened to bring me here, with her.

I make it up to my floor and pause in the doorway to the sitting room beside Peter. He's peering into the room with his hands folded behind his back. "As you can see, she's awake. Though, I'm not sure she's totally coherent. She seems to be in somewhat of a disorientated state, likely from being out in the cold rain for so long. I've laid some dry clothes out beside her, but she's made no attempt to change."

We both just survey her as if she's some bizarre life-form. "Thank you, Peter. Please have the cook make her some soup and hot tea."

Peter acknowledges me with a nod and steps around me.

I press both hands to the doorframe and just watch her. On the floor in front of the blazing fireplace with a white shag rug beneath her. She's curled herself into a ball with a cream-colored throw blanket wrapped securely around her. Her brown hair is now black as water drips, soaking the blanket on her back.

For a moment, I forgot that I'm also drenched. My shoes squeak as I move closer to her, but she doesn't even flinch at the sound of me drawing near.

Vulnerability at its finest. I could choose to beat her down a few more pegs and throw another reminder of the past in her face, or I can savor this serene moment of placidity between us. I've got little fight left in me today and I prefer not to rile her up and risk a slap in the face. No, I'll save that for the morning.

Right now, Bella needs out of these wet clothes. She needs warmth, food, and rest.

Crouching down, I slowly slide the blanket down her back. She offers no recognition of my presence in the room. My head tilts forward and I inhale the scent of her wet hair. She smells of earth and rain.

With a shaky hand, I touch the ends of her hair. Damaged remnants that probably took years to grow to this length. Twelve years, perhaps. Is it possible that these were baby hairs growing all those years ago? The last hair on her head I touched before she left me.

I'll never understand how this beautiful girl was ever a hand-me-down. Passed along from person to person because no one wanted to keep her. She's the epitome of perfection and grace, aside from that dirty mouth of hers.

Bending at the waist, I peer around her shoulder and look at her face. Wide open eyes with dancing flames in them as she stares into the fire. She's completely void of any emotion at this moment. Hands folded neatly in her lap, back straight as a board.

I move to the front of her, kneeling in my waterlogged clothes. Breaking her gaze on the fire, her eyes bore into mine, but she doesn't make a sound.

"I'm going to take these wet clothes off you," I tell her, making her aware of my intentions. I will surely have my way with Bella, but tonight is not the night for that.

In a gentle motion, I grip the bottom of her shirt and lift it up to pull it over her head. She doesn't fight me off as her chest is exposed to me. I drop the heavy shirt on the floor beside the rug and bite hard at my bottom lip as I ward off temptation. Her cleavage peeks out of her black bra and I'm mesmerized by her silky, peach-colored skin. There's an insatiable need to touch her. To taste every inch of her body and remind myself of what I've missed all these years.

It wasn't supposed to be like this. When I found Bella last year, I had a plan. Get her here and make her miserable for leaving me by keeping her forever. She ate right out of my hand when she signed that contract. I wanted to punish her, but not in the same way I punished everyone who hurt us. Her punishment was as simple as giving me the next twelve years of her life to make up for the lost time.

I watched her. I held back as I waited for the right time. Months passed as I witnessed her relationship blossom with that son of a bitch, Trent. I saw family dinners from the yard outside of her house. I stole glances as she slept peacefully in her bed. I fought off the urge to smother her with a pillow one night before the plan of taking my own life, just so we could hold true to the pact —*always stay together, until kingdom come.*

Months of misery that were nothing compared to the years of pure torture.

Now, she's here and the only thing I desire is her.

"I want to go home," Bella finally speaks through a cracked voice.

My fingers slide featherlike up her arm, leaving a footpath of goosebumps. "You are home," I whisper into the thin space between us. Taking her hand, I lift her up and she follows suit as we get to our feet.

"I'm going to take your pants off now." As I crouch down, I look up at her for approval, determined not to take advantage of her vulnerable state. She peers down at me with sadness in her eyes but doesn't fend me off when I tug at the waistband of her black cotton pants. They slide down with ease, leaving a trail of dampness behind. Her legs part slightly, allowing me to pass her thighs and when they reach the bottom, she lifts her foot and steps out of them. I place a hand on her calf and slide it up, sweeping away the water droplets.

Water continues to drop freely from the ends of her hair, hitting me in the face as she glances down at me. My heart rattles against my rib cage as I slide my hand up farther, stopping at her inner thigh. I squeeze slightly and draw in a deep breath, reminding myself that there will be plenty of time to explore every crack and crevice. And I will. I want to memorize every scar, blemish, and mark on her fragile body.

"Callum, I…" Her words come to a halt when my head snaps back up to look at her.

"You called me Callum. Why?" She never calls me Callum, even when I asked her to.

"I'm cold."

Of course she is. I push myself up and stand, bringing the blanket up with me. Airing it out with a fluff, I wrap it around her. It hangs freely over her shoulders as she makes no move to hold it.

"Come with me." I place an arm around her neck, holding the blanket in place. We walk side by side out of the sitting room, and my nerves begin to heighten as we approach my bedroom. I stop abruptly a foot away from the door and try to calm my racing heart.

I can't bring her there.

Yes. Yes, I can. This isn't just somebody, this is Bella. My Bella.

Trembling, I reach into my pocket and pull out the master skeleton key that opens every door in this place. I look at Bella before sticking it into the lock. She's still void of expression, but her color is starting to return.

I can't do it.

"This way." I jerk her by the arm and walk steadfast back down the hall to her bedroom.

The blanket falls to the floor and Bella stumbles, almost tripping over it, but I continue to pull her along, picking up my pace. When we reach her door, I open it up, give her a nudge inside, then slam it shut—with me on the other side.

Two hands hit the side of my head as I clench my hair and pull with all my might.

Fuck. That was too close. I was seconds away from allowing her into my sanctuary. The one place that is only mine—a place where I'm untouchable and free to unleash my demons.

I can't let my guard down like that again.

11

IT'S BEEN three days since I miserably failed at trying to escape. I've managed to stumble into this dark cloud that's draining me of purpose. Everything I had hoped for or planned for the future seems so unattainable. All my dreams, as far away as they were, have washed away in a matter of days. What's left of me lies hopeless in this fancy bed, when all I really want is to be home, curled up on my yard sale, full-size mattress.

There's a knock at the door, one of many over the last seventy-two hours. I ignore it, just like all the others. And, just like every other time, the door opens and Peter comes in, against my wishes. I'm not angry with him. He's just doing as he's told by his boss. The person I'm angry at is Callum.

"Ms. Jenkins, Mr. Ellis has requested your presence for lunch in the courtyard."

The courtyard? I roll over to my other side, so I'm able to see Peter. "What courtyard?" As far as I've seen, everything outside of this castle is just unattended landscaping and overgrown weeds.

"I'll show you to it if you'd like."

Rolling back over to face away from him, I tug the blanket up over my shoulders. "Tell Mr. Ellis I kindly said to fuck off."

My stomach growls loud enough for it to ripple through the room, but I ignore the cries of hunger.

The sound of Peter's shoes against the hardwood floor alerts me that he's coming closer. "You should consider eating. You need your strength."

"I'll survive."

When he occupies the space beside my bed, I look over my shoulder. Before I can even speak, he does. "He's very fond of you, Ms. Jenkins. Mr. Ellis is not fond of much."

Curiosity piques my interest as I push myself into a sitting position. "Your boss is an asshole. Not to mention, he basically kidnapped me."

"Legally, yes."

It's obvious whose side he's on.

My legs fold into a crisscross and I use this opportunity to quiz Peter, possibly while earning his trust. It could benefit me in the future. "How well do you know him?"

"Well enough to know that he'll be very upset if he knew we were having a conversation about him. He's a very private man and prefers to keep things that way."

"Okay then, we can keep this our little secret. How long have you worked for him?"

Peter looks at the ceiling, as if he's counting the years,

then he looks back at me. "I've been with the Ellis family for seventeen years."

"Oh, wow." That's long before Cal was adopted into the family. I figured Peter came on board after the death of Mr. Ellis Senior. There's a good chance he knows all the secrets to this mysterious man.

"So you knew him when he first came to live with the Ellises?"

"I did. In fact, I'm the one who escorted him from the home he was in to his new home in New York."

"New York, huh? I didn't know that."

"He was such a quiet boy. Had a very hard go at life, but inside of him, there is a heart that beats with good intentions."

"Yeah," I chuckle, "a hollow heart."

Peter glances behind him before leaning forward and whispering, "He can be a bit intense, but it's because he knows no better. He needs you to show him." Peter straightens and takes a step back. "He'll be waiting in the courtyard." He gives a curtsy, nods, and leaves me with my thoughts.

He knows no better. He needs you to show him.

No. Screw that. Cal is twenty-six years old. It's true that he had a hard go at life, but so did I, dammit. I'm not out kidnapping people who pissed me off and belittling them to the point of no return. He knows better and he, or anyone else who says he doesn't, is just making excuses for his behavior. He might be rich and insanely attractive, but he needs to earn back my respect and all the money in the world won't buy it.

Last night, for a brief moment, I looked into Cal's eyes

and I saw the boy I once knew. He undressed me with such attentiveness. Never once tried to take advantage of my defenseless state. But it doesn't change anything. Those moments were short-lived before he threw me into my room like I was a naked rag doll and left me in tears.

There's a monster inside of the boy who was once my friend and I'm not sure he'll ever break free from the chains that bind him to his past.

Kicking my feet out in front of me, I get up. My bare feet pad across the floor, then down the hall.

I'm wearing nothing more than a pair of black lounge shorts and a solid gray hoodie, twice my size, but I'm not exactly out to impress. It's apparent with the messy bun topping my head and the lack of makeup on my face.

I stop walking directly in front of Cal's bedroom door, wondering if it could be unlocked. Maybe I could get an inkling into the man he's become if I can find something in his room. Possibly something that shows what he's been doing the last twelve years to become such a deranged man.

Just as I go to reach for the doorknob, my hand jerks back when I see Peter.

"Oh dear," he says in a concerned tone, rushing to my side. He grabs me by the shoulders and walks me toward the elevator. "Never, ever, try to go in that room. Mr. Ellis is a very private man and he'd be very upset."

"Duly noted. It's just a room, though."

"A room that is off-limits. For your own safety, pretend it doesn't exist."

For whatever reason, Peter is very persistent, but it only makes me want to go in that room even more. To be that serious about no one entering, Cal has to be hiding something.

Peter continues to usher me to the elevator. He even presses the down button and makes sure I'm on, before letting the doors close with him on the other side.

Cal has waged a war and I'm prepared for battle—at least, in my head I am. Physically, I've got nothing. He could do whatever he wants with me on this island and I've got no defense.

When the elevator stops at the ground level, I look around, wondering where this meticulous courtyard could be. It has to be out back, possibly beyond the arch I saw when I was out here with Peter a few days ago.

Each step sends my heart deeper into my stomach. Something is different. I'm not outside yet, but I can see that the yard has been manicured. The grass is cut, and... is that the sound of a fountain running?

I pick up my pace and step outside.

My eyes widen in surprise. It's not what I was expecting at all. Everything I envisioned—all the ideas I told Peter I had for this back yard—it's all here. There's a fresh paved patio with a wrought-iron, glass table sitting in front of me with two chairs on either side of it. To the left is a beautiful garden blooming with wildflowers, even peonies, which Cal knows are my favorite. They had to have all been planted because they certainly did not grow.

Walking farther out, the sound of the fountain comes closer. I keep going until I'm on the finished, wood bridge. It no longer looks like it's about to collapse at any moment. It's newly built with a cherry finish with clear water running beneath it. I walk across it and gasp at the sight in front of me.

It's the courtyard. At least, I think it is. This is exactly how I would imagine a courtyard would look. A curtain wall wraps around the circular area. There are bushes with symmetrical tops surrounding the wall. The grass looks like it was laid, not grown. It's far too perfect, not a bare spot in sight. In the center is a large square of mosaic tiles and right in the middle of them is a fountain that takes my breath away. Made of five tiers with water running into sphere-shaped bowls.

"What do you think?"

I jolt at the sound of his voice. Spinning on my heel, I turn to face Cal. "It's beautiful." I continue to walk the grounds, taking it all in. The flowers and live plants offer a sense of calm. Everything here has felt so dead since I've arrived and it's twisted, but it sort of felt like that was my fate. While it's beautiful, it doesn't change that I'm still slowly dying inside.

"The cook has just brought lunch out. Come with me." Cal extends his hand. I look down at it like it's encased with poison.

"No," I say point-blankly, "I'm not going anywhere with you."

I shouldn't have even come down here, but Peter piqued my interest when he mentioned a courtyard. I had to see what he was so buttoned-up about. Well, now I know.

"I'm going back to my room." Crossing my arms over my chest, I hide the fact that I'm not wearing a bra, though it's not noticeable in this large sweatshirt.

"Bella, wait." Cal reaches out from behind me and grabs me by the arm.

"Get off me." I scowl, jerking away from him. "Don't you get it by now? I don't want to be here anymore. As soon as I can get a signal on my phone, I'm taking the first boat out." My words are harsh, but they have to be. Cal has not shown me the slightest bit of decency and I refuse to let him think I will stay here, just so he can make me feel like shit for leaving him twelve years ago.

"You're not going anywhere. Now, quit being a pain in the ass and eat."

"Why do you care so much if I eat?" It's getting really annoying. He treats me like I'm a child who's on the verge of starvation.

"Because you need your energy."

I'm trying really hard to keep my cool here, but I'm two seconds from lashing out at him. After years of therapy, I've learned, quite well, not to wear my emotions, but he's pushing buttons that he has no right to push.

Ignoring what he said, I storm back toward the castle.

"They'll never love you the way you love them," he hollers from behind me, in a last-ditch effort to get a reaction out of me.

Against my better judgment, I give him the reaction he's digging for. "That's where you're wrong. They do love me the way I love them. You're mistaking my family for yours." There's a smirk on my face that I hope he reads loud and clear. He once said he could read my thoughts just by looking in my eyes, so I glower hard at him, hoping he's hearing exactly what I'm thinking. The smile on his face says he's reading me all wrong, so I lay it out for him. "Fuck you."

Long strides bring him in front of me. "Oh, I will, and I'll love every second of it."

"I'd die before I ever had sex with you."

His tongue runs between his lips. "I prefer my women alive while I'm fucking them, but I'm willing to make an exception just for you."

He takes my hand in his, but I pull back, and in a knee-jerk reaction, I slap him across the face.

Unmoved, he warns me with a hard stare and before I can react, he's grabbing me by the waist and walking me backward, as my handprint forms on his cheek.

A low grumble climbs up his throat as he takes both of my wrists and pins them with one hand over my head. "I hate you, Callum."

"Quit calling me that," he bites back.

"Oh, now you want me to call you, Cal? I thought that title was saved for your friends and family." A shiver rides down my body.

"I have neither of those." Hungry eyes dart down to my lips and I lick them instinctively. He wouldn't dare.

I watch his mouth in anticipation and I despise the part of my brain that wants him to kiss me, just to see how it makes me feel. "Well, you know exactly who to blame for that."

"That I do. You." His face comes closer, and I catch my breath, right before his mouth lands on mine.

I should fight him off, but the pressure he's laying on me is too much. He pries my tight lips apart with his strong tongue. His hard cock grinds into my hip bone while my hands stay anchored over my head, unable to push him away—not that I'm sure I would.

My nipples pebble under my sweatshirt. No one has ever kissed me with such intensity or made my body feel weightless the way it feels now. We could leave the ground and float away and I'd be none the wiser.

Sweet mint seeps into my taste buds as it rolls off his tongue. His free hand slides down, gripping my waist. I'm miniscule and weak beneath him and there's not a damn thing I can do about it.

My pussy pulsates, begging to be touched, while I internally scream that this is not what I want. That deceitful little bitch.

My eyes open and I spot Peter carrying a pitcher of lemonade, but when he turns back around abruptly and walks away, my eyes close again. I try to pull back, so I can stop this, but there's no point. What Cal wants, Cal gets, and right now, he wants me.

So, I fall into the kiss and I give him all I've got. Lifting my knee between his legs, I rub it against his erection. He groans a sound of desperation, then moves his hand up my sweatshirt. I'm braless and he soon realizes that when he pinches the bud of my nipple and rolls it between his thumb and forefinger. My skin tingles and my logic is clouded, once again.

Cal moves his fingers steadfast down my side and immediately sticks his hands in my shorts. "Cal," I whimper into his mouth. He silences me by crushing it harder against mine, deepening our kiss.

I gasp when he unexpectedly shoves two fingers into my sex. A twinge of pain shoots through me, but it subsides quickly. My skin sears as my face reddens from the heat I'm engulfed in, just from his body pressing so closely to mine. Hesitation pokes at me, but I ignore it.

When Cal breaks our kiss, he looks me in the eye momentarily, possibly seeking assurance—something I refuse to give him—then he plants soft kisses all over the crease of my neck.

I'm sure he's confident that I won't try and run at this point, so he lets go of my hands. Unsure what to do with them, I set them on his shoulders.

I push away all hesitation and give in to what my body craves. If he wants to pleasure me, fine. But, I refuse to reciprocate the gesture and do the same for him.

Parting my legs slightly for him, he cups my pussy and continues pumping two fingers inside of me. The swooshing sound of my arousal makes me cringe, but at least it drowns out the thumping of my racing heart.

His venomous breath hits the shell of my ear. "Fuck. You're so wet, Bella."

My cheeks heat up again, but when his thumb begins rubbing my most sensitive spot, all modesty leaves me. I drop my head back and rest it against the stone wall. Cal bends his fingers and hits my G-spot, sending me soaring. My eyes close, my mouth falls open, and I relish in the insane amount of pleasure he's giving me. It's like nothing I've ever felt before. Trent has fingered me before, but it wasn't like this—not even close. At this point, I'm not even sure if I've ever had an orgasm before, that's how novel this feeling is to me.

"Oh God," I cry out when his pace quickens. My spine

grates against the wall, but the pain only arouses me further. "Cal, I'm—"

"That's right. Come for me, Bella." His voice is strained and husky. Holding a lust that sends my body into a frenzy.

Holding my breath, I clench my thighs and feel my insides contract while leaving me powerless. Ripples of electricity course through me and the next thing I know, I'm coming around Cal's fingers.

It takes me a moment to collect my thoughts, but once I do, I'm humiliated. I straighten my back and look to the right of me, avoiding eye contact. "That was a mistake." I pull at his arm, forcing his hand out of my shorts.

Cal puts his hand on my cheek, with the same fingers that were just inside me, and he turns my head to look at him. "It's a good thing you're not a regretful person then." His lips press against mine and nausea pools in my stomach.

"When do I get to go home?"

His eyebrows dip. "I've told you. You are home."

"Cut the bullshit, Cal."

"Oh. I'm Cal again?" He runs his fingers behind my ear and I push him back with two hands.

"You can't keep me here forever."

"Sure I can." His hand grabs mine and he pulls me like a disobedient dog on a leash, dragging me through the courtyard.

I look down and notice a wet spot on my shorts that looks like I've pissed myself. When I look up, I see Cal watching me as we continue to walk.

"Peter," Cal calls out. When he doesn't show his face, he yells louder, "Peter."

At his beck and call, Peter pops out from the archway of the castle. "Yes, sir?"

"Please bring Bella some clean clothes. She's made a mess in her shorts."

I instantly feel my cheeks flush and pinch my eyes closed. When I open them, Peter is gone. I swat hard at Cal's shoulder. "Why would you do that?"

He bites back a smile and my stomach somersaults. *Did Cal almost laugh?* I'd do just about anything to hear that sound again. One of his curled-over belly laughs. It was the best sound in the world.

Cal pulls out a chair and gestures for me to sit. "I'll wait until I change, thanks." My eyes roll as I try hard to maintain this hard-ass facade. I can't let him see how much of an effect he has on me. If he knew that I hated his guts one minute and internally cried to see a humane side of him the next, he'd use it to his advantage. All sociopaths do, and I'm almost certain that's what Cal has become.

It hurts to know that it's partially my fault. If I'd been there…no, I can't go there.

Cal slides a chair out from the table, the metal legs scraping against the cement patio. He takes a seat and sets a napkin on his lap. "I hope you still like spaghetti," he says, pouring himself a glass of lemonade and then another that I presume to be mine.

I press my hands to my hips. "If I eat your damn spaghetti, can I catch the next boat out of here?"

"No." He flips open a Manila folder on the table and

takes out some stapled papers. "But you can have your copy of the contract, like I promised."

I snatch it away when he hands it to me. My eyes skim over the first page, then the second, but I'm too riled up to read anything my eyes see right now.

"Thought you might want a copy of this, too."

I look up and see him holding out what looks to be a page from a newspaper. I take it from him. "What's this?"

"Insurance."

The headline on the paper grabs my attention immediately. **Hanafin Incorporated negotiates partnership with Callum Ellis, owner and operator of world-renowned Ellis Empire.**

"Okay," I say with sarcasm. "You want me to congratulate you or something." I hold up the paper. "I've got no idea why you think I'd care about this. You're rich. I get it."

"Keep reading."

I shake my head in annoyance but read the short paragraph.

Hanafin Incorporated, known for their subsidiary company, Office Pro, specializes in custom office furniture.

I don't even continue. Slamming the paper down on the glass table, I rattle the fine china sitting on top. "You son of a bitch."

"I never knew her, but I assume she probably was a bitch. I mean, you'd have to be to leave your newborn child next to a dumpster in an alley."

"Is this some sort of a joke to you?"

Cal re-situates his napkin and casually lays his arms

on top of the table on either side of his empty plate. "No joke. Strictly business."

"You bought my parents' fucking company!" I scream, grabbing the glass of the round table and flipping it up.

Cal springs to his feet as the glass crashes against the pavement.

"Why?" I shout, even louder this time. "It's a measly office furniture company. You don't even have offices."

"Sure, I do," he replies, completely calm and collected, and it only pisses me off even more. "But that's not why I bought it. I told you, it's insurance."

Cal begins picking the remnants of my outburst off his shirt. Spaghetti noodles drop off him. Red sauce coats the patio and glass is everywhere.

"Insurance for what? Me? I will never belong to you, Cal."

He stops, noodle in hand, and flings it to the ground as his eyes darken and the rigid cords of his neck bulge. "You already do." His jaw clenches, teeth grinding. "And now it's set in stone. You try to leave and your parents are out of jobs. They'll never find work in that rundown town. They'll lose their house, their cars, everything."

My head shakes in disbelief. "What the hell happened to you?"

I always knew Cal had a side to him that could be dangerous if it wasn't controlled, but I never expected he'd turn out to be this heartless.

"Life happened. When you're forged with no purpose in life, unwanted by the world, and hated by all, this is what becomes of you."

My heart aches. As angry as I am with Cal, I know that

gnawing feeling inside that tells you you're incapable of being loved. "You are wanted, Cal. You have a family. A very wealthy family, I might add."

He gives me a side-glance while wiping his sauce-covered phone with a napkin. "I didn't ask for this." Then he goes to leave, hollering over his shoulder, "Peter will bring food to your room."

"No," I holler back, "you can't just leave. I need answers, Cal." He doesn't stop, so I follow after him. "Cal," I try again. He picks up his pace, so I snatch his forearm. "Please." He jerks away and I feel defeated. Tears begin falling down my cheeks and I'm so damn tired of crying. I swipe them away violently. I fall to my knees on the cement foundation in the unfinished area of the castle. "I'll never stop trying to leave. You won't win."

Cal stops in front of the elevator, his icy stare held on me. "Then I'll be forced to destroy everything you love." The doors open and he steps inside, leaving me broken and helpless.

AFTER SPENDING an hour moping around the ground level and seeing if there is anything to help me make my escape, I come up with a plan. It's not foolproof, but it's better than doing nothing. I just have to break Cal down and use my charm to convince him to let me leave. Even if I do get a signal or a phone to use at this point, it's no use. He'll destroy the lives of everyone I care about and I'm not about to let that happen. So, tonight, I'll play the dutiful prisoner.

When I came back to my room, I found a dress lying on my bed with a note on top of it that said, *Meet me in the ballroom at eight o'clock.*

This afternoon I would have crumpled the letter and possibly lit it on fire outside of Cal's bedroom, but now, I'm stepping into a teal gown while Peter waits outside the door to zip me up. Fortunately, I did bring a strapless bra with me, so I don't have to go commando underneath this thing.

"You can come in now," I holler in front of the closed door.

The door opens and Peter steps inside. I glance over my shoulder and notice Peter's rosy cheeks. It makes me wonder how long it's been since this old man touched a woman. He's such a sweet guy and it's a shame his life has been wasted on this unhinged family.

With my hair bunched to the side, Peter zips the dress up, and I turn around to face him. "How does it look?" My fingers run over the satin fabric and I feel like Cinderella. If only I were about to meet my Prince Charming.

"You will most certainly take Mr. Ellis's breath away."

"That's what I'm hoping for." *With any luck, it will be the last breath he takes.* The thought crosses my mind, but I quickly sweep it away. I don't want Cal to die, or even get hurt, for that matter. I just want him to let me leave, so I can go back to my life in Rhode Island and begin searching for a new job. Of course, I'll have Trent telling me how I don't need to work.

Trent. Guilt gnaws at me when I think of what I allowed earlier today. I've always despised cheating and that's exactly what I did. I cheated on Trent. The sad truth is, it's the action that makes me feel guilty, not so much the thought of it breaking us apart or causing me to lose Trent's trust. I'm at the point in our relationship where, I think, 'it is what it is.'

Peter snaps me out of my thoughts. "If you no longer need me, I'll let Mr. Ellis know you'll be down shortly."

"Thank you, Peter. I appreciate your help. It's not like I have a lady-in-waiting here to help me with these things." I chuckle.

"If you'd like one, I'm sure it can be arranged. Magdalene did a lovely job for Mrs. Ellis and she was very fond of the family."

I was only making a joke, but it seems that this family really does hire all kinds of help. Peter is looking at me like he's waiting for me to answer him and I didn't even realize it was a question. "You're serious?" I finally say.

"If it would make you happy, I'm sure Mr. Ellis would be obliged to have her stay."

"No, that's not necessary. I'm fully capable of dressing myself."

"Very well. If you change your mind, please let one of us know. I'll see myself out." Peter goes to leave, but I'm left with a lingering question.

"Peter. What was she like? Mrs. Ellis, I mean." It's only natural that I'd wonder what Cal's adoptive mother was like. Was she nurturing? Kind? Sweet? Did she tend to him when he was sick?

Peter's face turns ghostly white and it's apparent that I've hit a nerve as he fiddles with his fingers nervously. "Mr. Ellis is waiting. I must go." He turns quickly and leaves the room.

That was strange. It was a simple question, and he couldn't even answer it.

I go into my en suite bathroom, that is actually pretty small for such a large bedroom. It's also old-fashioned with a clawfoot tub in the center and a basin for a sink that's attached to the wall, not the floor.

There's a small square mirror over the sink and I look back at myself while tying my hair into a bun. Remembering that my goal is to entice Cal, I pull it back down and give my head a twirl to fluff my natural curls. I dab on some light makeup and coat my lips in a nude gloss then smack my lips together.

Stepping into a pair of silver strappy heels, I straighten my posture and hope like hell that I don't break a leg in these things. It's been years since I've worn heels and I'm not even sure if I remember how to walk in them. I don't live the lavish lifestyle that Cal does. My life is average, at most. I prefer casual clothes and nights in with movies and popcorn.

Somehow, I manage to make it down the hall to the elevator without even stumbling. My confidence is soaring as I hold my head high and imagine that I'm on my way to some fancy gathering. The elevator beeps and I go to step in but take a step back when I see that it's occupied. "Umm, hi," I say to Byron, Cal's attorney, who's standing in the elevator in a three-piece black suit with a matching tie.

"Wow," his eyes skim over every detail of my body as he presses a hand to the door, keeping it open, "you don't see that on Cori Cove often."

Flattered, I feel myself blush a little. "What are you

doing here?" I spit out, likely sounding ruder than I intended to.

"I'm here to escort you to the ball."

This is just far too formal for my liking.

"Back to your original statement. You don't see girls like me here often, or ever?" I step inside and bunch myself into a corner.

"It's probably best if I don't answer that question," he says in a teasing tone, but now he has my wheels turning.

The door slides shut and Byron still has his gaze laser-focused on me. It's not my eyes he's looking at, though, it's my cleavage peeking out of the V-neck of the dress.

"Come on, you can tell me. It's not like Cal and I are dating. Or ever will, for that matter."

Byron stuffs one hand in the front pocket of his black pants and uses the other to run his fingers through his hair. He leans against the back wall and turns his head toward me. "Let's just say Cal isn't as lonely as you might think he is."

I'm not sure why, but my heart drops into my stomach. I guess it's because I never pictured him with a girl. From what I've seen, he's this dark and mysterious loner, who'd easily get annoyed with one. "Wait. Is Cal dating some-one?" I suddenly feel foolish for even dressing up to go meet him. I knew I should have burned the invitation. Probably all the dresses, too.

"Cal doesn't date."

The elevator stops, but I wish it hadn't. I hate that all I get are bits and pieces into who Cal is because everyone leaves me hanging.

I swallow my pride and ask the question that's eating me up inside. "So, who are these women that come here?"

Byron extends a bent arm toward me, and I hook my arm in it as we step off the elevator. It's pretty similar to the eighth floor that I'm staying on, but I imagine the rooms here are different. They're few and far between, which leads me to believe they are large rooms. They must be for one to be a ballroom.

"Cal's a single man with enough money to buy an island, obviously." Byron snickers. "You can't expect a bachelor like that to walk the straight and narrow all the time."

I can't imagine Cal walking the straight and narrow, ever. "So, they're hookers?"

Byron shrugs his shoulders with a lopsided grin and I get my answer.

I feel sick.

Of course Cal has sex. Byron's right. He's a single man and he can do whatever he wants, but it still disgusts me. If he'd just be a little less daunting, he could easily get any girl he wants.

"But, you didn't hear that from me," Byron continues. "Callum is a very private person, as you've noticed."

"Yeah. I keep hearing that. What I don't understand is why."

"Between you and me," he whispers, "it's not his fault he is the way he is. He's earned those stripes that allow him to do whatever the fuck he wants."

I blow out an exasperated breath. "So what you're saying is, he's earned the right to coerce people to an island and force them to stay against their will?" Byron goes to speak, but I'm not finished yet, so I hold up a finger. "In layman's terms, he's able to rightfully kidnap people because he's *earned his stripes?*"

"When you put it that way, it sounds pretty awful, but you did sign a contract."

"Ugh," I growl, unhooking my arm from Byron's and stomping, impetuously, away from him.

Everyone is on Cal's side. *Everyone!*

It seems he's forgotten that he's not the only one who's had a rough go at life. What about all the other kids at The Webster House or in any foster home, for that matter? None of us were wanted, but we don't go around behaving like the world owes us something. I was raised by a single mom who was a drug addict. I loved her fiercely, but my love wasn't enough to keep her sober. I found her dead and can still smell the foam that was coming out of her mouth. For years, I had the picture of her face in my head. Now, I don't even remember what she looks like. Life wasn't easy for me either. But nothing worth fighting for ever is.

"Poor Callum," I mock under my breath, right before my ankle twists and I fall straight to the ground. My legs sweep to the side and I yank off my shoe. "Stupid heels." I chuck it down the hall, then remove the other one. I lift it to aim and throw, but see Byron standing there.

"Whoa," he holds both hands up in surrender, "put down the shoe."

I drop it and go to get up. There's a twinge of pain shooting up my leg, but it's nothing I can't handle. Byron offers a hand, but I push myself up without his help. "I'm fine. But you can throw those shoes in the garbage."

Cal pops out of a room down the hall and it takes me a second to catch my breath. He's probably the most gorgeous man I've ever laid eyes on.

His black hair is messy, as usual, with glossy ends that are flipped carelessly to one side. A few hang in front of his forehead, but he makes no attempt to sweep them away. He's also wearing a black suit, similar to Byron's. A jacket buttoned halfway with a white button-up shirt underneath and a black tie. He stands tall with both hands in his pants pockets. His broad shoulders drawn back and his signature scowl on his face. It does things to me and I fucking hate it.

Regardless of how much I despise him right now, there's no denying his strikingly good looks or the way his masculine voice makes my pussy throb.

"Bella?" Byron says loudly.

I peel my eyes off Cal and look at him. "Huh?"

"I asked if you were coming. Callum is waiting."

Best not to keep Callum waiting. My eyes roll as I walk down the hall barefoot. It's going to be really hard because I'm stubborn as an ox, but it's time to play nice, if I ever want to leave this godforsaken island.

12

Callum

FUCK. She's breathtaking. All I see is her. Around the edges of her sculpted body, everything's a blur. The sounds I hear, all static. Just one look has consumed my entire train of thought. The closer she gets to me, the weaker my knees become.

I knew she was beautiful. Knew this wouldn't be easy, but damn, I never expected it to be this difficult. Every plan I had laid out perfectly. Every angry bone in my body was ready to fuse back together with the undeniable satisfaction of making her live a miserable life on this island with me. Now, it's taking everything in me not to lay her out on the floor of this hall and devour her body with my tongue while shoving my cock so far into her pussy that she walks bowlegged for days.

"Hi," she says with a softness to her tone. Her hands gathered in front of her while her thumbs drum together.

"You look…" my words trail off, unable to fulfill the compliment with the words in my head, "…nice." Giving it will make me appear vulnerable and weak.

It's something she can use against me. I can't give her that power—not yet. "Right this way." I place a hand on the small of her back and my semi-hard cock fully erects instantly, straining against the fabric of my pants.

Bella stops in the doorway and tosses me a glance. "Another piano?"

"We have three. The eighth floor sitting room, here, on the seventh floor, and one in the cellar."

Her eyes shoot wide open. "The cellar?"

"You'll see it someday." I wave a hand into the room. My head designer did a fantastic job throwing this together with only a month's notice. Open, hardwood floors with an eighteen-light, cut-glass chandelier hanging in the center of the room. The grand piano sits to the right overtop an antique Persian rug. The wall is layered with la fleur wallpaper and gold-encrusted vines. It was all part of the plan for the hotel—tailored to Bella's taste—but now, I'm not sure I want to share it with anyone but her.

I look at Bella for a reaction, hoping she loves it, but she gives me nothing. This is what she always wanted. Fancy dresses and formal dances. Is it not enough?

I always knew she was a tough girl, but she's been making this exceptionally difficult. Not just her presence alone—it's her inability to cooperate and let things happen as they are supposed to. She might not believe that this encounter was fate, but it most definitely was. Fate led me to her and I've led her to me.

"Say something," I bark out as an order.

Her fingers trail down the wallpaper and she looks at

me. "This wallpaper must have cost a fortune. Is it real gold?"

"Of course it is. Do you like it?"

Her shoulders rise then fall. "It's all right."

"All right?" I snap back. "I did this all for you and all you have to say is that it's *all right?*"

"For me?" She laughs. "Why in the world would you buy expensive wallpaper for me?"

"Isn't that what you always wanted? A life of luxury without worrying about money?" I reach into my pocket and pull out a rectangular box, then walk around her so that her back is facing me.

"What are you doing?" She looks over her shoulder as I take the top off the box and pull out the pearl necklace. Once I've got the clasp unhooked, I string it around her neck and fasten it.

She immediately spins around to face me, fingers rubbing the beads around her neck. There's a sadness in her eyes that takes me by surprise. "Cal, I never wanted any of this. Not the castle, the wallpaper, the fancy dresses, and certainly not the necklace."

"When we were kids, you gawked at the Beckhams' little girl and always said you wanted all the fancy things she had. You'd daydream about dancing in ballrooms to an orchestra. So, tell me, Bella, are you happy now?"

She turns to face me with pinched brows. "What I admired about them wasn't their things, it was their family. A mom, a dad, siblings, love. That's all I ever wanted. Sure, I would have loved to have one decent dress I hadn't outgrown or worn out but that wasn't what I dreamt of. I think you've lost sight of what's important, Cal."

"Me? How so?"

Gripping the sides of her dress so she doesn't trip over it, she walks closer to me. "You hated money, and now you're bathing in it. Ya know, I've always heard that men who flaunt their money have small penises. Is that the case?"

Dropping my head back, I let out a roaring laugh. "Oh, Bella, you're in for quite a surprise."

Her arms cross over her chest and she tilts her head, regarding me closely. "I've always hated surprises, so I think I'll let you keep that one to yourself."

The lights dim and Beethoven's "Für Elise" begins playing through the surround sound speakers, but it's not the song that was supposed to play. My blood boils at the uncanny ability for that new asshole guard to fuck everything up.

I'm not sure where Byron keeps finding these dumb-asses, but if he doesn't get me some help without burnt brain cells, I'll have to do the hiring myself.

Regardless, I offer my hand, placing the other behind my back. "Shall we?"

Bella's cheeks tinge pink and it's a look I haven't seen in a while. She's embarrassed. But, why? "Umm, actually…"

"You can dance, right?" My eyebrows elevate to my forehead. "You've played this song before. Tell me you can at least sway your body to the notes."

She laughs nervously. "My body can do many things, but swaying to notes is not one of them. Hard pass."

"Come here." I point and bend my finger, calling her in front of me. Hesitantly, she takes a couple slow steps. Still too far away, I scoop her by the waist and, in a swift motion, I pull her body to mine. I hold my hand up. "Hand in mine." To my surprise, she doesn't argue. I place my other hand on the small of her back while looking down at her lips as they move.

"I don't know about this. What if I trip myself, or you?"

"It's a quick waltz and it's already half over." I twirl her around to the beat then bring her back to me. "Besides, I've watched you fall at least three times since you've arrived. Once more won't hurt."

Looking down at her, I see that she's smiling. I catch myself doing the same and quickly erase the look from my face by pressing my lips together. Guiding Bella's movements, I do a chair and slip pivot while she follows my lead. "Curved feather, step," I say under my breath as we glide across the dance floor. "Now chasse." I walk her forward, then to the left, and back around. She misses a step and stumbles, but I grip her tighter, pulling her closer to me.

She looks up, our eyes catching, and it feels as if I'm staring into an open flame. The heat between us is fierce and I'm curious if she feels it too. When her expression becomes thunderstruck, I'm certain she does. Innocent eyes peer up at me, as if they're searching for clarity. Something I'm not able to give because I'm searching for the same in her.

The song stops and so does Bella. Her hands quickly

pull back as if she was holding on to hot coal. "All your bones are intact. I'd say you did pretty well."

"Wow. A compliment. From you." Sarcasm drips from her tone. "I don't know what to say."

"It wasn't exactly a compliment but take it as you will."

Bella walks over to the piano and I follow behind her while some Johann Strauss begins to play through the speakers. "Where'd you learn to dance like that?" she asks as she runs her fingers over the piano hood.

"Private lessons for a year."

"Oh," her eyes perk up as she looks over at me, "did your parents make you take them?"

"No. It was my own choice."

Vincent and Delilah only wanted me to do the things that Caden did, and dancing was not one of them. He was into physical sports—football, baseball, basketball. I never took up any them because sports weren't my thing, but if either of them had lived longer than they did, Vincent would probably have forced those hobbies on me.

"I shouldn't be surprised, but I am." She sits down on the piano bench and folds her hands in her lap.

I take a seat next to her, our outer thighs brushing against one another. "Why's that so surprising?"

"Just that you took the initiative to let someone teach you something. You always hated instruction. Always wanted to learn everything yourself."

"Well, there was this girl…"

My words trail off when her eyes shoot to mine. Curiosity piques her interest. "Go on."

I shouldn't have said anything. I want to slap myself for even having this conversation. The last thing I need is

Bella prying into my personal life. "Forget it." I go to stand up, but she pulls me back down.

"No. Tell me. Was it a girlfriend? A sister? A cousin? I wanna know about your life, Cal."

"I've never had a girlfriend. Never wanted one. The girl was a dance instructor who I met at a coffee shop a few years ago. We had a conversation about a charity event coming up and I told her I couldn't dance, so she taught me. That's it. That's the end of the story. Would you like to dance again?" I grab her hand and pull her up, feeling flustered.

There is nothing I hate more than talking about myself —past, present, or future.

"Actually, my ankle is starting—"

I cut her off by spinning her around. The tempo picks up and I don't stop forcing her along with me. We move in unison, flying across the floor, not even stopping for a beat.

"Cal, stop," she says, trying to pull away, but I don't allow her to break free.

Why does she ask so many damn questions? Why can't she just mind her own fucking business, live here with me and start a new life without worrying about what I've done in the twelve years we've been apart?

She's a royal pain in the ass and I'm getting tired of her poking and prodding.

"Cal, please. My ankle hurts."

Her dress snares underneath my shoe and she falls backward. I stumble right along with her, but I'm able to catch us before we both fall to the floor. "Dammit, Cal," she yells, jerking away suddenly and freeing herself from my claws. "What the hell is the matter with you?"

I watch her throw her little fit with a vacant expression while I stand there adjusting my tie. It's suffocating me, so I loosen it up a bit.

She's pretty sexy when she's mad. Right now I'd love nothing more than to shut her up with my cock down her throat.

"Say something, dammit!" she snaps. When I don't respond, she comes over to me and pulls my hand away from my tie.

I bite back, "What are you doing?"

"Quit being such a damn robot all the time. You don't have to pretend with me."

"I don't pretend, Bella. What you see is what you get."

She laughs in a mocking tone. "What you see is what you get? I call bullshit."

"You call bullshit? How about if I call bullshit?" I grab her by the waist and kiss her so deeply and so passionately that I can guarantee there's a puddle for me in her panties right now. Her chest heaves against mine as she melts into my arms.

She can pretend she's not affected, but I know the truth. I can see what I do to her. Which means, she can also see what she's doing to me.

It's scary as hell, but when I get into this mindset, where I'm consumed by only her, I don't fucking care. I will let my guard down, just one time, if that's what it takes to have her. And once my cock fills her pussy, there will be no going back—she will be mine.

"I want you to play the piano for me," I mutter into her mouth.

I've waited twelve years for this. Twelve long years wishing I could watch the way her fingers dance across the keys. The way her mouth parts slightly as she concentrates, every now and then her tongue sweeping across her top lip to wet it. The lust behind her eyes as the passion of playing consumes her.

She pulls back, peering up at me. "You want me to play the piano?"

My fingers slide underneath the spaghetti strap of her dress. "Take this off and play me that piece you wrote when we were kids."

Her pupils dilate with her fixed gaze on me. "You want me to take my dress off and play the piano?"

"Not just your dress. I want it all off—now." I pull the strap down, exposing her shoulder to me, then the other, until they're both hanging freely on her arm.

Bella clears her throat and runs her hands down her dress. "You're kidding, right?"

She should know by now that I don't joke, especially not when it comes to matters of her obedience. "No, I am most definitely not *kidding.*"

She will do what I say, or the repercussions will be much worse than her ridding herself of her clothes and pouring her heart into a song that I demand to hear.

Her trembling fingers attempt to adjust the strap of her dress, but I grab her hand and shake my head. "Now, Bella," I press.

"Cal," she takes a calming breath, avoiding eye contact as her eyes stay affixed to the door, "I'm not taking my dress off. That's absurd." She takes a step forward as if she's planning to make an escape, but I throw my arm out, grabbing her around the waist.

"Then I'll take it off for you."

Her eyes look into mine, searching for the darkness in them that tells her I'm, once again, not kidding. I glower, right before running my hand up the back of her dress. I pinch the zipper at the top and inch it down, exposing her bare back.

Shivers cascade down her arms. "Turn around," I tell her, my skin sweltering from the beauty in front of me. She does as she's told and I run my fingers over her shoulder and sweep her hair to one side. My lips press to the skin over her spine as I tug the zipper down all the way. The V of her thong peeks out, showing me a tease of her ass.

"Cal," she whispers, head tilting to her right shoulder.

My fingers skate up both of her arms until they're wrapped around her throat. I bite down hard on my bottom lip, warding off temptation. I could squeeze and force her on her knees right now. Shove my cock in her mouth until she gags on my cum shooting down her throat. Instead, I tug the strand of pearls aggressively, ripping them off her neck.

Her head straightens, body tensing in scrutiny. "Why'd you do that?" she asks with a hint of sadness in her voice.

"I don't give gifts to disobedient houseguests. Now do as you're told, or I'll stay true to my promise. I *will* remove every article of clothing on your body."

She orbits back around to face me, her eyes wide with discontent. "Please, just stop this. You're being so cruel."

"I never claimed to be kind. Now, go."

She takes a step backward, eyes deadlocked on mine. I watch intently as her chest rises and falls with each shallow breath. Tears prick the corners of her eyes, but she finally turns around and walks toward the piano.

She's right. I am cruel. I hate myself for what I've become—the monster the world created.

But she unleashed the monster in me twelve years ago when she broke the first promise ever made to me, and now, she gets to eat from my hand.

13

BILE SWIRLS IN MY STOMACH, threatening to climb up my throat. I'm repulsed. Downright sickened by the way he's treating me.

Get on his good side. It was supposed to be easy. This is anything *but* easy.

Can I really do this? Strip down to nothing in front of this man who is nothing short of a stranger?

I once ate a three-day-old sandwich from the trash. Got slapped by a drunk man my mom brought home when I was three—never even cried. I walked the streets for hours that night and no one even came to try and find me. I also turned my back on my best friend without thinking twice because I wanted a better life.

Hell yes, I can do this.

I take another step, pushing one strap off my shoulder, then another step, pushing the other strap down my arm. The silk fabric of the dress feels nice against my bare skin as it waterfalls off me.

Cal stands behind me, my backside fully exposed to

him. I lift the hood on the piano and position the leg, so it's in place, then rest the hood back down, so it's slightly open.

With my hair bunched to one side, I grip the strands tightly as a tear slides down my cheek. I dart my tongue out, sweeping it off my lip and swallow hard while pushing my pride down.

I grip the sides of my underwear and slide them down, stepping each leg out, then I sit down on the bench.

It's been over two years since my fingers have laid on piano keys. I didn't stop because of a bad experience or anything like that. The passion left me and no matter how hard I tried to force myself to play, the music didn't hit quite like it used to. Not like it did when I'd play next to Cal. I could no longer feel it in my core. The sounds were different, less satisfying.

I look over at him and I'm surprised to see his eyebrows pulled together with an evident crease. He looks as if his mind is tormented, held captive by the past. His Adam's apple bobs as he swallows and I find myself doing the same—swallowing hard, hoping he doesn't notice.

My shaky fingers hover over D and E. I blink away my tears then I press down and begin. It's been twelve years, two months, and thirteen days since I've played this song. Yet, my fingers gyrate across the keys like it was yesterday.

Memories flood me all at once.

"Okay. Are you ready?" I ask Cal as his eyes glide across the notebook. He's gnawing on his pencil and it looks like he's chewed the eraser completely off.

"Mmhmm," he grumbles, not even lifting his eyes from the page.

I don't begin. I just watch him, waiting, because I know he's not paying attention. His lips move as he silently reads the words he just wrote.

"Cal!" I grab his attention.

He drops his pencil into his notebook and closes it. "Sorry. Something just isn't flowing right."

"Don't stress about it. I'll help you. But first, are you ready?"

He nods. "Let's hear it."

I draw in a full breath and begin playing. Everything in the room is silent and still. The only sound is the harmony that surrounds us.

When I glance over at Cal, my heart quivers. He's not just listening; he's staring at me. His lips curl up in a smile and my cheeks flush with heat. I smile back at him then return my eyes to the keys.

I don't have the notes written out. I've been practicing for weeks and I've finally got it down, stored in my memory.

My fingers drum faster as I hit the chorus. My back steels as I pour my heart and soul into the composition.

Cal scooches closer, his leg brushing against mine and butterflies flutter through my stomach. I look over at him, wearing the same smile he is. His eyes light up, and for the first time in a while, I feel seen—heard, rather.

I wrap it up and end the song with a chord progression, then set my hands on my lap.

My nerves are heightened as I anticipate his reaction. "Well?"

"Wow, Bella. That was really good."

I perk up, tucking one leg under the other and turning toward him. "You really think so?"

"Probably the best sound in the entire world."

I open my eyes, not even realizing that they were closed. Cal is now standing to my left, his hand resting on the base of the piano. I stumble over a few keys but get back on track and keep going with it. I can't believe I even remember this song.

Cal takes a step closer and sits on the edge of the bench. I slide over a tad and I'm not sure if it's to get away from him, or to make room for him.

This moment is unlike any other since I've been here. So many emotions invade me and I try like hell to fight against them. My chest feels constricted—my lungs unable to fully inflate.

Another tear falls from the corner of my eye, but it's not because I'm scared. It's because I'm sad. My heart is breaking and it's because of this melody, this moment, and him.

My soul cries happiness for the years together— sadness for the years apart—and fear for the years ahead.

What does this life mean anymore?

I finish the song off and rest my hands on my lap.

Silence engulfs us.

Until Cal breaks it. "Are you going to ask me?"

My arms cross over my chest, hugging myself to hide my breasts as much as possible. "Ask you?"

"What I thought about the song?"

He remembers. I always asked him what he thought every time I played, sometimes, multiple times a day.

Once I woke him up just to sneak downstairs and listen, so I could hear his thoughts on a piece.

"Okay. I'll bite. What did you think?"

Cal brushes the stray strands of hair from my shoulder and begins to caress my upper arm. "I think it was the best sound in the entire world."

My heart pangs with agony. I feel dizzy and weak under his thumb.

"Why are you doing this?" I sniffle. "Beyond the anger and possible revenge. Why?"

Cal taps his finger to the C key repeatedly. I tuck my chin to my chest to see his face and there's a glint of a smile. "We were pretty brave back then, weren't we?"

I cover his hand with mine, stopping him from tapping the key. "We were just kids."

His eyes stay affixed to my hand that's touching him. "We were survivors."

There's no fighting the tears that fall from my eyes. *What have I done to him?*

"I'm so sorry, Cal."

Regardless of everything he's done to me the past couple of days—forcing me to strip down and sit here wearing my vulnerability—a mountain of regret has made a home inside of me. Maybe that was the point of all this. Maybe I deserve it. It wasn't until I sat down at this piano that it all hit me, full force, with enough pain to satisfy my worst enemy.

Keeping his hand in place, beneath mine, he tilts his head to look at me. Our eyes catch and a flame ignites inside of me. He has the most gorgeous dark eyes and I'm almost certain they can still read mine. I wish I could read his thoughts. If only I knew what he wanted from me.

My questions are answered when his lips collide with mine. His hands cup my cheeks as he devours my mouth like he's starving for my taste. It's passionate and unruly and I reciprocate by throwing myself into him.

Gripping the side of his head, I tangle my fingers in his mess of hair and give him what he's asking of me.

He tastes sweet, like apple-flavored whiskey. I haven't had anything to drink, but my head is spinning, my body reacting, like I've drank an entire bottle by myself.

Cal slides his hands down to my waist, placing them on either side of me, then lifts me up until I'm on his lap, straddling him.

It doesn't even matter to me right now that I'm completely naked while he's fully dressed. His erection pressing against my pussy alleviates all the humiliation I feel.

Tingles ride through me and I'm at his mercy, internally begging for him to do something—anything. I deepen our kiss, jutting my hips and arching my back.

A low grumble rides up his throat before he dips his hand between my legs and rubs his fingers in circles at my entrance.

God, I want his fingers inside of me so badly, and I hate myself for it.

I need him to touch me. Carry me to that high he took me to the last time his fingers were inside me.

I roll my hips again, forcing friction. He slides two fingers inside of me, giving me what I want, and my body jolts.

"Do you want me to fuck you, Bella?" he asks through a raspy breath.

I pull out of the kiss and look behind him, thinking. I want to tell him to shut up before he ruins this moment, but I don't out of fear of pissing him off.

Although, he's bound to get pissed one way or another. "No," I shake my head, "I don't."

It's the truth. I don't want to have sex with Cal, or any other man, until I'm married. It's a personal decision and one I've never swayed from. I'm all for foreplay and self-care, but when it comes to the unification of sex itself, I choose to wait.

"So, you're just a tease then? Is that what this is?" His fingers reach deeper, almost painfully so.

My heart jumps into my throat and I look at him with narrowed eyes. "A tease?" I breathe out a moan. "You're the one who made me take my clothes off."

He keeps digging, his nails scraping inside of me, but I crave more. "And you willingly did it. You climbed on my lap and spread your legs for me, never once fighting me off or saying you don't want this."

He's taking this conversation too far and I'm no longer in the mood. I go to swing my leg over him to get up, but he slaps his hand on my thigh, hard, leaving behind a stinging sensation.

I try again, to no avail, as he holds me in place. "I'm only human, Cal."

"And I'm not?"

With a crooked grin, I hold his gaze. "I don't know, are you?"

He grabs my hand, laying it on his erect cock. "I have human needs just like you do."

Cal squeezes his hand over mine, forcing me to feel his girth and my God, it is girthy. I can only imagine what that thing would do to my insides. It has the potential to spread me so far open that I would rip.

Cal moves his hand up and down, forcing mine to do the same. I take note of his length. At least eight inches that would fill me up. It sounds satisfying. His big cock sliding in and out of me while his naked, warm body presses to mine. I clench my thighs at the tempting thought.

No. I have morals. Having sex with Cal is the very last thing I need to do. What I need is to find a way to leave.

I jerk my hand away and try one more time to get off his lap, but this time, he grabs me by the throat. "Do my needs not matter? Only yours? You want to come around my fingers, only to have me go jerk off in my room, alone?"

The image of him stroking his cock flashes through my head and I pinch my eyes shut, trying to rid my mind of it.

What the hell is the matter with me?

"No," I choke out, his grip relentless.

"Then get on your knees and prove it."

"I…I can't, Cal. I have a—"

"What, Bella? A boyfriend?"

I nod slightly.

The veins in his neck flex prominently as he clenches his jaw. "Consider your relationship with *Trent* over." He emphasizes his name as if saying it is torturous.

Cal isn't wrong. My relationship is over. It was over long before I left home.

But even if my body is hungry for a man's touch—Cal's touch—as sadistic as it is, I've already been unfaithful once.

Another tear slides down my cheek and I'm so damn tired of crying. "If I do what you want, will you let me leave the island?"

"I can't let you leave, but I can promise I won't hurt you." His voice is tranquil as he observes the tear skating down my cheek. His jaw begins to unclench, the muscles in my forehead relax, and his posture goes slack. His eyes shift to mine and it's almost as if he was under a spell that he snapped out of, because now I'm looking into the eyes of the Cal I used to know. In a matter of seconds, the threat he held has disappeared, taking my fear along with it.

"Forget it. You can go back to your room now," he says, still staring deep into my eyes.

For a moment, I imagine myself leaving his lap and pulling my dress back on and walking out of this room, only to go in mine and spend the evening alone. It's been so lonely, and I think he's lonely, too.

"Maybe I don't want to," I whisper, raising my trembling hand and setting it on his cheek. The touch of his skin feels like fire against my palm.

My eyes close and I lean forward, gently pressing my mouth to his. The feelings that hit me all at once are obscure. So much doubt, but so much desire. Our lips never part as I hold this soft kiss in place. Chills ride up my thighs, never stopping until they spill into our kiss.

A soft, subtle kiss that escalates into two people ripping into each other without giving it a single thought —I refuse to let myself overthink this. Even if I know it's wrong, my body won't allow me to stop.

With both hands pressed to Cal's cheeks, our heads tilt, our teeth clank, tongues tangling haphazardly in a muddle of passion.

My want for him drips from my pussy onto his black trousers, seeping through them and coating his erect cock.

Cal puts his hands on both of my breasts and squeezes so hard that it hurts, but I want more. More pain, more pleasure, more of him.

He pinches my puckered nipples, tugging at them and stretching them. His teeth graze my bottom lip before he bites down forcibly. I cringe, pulling back to look at him, but he doesn't let my mouth leave his for long. He regains my lip and sucks hard, really hard. I whimper at the rush of pain. "Ouch, Cal."

He doesn't stop, just keeps milking my lip of blood until he licks his lips and I see a streak of red on them. Then, he kisses me, compelling me to taste it. It's metallic, mixed with his sweet, apple tang.

Something about it turns me on even more, causing me to roll my hips against his cock. My breasts perk up when my back arches and his lips work their way down from my neck to my chest before he takes my nipple into his mouth.

My head drapes back, eyes closed. Warm, dampened hands slide under my ass and he squeezes my cheeks while sucking on my nipple. "You should have left when you had the chance." His voice is husky behind an ominous tone.

In a swift motion, he stands, cradling my ass while seducing my mouth once again. My legs wrap around him and he kicks the piano stool backward, causing it to flip over.

Cal takes a few steps, holding tightly to me, our lips never parting. Once we're on the other side of the piano, he uses one hand to knock out the leg holding up the hood, then he sets me down on top of it.

He stands tall in front of me, my knees level with his abdomen. His hands slide up my legs, separating my thighs. My body infused with desire and lust as I watch him. Biting the corner of his lip, he gapes at my pussy. I should be mortified that he's studying my body like it's a science experiment, but all I want to do is grab his hand and shove his fingers inside of me while feeling his skin meld with mine.

When I go to grab his face to pull his mouth to mine, he retracts, pushing his hand against my chest to move me back. My brows pinch together, wondering why he suddenly won't kiss me. After all this, is he leaving me here unsatisfied?

"Lie down," he demands in an authoritative tone.

I do as I'm told, sliding back onto the piano. I close my legs and bend them at the crease beneath my knees, letting the lower half dangle over the side of the piano. Folding my arms up, I cover my breasts.

Cal slides off his jacket, then unbuttons his shirt, while watching me intently. His chest is exposed to me and I gasp at the sight. Not only at his rigid abs and pectoral muscles, but the mix of tattoos that are covering raised, pink scars. It's like he got them just to try and hide the marks. One side is completely covered in black ink and it looks like the same tree on the stained glass in his office. There's another that rests over his heart of an old pocket watch hanging from a chain that climbs up his shoulder.

Cal grabs both of my ankles and pushes them up until my legs are spread in front of him again. I lift my head to get a look at him, but just as I do, his face disappears between my legs.

His nose brushes my nub and shivers course through me. The stubble on his face tickles in the best way possible.

I lie my head back down on the piano, my chest heaving, legs falling open farther.

Cal runs his fingers up and down my pussy then stops and rubs vicious circles at my clit. He's a master at this technique, possibly even a god. No one has ever made me revel in their touch the way Cal does.

My lower half twitches as my mouth falls open. His stained touch shouldn't feel this good.

His arm reaches under my leg, one hand pressed to my stomach beneath my belly button. My body shivers when he brutally rams his fingers inside of me, He takes no care to be gentle. His force is rough and domineering. As if he's determined to make me come to feed his ego, not to satisfy my desire.

My body fills up with its own greedy needs. I'm forced to grab his hand on my stomach, squeezing tightly as the pressure inside of me builds. Heat pipes through my core, filling my veins, threatening to burst.

I am the greedy one here. Letting Cal get me off, once again, while giving him nothing in return. He asked for this. Dragged me here, forced my clothes off, and laid me on this piano. There isn't an ounce of remorse circling in my head, knowing that I won't fulfil his needs.

The walls of my pussy clench, tightening around his fingers. His tongue continues to flick feverishly at my clit and I wish I could drag out this moment for an eternity.

"Cal," I whimper, eyes closed, mouth wide open. I squeeze his hand harder, holding my breath and trying like hell to make this feeling last as long as I possibly can.

"Don't fight it, Bella. Come for me so I can clean up your mess."

His gravelly voice sends me over the edge. I hold my breath when I reach the height of my climax. A pinched moan climbs up my throat, rippling through the room and bouncing off the walls.

Exhaling my pent-up breath, I lift my head to see Cal's expression. He gasps, his breaths as heady as mine, as he watches his fingers orbit vigorously around my clit. My body twitches, tingles coursing through me as I orgasm again, this time it's like being zapped with a thousand watts of electricity.

My arousal runs down my leg, but Cal swoops down and licks up my inner thigh. I jolt when he begins sucking at my entrance, then my clit, cleaning me up, like he said he would.

I lean back down, my head resting on the piano hood as I catch my breath and steady my heart rate.

Regret begins to trickle through me and I know without a doubt that more is to come. I'll likely lie awake all night beating myself up for allowing this to happen again. The first time, it was due diligence. It had been months since my needs were met, and it was the least Cal could do to begin making up for holding me as a prisoner —not to mention, my hormones took control. This time, though, it was a mistake.

No matter how much I hold on to the moments of seeing the Cal I used to know, he's proven time and time again that he's as ruthless as they come.

I'm lost in my thoughts when suddenly all the air in my lungs comes out in one stuporous breath. I go to close my legs, but I'm too late. Cal grabs me by the waist and jerks me down until my ass is hanging off the piano and the head of his dick is inside me.

Unable to form a coherent sentence, I gasp when he shoves his full length in. It slides in with ease because I'm still drenched from my orgasm, but it doesn't hinder the pain.

"Cal," I finally say, in a raspy croak, "what…" My words trail off when he begins thrusting harder, faster, deeper. I go to lean forward to look at him, but he presses his hand to my chest, bearing weight on me.

No. This wasn't supposed to happen this way. Tears prick the corners of my eyes as I watch him. His mouth agape, his lust-filled eyes staring back at me. His cock strains against my walls and while it hurts, I imagine it would be much more painful had he not just had his fingers delving inside of me.

"Ugh," I cry out at the rush of pain shooting through me. To him, it probably sounds like a plea for more—a pleasurable moan.

I have to stop this. It wasn't supposed to happen. This was meant for my husband, and Cal will never be that man.

"Cal," I cry out again as the tears continue to shed. Just as I'm about to shout for him to stop, our eyes catch and something doesn't allow me to halt his movements.

A breathless groan escapes him as the corded veins in his arms flex. Sweat pools around his hairline, glistening in the dim light. In physical form, this man is an Adonis. He has the ability to make my heart skip a beat by just looking at him. Which is exactly what it's doing right now as we connect on this new level.

This is it. There's no going back.

He will forever be etched in my memory. Not because of our past, but because of this moment right here. Even if it was unknowingly, he stole something from me that I can never get back. But looking at him right now, I'm not sure I'd want it back. Maybe my innocence has always been meant for him.

Now that he has it, I hope he doesn't plan to shred me of my dignity too.

"Fuck, Bella. Your pussy feels so good." He leans forward, hands pressed to either side of me as he hovers.

His words vibrate through me as his face lingers over mine. Having him inside me feels like heaven and hell at the same time. Sin and benevolence. Wrong, yet right.

I'm taken by surprise when he presses his lips softly on mine. It's almost...sweet. Though, his movements never falter. His pelvic bone moves in a rhythmic motion. He thrusts in and out, assaulting my pussy and eventually the pain begins to subside, being replaced with something else. A feeling of contentment. A momentary unification between two people who came from the same broken path. There's a sense of attachment as his waist grinds against mine.

Cal grunts into my mouth, his breaths becoming labored. "God, Bella, I want to make a home between your legs and live inside of you forever."

Forever. Such an indefinite word.

He releases a few more husky moans before his movements slow, until he's motionless inside me.

My heart rate excels again at the realization of what just happened. He just came inside of me.

I push my hands to his shoulders, attempting to move him. His chest rises as he peers down on me with wide eyes. "What's wrong?" he asks, as if he has no idea why I'm suddenly agitated.

I need to get up. It feels like I'm suffocating beneath him. "Move, please."

He does as I ask and climbs down my body until his feet hit the floor. I spring up into a sitting position then hop off the piano and head straight for my dress lying on the floor while cum leaks down my leg.

As he pulls his pants up and buttons them, he walks toward me. "Why are you angry?"

Snarling, I snatch up my dress and wrap it around my naked body like a towel. "You came inside of me, Cal. You should have used a condom. Which I would have told you to do if I'd had a minute to think before you...began."

My heart begins rattling against my rib cage. Byron mentioned frequent female visitors and didn't deny that they were hookers.

I feel sick again.

"Calm down. It was one time." He zips up his pants and grabs his jacket off the floor. "I'm sure you'll be fine."

"You're sure I'll be fine?" I huff, stalking toward him and shoving my hands into his chest.

He takes a few steps back and smirks. "I'll have Peter take care of it. And if you're worried about STDs, don't. I'm clean and get checked regularly."

"Regularly?" I mutter. "How often do you have new partners? Wait," I hold up a hand, "don't answer that."

I really don't want to know because I really don't care.

"We all have needs, don't we?"

"Apparently yours are more important than mine because you didn't even ask before stealing something that was never meant for you."

Cal raises a brow, oblivious to what I'm talking about. "What the hell does that mean?"

Ignoring him, I gather up all my clothes and grumble before storming out of the room.

14

AS I WAIT for the elevator to take me up to the floor I'm staying on, I hold tight to the dress wrapped around me while clutching my bra and panties. There's no need to put anything on since everything would come off as soon as I get to my room. A hot bath sounds perfect right now. A stinging sensation is riding through my insides, and while it's expected after having sex for the first time, I wasn't prepared for that night to be tonight—or that person to be Cal.

My heart feels broken. All these years I have saved myself, just for him to sweep in and shatter every dream and moral I have.

The elevator comes to a stop and the doors slide open, but it's only the sixth floor. I backstep, my shoulders hitting the wall.

"What are you doing?" I ask Cal as he stands with a scorned look on his face. "How'd you even get on this floor?" There must be a staircase that I have yet to see. While the doors are still open, I look into a large library straight ahead. Floor-to-ceiling bookshelves encased in it. Cal always loved reading, so I'm not surprised.

He steps in the elevator and quickly eats up the space between us. His hands hit the wall on either side of me, causing my body to shudder. "Are you starting your period soon?" he asks point-blankly. The doors behind him close and the elevator climbs up again.

My period? "No. Why?"

"What the hell is this?" He holds up a pair of gray boxer briefs and I immediately notice the streak of dried blood on them.

"It's obviously blood, but it didn't come from me. I had my period a week before we got here." I know exactly what it is, but I don't tell him that.

"Then where'd it come from?"

We come to a stop and the doors open. "I don't know." I go to push past him, holding tightly to my bra and panties bunched in my hand.

He sidesteps in front of me, blocking my path.

"The doors are gonna shut. Move." I shove him to the side, but he's quicker than me. They begin to close and I blow out a frustrated breath. "Dammit. What do you want now?"

Cal glares down as he towers over me. "Have you fucked Trent?"

My chin hits my chest as I look down, avoiding eye contact. "That's not your business." I keep my eyes on my toes as I bend and flex them out of nervousness. Although, I shouldn't be nervous. So what if I was a virgin? It's not anything to be ashamed of.

"Have you fucked anybody? Ever?"

"Just get out of my way." I push him again, anger infiltrating my bones. I tap repeatedly at the button to open the doors, until they finally slide open.

I move quickly down the hall, trying to get to my room and away from him.

"Don't walk away from me when I'm talking to you," Cal calls out. I look over my shoulder and see him hot on my trail.

My pace quickens as I hold tight to the dress wrapped around me. I'm fully aware that my ass is showing, but I don't even care.

Once I reach my door, I glance over my shoulder one more time, and see Cal three feet away. He holds up the boxers and shouts, "Dammit, Bella. Just tell me you weren't a virgin."

I turn the doorknob and tuck myself inside, closing it gently behind me. My back presses to the door and my eyes close.

They shoot back open as my body rattles from Cal pounding on the other side. "Open the damn door or I'll come in without permission."

"Since when do you ask permission to enter? Sure as hell didn't ask permission twenty minutes ago."

"I just need to know because if it's true then I owe you an apology. Hell, I'll owe you a lot more than an apology."

My heart flutters at his words. They're not exactly endearing, but knowing he considered apologizing to me for anything seemed so far-fetched.

"Your first time shouldn't have been like that. On top of a piano, beneath an ice-cold heart. It should have been special. Just tell me I didn't fuck up. Please, Bella."

Why does he do this? This constant push and pull. He says hateful words and glares at me with threatening eyes, and then turns around and shows me the tiniest sliver of decency, forcing me to hold on to that fraction of a moment, where I know his heart isn't completely empty.

Pinching my eyes shut, I say in a placid tone, "You didn't fuck up, Cal."

Silence surrounds me. Not even an audible breath on the other side of the door.

I hear him. Or at least, I think I do. Maybe I just feel him. It's a strong sensation that tells me he's definitely still there.

"Can I come in?" he finally says, startling me. My heart jumps into my throat and I step away from the door.

I'm still wrapped in the dress and my hand is sweating from squeezing it so tightly to hold it in place. Probably shouldn't do what I'm about to do, but I do it anyway. I turn the knob and open the door for him.

I step aside, allowing him in. He glances at me as he walks in, then looks over at the bed and stops in the middle of the room. His hands in his pockets, again. I'm starting to think that's a quirk of his.

He's no longer holding the boxers. God, I hope he didn't give them to Peter to throw away. It's totally something Cal would do.

He turns around to face me and his complexion is pale, as if the very thought of taking my virginity is harrowing to him. "Thanks for letting me in."

"You're welcome. Now get this over with. I'd like to take a bath," I say, while walking to my bathroom. I leave the door open, so I can hear him, but I have to put something on.

"Are you on birth control, Bella?" he asks from outside the bathroom.

"No," I drawl. There's no reason to lie about that. There's also no reason for me to be on birth control right now.

"Why not?"

The dress falls to the floor and I grab a white, silk robe hanging from a hook in the bathroom. I didn't bring the robe here, but I've been wearing it, assuming it was placed in here for me.

I grab a scrunchie out of my makeup bag and wrap it around my wrist. Once the robe tie is fastened around me in a tight knot, I walk back out to the bedroom. "Because I choose not to be."

Cal is now sitting on the edge of my bed, his hands still in his pockets. His shirt is back on, but the top three buttons are undone, exposing a tuft of his black chest hair. "Because you and Trent want a baby?" His voice is strangled as if it was pure torture just saying the words. "Is that why?"

This would be a good opportunity to tell him the truth, that no, I don't want to have a baby with Trent, or marry him, but that really doesn't concern Cal. Maybe once he realizes that my heart isn't on this island and never will be, he'll let me go. "Yes," I lie, pressing my lips into a firm line.

Cal hangs his head and nods, as if he's accepting my lie. The tension in the room is so thick it's suffocating.

"Now, if you don't mind—"

"Actually," Cal stands abruptly, "I do mind." Long strides bring him in front of me. "I do mind because Trent doesn't deserve you. You're too generous and pure to be involved with someone like that. Why the hell are you even with him?"

"I told you—"

"Told me what? That he changed? That he's a good man? He's not, Bella. Trent Beckham was and always will be the enemy."

"I don't want to have his baby," I spit out in a fit of rage. "Dammit, Cal. Quit prying into my life. I'm not on birth control because I don't need to be. Trent and I haven't slept together." The words just spew from my mouth uncontrollably.

His mouth falls open as if my words have surprised him as much as they've surprised me. "Never?" he asks.

"Not yet."

"But you plan to marry him, right?"

I sweep the air with my hand and turn away from him. "I'm not listening to this." I walk over to the vanity set against the wall and open the jewelry box. The ballerina pops out and begins playing a familiar song. Just like the last time I opened it, I slam it shut again. "Why that song?"

"Quit changing the subject."

"No. How about you answer a few of my questions? Starting with that song. I know damn well Peter didn't pick that out and place it in the room I'd be staying in. Are you purposely trying to make me sad?"

He knows that's the tune to a song my mom used to hum to me when I was a kid. Even as she was on the verge of passing out with a band still wrapped around her arm and needles on the table, she'd rub my head and hum that tune.

"I'm trying to remind you who you are and where you came from."

"Why?" I shout, spinning back around. I shove my hands to his chest to push him away because I need some damn space. "Why would I want that reminder?"

I swipe away the tears on my cheeks aggressively, not even realizing that I was crying again.

Cal grabs hold of me and cradles my head while his chin rests against my hair. And I lose it.

I break down, letting it all come out until I'm ugly-crying in his arms.

"How are we supposed to get where we want to be if we don't remember where we came from?" he says, or rather, asks. I'm not really sure. "They took you away and fed you lies. They painted you this picture of a perfect life and stuck you in it then placed it on a shelf so you were out of reach. The world isn't pretty for all of us, Bella. Some of us are forced into ugliness." He brings the back of his hand to my cheek and brushes lightly. "You got Vango, while I got Caravaggio."

Caravaggio was always Cal's favorite artist. His work is Gothic and dramatic, but also full of emotion. Cal would flip through pages of his book and each picture would paint a new expression on his face.

I inhale a deep breath, filling my lungs before I say what needs to be said. "You need to let go of the past. It's the only way you'll ever be happy."

Cal tsks, "Easy for you to say."

"Ya know, it really bothers me that you act like you're the only one to ever have a bad start to life. At least you have a family and a home. Some never got that."

His brows pinch together, back steeled and shoulders drawn. "I didn't want this life."

"Well, too bad. You got it."

"You're right," he takes a step back, "I did.

My voice drops a few octaves as I try to sympathize with him. Something bad had to have happened. "What the hell happened to you, Cal? Please, just tell me."

"I didn't get the parents we always wanted. A year after you left, I was adopted by the Ellis family. A week prior, they lost their son in a car accident. His name was Caden. My adopted mother, Delilah, was a little crazy." His fingers loop around his ear. "Never accepted Caden's death and went into a manic state. So, Vincent took me in and forced me to pretend I was their son, just to appease his wife. Her mind was completely gone and she believed that I was really him. Most days, I pretended. Other days, my hatred for the old man wouldn't allow me to."

"Cal," I say, walking toward him, "I had no idea." I go to place a hand on his shoulder, but he swats it away. "Don't! I don't want your pity."

"I don't pity you. I just want you to know how sorry I am."

"Sorry?" He laughs. "You're sorry? For what?"

"I...I guess I'm sorry that you had to endure that."

"Because you left? Is that what you want to say? You left me after we made a solid promise to stay together. Do you realize that a week after you left, Nikki and Dante were adopted together? School teachers. If you'd just stuck to the plan, it could have been us. But you didn't because the pact meant nothing to you."

"If I could go back, I'd choose to stay." Am I lying? I'm not so sure. I love my parents and my brother, Mark, but if going back meant taking Cal down a different path, with me, maybe I'd do it.

"It's too late. The damage is already done."

I take a step closer, while he takes a step back. His legs hit the end of the bed and he's unable to go any farther, so I keep walking until we're face to face. "Did they hurt you?"

"Hurt?" He laughs monstrously. "They stripped me of my flesh and exposed my soul and coated it with salt. No, they didn't hurt me. They destroyed me."

My hands grasp my chest, holding tightly as my heart shatters into pieces. This isn't just about me leaving; this is about what happened after I left.

I go to speak, but the words won't come out. Cal glowers as he stalks past me for the door, slamming it shut behind him as he leaves.

"I had no idea," I mutter under my breath, on the verge of tears once again.

15

I SPENT hours crying in bed last night. It finally hit me that my future husband would not be my first. All through high school—many nights of temptation and pressure—I was able to hold on to my innocence and in one split second, it was gone.

Eventually, I sucked it up and convinced myself that it's not that big of a deal. Another part of me, a crazy part, even came to terms with the fact that it was probably always meant for Cal. I'm not angry, at least, not because of that.

I haven't been able to face Cal. Words cannot express how sorry I am for everything he's been through. I don't even know what happened, and I'm not sure I want the sordid details. No matter what Cal does, I will always have love for him. There is still a piece of my heart saved just for him, and maybe there always will be.

I've been sitting at the vanity mirror in my room for almost an hour, brushing my hair and thinking, when someone knocks on the door.

Shaking the thoughts that threaten to keep me under this dark cloud, I push the stool back and get up. I haven't walked around much today because my body is so sore. It feels like I ran twenty miles and had a jackhammer rammed up my vagina.

"Who is it?" I holler, while making my way to the door.

"It's Peter. I have something for you."

Please let it be food.

I opted out of breakfast this morning. I asked Peter to bring it to my room, but apparently, *Mr. Ellis* said if I didn't eat in the dining room with him then I could go hungry. My stomach has been growling ever since. For someone who worries so much about me eating, he has no problem starving me just to get his way.

I open the door and Peter is standing there with a tray holding a glass of water and a couple packets of pills. "What is this?" I ask, picking one of them up.

"Mr. Ellis asked that I bring you this. He said to take the single pills today and begin the others tomorrow."

I laugh, dropping the packet back down on the tray. "I'm not taking those."

Peter clears his throat. "He said it's a morning-after pill and your birth control."

"Well, you can tell Mr. Ellis that I'm not putting any pill in my mouth that comes from him, and certainly not a morning-after pill."

"If you'll just take the tray, I'll relay the message."

"Or," I emphasize, "you could give me the Wi-Fi password and some service on my phone and I could call and tell him myself."

Peter just stands there, dumbfounded.

"Fine. Gimme the tray." I take it from him, knowing that this isn't his fault. Boss's orders, after all.

Peter leaves and I close the door before setting the tray on my nightstand. I sit down on the bed and look at the little packets. I pick one up, the morning-after pill, and study it while I think.

The chances of me being pregnant are slim to none, but even if they were high, I'm not sure I would take this. I'm also not completely sure that I wouldn't. On one hand, it would be my baby. On the other, it would also be Cal's. We'd be connected for life, even more so than we already are.

Regardless, I drop the packet back down. Just as it hits the tray, the door flies open. "Take the damn pill, Bella."

"No!" I huff, getting to my feet. I'm tempted to pick the tray up and throw it at him, glass of water and all.

He pins me with a stare. "Why not?"

"Because it was your mistake, not mine. I shouldn't have to put something into my body because you couldn't take a minute to pull your dick out of me."

He tsks, "Don't act like you didn't enjoy it."

"Your ego is far too big for your head. You need to get that under control."

"And your mouth opens too much for someone who has nothing to say."

"Oh," I laugh, "I have a lot to say, but unlike you, I'm mature enough to know when to just keep my mouth shut."

"Fine. You want to risk having a baby with me. Don't take the pill."

My fingers tangle in my well-brushed hair. "God, you're so infuriating."

"And you're a royal pain in the ass."

I drop my hands and go to move across the room to get away from him. "Then just let me leave and..." My words trail off when a sharp pain shoots through me. I try to play it off like it's nothing, but Cal takes notice.

"What's wrong? What happened?"

I walk back over to the bed and sit down. "I ran into the bedpost earlier. I'm fine."

Cal comes to my side where I sit and crouches down, looking at my leg. "Where?"

I'm wearing shorts, so I probably should have come up with a better lie.

"There's no bruise. It's nothing." I grab a pillow and hold it in my lap.

"You're lying. You're in pain from last night, aren't you? Did I hurt you?" The realization that he did hits him and I'm shocked at his response. "I did."

"Just drop it."

"Peter," Cal calls out, "Come here, please."

Is this guy just lurking around every corner or what? He seems to always be there.

Peter comes into the room and Cal shifts his attention to him. "Please bring Bella an ice pack. Make it three or four. And some pain reliever and something to help her sleep tonight. Make it quick."

Cal's expression hardens as he kneels on the floor. "Were you a virgin up until last night?"

I take a deep breath and look away from him. It shouldn't matter. And I'm not embarrassed at all, I just don't want Cal to act as if this is some sort of a big deal, even though it is, to me. He didn't take advantage of me and I never tried to stop him, but I also didn't want it. I certainly wasn't prepared for it.

"Yes. Okay. I was planning on waiting until I was married."

Cal runs his fingers through his hair and growls, "Dammit, Bella. Why didn't you stop me?"

My shoulders shrug as I hug the pillow tighter. "Heat of the moment, I guess."

Cal runs his fingers through his hair, deep in thought. Finally, he looks back up at me. "I'm sorry. I had no idea. I'm sorry your first time had to be like that. I'm sorry I hurt you. Fuck!" he shouts. "I'm a monster. I'm a goddamn monster."

"No. You're not a monster, Cal. Not for that."

"I would have never—"

"I know. Or at least, I think I know. Please, don't make this into a big deal." Humiliation begins to take over. I'm no longer angry; I just hope he doesn't drag this out.

Peter returns at the perfect moment with the items Cal requested and I'm instructed to stay in bed for the remainder of the day with both Cal and Peter at my beck and call.

I had breakfast, ice cream for dessert, lunch, pie for dessert, dinner, a brownie for dessert, and even more ice cream before bed.

I really think that telling Cal the truth was the best decision I've made since I've been here.

I'M on my way to the fourth floor to go over some designs with Cal for the guest rooms, and it feels nice to be doing something productive today, although I'm sure the tension between us will be high. Today is all about business and I'm really hoping Cal can behave professionally.

He was so tender and attentive yesterday, so today, I'm holding on to that version of him.

I ended up taking the birth control and pain reliever but stuffed the morning-after pill into the drawer of my nightstand, along with the sleep aid. I suppose it's better to be safe than sorry with the birth control. I'm not sure if I'll ever have sex with Cal again, but if I do, I certainly don't want to have his baby.

The elevator stops on the sixth floor and Cal steps inside, clutching a book under his arm while I grip the notebook hanging from my hand. I take note of his book. *"The Great Gatsby*, again?" I say as the doors shut.

He holds the book out in front of him. It's the same hardcover first edition he had when we were kids. I swear he read it at least a dozen times in those four years.

"Our past is an anchor and a weight on us, no matter how hard we try to go forward," he quotes a line from the book. "Each time reading it is like the first." He tucks it back under his arm when we come to a stop on the fourth floor. "After you." He waves a hand in a gentlemanly manner.

I could debate that line and tell him that we're allowed to let go of the anchor, but I'm picking my battles today and that's not one of them.

When I step out of the elevator, Cal follows, eventually walking in step with me as we make our way down the hall. "Are you feeling any better today?" he asks, looking at my legs to see if I'm walking with a wobble.

"Much better. Thank you."

It's my first time on this floor and it's obvious there's a lot of work to be done. "What made you decide on floors two through five for the rooms?"

"Easy. Eight has the best view. I plan to spend a lot of time on this island and want my own living space. The sixth floor is for staff, as well as the library. The seventh is for entertainment. And you know that the first floor is the kitchen."

"Do you have your own space at all your hotels?"

"No," he shakes his head, "only my favorites."

We stop in front of one of the rooms and Cal opens the door, stepping aside to allow me in first. "All the rooms on this floor will be furnished with a bed, television, and a minibar. All the rooms on the east side have a private balcony. The rooms on the west do not."

They're good-sized and I see so much potential. "Do you have a theme in mind?" I pull the pen out of the binding of my notebook, ready to take notes.

"I've decided to go with a regal theme. We utilize the same theme at our most popular resort in Eastern Europe. My team thinks that having one in the states would attract American tourists from all over the country."

"Okay," I nod, "and the color scheme?"

"That's up to you. I'm not a fashion guru, or a designer."

"You mean, assuming you'll take my advice?"

Cal gives me a side-eye. "Assuming."

I bite back a smile. "Okay, then. Gold and burgundy it

is." I step farther into the room, decorating it in my head. "For the suites, I definitely think there should be working fireplaces. Maybe Tudor windows and clawfoot tubs similar to the one in my bathroom."

"I think we can work with that."

We finish going over some ideas for the guest rooms when my hunger pangs strike. Cal glances at his wristwatch as we're standing quietly in the elevator. He gives me a look. He must've heard my stomach growl. "Damn, it's already four o'clock. We didn't even have lunch. Where the hell did the time go?"

"Guess it's early dinner tonight." I look back down at all the notes I took today. Cal mentioned setting up a conference call with another designer, as well as the contractors who will be doing the renovations. My first week here has been a whirlwind of emotions and it feels good to throw myself into work. I can really use the distraction, and I'm sure Cal can, too.

"To make it up to you, I'd like to take you out for dinner tonight," Cal says as he pulls his phone out of his pocket. He begins tapping on the screen.

"Take me out?" I laugh. "We're on an island away from civilization."

"You let me handle that." He sticks his phone back in his front pocket when the elevator doors open. "Pick out a nice dinner dress and meet me in the sitting room in one hour." He steps out and begins down the hallway.

Stepping out behind him, I hang back, giving us some space.

Out for dinner? Like a date?

I'm not sure what to think. I'm also not sure where he

plans to go. He said 'out.' Maybe outdoors in the court-yard. It is one of my favorite places on this property and dinner under the stars sounds perfect; it's the company I'm worried about. Cal and I aren't able to go more than five minutes without butting heads.

Regardless of the plans, I'm excited to do something other than hang out in my room and listen to Mozart while pacing the floors. Last night I asked Peter if there was a television, with possibly Netflix or Hulu; he told me that Cal doesn't watch TV. Who doesn't watch TV? It's insane. I've got no idea what the staff does for fun, or even to simply relax, but it seems they just lie in bed and stare at their ceilings.

I'll never live like that—ever.

The realization that Cal expects me to stay here hits full force. A feeling of dread sweeps through me. Like a dark cloud lingering overhead waiting for a storm to ride in.

No. It's temporary, not a life sentence.

Once Cal is inside his room with the door closed, I continue down the hall to my room. I'm not sure what dress I'll wear tonight, but Cal said dinner, so it definitely won't be one of the ball gowns, even if I am itching to try on the peach-colored one with a sewn-in crinoline.

I get to my room and before I even open the door, I decide on the form-fitting black velvet dress. I've shuffled through all the dresses a few times and they're all so glamorous. Something I certainly am not. Naturally, I dreamt that one day I would be, but all little girls have those dreams. I guess Cal heard about mine, once or too many times, and decided it was his place to try and make them all come true, even if he is going about it the wrong way.

Making a beeline straight for the closet, I head for the black dress. They are organized by color, so it's easy to find since there are only a couple black ones. My fingers run over the velvety fabric and I'm assured that this is 'the one.' I pull it down and drape it over my arm while I search for a pair of shoes.

I pull a couple pairs off the shelf, sticking them all back on when I spot the perfect ones. They're also black with a small heel and straps that ride up the ankle; they'll look amazing with this dress.

This might not be an actual date, and I might possibly despise Cal, but there's no reason I can't have a little fun with it. Lord knows I'm not doing anything else during my stay, especially having fun. Well, aside from the three times Cal fingered me, and the one time he stole my virginity. I wouldn't say that was fun, as much as it was satisfying. The first time, I think he awoke something inside of me. A part of me that was hiding and craving to be unleashed. Not so much a freaky side, but a curious side. When I'm with him, intimately, I feel sexy—powerful and carefree.

Stripping out of my clothes, I drop them in the hamper next to my closet. Every evening when I return from dinner, the hamper is emptied and clean clothes are set neatly on my bed. I assume it's Paulina, although I have yet to meet her.

I step one foot into the dress then the other and slide it up my body. My arms go into the straps and I lift them into place, while admiring myself in the mirror. It fits perfectly, hugging my waist and hips. I'm not wearing a bra, since this one has built-in cups, leaving the perfect amount of cleavage peeking out the top.

My hands slide down my sides and I bite the corner of my lip. Something about this dress makes me feel provocative.

Reaching my hand behind me, I zip the back up as much as I can. I'll have to get some help to get it the rest of the way up.

Fortunately, after soaking in a nice long bath last night and wrapping my head in a towel while I slept, my natural curls are intact, so I opt for leaving it down.

After I dab on some light makeup, I smack my lips together and head out. It's been well over an hour and I'm sure Cal is waiting impatiently for me to meet him in the sitting room.

You'd think I'm on my way to my first date ever with how fast my heart is racing. I'm not sure why I feel so nervous. Maybe it's because I've never had a formal dinner with anyone before. Now that I think about it, Trent has never taken me on an actual date. We've gone to the movies, grabbed dinner, and gone to a few dance clubs, but they weren't dates—at least, it didn't feel that way.

Oh my God, I *am* going on my first date.

16

I GAVE her shelter and she gave me company. I gave her a dance and she opened her legs for me. Now I'm giving her this date, and she will give me a promise—a promise that she'll keep. She can pretend that her relationship with Trent is viable, but it died the minute she stepped foot on my island.

In life, we come across people with needs. We all have them. Bella has big dreams, dreams that I have the ability to make come true, and I can do that, but I never give without getting something in return.

My kindness is not out of weakness, and she will offer up her mind, her body, and her soul for the sake of her future.

We can do this the easy way, or the hard way.

"The boat is waiting," Peter says as he enters the open door of my office.

"Thank you, Peter." I set the contract down in the folder on my desk and close it. "Has she started the pills yet?"

"It doesn't seem so. I will check while you're out."

I give Peter an approving nod and he leaves the room. My hands press to the desk as I look at the door, waiting for Bella to come in. I can hear the clanking of her heels down the hall, so I know she's close.

I need Bella's cooperation, but more than anything, I need her trust. She needs to realize that I am not out to hurt her. I simply want *her*. Revenge is a broad term and can be carried out in many ways. I can admire her beauty, enjoy her company, and fuck her, all while knowing how much she hates it. I plan to take everything that she holds dear to her heart, everything she acquired over the past twelve years and replace it with me. That's my revenge. Forcing her to live the life I want her to live, instead of the one she wants.

Taking her virginity was not part of the plan. I had no idea she saved herself for me, even if she didn't realize she was. It's obvious, though. It was meant to be. Her pussy was never meant to be tainted by another man. And now, it never will be.

It's a satisfying feeling knowing that I laid claim to her in that way. She truly does belong to me in every sense of the word. My only wish is that I would have done it properly instead of in the heat of the moment.

"Cal," Bella says, knocking her knuckles on the wide-open door.

My back straightens as I take her in. She's as beautiful as the original Mona Lisa. Alluring, tactful, flawless. Primed to perfection in a sleek black dress. An hourglass frame that makes my cock twitch. Rounded ass and plump lips that would fit perfectly around me.

I'm no match for her beauty in a simple black suit with a matching black tie. My hair is in dire need of a cut, but I'm reluctant to bring Sage, my stylist, to the island. We have a history that I worry she will dredge up. It's the last thing I need now that I finally have Bella.

"Cal," she says again, snapping me out of the trance I was in, "are you ready?"

"Yes." I step around the desk and clear my throat. "You look...nice." My arm ushers out, and she hesitantly locks hers around it.

"Nice? Gee, thanks."

We leave the room and I close the door behind me. We get halfway down the hall when my phone buzzes in my pocket. I drop Bella's arm and take the call. "We're headed down," I tell Leo, before he has a chance to speak.

"The chef is getting antsy. Says the food is ready and he worries it will go cold before you get here."

"I said we're on our fucking way," my voice rises, "you tell him to keep it warm or he can get the hell off my boat and go cook for someone else." I end the call and stick my phone back in the front pocket of my pants.

Bella rolls her eyes at me, as if she's disgusted by my cruel nature. "Main floor?" she asks, her hand hovering over the down arrow.

"Yes."

The doors open and we step inside. They begin to close and it hits me that I forgot to lock up my room. "Shit," I holler, tapping the button to open the door, repeatedly. It does no good, we're already moving.

I pull my phone back out of my pocket and give Peter a quick call.

As usual, he picks up on the first ring. "I was in a hurry and left the door to my bedroom unlocked. Please use the master key to lock it up."

"I will do that as soon as I get to the eighth floor. The new guard was giving Paulina a hard time."

"Make it quick." I end the call abruptly.

It's rare that I forget to lock up. Actually, I never have, and the fact that I did goes to show that I'm far too distracted.

"Everything okay?" Bella asks as we exit the elevator.

I place a hand on her lower back and lead her to the main doors. "Everything is fine," I say sternly. "Have you ever been on a yacht, Bella?"

"No," she shakes her head, "I hate boats. In fact, I hate large bodies of water in general."

I look at her, surprised. "Really? Yet, you took a rowboat out in the midst of a storm, in the dark?"

"That was a matter of life and death." She picks up her pace, walking away from my hand that was resting on her.

"You're still here and very much alive. So call it like it is. You were trying to leave me."

She looks over at me with a scowl on her face. "I won't deny it. Of course I wanted to leave."

"Wanted to? Or want to?"

"Both." Her shoulders rise then fall dramatically.

I bite back a smile. "Well, I hope you can hold your stomach because we're going out on the bay."

She stops walking and jerks her attention to me. "We're leaving the island?"

"Leaving, but staying." I gesture to her to continue

toward the dock. She presses up on her tiptoes as she walks, trying to get a better view.

The yacht is lit up in a blue ambient glow and I can already smell the Lobster Thermidor.

"So, we're having dinner on a yacht?" Bella walks across the steppingstones and I follow behind her.

"Precisely. How do you feel about that?"

"I feel like there's a good possibility I'll be throwing up on your shoes. But I've never been one to shy away from a challenge."

When we step on the dock, Leo is waiting with his hand held out to Bella. She accepts his offer and steps through the hull doors.

"Good evening, sir," Leo says in his Italian accent, offering me his hand as well, but I snarl at it and step aboard on my own. I'm not a big fan of the guy, but he does what needs to be done, so I keep him on my payroll.

Bella stands in the middle of the deck and looks around. "This is nice."

"Nice?" I laugh.

"Yeah. You know, *nice*? Like the way I look tonight."

Touché. Those were my words. I wanted to tell her that she took my breath away and made my heart race, but I've never been good with words.

I join Bella's side and draw in a deep breath when I see Serena, one of the hired servers, on board. I thought I was strict on my orders with the crew that I did not want any of the ladies working tonight. I requested all men, yet there Serena stands. The last thing I need is for Bella to get a look into my past. I wasn't a womanizer, per se, but I have fucked many of the women who have accompanied me on the island. It was always consensual, and my partners always knew that it was strictly sexual.

"Right this way," Serena says with a glint of a smile. She walks ahead of us, assuming we're following.

I take Bella's hand against her will and lead her at my side. She doesn't fend me off as we head straight for the bar.

"We'll see ourselves to our seats, Serena," I say in a very serious manner. "You may go."

Serena pulls her lips between her teeth and sticks her hands in the pockets of her black waiter apron before spinning on her heels.

I look down at Bella and realize she's watching me back. "What was that all about?"

I shrug my shoulders, brushing her off. "I don't know what you're talking about."

Strips of blue lights run down a large mirror behind the glass bar and I'm able to see Bella's reflection as she stands beside me. Her fingers are still tangled in mine and I'm surprised she hasn't pulled away or pushed me out of her personal space.

Where the hell is the bartender? I lean over the bar and holler, "Can we get some damn service over here?"

"Sorry about that," Arabella says as she walks behind the bar. *Fuck my life.* What the hell is she doing tending the bar tonight? Either Peter or Byron royally fucked up and they're both on my shitlist right now.

"Two dry martinis," I tell Arabella, who is waiting for our order with a smug grin on her face.

"You got it, Boss." Arabella winks, warranting another glare from Bella.

Peering down at Bella while our drinks are being made, I rest one arm on the bar. I opt for a distraction rather than an explanation. "Still just nice?" I ask her.

She smirks then looks over my shoulder. Tipping her head, she asks, "Who was that girl back there?"

I look behind me, fully expecting to see Serena, but she's not there. "Who? Serena? Just help."

"And the bartender? Do you know her, too?"

"Neither of them are of any importance."

"Not of importance?" Bella blows air. "Help is important."

"You know what I mean."

"No. Actually, I don't. And the way you tensed up tells me they're both more than just hired staff."

Arabella sets our drinks on the bar and I release Bella's hand to grab them both. "Let's sit." I nod toward the only table in the open space. On top of the table is a ten-piece setting for a formal dinner. White cloth napkins, stainless-steel silverware, and fine white china.

I set the drinks down on the table, then pull out a chair for Bella. She sits down before I push her in a smidgen. "You're just gonna ignore what I said?" she asks.

Once I take my seat and position all my cutlery the way I like it, I take a sip of my martini.

Bella doesn't seem pleased that I'm brushing her off, and while it's not my intention, I'm hoping she drops this conversation.

"Did you fuck them?"

I cough, almost choking on my drink. "Excuse me?" I lick my lips dry, then set my drink on the table.

Her short, bare nails tap on her glass as she waits for an answer. "Well, did you?"

I believe in transparency, especially if we're going to make this work, so I give her the truth. "Yes. Many times." At this point, I'm mentally plotting the murder of my friend/attorney and butler/friend. Maybe a slow death—or quick and to the point. Either will be satisfying after this fuck-up.

Bella's eyes widen in surprise. "Wow, just a yes would have been fine."

Tilting my head slightly, I observe her with a grin. "Are you jealous, Bella?"

"No!" She says in a huff. "Not even a little bit." She tips her glass and takes a drink, a very long drink. In fact, she's downright slamming it.

"Whoa," I reach across the table and grab her glass, "slow down. Nobody enjoys drunk company."

She mumbles something I can't make out, probably an insult.

Serena joins us, and Bella reaches for her glass again, finishing it off while Serena sets down two bowls of hot soup.

"Could I get a refill, please?" Bella slides the glass toward the end of the table where Serena stands.

"Of course," Serena retorts, her eyes darting over to me. "And you, Callum? Would you like a refill?"

My jaw clenches, pinning her with a glare. "It's Mr. Ellis. And no, my glass is still full, as you can see."

Serena bites her lip and rounds the table. Coming up behind me, she leans down with a hand on my shoulder and whispers in my ear, "You got it, Mr. Ellis." She enunciates my name and my fingers clench around the cloth napkin in my lap.

When she leaves, I notice Bella scowling. I don't say anything because the last thing I want to do is feed into her assumption that there is something going on between me and Serena. It's sex. Plain and simple.

"Help, huh?" She laughs, reaching across the table and grabbing my martini.

"Hey! What the hell are you doing?"

"Excuse me if I need an extra drink. The *help* who has her ass hanging out of her black miniskirt and her tits threatening to break free has given me a complex."

"So this is about confidence and not the fact that I fucked her?"

"Multiple times," she adds. "And no, I couldn't care less that you slept with that hooker look-alike. As long as she didn't give you a disease that you passed on to me, we're good." She lifts her glass, or mine rather, and sucks half the contents down.

"I promise you she is clean and so am I. We have no worries."

Bella laughs and I can tell the alcohol is now coursing through her bloodstream. "Damn straight we don't because it won't be happening again. And how do you know she's clean? Do you have all your 'women,'" she air quotes, "tested?"

"As a matter of fact, I do. You can never be too safe. I also run a background check."

"Wow!" She laughs again. "Nothing like a hard cock waiting for a fax to come through before you can have a release."

My lips press together to fight back a smile, but it does no good. "You're just full of humor, aren't you?"

She raises her glass. "When life gives you lemons." The rim presses to her lips and I watch intently as she takes a drink then licks them. She notices me watching and darts her tongue out, sliding it around the rim of the glass, sweeping up the grains of salt.

My cock twitches in delight and I'd love nothing more than to have those lips milking me right about now. I could drag her down to the cabins and force her on her knees. The thought crosses my mind and I'm on the verge of getting up when Serena comes back.

Bella would probably put up a fight, but Serena would willingly do whatever the hell I wanted her to. I could sneak off and use the restroom, leaving Bella sitting alone. But that idea doesn't satisfy me. It's Bella I want.

Serena sets Bella's drink down and smiles politely at her. "Anything else, hun?"

"Actually," Bella holds up a finger, "I'd like to hear how you two met. Cal here tells me you're old friends."

My cheeks instantly flush with heat. Damn this girl. I need to get her under control and it needs to happen fast.

"Old friends, huh?" Serena looks at me and winks before returning her attention to Bella. "Yeah, we're old friends."

I actually do have to use the restroom, so I excuse myself while these two have a little heart-to-heart over the monster who's fucked them into oblivion.

As I'm walking away, I glance over my shoulder and see Bella watching me. She seems tense, but she's the one who started that conversation and now she gets to finish it. That'll teach her to keep her damn mouth shut.

Unzipping my pants after making it to the restroom, I press my hand to the back wall and take a piss in the urinal. My cock is still a fucking semi from watching Bella's mouth fuck that glass, so I point it straight down, taking care not to make a mess. God, she's infuriating and so damn sexy. I knew she was a knockout, but I never expected her to have this effect on me. I had every intention of fucking her when I brought her here, but I assumed it would be basic and partially fulfilling. Instead, I wanna bend her over every piece of furniture in sight. I need to hear her scream my name, so I know that piece of shit, Trent, is out of her head. I will fuck him out of her mind if it's the last thing I do.

I'm walking out the door, tucking my shirt into my pants, when I crash into someone, or they crash into me, rather. A low grumble climbs up my throat and I'm ready to lash out when I realize it's Serena.

"Callum, what a surprise," she says, looking left, then right, before pushing me back into the restroom.

"What the fuck are you doing?" I grumble, shifting away from her.

She grabs me by the collar of my jacket and pulls me close, her tongue skating across her lower lip. "I've missed you, baby."

"You shouldn't be here."

"Oh, come on," she chuckles, "you came in here knowing I'd follow."

"I came in here to piss and now I'm going back to my date."

"Date." She blows air, now gripping both sides of my jacket and pulling me closer. "Since when does Callum Ellis date?"

"Since the last time I fucked you and had nightmares of your saggy pussy. Figured I'd give monogamy a go."

Her hands drop, hanging at her sides. "Fuck you."

"Probably not."

I go to walk around her, but she slams her hand to the door.

"When you break her heart and she leaves, I'll be waiting."

Serena is desperation at its finest. She's a good-looking girl and can suck a mean dick, but it was never about more than a quick fuck for me and a good paycheck for her. She needs the money, but I no longer need the whore.

"Hello," I hear Bella say from outside the door. Serena purses her mouth into a satisfying smirk and moves her hand from the door so I slap mine against it, keeping it shut.

"In the stall. Now!" I mutter through clenched teeth.

Her hands cross over her chest and she just stands there, pleased with herself.

My jaw ticks in fury and I use my free hand to squeeze her upper arm tightly, so tight that the tips of my fingers hide in her skin. "Now! Or I will do very bad things to you."

Serena pushes herself up on her tiptoes and sweeps her tongue across my upper lip. "I like when you do bad things to me. That basic bitch out there, probably not so much. Enjoy your vanilla sex life." She drops down and yanks her arm away, then goes into one of the bathroom stalls, closing the door behind her.

My hands run down my suit, straightening myself out before I move my hand and open the door.

Bella takes a step back when we're face to face. "Everything okay?" I ask her.

"I'm fine. Is everything okay with you?"

The door closes behind me and I place an arm around her and begin to lead her back to the table. She steps away from my touch and stops walking. "I was looking for the restroom and heard commotion. Was our waitress in the bathroom with you?"

I've never had this feeling before—the need to lie to prevent an argument. I'm always straightforward, no bull-shitting, while taking none in return. Right now, though, I feel ten years old, meeting potential parents for the first time. Only this time, I'm trying not to piss off my future wife.

Since when do I care if I piss her off? I've done it daily, sometimes hourly, since she's arrived.

My fingers run through my hair as I choke on the words that want to come out. "Umm, about that..." Here comes the obvious lie. "She was lost."

Bella's eyebrows hit her forehead, arms crossed over her chest. "Lost?"

"That's right." What the fuck is the matter with me? Why do I feel like I'm on the verge of being scolded?

"Whatever," Bella waves her hands in the air, "let's just eat and get this over with."

Her heels clank against the hardwood floors as she walks back to the table. I watch her round ass rise and fall with each step and I'm suddenly enthralled again.

She's definitely jealous, and I'm highly turned on.

17

WE'RE HALFWAY through dinner and Bella still has a sour attitude. I asked her if she preferred to eat in the dining room in the house, or even in one of the cabins below deck, but she insisted we stay.

"How did you like the lobster?" I ask her as she sets her fork down and puts her hands on her full belly.

She holds up a finger as she finishes chewing then swallows down her bite. "Delicious. A little heavy on the parsley but still good."

I'm surprised she's admitting to liking something that I planned for her, although, it's not a compliment meant for me, it's for the chef.

I pat my mouth with my napkin, then set it on top of the table. "I'll be sure to let the chef know."

Serena comes over and offers to take our plates. I don't acknowledge her, while Bella, on the other hand, glares a warning in her direction. Serena takes notice and lets out a giggle. "Are you two lovebirds having dessert? Possibly something *vanilla*?" She looks at me with a crooked grin.

She wants to stir trouble and I won't allow it. Not with my date.

"We'll be having dessert on the sundeck. Please make sure everything is set and then you may leave for the night."

"But, Mr. Davis said—"

"I don't care what he said. You are finished for the night. See yourself off the boat and Mr. Davis will handle your final paycheck."

"You mean...I'm fired?"

I pick up Bella's plate and place it on top of my dirty one Serena's holding. "Precisely. Goodnight, Serena."

"Because of her?" Serena spits out in a fit of rage.

"This has nothing to do with Bella. This is due to your lack of professionalism on the job, as well as your poor bedroom skills."

Serena's face blares crimson as she stomps her feet like a child. "You know what, Callum, you might be a billionaire with a big dick, but you're the most selfish asshole I know." Her hands cup around her mouth, although she speaks loud and clear. "For the record, you never even got me off. You will pay for this. Mark my words." She storms off in a fury and I shoot Bella a look before she busts out laughing.

"Should have at least made her clean the bathroom first. I imagine she dirtied it while she was *lost.*" Bella smirks before finishing off her drink.

She's on her fourth martini of the night and the white of her eyes are now streaked with red.

"Serena," I call out. She turns around to face me with hope in her eyes. "Since you like to wander into restrooms, why don't you clean those before you go?"

Serena snarls in disgust. "You're kidding, right?"

"Do I look like I'm kidding?"

Once she stomps away, probably cursing me internally, I look at Bella who is laughing hysterically. "Let's have dessert then get you back to your room. You need sleep."

"Sleep?" she laughs, "I'm not even tired, besides, the sun just set ten minutes ago."

I push my chair back and stand, offering her my hand. She looks at it like it's diseased, before breathing out a hefty sigh and accepting it.

We pass by the bar where Arabella wipes down the counter, quietly. I'm sure she just heard the outburst from Serena, and if she wants to keep her job, she'll remain quiet.

"Are you enjoying yourself?" I ask Bella as we walk up the stairs to the sundeck. Granted, the sun has set, but there's an open view of the stars over the bay.

"As much as I can knowing that I'm trapped on an island by a man who hates me and won't let me leave. Oh, and stole my virginity."

"You sure do like to speak your mind."

"I'm not one to hold back, much like you. So, tell me Cal—why are you being so nice to me?"

Once we're at the highest level of the yacht, there's a nip in the air. Bella hugs her chest, shielding herself from the cold. I unbutton my jacket and slide it off, then wrap it around her shoulders. "Just because I'm a forward man doesn't mean I'm not a gentleman. I know what I want and I never stop until I get it."

"And I suppose *I* am what you want?"

Narrowing my eyes at hers, I make myself perfectly clear. "I already have you. What I want is for the people who hurt us to pay for their sins."

Her expression becomes solemn, eyes pinched together, shoulders drooping. "No one hurt us, Cal."

It's best if I just let this go. Bella never needs to know the truth about what happened that day and why I was punished, but that doesn't mean that those who had a part in my demise won't pay. It all begins with her, and here she is.

"Have a seat," I angle my head toward the small round table beside us, "I had the chef prepare something special."

"What?" Bella looks at me sideways as she lifts the lid on the silver platter. Her eyes shoot back to mine. "Blueberry pie?" There's a hint of a smile on her face and hope is not lost for the night.

"It was always your favorite." I grab the pitcher of lemonade—also her favorite—and begin pouring her a glass.

"Our favorite," she deadpans. I give her a look and she repeats herself. "It was our favorite. Don't you remember the day Mrs. Webster baked three blueberry pies for the town's pie cook-off that we weren't allowed to attend? We snuck downstairs in the middle of the night and took a pie to your room and ate it with our fingers."

I sit down at the table and Bella does the same. "And

the next morning when we denied it, she noticed your fingers were dyed blue and you took the full blame."

"You had just gotten in trouble for fighting Trent and I knew you were on your last strike."

If only she could have saved me the last time I got in trouble. Did I expect her to? No. But, I never expected her to just leave without even letting me explain what happened. All these years she's been a sister to Mark and a girlfriend to Trent, not even knowing what they did.

"I wrote you letters. A lot of them." Bella scoops a slice of pie onto her plate and I'm surprised when she does the same for me. She digs in while so many unanswered questions swirl in my head.

There's a sting in my chest, but I ignore it, while she keeps talking.

"It took me a couple weeks before I got the courage to do it, but once I did, I just kept writing them, hoping one day I'd find your address and I could mail them. I never did find it. I tried, though."

I had no idea.

This subject needs to change fast because I refuse to overthink this. It doesn't change the fact that she left me. If she did write letters, it was out of pity and that's something I do not fucking want.

"Why did you turn down Juilliard?" I shift to a lighter conversation, at least for me.

Bella grabs the bottle of whipped cream and begins topping her pie. "Why do you always change the subject when the conversation is about you?"

"Because I'd rather talk about you."

"Couldn't afford it. Plain and simple." She takes a bite,

her eyes close, and she moans at the deliciousness. "This is really good." She points her fork to the pie.

"You had a full scholarship."

Her eyes widen in surprise. "No, I didn't."

"Bella, you can't lie to me. I did an insane amount of research on you. School records, criminal records, medical records. By the way, I'm happy to see that the scar on your forehead is minimal from that rollerblading accident when you were fifteen."

There's a loud clank when her fork hits the ceramic plate. "Why would you snoop around in my life like that? Those things are private!"

"I wasn't about to let a hard-earned criminal move into my house. Or someone with a nasty venereal disease."

"You're crazy."

"Most of the time, yes. Why'd you turn down the scholarship?"

There's a brief moment of silence between us. Bella picks her fork back up and takes another bite, chewing sluggishly.

"I guess I just wanted to make up for lost time and leaving would only cause me to miss more time."

"Did they ask you to turn it down?"

Another beat of silence.

"No," she spits out. "They'd never ask me to turn it down. We all just thought it would be a good idea if I stayed. Mark was already accepted into law school and preparing to leave, since he was a year ahead of me. I didn't want them to be alone."

"So Mark gets to chase his dreams, but you don't?"

"Music is a hobby, not a career." She jabs the fork into her mouth, ripping off the piece of pie aggressively.

"You've got a career now in interior design, so maybe it's time to enjoy music again."

Bella blows a sarcastic laugh. "I wouldn't call it a career. A degree doesn't give me experience and even you were hesitant on my ideas."

"I think you had great ideas. In fact, when I set up the conference call with Barbara, I mentioned so."

"Can we drop this? None of it matters."

"Sure, it does. What if I told you that I could make your dreams come true?"

Bella slides her plate across the table while licking a smidgen of blueberry from her lips. "I'd say you're out of your mind."

"Maybe I am. But we both know that interior design is not what you're passionate about."

"You don't know anything about me."

"I know enough."

I won't stop tossing the bait. She'll bite when she's ready. If she lets me, I'll give her a good life, as long as she's with me and away from them.

"Are you ready?" I ask, before finishing off my lemonade.

She nods, then pushes her chair back and stands. I do the same, rounding the table and taking her hand in mine, without her permission. "I hope you enjoyed tonight."

"Aside from the deep conversation about my career choice," her shoulders shrug, "it was all right."

I smile at her snarky response. She's got quite the attitude, and it's due for an adjustment.

We're walking down the dock when my phone rings. I stop, forcing her to do the same by holding tightly to her hand.

Byron's name flashes on the screen. I hold up a finger to Bella, then take the call. "Why are you calling? You know I'm busy."

"Just thought you might want to know that there is a gentleman on the main island waiting to board a boat to Cori Cove."

I look at Bella, brows pinched together, while she stares up at the sky with her head tilted back.

"Who?"

"Trent Beckham. Want me to take care of him?"

"No," I growl. I tuck my phone to my side, covering the speaker, and grab Bella's attention by dropping her hand. "Why don't you go inside and I'll be in shortly."

"Okay," she drawls before turning and walking away.

I wait until she's working her way up the stone path before I put the phone back to my ear.

"Put him up for the night—someplace nice. Have Jeffery escort him before breakfast."

"You're sure?" There's a hesitation in his tone. "Isn't he the boyfriend?"

"Not anymore." I'm about to end the call when I remember that I'm pissed at Byron. "Oh, and I know that the female staff was no accident. I don't know what you're doing, but you know I don't play games."

"Oh, come on." Byron laughs. "One day, Bella might want to partake in the festivities on the island. I bet she has a freaky side to her. She might enjoy it."

Acid climbs up my throat at the thought. "She will

never *partake*. And if you pull a stunt like this again or even have a thought of her in that way, this friendship will be void."

"Whoa. Calm down, Ellis. It was a simple suggestion. Besides, this friendship will never be void, I know too many of your secrets."

Byron ends the call, purposely infuriating me. Gripping my phone tightly in my hand, I growl audibly, feeling the veins in my neck balloon while my pulse throbs in my throat.

Now that Bella is back in my life, she's all that matters. I'd bury my only friend before I let anyone touch a hair on her head.

18

CAL SEEMED tense when I left him on the dock. Whatever Byron was saying on the other end of the call made his fingers flex around the phone as he clutched it. He can be scary when he's mad, but when it's not directed at me, it's pretty sexy.

As I step off the elevator and make my way down the hall to my room, I unclasp the straps on my shoes and take them off, one at a time. With them dangling in my hand, I pass by Cal's room, but backstep to his door when I remember his call to Peter. Looking behind me and again, in front of me, I give the doorknob a try.

I'm taken aback when it actually turns. My heart begins galloping in my chest and my palm starts sweating against the glass knob. I look around one more time before giving it a gentle push. The door opens, and cautiously, I step inside.

I swear I can feel my pulse around my grip on the knob and I'm fearful to let go. It's pitch-black inside and actually pretty cold for being a closed space. At least, it's colder than the rest of the castle.

Chatter begins carrying from outside the room, so I shut the door quickly, latching it without a sound.

With my back against the door, I draw in a deep breath, quickly exhaling and spinning around in a breathless dismay when I hear a key slide into the lock from outside the door. I back away slowly, thinking someone is going to come in.

This is it. I'm caught.

I stand there frozen, waiting for someone to barge in and drag me back to my room before padlocking it shut so I'm not able to leave.

Seconds pass, until it's been a minute, and no one has opened the door.

Peter must have been locking it.

Taking a few steps back, I catch myself unintentionally holding my breath until my lungs feel like filled balloons. I exhale sharply and continue to step backward. It's completely dark, not even a glimmer of light shining into the room.

I gasp when I bump into the far wall. Reaching behind me, I press my hands to it and realize that it's not a wall. At least, it doesn't feel like it. It's cold—glass, maybe? I turn around, running my hands down it when, at the sound of a threatening hiss, I suddenly jump back.

My heart gallops into my throat as I hurry back toward the door to see if there's a light switch on the wall.

I should try and get out of here. Bang on the door for

Peter to let me out before Cal catches me. In my head, I know that. But, something doesn't let me.

I'm running my fingers up and down the wall near the door when I come across a switch.

Please be a light switch and not an alarm of some sort.

It wouldn't surprise me if Cal had this room armed with cameras and sounds.

Holding my breath again, I push up, breathing out a sigh of relief when the light shines into the room. It's dim and comes from a floodlight in the middle of the ceiling, but at least I'm able to see now.

I turn around, and the next thing I know, I'm screaming at the sight in front of me.

My hand claps over my mouth, shutting myself up. If anyone is on this floor, there is no doubt they heard me. Peter will likely be barging into the room any second.

Moisture coats my hand as I keep it in place, taking small steps toward the wall-sized tank, or cage, or whatever the hell it is. All I know is that staring back at me is the biggest snake I've ever seen in my life. It's all black, thick, and it has to be at least seven feet long.

I walk closer, closing the space between me and the caged reptile. My eyes are locked dead with his, or hers, and I feel like it's warning me off. Practically demanding I leave. But, I don't.

Instead, I go closer. With my hand out, I press it to the glass. The snake stays still, while I do the same.

Once I'm no longer afraid, I look at the other tanks beside it. There are three, horizontally lined up and running from the floor to the ceiling. Each one is at least ten-foot wide. Inside, there are branches, vines, and logs, and it reminds me of a little oasis. There are lights on top, but none of them are turned on, which is odd.

I look closer at the other cages and notice a smaller brown snake. I only see one, but there could be more hiding. In the cage at the end, there's another brown, but smaller one.

As long as they are in there and I'm out here, we're okay. Although, the sight of them does make me feel queasy. I'm not deathly afraid, but I'm certainly no friend to reptiles. If snakes can sense fear, that black monster would probably swallow my entire arm.

I had no idea Cal had a liking for snakes. I suppose there's a lot I don't know about who he is now.

It wasn't until this moment that I even realized that the bedroom walls are as black as coal with a black fleur print. Sconces are placed on all the walls around five feet apart. There's a very dark vibe to the room that slides chills down my spine. A king-size canopy bed sits on top of a black antique-looking rug. It's dressed perfectly in deep red, silk bedding. I walk closer to the bed, my fingers running along the wooden beams holding up the canopy. Engraved snakes slither down the mahogany wood and meet again at the footboard.

Are there no windows in here? I look around, thinking maybe there is one hidden beneath a curtain, but it's confirmed, there are none.

How strange.

Regardless, I still don't see why Cal would be so persistent on keeping people out of his room. Sure, it's Gothic and has me questioning if he's actually a vampire who eats snakes, but really, there's nothing that screams 'secretive' to me. If he were really that adamant about keeping others out, you'd think he'd have a better lock than one made in the early 1900s. Maybe even an alarm system. I suppose he probably doesn't need all that because most people obey his demands and don't sneak into rooms like I do.

There's a couple closed doors that I assume are a bathroom and a closet. Beside them is a floor-to-ceiling bookshelf packed full with classic books. I pick a door and turn the knob. It's the same glass, ancient knob that's on all the doors on this floor. I pull it open and it's a closet. A very large one at that. I step inside and flip on the light switch. There's two tall dressers, and a row of hanging suits, all black. A shoe rack, some shelves with shoe boxes, and… Cal's memory box. It's a weathered, wooden box with a metal clasp that's about the size of a shoe box.

He had that thing when we were at The Webster House. I can't believe he still has it. Pushing myself up on my tiptoes, I try to reach it, but I need something to stand on; it's too high up.

My eyes sweep the closet, looking for something that will raise me a few feet, but all I see that will work is the dresser.

I pull out the bottom drawer to get me a foot higher, then pull myself on top of it. I'm on my knees with my fingers touching the box when I hear something outside of the closet.

Quickly, I jump down and flip the light off in the closet and close the door gently. My heart hammers in my chest as I crouch down in the middle of the hanging suits.

When I hear the door to the room open, I pinch my

eyes shut, holding my breath and internally begging for whoever it is to turn and leave, so I can get the hell out of here.

The door closes and I listen to any sound that tells me someone is in the room. My heart begins to steady at the silence, but quickly accelerates when I hear Cal's voice.

"Did you enter my room?"

A beat of silence.

"The light was on so someone was here. Was it Paulina?"

Another beat of silence.

"Yes, she is well aware that it's off-limits but someone was here. I forgot to lock up, but I'm not distracted enough to leave the light on."

I swallow hard, hoping it wasn't audible on the outside.

Cal raises his voice to a near shout. "I don't give a shit. Find out who it was. And check on Bella. She had a little too much to drink."

He obviously doesn't realize I can hold my liquor. Even if I do feel like I'm about to throw up all over his Brunello suits.

"Who was it? Was it her? Did she wake you up?"

Is he talking to his snakes?

The hairs on my arms shoot up when I see the shadow of his feet outside the closet door. I have no idea what he'll do if he finds me, and I really don't want to find out.

I freeze, unable to breathe, let alone think, when the closet door opens.

I'm still hidden, but if he's looking for me, he will find me.

Cal just stands there, puzzled, as if he's searching for clues as to who was in his room.

A few moments pass before I hear the sound of his belt buckle. My mouth pools with saliva when his pants drop to his ankles, along with his boxer briefs.

Being the curious person that I am, I tilt my head slightly to the right, looking around a hung suit, to steal a peek at his own hung package.

Even soft, he's well-endowed. Thick black hair coats his pubic bone, running down to his smooth cock. Bulging blue veins and a plump silk head. My nipples pucker against my dress at the sight in front of me.

When he unbuttons his shirt at a leisurely pace, I once again find myself holding my breath. I gulp air as he slides off the shirt and is standing before me completely, butt-ass naked.

I don't even care what this man has done to me since I've been here. Part of me wants to dive out of this hiding spot and tackle him to the ground, just so he can shove his fingers inside of me again. I'd probably even let him fuck me—maybe. I'm still a little sore down there, but it's eased up quite a bit.

Cal pulls on a pair of gray sweatpants and I force the ridiculous thoughts away, even if there's a pool of moisture in my panties.

The light switches off and the door closes. I'm left sitting here, motionless, speechless, and totally fucking stuck.

Cal's phone rings on the other side of the door, startling me. I creep forward a bit to try and listen to the conversation.

"What the hell do you mean she's not in her room?"

Busted.

"Well, find her dammit."

I need to suck it up and walk out there, admit I screwed up and apologize for being nosey.

Just as I'm about to stand up, I stoop back down when Cal lets out a harrowing scream. Everything inside me comes to a halt—the blood in my veins, my heartbeat, the pent-up air in my lungs.

There's a loud bang that has my body shooting back into the corner I was tucked in. I hug my knees to my chest as shivers run through my body.

Cal tears open the closet door. I scooch back against the wall again. All I can see are his bare feet as he jerks open a dresser drawer then slams it shut. He walks back out of the closet, shutting the door behind him.

With my hands pressed to the floor beneath me, I notice my fingers sliding under something—an opening of some sort.

I wait a minute, then two, then three. Then the door outside of the closet slams shut and I'm left in complete silence, once again.

On my hands and knees, I crawl to the door. It's pitch-black and I can't see a thing, so I reach up and grab the handle, inching the door open so I can poke my head out.

He's gone.

I should run for the door, leave unscathed—but I don't, because I'm an idiot. Instead, I go back into the closet. I have to know what that lip on the floor was.

I flip on the light and push the hanging suits to one side and, clear as day, there it is.

A door.

There's a secret room? Or exit, maybe? I know this castle is old, but I thought those were only in movies.

I don't know what's behind that door, but I plan to find out.

19

"I DON'T CARE if you have to call in the goddamn coast guard, you will find her!"

Fucking imbeciles can't do their damn jobs if their lives depend on it. And they do. If she's not found, I'll bury every staff member on this island.

"I am powerful and I deserve power-filled things," I say under my breath, as I repeat the verse that I learned from my therapist when I was eighteen years old. It's the only useful thing that old wench gave to me. Because, I am powerful, and I do deserve power-filled things.

"I am powerful and I deserve power-filled things."

"Callum, you have to get control of your emotions, or you will do yourself more harm than good," Trudy, my thirty-five-year-old therapist says. Her legs are crossed properly, giving me no view of what's beneath her slate gray skirt.

Coming here was supposed to help me; instead, it's made me realize that I'm beyond help.

"I'm not scared of my emotions. I'm more concerned about the harm they will bring to others, instead of myself. I have this

rage inside of me that screams revenge on those who wronged me."

"Those thoughts are normal. You're not crazy, Callum."

"Wow. Never said I was, but thanks for clearing that up."

"You know what I mean." She giggles.

Is she flirting with me? I think she is. "I don't know what you mean. Care to elaborate?"

"Let's just move on. Have you memorized the chant I taught you?"

"Mmhmm," I grumble, my eyes sliding from her face down to her chest where her nipples pucker against her thin shirt.

"You are not a victim of your past. You are powerful and you deserve power-filled things."

Smirking, I look her in the eye. "You're right. I am powerful, and I will have power-filled things."

I slide my wheeled chair closer to her, my hand sweeps up her leg and separates her thighs. They uncross and both feet plant to the floor beneath her.

"Callum. This is very unethical. You need to stop this." She pinches her legs together, squeezing my hand between them.

"Maybe crazy is the word we should use," I whisper, watching my hand as I pry her legs apart. Her white cotton panties are exposed beneath her skirt and there's a small wet spot on them that has me grinning. "Trudy," I tsk, "I'm beginning to think that you don't want me to stop."

Her chest rises and falls rapidly when I sweep her panties to the side and puncture her pussy. Wetness pools around her entrance and my mouth falls open at the sight in front of me.

"Do you feel powerless, Trudy?"

My fingers slide in deeper, working her G-spot. She lets out a breathless moan. "Yes."

"That's because I have all the power here. Never forget that."

In a spurt of anger, I tear open the door to the hall and walk with heavy steps to Bella's room.

"I want them everywhere!" I blow out at Peter, who's working on the installation of the cameras. "Every floor. Every exit, entrance. I want to see the fucking dock if I need to."

Kicking open Bella's door, that wasn't even latched, I storm into her room. "Bella," I holler, knowing it's pointless.

There's no way she got off this island. She's here, somewhere. Byron is guarding the cellar. At least, he better be, or he's out of here. I told him that this shit stopped when Bella arrived, and it was recently brought to my attention that he's been carrying on as if he's at one of the main resorts.

I tear through the room, pulling blankets back, tipping her dirty hamper to see if she changed out of her dress—which is not inside—scope the balcony and look around the visible grounds from her room.

"Fuck!" I shout, heading back out of her room.

I pull my phone out of my pocket and give my head of security, Anders, a call. "Anything?"

"Nothing, sir. It's like she just…vanished."

"I want security heightened. Get at least three more guys here. With them and the new hire, you dumbasses better make sure this shit doesn't happen again."

I end the call and walk back down the hall to my room with long strides.

My light was on.

It hits me. I never forget to turn off my lights. Peter said he wasn't inside. It had to be her.

"Motherfucker." I stick the key in the lock and turn it so aggressively that it sticks and I'm forced to jerk it out.

I slam the door behind me, rattling the old clock on the wall. I don't even need to flip on the light to see because the closet door is wide open with the light on.

She was definitely here.

20

Bella

My ENTIRE BODY trembles as I grip the banister. My sweaty palm slides down it, and even though I know I should turn around, something doesn't let me. There's a reason why Cal is so protective over his room, and maybe this is why. If he's hiding something, this could be my only chance to find out what it is.

Thankfully, there's more sconces on the wall that are lit up, so I'm able to see where I'm going. The lights being on only reaffirms that something is definitely down here.

Fear courses through me when I think about what that something could be. It could be dead bodies—or imprisoned women. Oh my God, what if he plans to take me down here one day and tie me up? Maybe I really don't know Cal at all.

Saliva begins pooling in my mouth with each step down the spiral staircase. There's a familiar scent that only strengthens the farther down I go. It's that lemongrass scent that I smelled my first day here.

When I make the turn down the last few steps, I'm

shocked to see that it's just an empty room. The walls are painted all white. The floor is clean cement. There's nothing down here except for a door.

I walk over to it and wrap my fingers around the handle. Drawing in a deep breath, I give it a turn, but it's locked.

Dammit.

As soon as I turn around to go back up the stairs, I'm face to face with a very angry Cal.

"Umm. Hi," I say, stupidly.

Cal makes a growly noise before grabbing me by the waist and flinging me over his shoulder.

"Put me down," I holler, my hands smacking at his back.

I shrill when his palm slaps hard against my ass.

There's a bite to the imprint he left and instead of making me fearful, it pisses me off. "What the hell is the matter with you?"

"Didn't you ever learn that snooping can get you killed?"

I push my hands to his shoulders, lifting myself up as he one-arms me up the stairs. "Oh, are you going to kill me?"

"You'll be lucky if you get off that easily."

Was that a threat? That was definitely a threat.

"Why do you care? There's nothing down there anyways." I chuckle. "Does it make you feel like a villain to have a secret door in your closet?"

"You're about to learn how much of a villain I am. Now shut your damn mouth."

Pushing myself up farther, until I'm stiff in his arm, I

block his path with my body. "I'm not scared of you, Cal." I'm not sure that I've ever seen him look this angry. I should be scared, but I don't think he'd hurt me. "Will you just put me down? I can walk."

"You know, Bella. You've proven to be a pain in my ass. Therefore, it's time to reciprocate."

His jaw clenches right before his hand cracks my ass again.

Shrieking, I draw in a ragged breath. We're at the top of the steps; at least, I think we are. I don't even care. I grab Cal by the face and grit through my clenched teeth, "Don't ever fucking do that again."

His nostrils flare, warranting the threat of another blow. His hands wrap completely around my ass, fingers squeezing into the depths of my skin.

"What are you gonna do about it? Fight me?"

Jerking his foot out, he kicks open the door to the closet and carries me in. The suits are all pushed to the side, giving us a clear entry inside.

"I won't stop until I know what's behind those doors. So you might as well just tell me."

"Oh," Cal drawls, "you will stop if you know what's good for you. Would you like a preview of what will happen if you don't?"

Is that a question? Of course I don't.

Cal carries me over to his bed with shaky arms. He seems nervous, which is surprising for a man who exudes so much confidence. I look into his eyes, noticing he hasn't blinked since we stepped foot in his room.

Remembering that Peter said no one is allowed in

Cal's room has me wondering if that's the reason for his apprehension.

"Why are you so secretive with your room?"

Cal drops me onto the bed and takes a step back. Standing with an unnatural stillness, he stares straight ahead.

"This is my sanctuary. A place where no one can touch me and I'm in control. Don't we all need our own personal space as such?"

"I...um, I guess." Most people have bedrooms, but we don't treat them as a barrier from the outside world like he does.

Cal drops his gaze on the wall behind me and walks over to the snakes. He takes something attached to the side of the glass cage that looks like a remote. With the press of a button, the aquarium lights up.

It's like he called them to him, because all of the snakes come to the forefront of the glass. My insides shiver. There are so many of the brown ones, but it's that big black one that has my stomach twisting in knots.

Cal pushes another button that slides open the glass on the cage. He looks at me and the darkness in his eyes— the curl of his lip—causes me to scoot back on the bed. Hugging my knees to my chest, my dress drapes over my legs. My heart beats at an unprecedented rate when he reaches his hand into the cage and the sleek, black monster slithers around his arm.

"Cal," I say in warning, "what are you doing?"

He ignores me, walking over to the end of the cage where the other snakes are. He slides the doors open with the press of a button. Instead of letting the snake climb on his arm like he did the black one, he snatches it by the throat and pulls it out.

I gasp at the sight of him squeezing the smaller snake's neck.

The black one continues to slither up his body, its head nuzzling up to Cal's neck while it tangles around his arm.

Cal begins walking toward me. My heart beats faster, ruffling my rib cage. I'm as far back as I can go on the bed, but I continue to squirm, hoping to move further.

"Cal," I say again.

His knees press into the plush mattress as he slowly comes toward me. "You know what I love about snakes?" His brows rise as if he expects me to answer him. When I don't, he continues, "Any other pet would look down, tuck their tail, and run when they've done wrong. Snakes, on the other hand, they'll stand tall and look you right in the eye."

I turn my head, pinching my eyes shut as he kneels directly in front of me. "Please just put them away."

"You've proven my point. You were a bad girl, Bella. You went snooping around where you didn't belong and now we need to make sure that doesn't happen again. Look me in the eye," he says in a demanding tone.

I open my eyes and slowly turn back to face him.

"You're wearing your fear and snakes feed off that."

He comes closer as my breaths become delayed and my head gets dizzy from the lack of oxygen.

The snake stretches his body, stiffening with its head in the air, and Cal brings his hand down to the bed.

"Please don't put it down," I beg him. He doesn't listen

as the snake slithers off his hand and onto the silk comforter.

The other one is wrapped around his hand, but that one doesn't worry me as much. It's on the smaller side and looks more like a rat snake.

With the snake in his hand, Cal climbs up the bed to me, getting as close as he can with my knees blocking him.

"What are you doing?"

His hand, while holding the snake, slides up my leg and he pries them apart, but not without a fight on my end. I squeeze them tightly, forcing my knees together.

Cal looks up at me and smirks before allowing the brown snake to slide off his hand and around my calf.

"Cal, please. Get it off me," I cry out, tears rolling down my face.

With my attention on the snake, he's able to push my legs apart, and his body slides between them. "Are you done sticking your nose where it doesn't belong, Bella?"

"Yes. I promise. I'll never come in here again. Just get that damn thing off me."

I look at the other snake that's sliding slowly around on the comforter. It seems docile, but I know they can strike at any moment. I don't know much about snakes, but I do know that.

I'm afraid to move, so I don't fight Cal off as he slides my underwear down, over the snake and off my legs. Long fingers skate up my inner thigh, pushing my knees farther apart. His face nuzzles in, warm breath riding up my legs.

This is really happening. I have a snake latched onto

my leg while Cal is preparing to feast on me. I take a deep, ragged breath when his nose brushes my sensitive clit. I close my eyes but open them again quickly when I feel the weight of something on my chest.

"Oh my God. Move it. Please, Cal. Just get it off me." My chin is pressed to my chest as I watch the snake slither over it. Its head level with mine, staring me straight in the eye, as if it's telling me that it is the one with the power.

"Snakes are powerful. And we both know I like power-filled things." His long tongue stretches out, sliding inside me like an unhinged snake, flexing and flicking feverishly while he sucks my clit.

I blow out a breathy moan, hating that I'm instantly turned on by the thrill of this. I don't dare move; I don't dare make a sound, but the way he's licking me up and down like I'm his favorite taste in the world, it's damn near impossible.

Cal pushes my dress up farther until the bottom half is bunched at my stomach. "Get rid of the dress," he barks out the order.

"I can't," my words come out in a quivering whisper, "the snake."

"She'll move. The little guy, on the other hand, he'll latch on for dear life."

My hands shake uncontrollably as I slide my fingers under the straps on either side of my shoulders. I push them down, taking care not to piss off the snake. I'm staring straight into the eyes of danger, gambling with my life. Even if she's not venomous, she could choke me out in two seconds flat.

The straps fall to the side and the snake worms its way

up to my bare chest, sliding across my exposed breasts. With a straight back, I push my dress down until Cal removes it.

Two fingers pinch my throbbing clit, causing me to whimper at the mix of pain and pleasure.

The snake writhes against me, resting on my collarbone while Cal works his magic.

All I can focus on is the greedy feeling washing over me. I buck my hips up, needing more than what he's giving me. I feel like a whore at his beck and call. A weak and miserable slut who spreads her legs for the thrill of the ride.

Cal has awoken something inside of me that I didn't know existed—sexual needs, unfulfilled desires. He's a master at his technique and I'm a mere peasant begging for his touch.

When he removes his shirt, I gaze open-mouthed at his shapely chest covered in black ink. A coat of black hair runs down the V of his abdomen and when he takes off his sweatpants, his cock springs free. Hard, with bulging veins and a plump head that I want to wrap my lips around just to see how it feels in my mouth.

Cal leans forward, his hands pressed on either side of me. His mouth falls to my breast and he sucks my nipple in his mouth. He's a man who knows what he wants and I'm so turned on by that fact.

My eyes close as the snake begins slithering again, while the other latches onto my leg like I'm its lifeline.

"Do you like when I suck your nipples, Bella?"

I nod without giving it a thought. I like everything he

does to me. I never know what to expect, but every touch is an electrical current running through me.

He gives my nipple a flick and I shudder while he watches my reaction. Biting his lip, he reaches down and I feel him unravel the snake from my leg. Bringing it up between us, he puts it right in my face, which instantly stirs the black snake. "Kiss it goodbye."

Thank God!

I breathe out a sigh of relief that he's putting them away. But there is no way in hell I'm kissing that thing.

I turn my head in disgust. "Not a chance."

"If you want him to leave then kiss him goodbye."

Chills shimmy down my body. I close my eyes tightly, pucker up, and hope like hell that thing doesn't bite me.

I'm thrown off guard when it's Cal's mouth that meets mine and not the head of the snake. I feel the weight of the snake drop beside me and the one on my chest instantly leaves. Cal cups my face in his hands and kisses me forcefully while I feel the snakes squirm against my side. There's a hissing sound that signals alarms in my head, but Cal doesn't allow me to break free to see what's going on.

Seconds later, he lets me go, and I look to my side but turn away abruptly, burying my face in Cal's neck when I see that the bottom half of the brown snake is hanging from the mouth of the other.

She ate him. She really fucking ate him next to us while we're lying here naked.

"Are you insane?" My words are muffled against Cal's skin.

He doesn't react; instead, he shoves his cock inside of

me, causing my lungs to deflate in one breath.

"Do you want this, Bella?"

God, the way he says my name with that gravelly tone makes my pussy twitch.

"Yes. I want this."

He doesn't move. Just holds his cock still inside of me, filling me to the brim while his balls rest against my ass cheeks.

"Say it. Tell me you want me to fuck you."

I don't respond. Not because I'm embarrassed to admit I want him to, but because the words feel degrading, like I'm begging. Maybe that's what he wants.

He pulls back and rams his cock in so hard that my head reverberates off the headboard. "Ugh," I cry out.

"Tell me."

He does it again, kinking my neck in the process.

"I want you to fuck me."

He pushes himself up so that his face is hovering over mine. He's wearing a grin, proof that he got what he wanted.

In one fell swoop, he pulls his cock out. Proof of my want for him drips from its head onto my parted lips.

His body slides down again while the black snake climbs over my rib cage. I can see the bulge in her from swallowing the other snake whole. I hold my breath as she makes herself comfortable in the crease of my neck, like it's a warm bed for her after finishing a meal.

Cal pushes my legs open until they are widespread. He slides one possessive finger inside of me with ease then adds another. Working them just right, I begin to relax and enjoy the feelings coming over me.

Just as I start to get into it, he pulls his fingers out. I brace myself up on my elbows with a raised brow. "What are you doing?"

He pinches my clit again, this time so hard that every cell in my body is alerted. "Do you plan on snooping in my room again?" He doesn't stop as he awaits my answer.

"No. Never again." It's very possible that I lied, but he doesn't need to know that. He just needs to hear what he wants so he'll give me what I need.

His fingers penetrate me again, long, curled, and deep. His palm cups my crotch as he pumps them inside, hitting my G-spot while his thumb rubs my aching clit.

This time when I relax, he doesn't stop. My hands slide down to my stomach, grazing the soft skin as I lick my lips. Modesty eludes me. Time has stopped, the world has ceased to exist, and it's just this moment of heightened energy. My hips rise, then fall, up and down, while Cal finger-fucks me. The sound of moisture coating his fingers as he fills me to the brim. His palm slapping against my pussy, thumb circling my clit.

"Oh God," I cry out, grabbing his full head of hair and tugging. Everything washes away. I'm filled with a burning agony and a dire need to release. I squeeze my walls around his fingers, arch my back, and... "What the hell? No!"

Why did he stop? My hands begin to shake like an addict in need of a fix.

Cal comes up on his knees, grinning from ear to ear as he grabs the snake.

"You asshole!" I spit out.

"Punishment is a bitch. Now, roll over."

21

I GRAB Bella by the waist and flip her over onto her stomach, then lay Amira on her back. Goosebumps shimmy down Bella's spine as Amira slides across the uneven surface.

My legs straddle hers as I slide my cock up and down the slit of her ass. "Have you learned your lesson yet?" I ask, eyeing her round cheeks that hold a faded imprint of my hand from earlier.

Her toes curl into the bed and she makes her head comfortable on her folded arms. "Yes. Please, just fuck me."

She's lying. Bella has proven that I can't believe anything she says. I tried to give her freedom to roam, but she's proven twice, not once, that she's incapable of being trusted. She tried to escape by boat in the middle of a storm, and now she's snooping around.

I raise my hand and smack it hard against the same cheek of her ass as last time. Her skin welts into the shape of my fingers.

Her head shoots up. "Ouch," she whimpers, but she doesn't move. I'm not sure if it's fear of Amira, or fear of me. I like to think it's a little of both. The more worry instilled in her, the more manageable she'll be.

"I don't believe you." I part her ass cheeks and slide my cock in between them. "I want you to tell me you're sorry."

She shifts nervously but doesn't try to get up. Bella isn't a virgin anymore, and that I am certain of. I wasn't aware the first time and should have been gentle, but now, I am free to fuck her with everything I've got.

"I'm sorry," she finally chokes out, "I won't come into your room again."

"You're right, you won't. But that's not what I want an apology for." I bite down on my bottom lip, piercing the skin as blood seeps into my mouth. My eyes widen in anticipation as I raise my hand and smack her ass again, only this time, I put all my strength into it.

"Ahhhh," she bellows, shoving her face into the pillow and forcibly gripping the sides of it.

Once the sting subsides, she lifts her head and twists to look at me with tear-stained eyes. "What am I apologizing for?"

"Leaving me."

We can pretend all we want—ignore the elephant in the room every time we're together—but we both felt the pain that day. The only difference is, I still feel it. I tried everything to forget, to diminish the anger and live life to the fullest. I've fucked random women to feel close to someone. I've killed to rid myself of the toxicity. I've cut, I've bled, I've cried. Nothing worked until she came back.

I'll do whatever I have to do to keep her here.

She won't run. She can't hide. She will live this life with me and learn to love the darkest corners of it.

Her fearful expression is replaced with one of empathy. I can see it in her eyes. The sorrow, the regret, the hope that one day I'll forgive her.

Maybe I will.

I grab her by the waist, hoisting her onto her knees, and in one breath, I stick my cock inside her pussy. Her head drops down, back bridged, and ass up. When I begin thrusting, Amira slithers over Bella's side onto the bed.

Pinching her waist, I use it as cushioning to drive myself deeper. "You're so fucking tight. So warm. So wet." She hugs my cock like she never wants to let it go. I push myself up onto my feet, crouched behind her, while crushing her ass with my pelvic bone. My balls swing back and forth, so I grab her hand and pull it between us so that she's cupping them.

She squeezes and releases, repeating the action, and it feels so fucking good. With one hand on her waist, I use the other to grab her hair and tug enough to raise her head. "Does that feel good, baby?"

"Yes."

An electrical charge roots in my cock, releasing and traveling through my entire body. I pull her hair harder, squeeze her waist tighter, and fuck her faster. My cock slides in and out, sloshing in the mess of her arousal. I'm close. So damn close, but I'm not ready.

Stopping my movements, I'm warranted a stink eye from Bella.

I ease my hold on her hair, but still have a good grip as

she drops her head down. "I hate you." Her words are muffled by the pillow she's pressed against.

Jerking her head back up, I cover her body with mine. "You wanna come? Get on your knees and say you're sorry around my cock, then maybe I'll let you." I pull her up by my hold on her hair and she gets on her knees. "On the floor." She looks at me, curious to see if I'm serious or not, so I give her a look that says how serious I am. "Now."

She obeys me, and I'm actually surprised.

Kneeled on the floor, she places her hands in her lap. I stand in front of her and grab her by the back of the head, shoving my cock into her open mouth. "Say you're sorry, again."

"I'm sorry," she chokes out around my cock.

"Good girl. Now suck."

My head drops back, hand resting on her head, guiding her motions. There's no way in hell this is her first time sucking dick. Not with the way she's flicking her tongue and using her own saliva to lubricate me as her hand slides up and down with her mouth. The thought of her even looking at another man's dick infuriates me. Never again. She's all mine now.

I grab her and flip her over the end of the bed. She gets on her knees, so her ass is level with my groin, then I feel the heat of her pussy around my swollen cock as I enter her.

My hips move violently as I slide a finger between her ass cheeks and roam around her tight hole.

She whimpers in delight and I'm pretty sure she likes

it. "Have you been fucked in the ass before?" I ask her out of sheer curiosity.

She shakes her head no. "Good." Another first saved just for me. But, we'll keep that for next time. I'm too close right now and if I pull out, I'll likely spill all over her when I really want to fill her up with my cum.

I slide my free hand underneath her and begin flicking her clit until it drives her wild. A loud moan rips through her as she comes, sending me over the edge with her cries of pleasure.

"Fuck," I grumble, thrusting deeper and faster. My breaths become heady as she clenches my cock and milks me.

Standing still, I release inside of her.

My hands drop before thrusting a couple more times, then I pull out. Evidence of our orgasms spill onto the bed.

Bella drops down heavily and catches her breath.

I hope she learned her lesson. Then again, part of me hopes she fucks up again just so I can punish her even harder next time.

BELLA IS in my bathroom cleaning up, while I make the bed with a clean blanket. It feels surreal having someone in here. She doesn't know this, but no one has stepped foot in any of my bedrooms since I was eighteen years old. I clean up after myself and set my laundry in the hall for Paulina. Even Peter knows to stay away. She'll also never know that she's the first girl in my bed. I've been with many other girls, but I have different beds for that.

Tonight was a close call. I have every intention of telling Bella about The Grotto and The Dungeon, but it won't be today.

She needs to ease into things here. If I force too much on her too soon, she'll try to escape again and next time, she might not make it out alive.

Bella is a firecracker and I didn't anticipate that. All of my research suggested that she grew up to be a book smart, family-oriented Christian. Her parents are members of the school board, both well-known in their small community. Although they work for pennies and live in a three-bedroom ranch house, they seem pretty normal and happy. Proof that money is not what makes the heart flutter.

I've always hated money. Just because I keep it and use it to my advantage doesn't mean I wouldn't have given it all up for a little normalcy. I didn't want this life. I wanted the life she got—the life Mark got. It was stolen from me, just like my dignity. Now I keep the power because I knew how much Vincent didn't want me to have it. He wanted to see me fail after Delilah died.

"All done," Bella says, closing the bathroom door behind her. She folds her hands in front of her waist. "Mind if we talk before I go to bed?"

Fuck. She's one of those. A talker, probably a cuddler. What's next—a foot rub?

I blow air out and shrug my shoulders, smoothing my hand over the comforter, black this time.

Bella walks into the middle of the room and stops

about five feet away from me. "Are you ever going to tell me where that secret door goes?"

I should have expected this question. "Yes. Eventually you will know everything about the businesses I run."

"Businesses?"

"Did I stutter?" I turn around to look at her, crossing my arms over my bare chest.

I can see her throat bob as she swallows. "You're so rude!" she stammers, eating the space between us.

With her eyes locked on mine, she runs her hands down my arms. I flinch at the foreign sensation. "Let me help you while I'm here. With the businesses, with whatever is eating away at you."

My brows furrow as my gaze drops on her. "What makes you think something is eating away at me?"

"Come on. You're so obvious. You go from hot to cold in the blink of an eye. There's a constant push and pull between us. I don't know if we're friends, enemies, or lovers."

My fingers sweep her ear, tucking her hair behind it. "If I remember right, you have a boyfriend. So, it's certainly not the latter. Friends share secrets and all you tell me are lies. Enemies would be suitable, but the way I make your knees wobble, I doubt that title works on your end."

"I'll tell you a secret, if you tell me one."

Share a secret? I haven't shared a secret with anyone since...her.

"Okay. You go first."

I take a seat on the bed, and she sits down beside me. For a brief moment, it feels like old times, even if we are older. I'm not sure that I've gotten wiser, but I've definitely learned to cover my tracks when I do something stupid.

Her hands fold in her lap, and she looks at me, so I look at her. "I didn't say yes to Trent."

"Wait a minute. You mean you're not engaged?"

She shakes her head. "I care about him a lot, but there has always been something missing between us. A connection, a spark, maybe? If that sort of thing even exists."

"It does," I spit out on impulse.

Surprised, she turns her whole body toward me and pulls her knees to her chest. "You've felt it?"

I feel it now. I don't say it, though. Vulnerability is scary and something I'm not used to.

"No, I haven't."

"Hmm." She bites at her lip. "Well, hopefully someday we both get to."

My heart quivers, another foreign feeling. Our eyes lock and I'm mesmerized by her beauty. Twenty minutes ago I was punishing her and now all I want to do is wrap my arms around her just so she'll do the same. I forgot what it feels like to be held in the arms of another person.

"Your turn," she says, pulling me out of my thoughts.

I wouldn't call it a secret, but since it's heavy on my mind, I give it a go. "You're the last person I hugged." There's a bite in my stomach as the words leave my mouth, and I instantly want to take them back and swallow them.

Her eyes widen. "You haven't been hugged in twelve years?"

I look away, unable to see the pity in her eyes. It will only make me angry. "It's not a big deal. Just drop it."

"Not a big deal—"

"I said drop it," I shout, getting to my feet and crossing the room to Amira. I got her the day of Vincent's funeral. Amira stared me right in the eyes, challenging me. She stood straight up against the glass, exuding power and dominance. I didn't know a thing about king snakes, but I learned quickly that they are one of the few snakes that will eat their own kind, and that appealed to me. Along with her, I purchased a dozen rat snakes to dump into Vincent's final resting place. My hope was that they'd get hungry and feast on his remains.

Everyone had left the burial site and I asked for a moment alone with my father. Well, I paid the undertaker a grand to open the casket and leave me alone with him.

It was just me and the man who took me in and tore me apart.

"You're in good company, you rat bastard, or should I say, you dirty fucking snake. Rest in hell."

Then I dumped the bucket in and told the undertaker to close him up and put him down.

Bella comes up and wraps her arms around me from behind. Her head rests on my back and I freeze. "What are you doing?" I ask in an authoritative tone.

She squeezes tighter, forcing the air out of my lungs. "Please don't shut me out."

"Let go of me."

"No." I can feel her shake her head against my back.

"Dammit, Bella. Let go of me now."

"I'm not letting you go."

"I don't want to hurt you, but I will."

"No, you won't. I told you, I'm not scared of you."

"You're a fool then." I turn around to face her, but she doesn't back up. I walk around her and she grabs me like she's the one with the upper hand. I snarl at her, grasp her bicep and jerk away. "Quit acting like you care."

I don't know what the hell is wrong with me. Actually, yes, I do. I'm fucked up beyond repair and she's the crazy one for thinking she can pry me open and force me to expose my wounds for her.

"I do care. I always have and I always will. Please," she grabs my other arm so that her body is flush with mine, "let me in."

Tears prick the corners of her eyes and I search them, wondering if they're real or if this is all just another act. For all I know, she could be warming up to me so I let her go. Not that I would. But she doesn't know that.

"I let you into my room. I think that's enough for tonight." I walk past her toward the door. "Goodnight, Bella." I pull it open, waiting for her to leave, but she stands there, looking at me like I'm this sad, broken boy in need of twelve years' worth of hugs.

"Go!"

She shakes her head. "No, I'm not leaving you this time." Her feet move, but not toward the door. Instead, she goes over to the bed and flops down like she owns the damn thing.

A low rumble climbs up my throat as I slam the door shut. "Get off my bed."

She was really good at obeying my commands when she wanted to get off—now, not so much.

"You were right," she says, like I'm supposed to know what the hell she's talking about. "I didn't accept the scholarship because they made me feel guilty for leaving. It wasn't their intention, but their words made me feel it anyway."

She's talking about her parents. I do know that.

"I enrolled at a local university. Recognized Trent in a language arts class and I've been under his thumb ever since. Before I came here, I started to realize my dreams didn't matter to him. He just wanted me by his side while he lived out his own dreams."

Damn her for doing this.

I round the bed and sit down on the edge, my feet still on the ground. "So you turned down Juilliard, stayed with Trent, but still accepted an offer to work on a private island. Why?"

"To finally get away. I was hoping to come here and find myself. I've been searching for the girl with ambition that was heading into foster care—but I still haven't found her."

"I thought you had everything you've ever wanted."

Bella sits up and crosses her legs into a pretzel. "It's not always black and white. I love my family, but I'm more than just a daughter or a sister."

"If you could go back, would you take the scholarship?"

"Without a doubt." She doesn't even think on the question, just spits out the answer like she's known it all along.

There's a beat of silence before I break it. "My adopted mother committed suicide when she realized that I wasn't her son and he was never coming back. I watched her stuff her mouth full of pills and didn't stop her. It was one less person I had to fend off before making my escape."

Her void expression doesn't falter. I see no sign of judgment or hatred in her eyes. "And your dad?"

"I killed him. A little hydrofluoric acid in his evening shot of Scotch and I watched as it ate away at his insides. He screamed in agony as it burned his esophagus, but that was only the beginning."

"Help me," he cries, a harrowing sound that only makes me laugh harder.

"Help you? Why the hell would I do that? I'm enjoying this too much. How's it feel to be burning from the inside out? Not quite as bad as I felt every time you tried to give me a fever because your wife always thought I had one. You're a loyal husband, I'll give you that. That's why she thought I said those things. Because I was sick! No. The only sick person in this house is you. I almost died three times, but you wouldn't know that."

"He curled over and dropped dead, then I had his own men come and take his body out and make it look like an accident."

This time, I see it. The judgment. The fear. It's written all over her pretty face.

"Go ahead and tell me what a sick bastard I am. Not like I don't already know."

"I...I'm not saying that. It's obvious you went through some things that made you do what you did."

Now she knows the monster I became when she left me. And for that, she can join me in the darkness.

"Get some sleep, Bella. We have a busy day tomorrow."

I stand up, thinking she'll jump at the opportunity to run out of here, so she can get as far away from me as possible.

Instead, she slides under the blanket and makes herself comfortable. "Just one night? For old times' sake?"

I've got no fucking idea why she's not hauling ass, and I don't like this unpredictable action, but I also don't make her leave. Instead, I kill the lights, leaving the middle aquarium light on, and go to the other side of the bed.

I don't lie down. I just sit there and watch her until she's fast asleep. Then I watch her some more. Every twitch of her lips and crinkle of her nose. I admire the crease in her forehead when she dreams. I take it all in, wondering how I expect a girl like that to ever love a monster like me.

22

"Good morning." Cal closes the book in his hand and sets it down on the nightstand. He's no longer shirtless and in gray sweats. Instead, he's wearing a white button-up shirt with the sleeves rolled up and a pair of black dress pants with matching socks. The tips of his hair glisten, so I assume he took a shower not too long ago.

I push myself into a sitting position and lick my dry lips. "Did you sleep at all?" I turn my head slightly, trying to avoid him smelling my nasty morning breath.

"Few hours."

The bags under his eyes tell me he's lying. If I had to guess, he stayed up and read all night.

Something feels different this morning. A new excitement inside of me, this feeling of contentment. My heart somersaults when he cracks a smile, and it's a look I'll never get tired of.

Right now, I don't feel like a prisoner kept here against her will. Today, I want to be here. And tomorrow, and possibly the next day. There's something undeniable between Cal and me and I can't wait to explore the possibilities. Maybe he was right. Maybe fate did bring us back together. It's possible that he was the one meant to fill that emptiness inside of me all along.

Climbing off the bed, I stretch my arms up and yawn while covering my mouth. I would have thought waking up next to Cal would be awkward and uncomfortable, but it's not. Regardless, I feel disgusting and need a shower. "I'm going back to my room to get cleaned up. See you at breakfast?"

"You sure will. In fact, we'll be eating in the courtyard this morning."

"Oh, that will be nice."

There's something about the way he's looking at me. He seems happy, way too happy. He's blazing confidence and I get the feeling he's got something planned for us today. Normally I'd dread it, but now, I'm pretty excited.

I go to leave but stop to give him a double take. Smiling, I finally unlock the door and leave, closing it behind me.

My back presses to the door and I'm lost in thoughts about how much of a breakthrough we had last night. It started off intensely. I thought for sure Cal was going to be furious when he found me in the secret passage. Then came the punishing sex, which I thoroughly enjoyed, aside from the snakes. Cal was dominant, possessive, and so damn sexy. It opened my eyes to a new world of pleasure that I'm anxious to revisit. Not to mention, the passion. God, did I feel it.

That wasn't the best part of the night, though. The best part is when he opened up to me and shared secrets that I don't think he's ever told anyone. It made me feel special and I was able to remember that, deep down, Cal is not a bad person. He never was. He just doesn't know any better. It's no excuse for murder, but I don't know the whole story. I'm not sure anyone does. It's apparent he faced some traumatic events and I'm hopeful that one day he'll tell me all about them. Even if he wanted to, even if I wanted him to, he can't go back and change his past. I just hope that with me by his side, he doesn't have to live there anymore. I want to help him heal—I want us to heal together.

"Good morning, Ms. Jenkins," Peter says, startling me.

I peel myself off the door with a permanent grin plastered on my face. "It is a good morning, Peter."

"I couldn't help but notice your bed was made this morning. And now I see you're leaving Mr. Ellis's room. I assume things are well with you two?"

My lips press together as I try to bite back the smile that won't leave my face. "You assume correctly."

"That's quite a compliment coming from Mr. Ellis. He doesn't allow anyone in his room."

Peter had mentioned that before, but it didn't really register, and now I'm curious what he means by it. "Not even the women he brings home?"

Peter leans forward and whispers, "In all my years with Mr. Ellis, twelve to be exact, he has never had a woman in his room."

My eyes widen in surprise. "Really? That's so strange for a man who entertains women often."

"You didn't hear it from me." He places a hand on my shoulder, steering me away from Cal's door. "The cook has prepared a special breakfast. I'll see you later, Ms. Jenkins."

I thank Peter with a smile and continue down the hall, stopping when I notice the small black camera on the wall outside of my door. I look behind me and see a couple more. They're everywhere.

Just when I think Cal and I are making progress, whatever that means for us, he proves that he's still all about keeping me as his live-in prisoner. I shouldn't be surprised, considering there was a manhunt for me, covering the entire island last night. I'm just hoping that, eventually, I can earn his trust. Now I just have to decide what I'll do when I get it. Now that Cal is back in my life —as much of a roller coaster as it has been—the idea of him not being part of it hurts. Then again, the idea of never leaving the island hurts, too. There has to be a common ground we can reach, assuming Cal is keen on compromise. I'm not holding my breath, but I'm also not giving up hope.

MY HAIR IS STILL wet from the quick shower I took. After I brushed it out, knowing that it would be extra frizzy and curly since I didn't dry it, I put on a pair of yoga lounge pants and my old Hickory Knoll High 'Class of 2016' sweatshirt. I'm hoping Cal doesn't plan to do much work today, because as the morning goes on, the sorer I begin to feel. My first time hurt, but this is a whole new level of pain. Each step has my lower half aching, while a sharp pain shoots from my vagina to my abdomen. Cal gave me quite the beating last night—I'm pretty sure there's even a bruise on my ass from him slapping it three times—but damn if it wasn't worth the pain.

I go over to my nightstand and open the drawer to take my birth control. They're tiny pills, so I'm able to swallow it down without water.

My mind wanders to Trent and how he's going to react when he finds out what I've done. There's no way I can't tell him. It's also going to be my opportunity to end things for good. Being here, away from him, has made me realize that it's time to chase my own dreams while he lives out his. I'll always care about him, but the way my heart is beginning to open up to Cal assures me that I never really loved Trent.

I'm sure by now he and my parents are wondering why I haven't reached out. I did tell them there was a chance service would be sketchy and not to worry if they didn't hear from me for a while. It's been almost two weeks, though, and by now, I'm sure worry has set in.

Thanksgiving is in two days and I'm not sure what that looks like here, but I know I'll miss the family dinners I have back home. Maybe I can assist the cook and make a good old-fashioned turkey dinner for Cal. I'm not even sure that he's had one since The Webster House. Even though Thanksgiving there wasn't exactly memorable. It consisted of two dozen kids fighting to get the last slice of turkey before we were sent to our rooms, so the adults could settle their stomachs without the commotion of us kids.

Sliding my feet into my house slippers, I leave the room, closing the door behind me. As I'm walking to the elevator and passing Cal's room, I think back to the secret door in the closet. Obviously I know Cal didn't put that door there and, of course, he'd use the extra space that's given through it, but I can't help but wonder what he could be hiding that would require a passcode for entry. Eventually I'll find out, but right now is not that time. Right now, my hunger pangs are reminding me that I need to eat.

The elevator doors open and I expect it to be empty. I'm surprised to see that Peter is onboard. "Oh, Hi, Peter. Going down?"

He's standing next to the panel with his hand hovering over the G, for the ground level. "Yes, ma'am. And you are as well, I assume?"

"Sure am."

He presses the button on the elevator then looks at his phone, there's a static noise and muffled voices coming from it that has me peering over his shoulder.

It's a video of some sort. It looks like camera footage, which doesn't surprise me since they armed the entire castle last night.

We make it to the fifth floor, then fourth, and that's when I hear Cal's voice on the phone. He sounds angry. Peter immediately goes to silence it, but like a savage child, I snatch his phone from his hand.

"When is this footage from?" I hold up the phone, wondering why the hell Cal is walking out of the mystery door on the main floor with a girl. Wait...not just any girl. That was our waitress—Serena, I think, was her name. She's wearing some sleazy-looking, leather skirt that barely covers her ass and a top that looks more like a bra, with a large black duffel bag hanging over her shoulder. That's not what gets to me, though. It's the way she's rubbing up on him and he's not pushing her away. His head turns slightly as she kisses all over his neck and I can feel the heat rise in my cheeks.

My stomach twists in knots, and for the first time since I've got here, I'm jealous. Really fucking jealous. In fact, I might just go claw the bitch's eyes out once this elevator stops.

"Please give that back to me."

"Is this live?"

"Yes, Ms. Jenkins, and Mr. Ellis would not be happy if he knew you were viewing security footage." He holds his hand out, but I grip his phone like my life depends on it.

I shake my head no. "Not until you tell me where that door goes."

"I can't do that."

The elevator comes to a stop, but I squeeze my body between him and the panel and press the button to hold the doors shut. "Then I can't give you your phone. Where does that door go?" I look back at the screen and both Cal and Serena are gone from the camera's view.

"It's a private room that's off-limits for staff, as well as…you."

"But Serena is a staff member, or at least she was, until Cal fired her." *If he really did fire her.* "Why was she in there if it's off-limits to staff members?"

It seems the cat's got his tongue. I remove my finger from the button and hand him his phone. "Fine. I'll just find out for myself."

The doors open and my heart is pounding. Instead of

going to the courtyard, I turn in the opposite direction and walk straight to the door. Knowing that I'll have no luck, I turn the handle anyway.

Locked. Of course.

"Cal," I holler, walking toward the main entrance, curious if that's where he shuffled Serena to in an attempt to hide her. Or maybe he doesn't even want to hide her. Maybe she's here so they can flaunt their past in my face. "Cal," I holler again, once I'm on the front side of the castle.

I can hear Peter talking to someone behind me, likely ratting me out for taking his phone. I spin around and see him talking to Cal as they both move at a steady pace toward me.

"Bella, what's going on?" His eyebrows are dipped into a sharp V. The top three buttons on his shirt are undone and I try to remember if that's the way they were when I left him this morning. Cal stops directly in front of me and places a hand on Peter's shoulder. "I've got things from here. Please tend to our guest."

Rage cripples me. "Your guest? As in, Serena? So you fire her but let her stay as a guest?" Cal lifts his lip in a knowing smirk, only fueling the flames. "Why are you smiling? This isn't funny."

"Didn't you learn your lesson last night? Or do I need to remind you of what happens when you start snooping?"

I give him a shove and he takes a few steps back, but I quickly eat up the gap between us. "Why the hell is that waitress still here and what were you two doing?"

Cal grabs both of my wrists and that cocky grin is still plastered on his face. "Someone's jealous."

"I am not," I huff, "but I would like to know what's behind that door and why you two just came out of it together." I eyeball the door and he looks to our right, acknowledging it.

"More guest quarters." He begins pulling me toward the back exit to the courtyard. "Come on. There is someone here to see you."

"No," I snap, jerking my hand away, "did you have sex with her just now?"

He wears a defensive but also perturbed expression. "What? No!"

"Have you slept with anyone else since I've arrived?"

The door to the mystery room opens and the bartender from last night stands in the doorframe. Her movements freeze as she looks from me to Cal and quickly shuts it. Cal gives her a warning look and clenches his jaw.

"You've got to be fucking kidding me," I grumble. "You really are a manwhore, aren't you? Byron wasn't lying."

Cal instantly becomes agitated. "What the hell does Byron have to do with any of this?"

"He told me you aren't as lonely as I think you are and didn't deny that you sleep with hookers."

Cal laughs. "Hookers? Byron's a damn idiot. I don't have to pay women for their company." His lip curls. "They beg for it."

"Of course they do. Because you're such a catch." I push past him.

"Bella, would you wait a damn minute?"

"No." I look him dead in the eye as I choke back the tears begging to break free. "This was all a big mistake. We never should have—"

"Nothing is ever a mistake. You coming here was always meant to be. But we all have skeletons in our closet and you can't expect any less from me."

His words hit hard. Like a knife digging into my chest, twisting and turning. I don't know what I expected from him, from us. Certainly not a relationship. That's insane. A happily-ever-after? It's not possible with Cal.

"Now who's this guest you were going on about? A new maid in a skimpy dress with a feather duster?"

He never answered my question when I asked if he's slept with anyone else since I've arrived. He doesn't need to. It's apparent he has had the company of other women, as he'd put it. In my words, he's fucking them.

I'm disgusted as I walk quickly to the courtyard. My hunger has subsided and been replaced with nausea. I was starting to feel settled here. It was beginning to feel like home, even though it's temporary. Part of me was excited that Cal and I were moving in the right direction. The undeniable spark was there and I couldn't wait to see him this morning, ready to spend the day only growing closer. Then I saw the cameras, and after that came the footage.

I'm so lost in my thoughts when I enter the new court-yard that I don't even notice the man seated with his back to me until Peter snaps me out of my trance. "Right this way, Ms. Jenkins."

"Who is that?" I ask, while we make our way to the table.

"Your guest."

My guest? Nervousness sweeps through me. The man sits there quietly in a slate suit, not even turning around when he hears us coming.

Part of me knows before we get there. Call it intuition. I hoped I was wrong, but my guess is proven to be right when Trent looks up at me from where he's sitting.

"Bella," he stands and wraps his arms around me, "God, I've been so worried."

I'm rendered speechless as I stand there with my hands at my sides. I slowly raise them, embracing the hug while my heart pounds against his chest cavity. "What are you doing here, Trent?"

He pulls back, looks at me, and smiles. "I came to see you. We've all been worried sick that something had happened. I called the ferry company on the main island and they confirmed that you made it here safely, but no one's heard from you."

If he's here, that means Cal allowed it. He let Trent come on his island, even after claiming to hate him. I wish I could have seen the reunion between the two of them. It's possible that they patched up old wounds from the past and are ready to move forward, much like Cal and I were trying to do.

"Let's sit." I gesture to the chairs. "I told you that I wasn't sure I'd have service and not to worry." I force a smile on my face, as hard as it is. It feels like Trent just walked into my new world, but he doesn't fit here.

"I figured you'd be a little happier to see me, considering I took the time off work and came all this way. A thank-you would be appropriate."

"Thank you?" I say it as a question, not a statement.

"You're welcome. Now, let's eat, then you can give me a tour of this place." He glances behind him, looking up at the castle. "It's nothing like I'd expected when you said you'd be designing a hotel."

"It's not what I expected either." The words coming out of my mouth couldn't be truer. I never expected my boss to be the only best friend I'd ever had. I thought I'd come here and put in laborious hours, staying up until the next morning working on designs and having meetings with contractors. I also never expected to fall out of love with Trent and give myself to another man. I came here a virgin, with imponderable dreams. No idea which direction I was headed in. I played the piano again. I looked in the eye of the storm, and I conquered it. My heart began to open and ten minutes ago, I was reminded why I've kept it closed all my life. I was a fool, and I still am.

"I told you it was a pipe dream. Come home with me, Bella. Let's start our life together."

"Trent, can you excuse me for a minute?" I push my chair back, scraping the legs against the cement. I don't even wait for his response as I put a hand over my mouth to stop the sounds of my shattered heart from spilling out.

I'm looking down at my feet when I crash into someone. I peer up, my tear-soaked eyes looking into Cal's.

His hands set on either side of my waist. "What the hell did he do to make you cry?" His gaze shifts behind me, locked on Trent.

"It's not him. It's you." I step around him and walk back into the foyer of the castle. I keep going until I'm at the front doors. With both hands, I swing one open and walk outside. When I think that Cal is going to talk to Trent, he surprises me and follows me instead.

This time, I don't run away. I turn around and shout with a pointed finger, "Why in the world would you bring him here?"

"I didn't bring him. He came on his own free will."

"And you let him? I thought you hated him."

"I do, which is exactly why I allowed it. He needs to know it's over between you two. Now go out there, tell him you're fine, so I can send him on his way."

A dry laugh scales up my throat. "No."

"Excuse me?"

"I'm not telling him that. In fact, I should go out there right now and tell him everything. How you lured me here with the perfect job wrapped in a shiny box with a glittery bow. I can even tell him how you forced me to take my clothes off and stole my virginity from me without my approval."

He gives me a side-eyed glare. "Hey now, you never told me to stop."

"You never asked me if I wanted you to."

"Does a thief ever ask for permission?"

My mouth falls open at his arrogance. "You're such an ass. I can't believe I was actually starting to like you."

"Like me?" He chuckles. "I had you eating out of my hand, Bella." He closes the space between us and presses his body against mine. His groin digs into my hip bone, igniting every cell inside of me with a burning desire.

His way with words is repulsive, but the chemistry that sizzles between us when we touch is undeniable.

"Maybe I should go out there and accept Trent's

proposal. Your contract says I have to stay, it doesn't say I can't have company. He can live here with me until my time is up."

Cal grinds against me, his lips ghosting over mine as he cups my cheeks in his hands. "Your time is infinite and if he stays, I'll kill him and make you watch while I do it."

I swallow hard. "You don't have any power over me. I can get out of the contract."

"And allow your parents to lose their jobs. Go for it."

Damn. I forgot about that.

"Now, I want you to walk back out there like a good girl and end things with Trent, so we never have to deal with his uptight ass again. And if you dare tell him anything about our agreement, or anything else that's taken place on this island, your family will suffer." His lips crash into mine in a tantalizing manner. Hard and force-ful, as if he's the one I'm kissing goodbye.

He's so bitter, but he tastes so sweet. Like temptation on a platter—a forbidden fruit. But I've bent over back-ward for him since I arrived. Maybe he needs to bend a little, too. I'll go back out there, and I'll keep my mouth shut because I love my family, but now it's time for Cal to feel the sting of rejection. He's fucking other girls, so why should he care if I have relations with other men? If the other women stay, so can Trent. I might not want him here, but Cal doesn't know that.

I break the suction of our mouths and smile coyly. "Will you be joining us for breakfast?" My fingers sweep across his bottom lip, wiping the excess saliva from our hard-pressed kiss.

"You think I'd leave you alone with that animal? Of course I am."

"Good. Let's get this over with." I walk around him and pull open the door. He presses a hand to it, allowing me to enter first.

"Let's."

23

THAT WAS EASIER than I thought it would be. Bella is becoming more compliant each day, which is a step in the right direction. Last night we had a little mishap when her curiosity got the best of her—and again this morning, when Peter let his guard down—but as long as we're moving forward, we're on track.

It's possible we may be ready sooner than I thought. Regardless of whether or not she has a say in her future, I would like it to be a pleasant one. I've always heard spring weddings are beautiful. It won't be long until she's bound to me forever and the pact is carried out on both our ends —a vow to never part. Until kingdom come.

Before joining them, I make a quick call to Byron. It goes straight to voicemail, which pisses me off more than I already am.

"Get those damn women off this island now or you're done, this friendship is done, and I'll hire a new attorney to change my will. You won't get a fucking dime."

The space downstairs is complete but wasn't supposed

to be in use until after the grand opening. Byron, being the nympho that he is, can't seem to keep his dick in his pants long enough to grasp that concept. Serena and Arabella were supposed to be gone after my night with Bella on the yacht. In fact, they were never supposed to be here in the first place, but Byron brought them for his own personal gain. Now I can see that he kept them here and he's been using The Grotto as his own sexual playground.

He was scarce for a while, but now that he's around, it's obvious he's trying to get under Bella's skin. Bringing the girls here, telling her about my previous hookups. He sees her as a threat, so he's making himself one.

I tuck my phone in my pocket and rejoin them in the courtyard.

"Trent," Bella says, grabbing his attention.

He dusts his hands off on his gray slacks and gets up to face where she stands. His mouth is stuffed full of muffin and while I wish he'd choke on it, I prefer he lives to hear what Bella is about to say.

"You remember Cal...Callum, right?"

Looking me in the eye as he chews, his mouth likely becoming drier and drier with each passing second, he seems stunned.

His gaze shifts from me to Bella. "What is he doing here?"

"Cal owns the property. He inherited Ellis Empire when Mr. Ellis Senior passed away. He was adopted by Vincent and Delilah Ellis when he left The Webster House."

Trent looks like he's seen a ghost, and not a friendly

one. He reaches his hand out and grabs Bella, pulling her closer to him with his eyes cemented to mine. "You never mentioned that." He still holds my stare, although he's speaking to Bella.

"I had no idea until I arrived."

"Could you give us a minute alone, Callum?" He finally looks at Bella. "My girlfriend and I have a lot to discuss."

"Actually," I reach the table and grab a muffin, peeling back the paper, "I'm pretty hungry."

"Me, too," Bella chimes in. She takes Trent's hand in hers and I watch intently as she wraps her fingers around his. "Let's eat."

Trent follows her lead and sits back down in his chair. I pull out a seat for Bella and take the one to the left of her. "This is nice. Like a reunion of old friends." I bite into my muffin, challenging Trent with a glare.

"Cut the bullshit, Callum. We were never friends and you know it. Wouldn't surprise me if you purposely hired Bella just to get under my skin."

I hold up a finger, putting him off while I chew the food in my mouth because, unlike him, I have manners.

"Actually, honey," Bella says to Trent, "Cal had no idea."

Honey? Is she buttering him up before leaving him high and dry?

"Here," she hands him a croissant, "try these. They're like no croissant you've ever tasted before. In fact, Cal has the best cook and every meal is divine. Wait until you see what's for dinner."

Dinner? I toss my muffin down on the small round plate. "Bella," I warn, "isn't there something you wanted to tell Trent?"

"Oh yes," she giggles, "how could I forget? Our room has the best view on the island. It's on the top floor. Well," she corrects herself, "there's one floor higher up, which I think is the turret. I've been wanting to go up there, but the elevator stops on the eighth floor and the stairs are closed off. We should—"

"Bella," I snap, "what the hell are you doing?"

"Whoa. Don't talk to her like that." Trent raises his hand, then rests it on Bella's lap like he's trying to comfort her from my outburst.

I clear my throat, steady my pulse, and glower at her. "Do it."

She sits there poised with a twitch of humor on her lips. "I don't know what you're talking about. I want Trent to feel at home here. After all, he'll be staying. Right, honey?" She looks at him with fluttering eyelashes.

"Well, for a couple nights. I'll have to leave the day after tomorrow. It's Thanksgiving and all. I was hoping to convince you to come home with me."

"Holidays in Hickory Knoll are my favorite." Bella rivets her eyes to me. "There's nothing like being surrounded by people who love you."

I feel like that was a jab. Is she insinuating that no one loves me? That I'm incapable of being loved? If so, she's correct.

I've lost all control of myself when I jump out of my chair and grip her by the arm until she's standing. "We need to talk." I pull her away, although she doesn't put up a fight, and follows my lead.

Trent shifts in his seat and mumbles something that I completely ignore.

"It's okay, Trent. My boss is an asshole and my job is demanding."

"You got that right," I growl in a whisper.

Once we're back inside, I pull Bella into a small alcove. "You've got some fucking nerve."

"So do you. Screwing other girls while you're sleeping with me. Real classy, Cal. And to think, I was starting to feel like I belonged here."

"I'm not fucking anyone else. But if you keep this shit up, I'll lay Serena out on your bed and let her cream on your clean linen."

Bella raises a hand and slaps me across the face. I snarl at the sting, tightening my grip on her. Her shallow breaths hit the nape of my neck when I lean forward and whisper in her ear, "Then I'll put your face in her mess while I fuck you from behind."

"I hate you."

My erection threatens the fabric of my pants and there's no doubt that I could come just by grinding into her while she trembles beneath me. "I don't believe you. I think you hate that you want me."

She doesn't respond, but her labored breathing and the way her heart is vibrating against her sweatshirt is proof enough.

"Get out there and end this now, so I can take you to the turret and fuck you while we watch him leave."

Her head cocks to the side and she thinks hard. A minute later, a smirk grows on her face. "You tell me what's behind that door and the one in your closet, and I won't fuck Trent tonight."

My jaw ticks, knuckles clenched. Just the words—the

thought—sends my blood to a boiling point. "You wouldn't dare."

"Try me."

"Don't push me, Bella. I will kill him. I told you what I did to my parents. It's nothing for me to end the life of the guy I hate more than anyone."

"You say you hate him, but I think you're just jealous of him."

I bite down, my teeth grinding so hard that I feel the crunch against my tongue. I always knew I'd tell her, I just didn't want it to be this soon. "It's part of the hotel. A separate area we call The Grotto. All of Ellis Empire resorts have a grotto area. My guests pay a large amount of money for a retreat that offers luxurious accommodations, as well as the opportunity to become a member of a VIP club."

"VIP club? What does that mean?"

"Make him leave and I'll show you. I'll open your eyes to a world you never knew existed." My eyes wander to her tempting mouth.

"Tell me now or I'll go climb on his lap and ride him right in the courtyard."

I laugh. "Seventy-three hours ago you were a virgin. You're far from having the nerve."

"Watch me," she titters, grinning from ear to ear as she slides out from under me.

"Don't you dare, Bella."

She keeps walking, adding an extra shake to her hips. Trent meets her halfway and his voice raises as he speaks, "Where were you? I looked everywhere. This place is a damn maze."

I adjust my erect cock in my pants and go to where they stand. Just as I'm about to grab their attention, Bella crushes her mouth to Trent's.

Rage consumes me. Every nerve inside me feels obstructed as I join the two of them and rip Trent away from her. "Breakfast is over."

"Get your damn hands off me," Trent barks. "Come on, Bella. Let's go to your room, so we can have some privacy."

I hold up a hand. "Not so fast. Peter will show you to your room." I look at Bella. "We have a scheduled conference call with Barbara in twenty minutes."

Bella cocks a brow. "I didn't know about that."

"You do now." I holler over them, "Peter." A second later, he's there, waiting for my instruction. "Please show Mr. Beckham to his room on the sixth floor. He'll be staying in six-twenty-two."

"Yes, sir." Peter nods.

"We'll see you later, Trent." I enunciate his name, hating the way it sounds. I despise everything about that man, and not because I'm jealous of anything he has. It's because he stole everything *I had*.

24

"THIS IS RIDICULOUS. Trent just got here an hour ago and you expect him to just go off on his own in this huge place?"

"Why do you care? You told me something was missing between you two anyways."

"That has nothing to do with human decency. The guy came all this way because he was worried about me. That means something."

"It means he wants to deflower you then leave you. I know men."

"You know how you are. Not all men are womanizers."

The door to Cal's office closes behind us and I take a seat on the couch against the back wall. I pick up one of the chess pieces, look at it, then set it back down on an empty square.

"Can we just get on with this conference call, so I can at least do some sort of work while I'm here."

He takes slow steps in my direction, each one causing

my heart to flutter. "The call isn't until seven o'clock tonight. Barbara is on the West Coast."

"So you lied, even though you claim to be truthful."

"I lied to get you away."

Cal kneels down in front of the round glass table holding the chessboard. Picking up a rook, he moves it up. "He's not staying. You do realize that, don't you?"

I pick up another piece and move it. "You just put him in a room, didn't you?"

Cal moves another rook, likely guarding his queen. "You're making this harder than it needs to be. If you want him to go home and tell your parents about how miserable you seem here, fine. Let them worry. Otherwise, you can send him on his merry way and tell him you'll see him when you get back."

The last thing I want is for my parents to worry or lose their jobs. I truly believe Cal would go to those lengths to keep me here. I still haven't read over the contract because he basically spelled it all out for me. My hands are tied for the next six months.

"He'll be more worried if I make him leave tonight. Give it until morning and I'll break things off."

Cal chastises me when he thinks I screwed up. Now I get one night to punish him, but I can promise it won't be as satisfying as the decree I received.

"Fine. But you stay the hell away from his room. You two will only communicate if I am there."

"Controlling much?"

"Yes. Yes, I am." He sets his pawn down, taking my king. "Check."

I look up at him as he stands, rounding the table with

his gaze set on me. My palms dampen as I drop back onto the couch in defeat.

Using his thumb, he tips my chin and hovers his lips over mine. "I didn't like seeing you kiss him."

Tingles ride downward from his touch. "I don't like seeing you leave strange rooms with women."

"So you were jealous?" He smirks against my mouth.

"Were you?"

"More jealous than I've ever been in my entire life. I could have killed him with my bare hands."

Cal drops the weight of his body on me and devours my mouth like he's trying to make me forget my kiss with Trent. Not that it was anything like this. Kissing Cal is like nothing I've ever felt before.

His knee presses between my legs, grating against my crotch. "Let me fuck you so good you never want to look at another man again."

I moan into his mouth when the friction of his knee intensifies. I'm a terrible person for wanting this while Trent is here. Regardless, right now, I want Cal inside of me more than I've ever wanted anything.

I'm anticipating it will be painful. My insides feel bruised and swollen, but I don't stop him as he grabs me by my waist and flips me over onto my knees. My hands grip the back of the couch as he teases the skin of my lower back with the tips of his fingers, leaving goosebumps in his path. My pants come down, along with my underwear, hugging my knees. The sound of his zipper going down has my nipples puckering against my bra.

"Are you still taking the pill?" he asks from behind me.

"Mmhmm."

"Good girl." He groans before curling his fingers inside of me.

My back bends as he pumps them at just the right pace, sending a rush of adrenaline through me. I roll my hips as he swirls his fingers inside, loosening me up for what's coming next.

I reach my hand back in search of his hardness and find it pressed against my ass cheek. My fingers wrap around his girth and I stroke him to the best of my ability in this position. A pleasurable moan rips through me when he uses his thumb to circle my clit.

With the way he's working his fingers, I'll be coming before he even puts his cock inside of me. Cal takes my hand off him but doesn't stop fingering me.

I look over my shoulder to see if something's wrong.

"You keep that up and we'll be finished before we start."

Suddenly, he picks up his pace, bringing out another moan from me, this time louder. No matter how hard I try to quiet myself, even with my face pressed into the couch, it's no use. Everything he does feels so good, and when I think it can't get any better, he flicks his finger just right, sending me over the edge again.

"Scream for me, baby."

He goes knuckle-deep, and I feel my walls close around him. Not holding back, I cry out in euphoria. "Ugh. Oh God, Cal."

"That's right. Say my name." He smacks a hand to my ass and I roll my hips.

Just as I'm about to come, he pulls his fingers out and slides his dick inside of me. "Come around my dick,

Bella." His fingers grip my hips, and he power drives himself into me.

He completely fills me up with his dick, and it fits perfectly. It's like I was molded just for him. Arching my back, I lift my head and close my eyes while my nails burrow into the thick leather of the couch.

Something cold on my skin alarms me and I turn my head to see Cal dragging the queen chess piece over my ass cheek. He's wearing a shit-eating grin, and I immediately know he's got something planned.

"Take a deep breath." His voice is raspy and his eyes offer a warning.

I do as I'm told, anxious for him to continue so I can come, although my hands begin trembling out of worry of what he's about to do.

The tip of the chess piece enters my asshole and my lower half jolts. I tug forward slightly, but he grabs my hips and pulls me back into place and begins fucking me again.

"Cal?" I say in question, "What are you doing?" It's a dumb question. I know exactly what he's doing. I may have been a virgin up until recently, but I do know what an anal plug is, although, I've never had one inside of me and never cared to, but Cal makes me do a lot of things I never thought I'd do.

It's cold and foreign, spreading me apart slightly with a tinge of pain, but nothing unbearable. As he picks up his pace, moving his cock in and out of me, he pushes the chess piece deeper, causing me to shriek. He begins twisting and turning it, but the pain subsides quickly and all I can focus on is his pelvic bone writhing against mine as he fucks my pussy.

My hips roll and I meet him thrust for thrust. He picks up his pace, and I bite down on my lip, trying to control my outburst as I orgasm around his dick.

Cal grunts, his breathing rapid and labored. He digs so deep inside of me that I can feel him in my stomach. Freezing, he fills me up with his cum and stops turning the chess piece.

In a swift motion, he slides his dick out and replaces it with his fingers. I revel beneath him. A new and exciting sensation flows through me and I feel myself gush with liquid into his hand. I'm not sure what happened, but it feels so damn good, and I don't want it to stop.

Sounds I didn't know I could make escape me as I come undone around his fingers.

I feel out of control, like my body is not my own as I'm struck with insatiable heat.

Cal moans in delight and keeps going until I do it again, squirting my juices all over. It hits the couch and my legs and doesn't ease up as he digs his fingers farther inside of me.

"Fuck, Cal. I'm... Oh God," I scream in ecstasy.

He growls like a beast and I finally pull away, stopping him, because I'm not sure my body can take much more. My head is spiraling, my mouth parched.

Once I settle down a bit, I feel embarrassed about the mess around me. I drop my ass and turn around, tucking my knees as I sit on the liquid spill. "I'm sorry."

Cal chortles, which calms my nerves a tad. "What the hell are you sorry about? That was sexy as hell."

"Is that normal?" I feel stupid for even asking, but I didn't know it was possible for a woman to...ejaculate.

"Yeah, it's normal. It means you've got a gift, and I happen to love the fuck out of it. Not all women squirt, but those who do experience the best orgasms."

Squirt? God, just the word itself makes my cheeks blush.

Cal walks into the bathroom and returns with a towel and hands it to me. I fold it in my lap as I tug my soaked pants up and adjust my shirt back in place. I still feel like my head is in a cloud, like I'm stuck in this euphoric state. "I've never felt anything like that."

Leaning forward, he presses his lips to my forehead. "Then I can't wait to make you do it again."

My heart squeezes at the gentleness of his kiss. The softness in his words. It's eye-opening and right now, all I want to do is take a shower then lie in bed and let him hold me until I fall asleep.

One day. Maybe.

"Trent is in his room, so you can go to yours and get changed." He begins tapping on his phone as he talks to me. "Paulina will be doing rounds soon for laundry, so we can get those cleaned for you." He looks up. "I meant what I said, Bella. You are not to be alone with him."

Then he leaves. He just leaves me sitting on his couch in my own fluid.

"Thanks for the multiple orgasms," I mumble as the door latches shut.

25

I'M PACING The Grotto floor, watching my app where I have the live footage pulled up, so I can see Bella's bedroom door. So far, she's obeying me and staying put.

I'm tired as hell. Haven't slept in two days, and it's not looking good for tonight either. Now I've got to watch her ass and his to make sure no funny business is pulled. I want to trust Bella, I really do, but the way I've been duped by her in the past has me wondering if her sincerity lately is a ploy to try and leave. Unfortunately, if she does try that, I'd have to be the bad guy and carry out my threat to destroy her parents' lives.

A call comes through, interrupting the live stream.

Byron. It's about damn time.

"Where the hell are you?" I huff into the speaker of the phone.

"Had to go take care of something. I'll be back later tonight. Where are you?"

My lack of patience gets the best of me. "The same

damn place I've been for the last two months. Now get your ass back here. We need to talk."

"I'll be there around ten. Meet me downstairs. And you're right. We do need to talk."

He ends the call. His ass really just hung up on me *again*. I'm getting real tired of this shit he's been pulling lately. I know he's trying to turn Bella against me. He wants her gone, and he's making it known.

I get to the dining room, just as the cook is setting the table for dinner. Nothing like a nice dinner with my future wife and her boyfriend to end this day on a good note.

"Good evening, Mr. Ellis," Peter says as he enters the room with his hands behind his back. "Ms. Jenkins has informed me that Mr. Beckham refuses to join you for dinner tonight."

My fists ball at my sides as I try to remain calm. There is no one I hate more than Trent Beckham, and nothing I hate more than an ungrateful guest. "Then you can relay to *Mr. Beckham*," I growl his name, "that he can go hungry tonight."

Peter tips his head. "Very well."

I walk so fast out of the dining hall that my body can barely keep up with my feet. Bypassing Peter, I head straight for the elevator and jump on, not even holding the door for him. He's much more agile than most men his age, but he still moves slowly and right now, I'm in a hurry.

Instead of stopping at the sixth floor to confront Trent, I go to Bella.

My knuckles pound against her door repeatedly, until

she finally pulls it open. Brushing past her, I enter her room. "It seems your..." I stop, completely caught off guard when I see Trent sitting on her bed. "When did he get here?"

I watched the cameras and didn't see him come up. *Dammit!* It must have been when I was on the phone with Byron. Two whole goddamn minutes and he found a way to weasel his way into her room.

Trent stands up, his shoulders drawn back like he's challenging me. "Is there a problem, Callum? I am Bella's soon-to-be fiancé, and guest, and to be honest, I'm not too happy with the way you've been talking to her. Seems a little unprofessional, if you ask me."

"I didn't ask you, but thanks for your input, *Trent.*" His name alone makes me want to break things.

It's ironic that the boy I've hated since I was eleven is now standing in my kingdom, telling me I'm unprofessional.

Trent takes a step forward and places an arm around Bella's waist. "I think you need to leave this room. It's Bella's private space and you shouldn't be in here."

Gnashing my teeth, my gaze skates from his hold on her to his eyes. "Actually, I think you need to leave. Your trip has come to an end. Bella, please see him out."

"What? No!" she stammers, stepping away from him and into my space. "Please, Cal," she whispers, "let me handle this."

I stare into the eyes of my enemy before looking down at her. "You're not handling it very well. End this," I mumble.

Her doe eyes peer up at me and it's hard not to fall under their spell. "I will. I just need some time."

"Fine. I'll see you both at dinner. The cook will be off duty in an hour and if you'd like to eat, now is your chance. Otherwise, you can both starve, for all I care."

Bella glances over her shoulder. "Is that okay?" she asks Trent.

Why the hell is she asking his permission to eat?

"No," Trent retorts with a glowering look. He takes another step forward and pulls Bella back by her hips. Her back hits his chest while his hands stay locked on her waist, his eyes on me. "Bella and I will be eating in here tonight."

Don't kill him.

Not yet.

Look at Bella.

She can calm you down.

She can end the deranged thoughts swirling in your head.

I look at her and see those sad, begging eyes. There's a tremble to her bottom lip that tells me she's scared. She should be. She knows what I'm capable of and I won't hesitate to show them both.

Collecting my composure, I stand tall. "You eat downstairs or you don't eat at all. You sleep in your own room or you get the hell off my island. Got it?" I'm talking to him, not her, but there's a good chance he thinks I'm speaking to both of them.

"Who the hell do you think you are?" Trent grumbles. "You get a few bucks in your bank account and, suddenly, the orphan has all the power?" Bella turns around and begins whispering something, but Trent snaps at her, "Don't interrupt me when I'm talking."

Unable to refrain any longer, I step up to him. Moving Bella out of the way, I get in his face. "Do you have a death wish, Beckham?"

I reach out and grab Bella by the hand, trying to get her away from this lunatic. "Come on, we're going to eat."

Her eyes beg for mercy as she tries to free her hand to no avail. "Just give me a minute. He needs to eat, too. Please."

"You've got two minutes." I drop her hand, throw Trent a warning glare, and head out the door, leaving it ajar.

My back presses to the wall beside the open door and I kick my foot up behind me. One night. One more night and she will never see him again.

"We're leaving this place right now or I'm going back and telling your parents you're working for a psychopath."

I reach into my pocket and pull out a tube of toothpicks, then pop one in my mouth with a smirk on my face.

Oh, if you only knew, Trent. Bella isn't going anywhere with you.

"Trent, please just stop this. This job is important to me."

"You don't need this job, or any job, for that matter. In fact, once we're married, I'd like to start our family right away. You can stay home with them and I'll work."

"Don't I have a say in what I want? Maybe I don't want kids yet. Maybe I *want* to work."

"My future wife will not work some ridiculous nine-to-five job for little pay while someone else raises our kids."

There's a beat of silence that has me leaning closer to the door.

"Trent, this just isn't working anymore. I think you should go."

Trent laughs menacingly. "You're kidding, right? I take time off work to come here and you think you're going to break up with me. For what? This lousy job? For him? He might have money and connections. But I do, too. If you're scared of him, we can take him down. I know a guy—"

"Why are you talking like this? Are you seriously talking about having Cal killed? Have you lost your damn mind?"

Instead of an answer, all I hear is the shuffling of feet. "Let's go. We're leaving this damn place."

She stops in her tracks, not allowing him to usher her any farther. "I'm not leaving with you."

The scuffing sounds against the floor has me pulling the door open the rest of the way. Just as I do, I watch as Trent raises his hand and flattens it across Bella's cheek. The National Guard couldn't even stop me as I make a beeline right for Trent. I grab Bella, who's cupping her tear-soaked cheek, and give her a push to the side. My fist cocks back and I lay it straight on his nose.

"You're a dead man," I scream, as I continue to hammer his face with my fist, rotating from left to right as he falls to the ground. My legs wrap around him. His arms cross in front of his face as he tries to stop me, but I'm unstoppable. Blood splatters around the room. Bella cries out, begging me to stop, and Trent moans beneath me, but I don't stop. I keep going. Punch after punch. Blow after blow. Hearing bone meet bone as my knuckles grind into his flesh. Feeling the slippery mess of his blood —tasting it, smelling it. I'm a man hell-bent on retribution, especially from the asshole who took everything from me.

"Help. Someone help." I hear Bella holler from outside the room.

Trent reaches up, trying to grab my throat, but it's useless. He's too weak. The strength and the power are all mine. His demise will be my dawn. My fresh start. A new beginning. A life with the woman he claims to love.

I've waited years for this. Years of knowing he was living his best life. He had it all. The perfect family, unconditional love, inherited wealth. Then I found out he got her. He got the girl that was meant to be mine. He stole her from me in a dirty power play.

Now, I'm taking it all back. The sweet taste of revenge sits heavy on my tongue as I watch him crumble beneath me.

"I lost everything because of you," I scream so loud my words echo off the walls. "For twelve years, you and that asshole lived a life that should have been mine. Everything we wanted, everything we dreamt, you stole. Now you get to pay. Bella is mine and there isn't a damn thing you can do about it."

I hear her.

"Please stop, Cal. I'm begging you."

The voice of an angel.

"Please," she cries out.

My blows become sluggish. The pain in my hands begins to creep in.

"Please," she says one more time, her hand resting on my shoulder.

I look behind me and see her standing there, tears streaming down her face.

"Please don't kill him."

My chin hits my chest and I sit there, on an unconscious Trent, for what feels like minutes.

"Would you like me to take care of him, sir?" Anders asks from behind me.

"Take care of him?" Bella howls. "I know what that means. No, you will not *take care of him*."

I push myself up, feeling lightheaded from the sudden adrenaline shift. Looking at Anders, I nod. "Take him to the cellar. I'll be there in five."

"No!" Bella screams. Her fists hit me over and over as she cries before falling into my arms. "I won't let you kill him. He's a person, Cal. He might be cruel, but he doesn't deserve to die."

"Now," I say to Anders, before scooping Bella up and tossing her over my shoulder.

She fights me the entire walk down the hall. Her fists whale on my back. Legs kicking, mouth running.

We stop at my room and I squeeze her body tighter, so she's unable to get away. Reaching in my pocket, I pull out my key, unlock the door, then open it. Once we're inside, I go straight to my closet and pull open a drawer.

Bella stops moving, watching as I pull out a thick bundle of rope. "What are you doing?"

"It's for your own good. With him gone, we can finally live."

"No!" She begins kicking and punching again while she screams at the top of her lungs.

"It has to be this way."

I set her down on the bed and bind her wrists together. She doesn't make it easy as she jerks and squirms to try and free herself. Once the rope is tight enough that she can't get free, I tie the loose end to the pole on the footboard of the bed.

"Why are you tying me up?" She sniffles. "I already know you're planning to kill him. Why are you doing this?"

"Because I don't want you to stop me. He hurt us. Everything that happened is because of him." I give the rope a pull to make sure it's secure. Once I'm sure it is, I kneel in front of Bella. "Everything will be okay. I promise."

Her lips curl in a snarl. "If you kill him, I'll never forgive you."

"With time, you will." I stand up and head for the door. "Scream all you want. This room is soundproof, so no one will hear you."

I walk out and lock the door behind me. Vengeance awaits.

26

"Nooooo!" I repeat, over and over, until my cries feel helpless. I'm sure he didn't mean to slap me, and it's not like he ever has before. It couldn't have been easy for him to step into this environment. Me, his girlfriend, along with his former enemy, who is suddenly so jealous he can't even blink out of fear someone will touch me. I should have just told Cal no, that we weren't eating in the dining room. I was scared, though. He's hanging my parents' careers over my head—he holds my future, and theirs, in his hands.

Sometimes I see the person he used to be. It's a miniscule amount, but he's in there. I was ready to end things with Trent and make myself live in this world Cal created for me. After six months, maybe I could fall in love with him. I might not want to leave once he sets me free, and even if I did, I'd know I at least tried everything I could to repair what was broken between us.

My body is depleted of strength as I twist and turn, trying to break free from this rope that binds me. I look over when I see that black snake looking at me. I hold her stare, challenging her to look away first.

A minute passes, then another, but she wins.

I'm weak.

All my life I've done what everyone else wanted. The one time I made a choice for myself by taking this job, it was the wrong one.

I try again. Tugging and twisting the rope, hoping it will snap and I'll be free. It digs into the skin of my arms with each pull, but I don't stop. Not even when it burns. Even when I begin to bleed, I keep going.

"Ahhhh," I scream, yanking harder and faster, cutting myself while trying to free myself.

I look back at the snake who's still fixated on me. It's like she's laughing. Mocking me and telling me I can't do it.

I will get out of here. I might not be able to save Trent, but I swear if Cal kills him, I'll leave. He can make good on his threats against me. I'll buy my way out of the contract and my parents can get new jobs. I will not live with a man who kills someone just because they upset them. Yes, he killed Vincent, but the man tortured him and left him no choice. If anything, Cal was brave in that moment. Right now, though, he's being a coward.

With my eyes deadlocked on the snake, I pull again. My body crashes to the ground, and I realize I did it. *I'm free.*

In that instant, the snake looks away and slithers down a branch. I'm not sure why, but I smile.

I won.

Without wasting another minute, I go straight to the

closet where the secret door is. Pushing the suits to the side, I turn the handle and open the door. My feet get away from me as I hurry down the winding staircase.

For whatever reason, Cal told his guard to bring Trent down here. He mentioned a club of some sort. *Oh my gosh!* My stomach clenches. What if Cal is involved in some shady organized crime that involves killing people, or even torturing them?

I'm fearful of what I could potentially walk in on. But when I turn the handle on the door to the room at the end of the staircase, I'm reminded that I won't be walking in on anything. This door is locked with a passcode.

"Dammit!" My hands fall from the door in defeat. Just because I never want to see Trent again doesn't mean I want him to die. If I don't get in there soon, that is a very real possibility.

I hurry back up the stairs, feeling like time is running out. If there are plans for a club down there, then there has to be another entrance. Surely guests won't be going through the secret door in Cal's bedroom closet. This isn't *The Lion, the Witch and the Wardrobe.*

Wait a minute. The door on the ground floor by the main entrance had the same keypad. Serena and the bartender both came out of that door. It has to go somewhere important. That must be it. It has to be. I can't imagine the password is the same because there is no way Cal would let anyone have immediate access to his room. There is no lock on the closet door, so it leads me to believe Cal is the only one who uses it. He may be the only one who knows about it.

Tearing through the closet, into Cal's room and out

the door to the hallway, I don't stop moving. I go straight to the elevator and hit the down arrow, over and over, until the doors slide open. I'm in full-blown panic mode and don't even notice it's occupied when I step in. Taking a step back, I stumble over the edge of the door.

"Cal. I…umm—"

"I can see I didn't put enough faith in you. You're free."

I look down at the elevator floor and notice the blood dripping from his hands. It's been almost an hour since Cal attacked Trent. The blood from their fight should be dried.

Cal scratches his neck, leaving a trail of the fresh blood on his skin. His white shirt is covered, all the way down to his shoes.

"Well, are you getting on or are you just going to stand there and stare at me?"

Swallowing hard, I step in with apprehension.

"Where are you going, Bella?" His expression is desensitized, hands in his pockets.

I hit the G for the ground floor and press my back to the wall. My arms cross over my chest as my eyes scan his body. He's acting very strange, but that would be expected after murdering someone.

"I just need some fresh air." My fingers graze over the rope burns and deep gashes on my wrists.

Cal takes notice and grabs my arm. "Why the hell did you do this?" He looks at the marks, then to me. "Don't you know stubbornness can get you hurt?"

"Did you kill him?" I spit out, my arm still in his hand.

He just stares at my wrists for a second, deep in

thought. Finally, he snaps out of it. "Trent won't be bothering us again."

"Us?" I laugh tensely. "As if there is an us. I told you if you killed him, I'd never forgive you and I meant it."

Snapping my arm away when the doors open, I step off the elevator. Cal follows behind me at an amble pace. I know he's waiting to see what I'm doing, so it looks like, right now, I'm just going for fresh air.

I head straight for the exit, glancing at the keypad on the mystery door as I pass by it.

"You can go clean up. I don't need a babysitter."

Cal joins my side, walking in step with me as the fresh, cold air hits my face. I take a deep breath and keep walking.

"You've proven that you do. First the snooping and now the disobedience. I told you to stay put, yet here you are."

When the sound of a boat engine roars to life, I pick up my pace. Walking steadfast down the steppingstones. "That's a boat. Where is it going?"

"Somewhere you're not." Cal grabs me by the arm. "You can't escape me, Bella. We were so close to where we're supposed to be until Trent showed up. We will get there again, and you will forgive me. He's gone and now you can move on…with me."

I stop moving when Cal holds me in place. A ripple in the clouds tells me another storm is coming. Dread washes over me. I'm so confused and so lost; I have no idea what to do.

"Please just tell me he's okay."

"He hit you, Bella. He talked to you like you were a dog and he struck your face. He wants to control you."

"And you don't?" I shout. "Isn't that what this is?" I jerk my arm away and look at his blood-soaked skin. "Look at you, Cal. You're obsessed with this idea of us living here and falling in love. So much so that you're willing to kill anyone who gets in your way. If anyone is controlling, it's you."

His shoulder shrugs while he stands there, still lacking any emotion that says he's remorseful for his actions. "You're right. I am. It's because I know what I want and what I want is you. I will bleed for you, Bella. I will kill for you. I would walk to the darkest depths of the world to carry you to safety. They don't deserve you."

"And you think you're protecting me by keeping me away from *them*? Or is this just your way of punishing everyone who wronged us?"

"Both," he simply says. He takes a step forward, his chest flush with mine, and he looks down at me with his hands at his sides. "Together forever, until kingdom come."

"Let the past go, Cal. We don't live there anymore."

Cal chuckles obnoxiously. It's his way or the wrong way. "I can only overcome the past by facing it head-on. Only then will I be able to focus on the future. We're getting closer. Now," he says, turning me around toward the castle, "I need to take a shower and get some sleep. It's been a long day. Peter will bring dinner to your room, you have a call scheduled with Barbara in an hour, and I'd appreciate it if you stay there for the remainder of the night."

"But it's only six o'clock. I don't want to sit in my room alone."

"Fine. I'll allow you to go to one of the floors to play the piano. Or, you're welcome to visit the turret."

My eyes light up. "I am? But the elevator doesn't go that high. How do I get up there?"

"Peter can take you."

I'm furious right now, but I've wanted to visit the turret since the day I arrived and saw it sitting so high in the clouds.

"This isn't over. I will get answers, if it's the last thing I do."

Cal smirks. "I don't doubt you'll try."

27

DINNER WAS…MEH. Cold and not exactly what I'd call a meal. Once I lifted the lid on the platter, I knew Cal had it made special for our guest, Trent. Clam chowder, which Trent hates, salad covered in onions—he also hates onions —and dry rolls.

I'm not even sure how he knew the foods Trent despised. Then again, Cal seems to know everything about everyone, so I shouldn't be surprised.

My call with Barbara went great and I'm really excited to get the contractors here after the holidays, so we can begin the renovations on the guest floors. We even went over some plans for the ground level that include an indoor swimming pool and a cozy entrance with an orna- mented welcome center.

Hearing a knock has me dropping the book I've been reading—*Wuthering Heights*—and fleeing for the door. Peter is taking me to the turret and I'm grateful I let my phone charge, so I can take pictures. Not only that, but it's also an opportunity to try and get a cell signal. I just need to call Mark and have him try and reach Trent. I imagine if Trent is alive, he's in a hospital being treated for broken bones in his face, possibly even some ribs, but eventually, I'm hopeful Mark can reach him.

Mark and Trent have been friends since I left The Webster House, although it wasn't until college that Trent and I got together. It was exciting at first. I saw him in a new light. He was sweet and attentive. When the honeymoon stage ended and things got difficult, my family pushed me to try and patch things up. They didn't know how controlling Trent was and only saw what they wanted to see—a good man who could take care of me.

Unfortunately, that doesn't result in love, and I now know Trent is not the man I want to spend my life with.

"Are you ready, Ms. Jenkins?" Peter asks when we come face to face in the doorway.

"Yes, I am. I can't wait to see the view from up top. So, how do we get there?"

"Follow me and I will show you."

A few minutes later, we're standing in front of the mystery door downstairs. My palms are sweating as I push myself up on my tiptoes, peering over Peter's shoulder. He punches in the code without a care in the world, but his fingers move so fast that all I caught was the first number—six.

The door buzzes, then opens. We're standing in, yet another, empty room. Although, this one has an elevator. The door is exactly the same as the one I've been using every day since I arrived. It's eerie to think that after weeks here, there is still so much of the castle I have not seen. There could be just about anything behind these walls. Bodies, killers, ghosts.

Peter calls down the elevator with the push of a button. We step inside and I notice all the floors are on the panel. There must be access to each floor from this elevator.

"So this can take us to any floor?" I decide to ask, rather than wracking my brain trying to figure things out.

"Yes, and no. It's only accessible to people with the passcode, which is very few. This elevator stops behind the door at the end of each hall where the staircase is and the only way through the door is with a passcode."

So this entire time people could have been coming and going into the cellar and I wouldn't have even noticed. It really has me wondering how many different women have been down there.

"It has to be hard to remember all these codes."

"This is the only one here at Cori Cove, but there are others at the various hotels. After you punch them so many times, though, they stick. I'll probably have them all in my memory until the day I die."

"Aren't you worried you'll forget? I mean, you have to keep a record of them somewhere."

"Mr. Ellis doesn't believe in a physical trail. But, between us, I keep them in a notepad."

I smile inwardly. *That's exactly what I wanted to hear.*

It's a short ride up to the turret level, and even though the main reason I want to be up here is to check the signal on my phone, I am excited about the view. I haven't traveled much, well, at all, really. In fact, I've only visited two states and never left the country. There is so much I've missed out on and as I step out of the elevator and immediately look at the view, I'm reminded of the beauty in this world that I have yet to see.

At this moment, everything slips away from me. My feet take me to the covered balcony and it's like I'm staring into the sky. There is so much out there that I want to explore. Our world has so much appeal and I feel like a caged animal, getting her first nip of the fresh air. As much as I love the life I live, I want more. More of this. More of everything. I want to travel and find beauty in the little things. Seashells and rare flowers. Untouched land and geodes.

All along I thought I was selfish for wanting to leave my parents and Trent, to follow my dreams, but now I realize that I wasn't selfish. I have to live my life for me, not them.

I hold my phone up to look for a signal, but as I should have guessed, nothing.

"What do you think?" Peter asks, standing next to me. I didn't even realize he was there while I was lost staring into the abyss.

"I'm speechless. It's…amazing."

"Sometimes I come here alone when the nights get lonely. My late wife and I loved to travel and of all the bell towers I've been in, this one reminds me of her the most."

Peter has never mentioned his wife and now that he has, I want to know more about her. About him. About them.

I take a step back and look at Peter. "Why this one?"

"Because it's where we fell in love."

My heart squeezes and chills slide down my back. "You mean, you were here before Callum bought the place? I thought you'd been with his family for years?"

I know that sometimes a groundskeeper will stay at a location, even after the property sells, but Peter has been with the Ellises since before Cal was adopted, so how was he here all those years ago?

"When I shared the story about how Carolina and I met, Callum, err, Mr. Ellis," he corrects himself, "was intrigued. He was only fourteen, maybe fifteen years old, and I think it gave him hope that true love really does conquer all. He's not as hard on the inside as he is on the outside. The boy has a heart. In fact, sometimes I think it's too big for that small head of his." Peter chuckles.

"Tell me. Please tell me the story of you and your wife."

Peter gestures toward a concrete bench beneath the giant bell that hangs overhead. "These old legs can't handle my weight as long as they used to. Mind if I sit?"

"No. Go right ahead."

Peter takes a seat and I join him on the bench. "She was the most beautiful woman I'd ever laid eyes on. I was thirteen years old when my family came to work for the Bromley family. My mother was a maid and my father tended to the landscaping. My brothers and I were always causing mischief and I'm pretty sure we almost cost my parents their jobs a time or two."

Peter smiles at the memories and my heart floods with happiness for him. "Carolina was an only child and her father was adamant that she was not allowed to fraternize with 'the help.' So we steered clear. One day, my father became ill and missed his chores for the day, so I wanted to help him. I snuck out in the night and tended to the garden, collecting all the vegetables for the next day's dinner. That's when I heard her. My name whispered in the wind and it was like an angel singing. I looked up and saw Carolina on that very balcony. She was a mere shadow in the night, but I knew it was her. She called me up and I flew up those stairs so fast that I'm pretty sure I tripped at least a dozen times. But it was worth it. We stayed up talking all night. Then each night after, we met up here, until so much time had passed that it felt like our conversation had just started.

His hands slap to his legs and I assume he's finished with the conversation. I need more, though. "And then what happened?"

"When Carolina was sixteen years old, me being eighteen, we were caught. Her father forbade us to see one another, so we planned to run away together. She was the love of my life and the thought of never seeing her again was too painful to bear. We never got away."

The sadness in his eyes sends a tear sliding down my cheek. I quickly wipe it away so he doesn't see how emotional his love story is making me.

"Her family moved and took her away before we could make our own escape. Before they did, though, we made a promise that we would meet back here exactly two years later when she was eighteen. It was still owned by the Bromley family, but there were no plans to occupy the space."

"You did, right? You came back?"

"I came back," he smiles, "and so did she. She escaped the clutches of her father and we married two weeks later and moved to Boston where we lived until she passed away seventeen years ago, and I've missed her every day since."

"So that's where Cal lived? Boston?"

All this time he was so close. I swear there were times where I could feel him near and I just knew he wasn't on the other side of the country, or the world.

"Carolina and I were fascinated with castles and historical landmarks. We traveled the world together. When I heard that the Ellis family was looking for a footman, I contacted him immediately."

"And then Cal's father bought Cori Cove?"

"No. It wasn't until Mr. Ellis Senior passed away that he purchased the island. And here we are."

"And you're okay with him turning it into a tourist hot spot?"

"I'm just happy to be here. It doesn't matter what I see on the outside, it's the feeling this place brings me on the inside."

"It is a beautiful place. It's just a shame that you have to share it."

"If I had to share it with anyone, it would be Mr. Ellis. He, too, deserves to find his one true love."

"That may be true, but, Peter, I don't think that person is me."

"Oh?"

"I'm not emotionally equipped to handle his mood swings or his possessive nature."

"You slept in his room, did you not?"

"Well, yeah—"

"You've gone against every rule he's set in place and you're still here. Something tells me, you're stronger than you think. The heart wants what the heart wants, Ms. Jenkins. Don't fight it."

The heart wants what the heart wants.

Butterflies swarm in my stomach when I think of Cal and his unruly ways. He can be irrational and monstrous, but I suppose he's always been that way. He was always gentle with me when we were kids. Always wanted to protect me and save me from hurt feelings. Time changes people, but people are part of that change. My Cal is in there somewhere and I'm not going to stop until I bring him back.

I don't even think as my arms fly around Peter and I pull him in for a hug. He reciprocates with a gentle pat to my back.

"Thank you, Peter."

Peter has been such a blessing in this scary place. He's a reminder that I'm not alone, even when I feel like I am. He might work for Cal, but I'm starting to think I have a friend in him. It's unfortunate that tonight, I have to do what's necessary to steal from him.

"It's getting late and I'm pretty tired. Would you like to have a bedtime cup of tea with me?"

"I'm not sure Mr. Ellis—"

"Oh, come on," I chuckle, "it's just tea. He won't mind, and if he does, I'll take full blame."

Peter thinks for a moment but finally says, "Okay. That

would be lovely. I'll prepare some now and meet you in the sitting room."

I smile at his response while my heart is crying at the fact that I have to swindle this sweet, old man.

28

AFTER A QUICK STOP at my room, I'm headed down the hall to meet Peter for tea. I don't even drink tea, but I've seen him drink it a couple times, so I knew it was a good call.

I stick my hands in the front pockets of my sweatpants and roll the sleeping pill between my fingers. It's been in my drawer since Peter brought it to me the day after Cal and I first had sex. It was a rare time that Cal was catering to my every need, and it was actually pretty sweet.

No matter how much my heart tells me that Cal is not this monstrous guy he wants the world to see him as, it still doesn't change the fact that he's keeping secrets. He should know by now that I don't roll over when I suspect something is going on. I dragged him on so many wild goose chases when we were kids that there's no way he's forgotten. I once suspected the mailman was having an affair with Trent's mom and made him go with me to peek in the window. It turns out it was her brother. I laugh at myself for being such a nosey little shit every time I see Trent's Uncle Bob at his family gatherings.

Peter is sitting on a chair in front of the fireplace. Startled at the sound of my footsteps, he turns his head quickly. "Goodness, dear, I didn't hear you come in." He's clutching a cup in his hand and brings it to his mouth.

"Sorry about that." I reach down and grab my tea then take a seat in a chair on the other side of the fireplace. I stretch my hand out in front of me, feeling the heat of the flames from the blazing fire. "Feels nice."

Peter nods. "It does."

I take a couple sips as we sit there in silence, my anxiety getting the best of me. Maybe this is a bad idea. Knocking the poor guy out, disarming the cameras on this floor, and stealing his key just so I can go search his room for a notebook of passcodes. Maybe I am in too far over my head.

No, I have to do this. If I ever want to find it in my heart to move forward with Cal, I need to know the secrets he's hiding.

"Peter, would you mind fetching me a blanket? Even with the fire, it's still so chilly."

My eyes follow Peter's teacup to the small round table. "Of course."

He stands up slowly and walks behind me. I peer over my shoulder, and once he's out of the room, I get up quickly and walk over to drop the pill in his tea. It sinks to the bottom and I begin to panic when I can see it through the light caramel-colored liquid.

"Dissolve, dammit." I look at the door and back at the tea. It's still there.

Peter comes back in with a white blanket in his hand and I jump back into my chair. There's no way he missed my speedy movements, but he doesn't even bat an eye.

"Here you go." He hands me the blanket and takes his seat again. He picks up the tea and to my surprise, he takes a sip without noticing.

I watch intently as the minutes go by and he drinks at the speed of a newborn baby, never once noticing the pill.

A few more minutes pass and Peter lets out a big yawn.

This could take a very long time, but I have to wait it out.

Watching Peter continuously yawn while he stares into the fire like he's under a spell from the glowing embers, I yawn myself.

I'm about to just give up and go to bed because it's apparent this guy is *not* falling asleep.

I look back at him again and notice his eyes fluttering.

It's working.

The next thing I know, they're closed and he still has his cup in his hand. I give it a few minutes, letting him fall into a deep sleep, then I stand up quietly and tiptoe over to him. I take the cup and notice there are just a few more sips left of tea so he must have drunk the pill. I set down the cup and take a deep breath before patting his pants pocket. I can feel the bulge from his phone, so I slide my hand and grab it, being very cautious not to stir him.

I breathe a sigh of relief when I see that his phone doesn't have a passcode. It seems to be the only thing in this place that's not protected.

After swiping through his apps, I finally find the one

used to view live streams and saved footage. There are twelve different cameras, all numbered by floor. Once I've disarmed all three of the cameras on the eighth floor and the one on the sixth floor, I reach in his pocket and pull out the key. If I remember correctly, this is a master key. Right now, though, I only need it to get into his bedroom. I tuck his phone back in his pocket and haul ass out of the room.

Ignoring my rapid pulse and the sweat collecting on my forehead, I go straight to the elevator. I don't even blink as I pass by Cal's room. Hopefully he's asleep. He looked exhausted, so I'm sure he is.

I make it to Peter's room on the sixth floor and slide the key in, internally cheering when it unlocks. As soon as I'm inside, I close the door behind me, flip on the light, and begin my search. It's actually pretty empty, aside from a twin-size bed, a dresser, and a nightstand. There's a somber feeling to his room. Poor Peter is so lonely.

I'm a terrible person for doing this. But, I do it anyway. It doesn't take long before I find a notebook, well, it looks more like a journal, in his nightstand drawer. I begin flipping through the pages when I realize that this isn't just any old notebook, it's a journal. My eyes skim down one of the pages, reading the passage quickly to myself.

Dear Diary,

I saw him again today. My heart fluttered in my chest and the feeling of a thousand butterflies danced through my stomach. We sat at the tower and counted the stars while holding hands and sipping on a bottle of Father's bourbon. Just as a star shot across the sky, he leaned over and kissed me. It was at that moment that I knew nothing would keep us apart. We were meant to live this life together, or we would die trying. Never in a million years would I imagine going against Father's wishes. That's what love does to you. It makes you crazy. You do things you never thought you were capable of. All I know is, I am crazy in love. Tomorrow we're carving our names into the tree at the backside of the island. Maybe one day, it will show proof that love existed here, and true love conquers all.

I clutch the diary to my chest and hug it tightly. Someday I hope to find a love like Peter and Carolina had.

I continue to flip until I'm at the very end and that's when I see them. An entire page of passcodes with various hotel and island names. I search for Cori Cove and there it is. One passcode for one door. That's all I need.

I memorize the numbers in my head, repeating them over and over again, as I put the diary back and close the drawer. *Six-three-two-eight-eight.*

With hurry behind my steps, I leave Peter's room and go straight to the end of the hall where the door to the private elevator is located. I punch the code in, and the door buzzes. I shriek, looking behind to make sure none of the other staff heard it. The coast is clear, so I go inside.

The elevator doors open for me, and I press the C, which I assume means cellar. I feel like such a rebel, knowing that if Cal catches me, I'll be punished again. After I'm done with my search, maybe I'll get caught on purpose—assuming Cal isn't some crazed killer or rapist. No, Cal is many things, but he's definitely not a rapist.

When the doors slide open, I feel like my heart is about to jump out of my chest. My entire body is shaking and I'm suddenly afraid of what I might find. What if Trent is dead down here? What if there are others?

Cautiously, I step out. That's when I realize I'm in another empty room. *How many empty rooms does this castle have?*

There's a door straight in front of me. I creep over to it and I'm happy to see that there is not a passcode for this door; it's also more modern than any of the others here. It's all white with a silver knob. I give it a turn and slowly pull it open.

I never would have guessed that what I'm looking at right now has been down here this entire time. It's so fancy and well-lit. Everything is blood red and crow black. Red lights are strung around the room. A large bed that looks like a triple-king-size is pressed against one wall. There are curtains separating one section to the next.

Keeping on my way, I take it all in. There's a large swing hanging from the ceiling. "Oh my gosh," I mumble, running my fingers down a floor-to-ceiling pole. There are three of them. Dancing poles. Velvet sofas are positioned around the room. A bar with a lit-up sign that says *The Grotto*. There's even a dance floor. This looks like some sort of club, but not just any club. If I had to guess, it's some sort of sex club or swingers' area.

A VIP club.

I keep walking deeper into the room. There are a few more private sections with small beds. All the bedding is either black or red. My fingers graze over the back of a chair and the touch of the velvety fabric gives me this sexy feeling inside.

I immediately stop walking when I hear voices. Someone is down here. It's coming from behind a curtain at the end of the wall. I slowly walk a little farther but stop when I hear the conversation.

There's two men, at least.

One is definitely Cal.

The other sounds like Byron.

The smell of cigar smoke invades my senses and I almost gag but stop myself. My biological mom's boyfriend always smoked cigars and the smell alone makes me nauseous.

"I know what you're doing. You know what you're doing, and it ends now," I hear Cal say in an aggressive tone.

"It's all for fun," Byron laughs, "besides, I think she'd be a good fit next to this ass here."

There's a quick sound of skin slapping skin, then a girl howls. "Damn, baby. Do that again."

My heart jumps in my throat. *There's a girl with them.*

"You just do what you're told and keep sucking her clit, then maybe I'll give you a little attention."

A moan ripples from behind the curtain and I have the nagging desire to look and see if Cal is with another girl.

"Mmm. That feels so good." It's a different girl and it sounds like Serena.

That bitch is still here.

I creep closer until I'm only inches away from the thick curtain. It's the only thing separating me from them. The only thing hiding me. If I'm caught, I could be forced into the receiving end of Byron and Cal's little sexcapade.

I grip the key in my hand so tightly, the sharp edges dig into my skin.

This could be Cal's entire reasoning for me being here. He wants to train me to be one of their little toys like these girls are. With a club like this, there has to be more of them. Hell, it wouldn't surprise me if this is going on beneath every one of the Ellis Hotels.

"One more stunt and you're gone. This is the last time I'm telling you," Cal finally speaks up. "She's off-limits and will never be part of the club.

"Never know, she might love it. These two sure do."

There's a small opening and I lean over to try and get a better look, and that's when I'm able to see Byron and the two girls. He's fucking one from behind, moving at a slow pace while sucking on a cigar, while another girl is spread out on the bed with her legs bent at the knees. The girl he's fucking is feasting on the other girl's pussy.

"She's not ready. And when she is, she will only be with me. You touch her, you're a dead man."

Something doesn't let me stop watching. It's not that I'm into that sort of thing; in fact, a small-town girl like me has never even seen it. But, my body reacts in a way I can't even explain to myself. I can feel my panties dampen as the girl begins swirling her tongue at Serena's entrance while Serena squeezes her own breasts.

"You can throw out all the threats you want, Callum. We both know I'm your only friend and you need me."

"Need you?" Cal laughs. "I don't even like you. You're not a friend to me. Not anymore."

I try to get a better look to see where Cal is and I'm

terrified that I'll find him in a similar position as Byron, so much so that a lump lodges in my throat.

Leaning over a tad more, I see him.

He's there. Sitting all by himself in a chair, watching Byron and the girls with a cigar of his own.

"Like me. Hate me. Doesn't matter to me. Doesn't change the fact that I'm one-half of the beneficiary of your entire estate and there isn't a damn thing you can do about it. I helped you, remember?"

"Oh, but there is. Once Bella is my wife, you lose that title."

My hand claps over my mouth, muffling the sound of my gasp. *His wife?*

"Yeah. Good luck getting Mary Magdalene to marry you. Even with the contract, you'd have to drug her to say, 'I do.'"

"If needed, that can be arranged. She will marry me and then she will give me a child."

Ignoring all the moans and groans, I think about what I just heard.

I back away from the curtain slowly. *Marry him and give him a child?* Am I some sort of business transaction? Is this all about his revenge against the people who he claims hurt us? Whatever it is, it's not love.

It's never been about love.

I'm on the verge of breaking down when I hear a phone ring.

"Yeah," Cal says. "What? Well, you better fucking find out why."

"What'd she do this time?" Byron asks.

"Cameras are out on the sixth and eighth floor. Peter is passed out in the sitting room."

"That bitch is trouble and you're a fucking idiot for even thinking about marrying her."

"Shut your damn mouth," Cal shouts. "I'm warning you. Now get your dick out of her ass and do something productive or get the hell off my property."

I tuck myself into the corner, between a couch and the curtain, and hide when Cal storms past me.

"Don't worry, ladies. We'll all get a little piece of what that bastard owes us." Byron lets out a deep grumble and I can hear the sound of him smacking the girl's ass again. She moans loudly and I find myself looking again. He's moving at lightning speed, ramming her from behind. Her mouth drops open as her tongue slides up and down Serena's pussy. Her fingers spread her lips farther apart, in the shape of a V, and she uses her other hand to shove three fingers inside of her.

They all three expel cries of pleasure as their orgasms tear through them. The sudden urge to touch myself has me looking away. No. I can't.

If I watch any longer, I just might cream my panties and come right along with them.

Just as I go to get up, I hear Byron. "Get your asses cleaned up and go out the back door. Callum will have a fit if his girl sees you around again."

His girl? Or his forced, future wife?

Bile climbs up my throat.

I sit there waiting impatiently while they all get dressed. I can't risk leaving this spot until they're all gone.

Once the girls are gone, Byron walks past me, leaving

out the door I came in. I stand up, stretching my body that's tense from being curled into a ball in the corner. I play it safe and give Byron a minute to get farther ahead of me before I leave.

Using this time, I look around the place. It's most definitely some sort of sex club. If what I just watched wasn't proof enough, then the wall-sized shelves of lube sure are.

I'm not bothered by this. If anything, I find myself curious. What bothers me is all the secrecy and lies. I've dealt with enough shady people in my lifetime. I refuse to let one of them into my heart. Cal plans on us getting married, but at this point, that's impossible.

I turn around to leave when the door behind me flies open. I gasp when I'm face to face with a very large, very angry-looking man.

"Don't be scared, little girl, I don't bite...hard." A devilish smirk spreads across his face and alarms sound in my ears.

He's at least six-foot-five with a full beard, yellow teeth, and a mullet cut. His arms are three times the size of my thighs and if it comes down to having to fight this man off, I will lose.

"I was just—"

"Just what? Coming down for a little fun?" He grabs his dick and shakes it. "I've got some fun for ya right here."

"Get away from me," I say, taking a few steps backward. My legs hit the end of a bed, and I fall onto it.

I've seen this guy around. He's the new guard Cal hired. He keeps coming closer, and fear sweeps over me.

"Mr. Ellis is going to come down here. He's going to find me."

The guy laughs. "Mr. Ellis is searching outside. No one's coming down here, baby. They're all looking for his little runaway."

His knees hit the bed and I scooch backward until I can't go any farther. He crawls to me with a scary smile on his face.

"I'll scream."

"I like when they scream. Make it loud for me, okay?"

The sound of his zipper dropping has me holding my breath. The next thing I know, his hard but small dick peeks out.

"Stop." I hold up my hand, not letting him near me. I'll die before I let this man touch me.

With a hoarse breath, he grabs me by the waist and fights to pull my pants and underwear down. "Stop," I scream, tears rolling down my cheeks. The scent of stale beer and cigarettes rolls off him and repulses me even more.

My legs kick and my hands flail around, but he's relentless. They make it all the way to my ankles and, at this point, it's no use. The full weight of his body crushes me. His gross dick, ready to go in. I pinch my eyes shut and internally cry tears of hate for the world. Hate for him. Hate for mankind.

"Get off me," I scream again. Using the key in my hand, I bring it to his face and scream as I slide it down, digging as deep as I can while leaving a trail of blood.

Suddenly, a loud *pop-pop* rings through my ears, and

he drops down on top of me. It's not until I open my eyes that I see Cal standing there with a gun at his side.

He jumps onto the bed. "Jesus, Bella. Are you okay?" He rolls the guy onto the floor, but I'm frozen in place.

I go to speak but nothing comes out as I look down at my sweatshirt and see the round blotch of blood. My stomach sucks in, trying to stop the liquid from seeping into my skin. My hand clutches the key in my hand as if my life depends on it.

"Did he..." Cal turns his head and bites his bottom lip, "did he touch you?"

"He...he touched me, but he didn't...you came just in time."

Cal scoops me into his arms and lifts me off the bed. "Dammit, Bella. What were you thinking coming down here?"

Suddenly, coherency returns. "Are you saying this is my fault?" My words come out in a hushed choke.

"No. God, no. This isn't your fault. If anything, it's my fault."

"I...I'm sorry, I—"

"Don't you dare apologize. I'm taking you upstairs and drawing you a bath. I'll have Peter... Never mind, Peter is passed out. But you probably know that, don't you?"

I don't respond. My words keep getting away from me and I'm not sure I could explain anything right now.

"You can sleep in something of mine tonight."

Cal carries me up the winding staircase to his room and I stuff Peter's key into the front pocket of my hoodie. My head rests gently against his chest, and as angry as I am with him, I feel safe. He killed a man to protect me. Aside from the whole arranged marriage talk, I think he really does want to keep me safe. Or at least, away from all other men.

THE IMAGE of that man's face keeps popping into my head as I soak in the bathtub—Cal's bathtub. In his room. Every minute or two, he pops his head in the door and checks on me, but my response is always the same. "I'm fine," I tell him when he does it again.

Am I, though? Will I ever be *fine?*

Cal plans on us getting married, which means one of two things: he always planned on keeping me forever. Or, he just needs the title for his self-image, and/or final will. If that's the case, it's possible he planned to let me go as long as I maintained the title of his wife.

"Cal," I holler, calling him back in here. I'm soaking under white suds with only my head above the water. It's the perfect temperature and seems to be helping me calm down. I've never seen a dead body before and I'm not sure I'll soon forget what happened. I was centimeters away from being raped and the thought alone makes me never want to leave Cal's side again.

"I'm here. What's wrong?" His eyes are alert, and I can tell he's ready to take action at whatever I need.

"Tell me about the contract."

He steps through the opening of the door and into the bathroom. "You got a copy. You're free to read it." Pressing his palms to the sink vanity behind him, he watches my hands as I scoop bubbles and drop them down, repeating the process.

"It's over a hundred pages. You know damn well I didn't read that thing. Honestly, I thought I knew the terms after it was made clear I wasn't here for just a job. Lay out the main points. Why am I here and for how long?"

Cal grazes his chin with his thumb and thinks before he finally speaks. "You're here as long as I decide for us to stay."

"Ugh," I growl, "you're so frustrating. Just tell me the damn truth. Do I have to marry you?"

He looks stunned. Completely caught off guard. "Why do you ask that?"

"I was down there while you were talking to Byron. Also saw him fucking your old flames. Now tell me the truth."

"Yes," he says point-blankly. "You will be my wife."

"And if I don't marry you?"

"Then you breach the contract and pay me a lump sum of two million dollars, plus punitive damages."

"You know, I could fight that. I was coerced into signing the contract."

"You could," he shrugs, "but good luck finding a lawyer that will top mine or a judge that's not on my payroll."

Fuck. He's probably put so much thought and planning into this that I really will have to marry him.

Cal pushes himself off the vanity and takes slow strides toward me. His sweatpants hug his hips so perfectly and the eye-level bulge in his pants has my nipples puckering beneath the suds.

"Is the thought of being married to me really that bad?"

I laugh in a sarcastic pitch. "You just shot one of your men, who was trying to rape me. I just found a secret swingers' club in your basement and you have a secret staircase that takes you to it. For all I know, you're sneaking down there and screwing girls every night. I don't trust you anymore and I can't marry someone I don't trust. And let's not get started on love."

Kneeling, he puts his hands on the ledge of the claw-foot tub. "You don't love me?" The way he asks the question—the look in his eyes—it's like he thought I loved him all along.

Maybe I did.

Maybe I do.

"I've always loved you. I'm not sure I ever stopped. What we had as kids wasn't your normal elementary/middle school friendship. We were closer than that. We were closer than siblings. It's like you were my—"

"Soulmate?"

I nod. "Yeah. Exactly."

"That's because I am and you are mine. I told you, Bella, fate brought you back to me. I'm righting my wrongs while you're doing the same. Words can never explain the pain I felt the day you left me. I wasn't sure I'd ever get past it. Even once you arrived, I still felt the sting of that day. But I found a way to move on and it's in my own selfish way, but it's the *only* way. Marry me, Bella."

"But why? What does marriage solve?"

"Because I have to get married and you're the only person in the entire world I'd even consider taking as my wife. And because it will allow me to finally forgive you while also getting my revenge on the people who hurt us."

Each day I get more and more confused. The more I learn, the more confusing things become. If I'd just stay in my room and ignore all the cracks and crevices in this damn place, my mind wouldn't be going a million miles a minute, trying to decode what this man is saying.

My head rests back and it hits me that Cal just proposed to me and I totally blew him off. I'm not even sorry because it was the worst proposal in the history of proposals. "Please stop beating around the bush. Just say the damn words."

"If you were downstairs when Byron and I were talking, then you heard about my will and how he's one-half of my beneficiary. Vincent never intended to leave me a penny. Everything was left to some woman he knocked up years ago and his bastard son that Delilah never knew about. Byron wasn't only Vincent's attorney. He was also his business partner."

"Business partner? Byron's only like five years older than you."

"Nine. He sees a damn good esthetician and has the best plastic surgeon in the country. Anyways, eight years ago, I went to Byron's office and I struck a deal with him. Change Vincent's will and leave me everything, continue the 20/80 partnership, and pay him a lump sum of three million dollars. It wasn't enough for him, though. He called me reckless and savage and was sure I'd get myself locked up or killed before I turned twenty-one and the business would suffer. He countered and requested he be the sole beneficiary on my will. I agreed to his demand with a clause that rescinded the deal if I were to marry."

"You're saying when you die, Byron gets everything?"

"Half of everything. Peter is a joint beneficiary. Everything will be split between the two of them."

"And you hate him that much to go to all this trouble just to get him out?"

Cal leans forward and the expression on his face sends chills down my spine, even in the one-hundred-degree bath water. "Byron's playing dirty, Bella. I caught wind of some shit he's involved in and if he's not out soon, I risk losing everything. I didn't take this empire from Vincent. I earned it, and I'll be damned if some washed-up attorney, who fell into luck, is going to take it from me."

"You're scaring me, Cal."

"I'd die before I let him or anyone else hurt you. I promise you that."

The look in his eyes, the expression on his face, I believe him.

There is still so much I don't know or believe, though. His answer to this question could make us or break us. "Did you kill Trent?"

There's a long beat of silence as Cal stares at the floor. He knows the answer, so his hesitation has me wondering if I should even believe what he says.

"No. I didn't kill Trent."

I'm not Trent's biggest fan but a rush of relief washes through me. "And the club downstairs?"

"They've been part of Ellis Empire long before I came along. We're known for our top-notch resorts as well as the unique experience we offer. Sex is a natural and beautiful thing, Bella. It's nothing to be ashamed of."

"But with complete strangers?" It just seems odd to me. Granted, I'm a small-town girl who's been blind to this lifestyle. It just seems degrading. Then again, I did see Byron with those girls and there's a part of me that was slightly turned on.

"Some guests just like to watch, some prefer to engage, and others prefer not to take part in the club aspect at all."

"I know for a fact I'll be avoiding that part of the hotel once it opens." At least as a participant. I'm not completely opposed to watching—maybe learning.

"It's not for everyone and I actually prefer you stay away from there. We do extensive background checks on members, but it doesn't mean I trust them." Cal rests a hand on my thigh and looks at me with a quizzical expression. "Unless, of course, it's you and me."

My interest is piqued. "While others watch?"

"Or while we watch them."

My heart jumps into a frenzy at just the thought. The thing is, I'm not sure if it's because I'm surprised he'd suggest such a thing or intrigued because I'm interested.

29

BELLA ASKED if she could sleep in my room tonight. Before the complete sentence left her mouth, I was immediately hit with a rush of panic. She slept in here before, but I stayed awake the entire time. A handful of caffeine pills and a book and I stayed awake with no problem. Although, I did pay for it the next day.

Tonight, I have to sleep. If I'm not at my best tomorrow, things could go very bad. I need to be alert and focused and make sure my plans are made clear at my meeting.

Bella comes out wearing nothing but the white tee shirt I gave her. If I thought she was beautiful before, then there is no word for the way she looks right now. She's a mixture of terms rolled into one perfect body. Stunning, alluring, bewitching, and beddable. The way her wet hair hangs down, dampening the shirt until it's see-through. Her perky tits look at me like a delectable dinner waiting to be devoured. And don't get me started on those long legs. They're squeezable, bitable, and fuck if I'm not rock-hard.

She walks toward the bed and I straighten my back against the headboard. My book slowly closes and drops to my side. I clear my throat. "Feeling better?"

She shrugs a shoulder and sits down in the same spot she claimed last time she slept in my bed. "Little bit. I think my nerves are just shot for the night. Hopefully sleep will help."

I wanna grab her and claim her. Pull her on my lap and let her ride my cock. But, it's not the right time. She's depleted and she's right, she needs sleep, as do I.

Her head rests against the pillow and her eyes close. Sitting there beside her, I watch her, wondering what thoughts are circulating through her mind right now. Is she remembering the attack of that sadistic man? His body falling lifelessly on hers? Is she thinking about marrying me? Or running away somewhere I'll never find her?

That last thought is like a knife to the chest and I think I'd take the knife over the possibility of never seeing her again. I know things can get dangerous here, but I'm fixing it. I'll make it safe. I'll protect her at all costs.

Minutes later, she's fast asleep. I slide down on my side and lie there, watching her. Until I can no longer keep my eyes open, and she drifts into my dream.

"No!" I scream at the top of my lungs. "Put it down. That's mine!"

Vincent holds up the picture and shreds it, piece by piece by piece. I watch as fragments of my picture fall slowly to the ground.

"You're delusional if you think any girl will ever love you. You're unlovable. But mostly, you're nothing but a fuck-up. You can't even follow one goddamn rule, Caden!"

"My name isn't Caden. I'm Callum."

"You're Caden Ellis," he shouts so loudly his voice echoes through my head, leaving me with a splitting headache.

My head wobbles as I try to brace it on my neck and I realize the pain isn't from his screams, it's from the punches he's laying on my skull.

"You're worthless. Scum. A piece of rotten shit. Now pull yourself together and get your ass downstairs. Your mom wants to have dinner with you."

"Cal," I hear Bella say, "Cal, please. Stop."

I blink a few times, adjusting my eyes to the light she must have turned on. "I'm awake," I spit out. "It's okay. I'm awake."

"What just happened?"

I can see her chest heaving and it tells me all I need to know. She just witnessed me at my worst.

"It was just a bad dream." I take her hand and lead her back to the bed.

Instead of lying down, she sits, so I do the same. "Dreams happen when you're sleeping. You were not sleeping. You were scrambling through the room like you were trying to get away from someone. You were crying, Cal." I notice a tear slide down her cheek and I sweep it away with my thumb.

Cupping her face, I look into her eyes. "I was sleeping."

She shakes her head, not buying it. I was sleeping, though.

"I have night terrors," I tell her. "It's happened every night since I killed Vincent. Nothing I do makes them stop." Bella throws herself into my arms and begins sobbing. "Hey, it's okay."

"No," her head rests on my chest, "it's not okay. It's all my fault. If I'd never left, you wouldn't have endured all this pain. He destroyed you."

I tip her chin up until she's looking at me. "He broke me, but I'm putting myself back together now that I have you."

Bella presses her lips to mine. The taste of her salty tears seeps into my mouth and I welcome them because they're hers. I welcome all of her as her hand slides down my pants, grabbing hold of my cock.

Then I remember what she went through tonight, what she just witnessed. "Are you sure?"

"More sure than I've ever been about anything." She presses her lips to mine again, chastising my mouth like it's not meant to speak. As if it's only meant for her to kiss.

Slowly, I lie her back, blanketing her body with mine. Her hips buck upward, seeking friction from me as I rest between her legs.

"Yes," she says. I pull back and look at her with questioning eyes. "I'll marry you, Cal."

Every thought escapes me as I fall into her.

I'm not even sure when I got rid of our clothes. Lying there on top of her, naked and hungry, I need to give her something she should have gotten the first time. As rough as I'd like this to be, as much as I want to sink my claws into her flawless skin, she deserves to have what she should have gotten her first time.

Her legs are bent at her knees around me, arms draped at her sides. I pick one up and press my lips to her wrist while watching her. Curious eyes stare back at me as I softly kiss my way up her arm.

Bella sucks in her bottom lip. "What are you doing?"

"Shh," I say, pressing a gentle finger to her lips.

I'm not sure if I know how to be tender, but since I am the only man Bella will ever be with and she didn't get sweet her first time, I'm going to try like hell for her.

My mouth glides to the shell of her ear. I set her arm back down then move to the next one. Sliding up and down, my cock rubs against her. My attention is all on her —on us.

I don't want her to be miserable. I need her to take me out of my own misery. I set her other arm down and draw in a deep breath, filling my lungs with her scent, then I exhale into her mouth. She reciprocates the kiss, sliding her tongue in and tangling it in a web of desire with mine.

Sliding down her body, I kiss every inch in a trail until I get to the parted lips of her pussy. Sucking hard on her clit, I don't stop as she cries out in moans of pleasure. Her fingers tangle in my hair, tugging and pulling as I push two fingers inside of her.

She's so wet for me. Just for me. Only ever for me. Mine.

My tongue sweeps up and down, my taste buds smoothing against the sensitive skin.

Her back lifts off the bed and she pushes my face further into her. My fingers move faster, pumping in and out, and I let out a low growl when I feel her clench around them. I catch myself grinding my dick against the mattress, but it's not enough. I need to be inside of her.

"Come for me, baby."

And she does, proof of her orgasm spilling out of her. I keep my fingers moving and she keeps riding my face as I lick up her sweet juices.

Once I pull them out, I slide up her moistened body and give her a taste of herself. She takes what's given to her and pulls my head closer, tangling her tongue with mine.

My hand moves up her side sluggishly, her skin shivering beneath my touch. "Fuck me, Cal." Her words whisper against my lips.

My hand keeps moving until I'm cradling her head in my palm. With my other hand pressed to the mattress, I line my cock with her entrance and slide in.

I move in slowly and subtly. Taking in every second of the warmth surrounding me. Moving in and out, up and down, circling my hips and letting her pussy engulf me.

"Fuck, Bella."

My senses become keen. Every touch is like fireworks igniting inside of me. Every taste is like a gourmet meal after starving for weeks. She's inevitably the most perfect, most beautiful thing I've ever seen in my entire life.

Our sweaty bodies meld together as we move from the bed to the floor until she's pressed against the wall and

I'm behind her naked body. My hands lay over hers on the wall as I slide out, slow and steady, then fill her back up. Her head drops back onto my shoulder and I suck at the thin skin of her neck.

"Cal," she groans when I fist her hair and pick up my pace.

My entire body fills up, ready to combust, and we release together.

Slowing my movements, until we're both standing still with me inside of her, it hits me that she said yes. It might not be for love, yet. But one day, Bella will love me the way a woman loves her husband. She will give me kids and I'll give her an heir to a billion-dollar fortune. They will never want for anything.

"So, we're getting married?" I smile through a kiss on her shoulder.

I pull out and Bella turns around to face me while my hands rest on her hips. "It seems I don't have much choice. I'll help you free yourself from Byron's chains, under one condition. You have to tell me everything. About your family, about my family, about Mrs. Webster. I need to know where Trent is. I don't like him, but I want to know he's not dead. I need you to tell me what you meant when you said Mark and Trent were the reason we weren't together."

I kiss her again and again, speaking against her mouth. "I'll tell you everything you need to know tomorrow. I have to take a short trip to the main island in the morning, and when I return, we will talk. Right now, you need sleep."

She nods in agreement.

I will tell her everything. *Tomorrow.*

That night, I fell asleep and slept through the night for the first time in eight years.

30

I ROLL over to my side and feel the crumple of paper under my cheek. My eyes blink open, and I realize I'm alone. Pulling the paper out from under me, I read it.

Last night was amazing and I look forward to many more nights with you. Breakfast is waiting in your room. When I return, we will talk, as promised. It's time to live! -Cal

A smile grows on my face as I clutch the paper to my chest. Last night was amazing. It felt like the first day of the rest of my life. I have no idea what's in store for me, but that's the beauty of it. I've always planned everything out perfectly and end up disappointed when things don't go my way. When Cal and I talk, he needs to know my family will still be a big part of my life. This marriage of convenience needs to benefit us both. Is that what it is? A convenience? I said yes to Cal because I want to help him. In some ways, I think I owe it to him. But I also said yes because I cannot imagine my life without him. I love Cal. I really do. This thing we have going on is unconventional at best, but it works for us and that's all that matters.

After lying in Cal's bed, thinking about the future for a good twenty minutes, I have no regrets as I get up and leave to go shower and have breakfast in my room.

Sometime today, I plan on apologizing to Peter for last night. I feel so bad for manipulating such a sweet person. He seems like the forgiving kind, so hopefully it won't change things between us. Peter has been good to me while I've been here, and I don't want that to change now.

As soon as I open the door to my room, I'm grinning from ear to ear. I walk to my bed where a tray is placed on top and run my finger over the stem of a single peony in a crystal vase.

I planned to take a shower first, but the rumble in my stomach has me lifting the lid of the platter and diving into a stack of pancakes, bacon, and fresh fruit.

All I need is some Netflix and this would be heaven. I make a mental note to tell Cal today that I want a television and the Wi-Fi password. If I'm going to be his wife, I'm not going to be treated like a prisoner.

One more bite and I move the tray to the side and get up to take a shower. A knock at the door has me turning around. I pull the door open and Peter is standing there.

The disturbed look on his face tells me he's upset about last night. I never put his key back and he has to know I stole it.

"Hi, Peter."

"Ms. Jenkins," he acknowledges me with a nod. "Mr. Ellis has given me strict instructions to escort you off the island immediately. You'll need to pack your things and meet me at the dock in ten minutes."

"Wha...what? Cal didn't say that." I'm so confused that I'm not even able to form a coherent sentence.

"Something has come up and I'll explain on the way. Please, hurry, Ms. Jenkins."

"Peter, if this is about last night, I'm sorry."

"Last night?"

"Tea in the sitting room? Your—"

"If anyone should apologize, it's me. I was more tired than I thought and it was rude of me to fall asleep in your company."

Huh? He doesn't know about the key or any of the events of last night? Peter thinks he fell asleep because he was tired.

Now I feel even more guilty, but if this isn't about last night, then why am I being forced off the island?

"No time to waste. I'll see you at the dock in ten minutes." He turns and heads down the hall.

I step out the door and holler behind him, "But, Peter. I don't want to leave."

He doesn't respond, just continues walking at a steady pace until he reaches the elevator.

"What the hell?" I grumble under my breath. Is Cal really letting me leave? Not just letting me, but making me?

I begged for this for weeks, but now that it's happening, I don't want to go. I want to stay and be with him. Something isn't right. There has to be an explanation.

Peter disappears into the elevator, so I go back to my room, wondering if I should do as I'm told and pack up my things or if I should just stay here and wait for Cal to return. Unless...unless Peter is taking me to meet Cal somewhere. That has to be it. He wants us both to leave the island.

After carefully deciding to pack my bag and follow instructions, I'm standing in the doorway of my room, staring into it. I hope we get to come back someday. This place has begun to feel like a home away from home. The thought of leaving and not returning has me fighting back tears.

One last look, and I'm closing the door behind me, dragging my suitcase down the hall to the elevator.

I make it to the ground level and see Peter waiting for me.

"Peter, please tell me what's going on," I say as I hurriedly drag my suitcase to where he stands.

He takes my suitcase and drags it behind him but doesn't say a word as I follow. There's a small boat waiting for us and I see it's Jeffrey, the same guy who brought me here.

"Take care, Ms. Jenkins. I hope to see you again soon, for Mr. Ellis's sake. He needs someone like you in his life." He presses a chaste kiss to my cheek and walks past me.

"You're not leaving with me? But where am I going? What happens next?" I chase after him, refusing to leave without knowing why I have to.

Peter stops, turns slowly, and places two hands on my shoulders. "You're in danger, Bella. Don't ask questions. Just go."

My eyes widen, chills cascading down my body. "Danger?"

He nods. "Mr. Ellis will keep you safe if you let him. So, please, go."

Peter disappears and I'm left as confused as ever while Jeffery lifts my suitcase on the boat. "Do you know what's going on?" I ask him.

He shakes his head. "I just do drop-offs and pickups, dear."

I feel like I just got here and now I'm leaving. I want to stay. I want to stay here with Cal. There's a pinch at my heart, a nagging and painful pinch that stays with me the entire ride to the main island. My fear of water doesn't even touch what I'm feeling inside. I'd swim back if I knew he'd be there waiting for me.

If I'm in danger, that must mean someone wants to hurt me. Or, what if someone wants to hurt Cal? Oh my God! And I just left without doing anything to help him. I have no way to contact him. No way to find him. All I have is his name, an island, and the number to the assistant who set me up with the job. That's all I know about the man I've falling in love with.

AFTER JEFFERY DOCKED and I was handed a ticket for the ferry, I ended up back where it all began. The parking lot of Falcon Ferry. I didn't go home to Hickory Knoll. There was nothing I could do from there. Instead, I took the first flight to New York and I'm walking up to Mark's apartment door, ready to find at least one of the answers I need.

With no call letting him know I was on my way, I came completely unannounced. I knock a few times before the door flies open.

"Bella? What's wrong?" he asks, likely noticing my red, puffy eyes from hours of crying.

"Can I come in?"

He steps to the side. "Of course."

Sheer exhaustion has me wanting to plop down on that white leather couch in the middle of the living room, but Mark and I aren't close. We don't invade each other's space. There's never been a solid friendship, hangouts with friends, or even small talk. Everything we did together was as a family and we sort of just existed together. He's not cruel, by any means. In fact, he's always been kind to me. Don't get me wrong, I love my brother, but he's always been a very standoffish person. I suppose we all deal with our past lives in our own ways.

"How's law school going?" I ask as I look around the small apartment.

Mark closes the door and enters the room, standing next to me. "Look, if you're here because you heard, let me start off by saying I planned to tell them."

I've got no idea what he's talking about and I'm sure the expression on my face says so.

"It's only been three months and I was just giving it some time until I got my fitness club up and running. Things are going slow—"

"Did you quit law school, Mark?"

"Yeah. Isn't that why… Why are you here, Bella?"

My hand falls from the handle of my suitcase and I'm unable to hold it together anymore. Tears start falling and I sniffle. "I found Callum."

His eyes perk up. "Callum, Callum?"

I nod. Saving time, I get straight to the point. "We

reconnected and things have been…well, weird, but that's beside the point. I need you to tell me what happened before we left between you, him, and Trent."

"Wait a minute. Does Trent know about this?"

I nod again. "He came to see me. I'm sure you'll hear all about it." And of course, he'll go and tell our parents and they'll sit me down for a talk about self-respect and making good choices. "Did you know Cal got in trouble that day?"

Mark runs his fingers through his hair and blows out air. "Damn, Bella. This all happened ages ago. I don't even remember." He walks over to a coffee pot on the counter and fills a mug in front of it. "Want some?"

"Yes, please." I'm not a big coffee drinker, but I could use some caffeine right about now.

Mark gets me a cup and we sit down at a small, round table. "So where'd you find him?"

"Ever heard of Ellis Empire?"

He shakes his no, and I'm not surprised.

"He owns a ritzy hotel chain. Inherited the company and billions from his late father."

"Damn, he made out well." Mark looks around his tiny living space. "If only we could all have that luck."

I don't tell him what Cal had to go through to get where he's at in life, but I don't need to. None of it matters. "I accepted a job and he ended up being my boss. Talk about a surprise."

"No kidding. That couldn't have been a coincidence."

"It wasn't." I take a sip of my coffee, burning the tip of my tongue. "While I was with him, he mentioned a couple different times how you and Trent were the reason for some things that happened. Obviously, you left Mrs. Webster's when I did, so I know it wasn't after the fact."

Mark is silent for a minute. He takes a few drinks of his coffee, taps his fingers to the mug, then finally says, "Trent would be pissed if he knew we were talking about this."

"Fuck Trent."

It seems I've caught him by surprise. "Aren't you two getting engaged?"

"No. I never told him yes and I was never going to. Trent and I are done."

"Wow," he nods, trying to read my expression, "so are you and Callum like a thing now?"

Ignoring his question, I get to the point. "Tell me what happened before we were adopted, Mark."

"Come on, Bella. You're putting me in a really shitty spot."

I don't want to play hardball, but I will. Pulling my phone out of the pocket of my hoodie, I hold it up. "Tell me now or I'll call Mom and Dad and tell them you quit law school."

Mark pushes his chair back and gets up, pacing the small space of the kitchen. He fidgets with his fingers, then stops at the chair he was in and rests his arms on the back of it. "It was all Trent's idea. We were out back following deer tracks late at night and saw Callum sneaking through the living room window into Trent's house. I made some snide remark about how I wouldn't have to deal with the asshole much longer because you and him would probably get picked and go off to live your best lives while I was stuck for another four years."

When he stops talking and begins fidgeting with his hands, I push for more. "Okay. What happened next?"

He looks up and continues, "We confronted him and he told us some bizarre story about how he was doing it for you. Trent knew Callum was always getting into trouble, so he had the grand idea to tell Mrs. Webster he broke into his house and stole a wad of cash from Mr. Beckham's safe. It was supposed to be a joke, but we also thought maybe it'd help my chance. Which it did."

My jaw drops. "So you lied?" I should have known someone stirred the pot and intentionally ratted him out.

"Yeah. Sort of. I mean, he did break in, but he didn't really take money. Trent went to his parents with the money *he* actually took and convinced them to go to Mrs. Webster. Sure enough, she punished him to his room for three days, making him miss out on the meeting."

I take a deep breath, trying to process all this. My heart hurts so bad for Cal. He didn't do anything wrong.

"Wait. What was the bizarre story? How was he doing it for me?"

His shoulders rise and he throws his hands out. "No idea. He said he needed to get something for you to impress 'your new parents.'" Mark laughs. "Even though they were never his parents and never will be. We didn't see anything in his hands, so he must've been hiding it."

"He never told me about that."

"Probably never got the chance. Two hours later, we were on our way to new and better things. Come on, Bella," his voice rises a few octaves, "don't sweat it. We have a good life—good parents. Leave the past where it belongs. Leave that loser where he belongs. Trent is your future. Go make things right with him."

I shake my head, getting angrier and angrier with each passing second. "First of all, I never want to see Trent again, let alone make things right with him. Second, Cal is the furthest thing from a loser. He is a man who is honest and loyal. Unlike you and Trent," I snarl, curling my lip before grabbing my bag and storming out.

I END up in a hotel about a block from Mark's apartment in the Upper East Side of NYC. I'm physically and emotionally drained and right now, I'm not sure I even have the strength to take a shower. I've cried, I've screamed, and I've dropped to my knees and begged for a sign of what I should do next.

Everyone in my life has been lying to me. Mark, Trent, Cal. The three men I thought I could trust. I have no close girlfriends, I have no cousins I grew up with, or grandparents I talk to. I have my mom and dad and those three guys, and that's it. But now, all I have is my parents.

Somehow, I manage to stay on my feet as I wash this horrendous day off me. I've been on a boat, a plane, and walked down the streets of the city, carrying my damn suitcase. I haven't eaten, I haven't slept, and I'm on the verge of throwing up from coughing through the tears so much.

My mind has gone over so many scenarios of what I should do and it's come down to the final two: go home or go back.

I finish cleaning up and crawl into bed, lying there for hours with my eyes wide open.

The next thing I know, I wake up and the sun is peeking through the blinds. My body jolts up when something outside the window catches my eye.

"No way," I mutter. My feet hit the floor and I walk over to the window. Pressing my hands to the ledge, I look at the sign directly in front of me. *Snake Pit Lounge and Bar.* It's not the name or the sign, it's the snake head looking back at me. With emerald green eyes and a challenging stare. Its tongue is out in a hiss and I realize, this is my sign.

I'm not giving up.

31

"THANK YOU, Jeffery. I promise, this stays between us."

"I trust you, dear. But, please be safe."

I give Jeffery a smile before getting off the boat and practically running up the path to the castle. It feels good to be back, and I'm anxious to see if Cal is here. I'm just as nervous as I was the first time I arrived on this island, but this time, my nerves are for good reason. I'm ready to tell him I love him. That, really, I never stopped. Our futures have been carved in stone since before we even met and this is the way it's meant to be. It was always him. It was always us.

Pulling open the door, I step inside the main entrance. "Cal," I call out. My feet don't stop moving as I go to the elevator. "Cal," I try one more time, just in case he's out back somewhere.

The elevator doors slide open and I step inside. It feels strange, but it also feels right.

With no hesitation, I go straight to Cal's room with the key I stole from Peter. The door unlocks and I shove the door open. "Cal, are you here?" I scope out the entire room, the bathroom, even the closet. But it's useless. He's not here.

Just as I'm about to leave and go search the rest of the place, I turn back around and go to the closet.

I pull out the bottom drawer of the dresser and stand on it, pushing myself up until I'm kneeling on the top. Stretching as far as I can, I grab Cal's memory box and jump down.

Carrying it over to his bed, I take the top off and sit down. That's when I see it. My heart squeezes as I begin to sob.

It's been here all along. If I'd only just looked.

I pull out the pink dress and it's exactly as I remember it. Baby pink with ruffles on the seam. Lace embroidery that hangs around the collar.

Cal broke into the Beckhams' house that night to steal this dress for me. He knew how much I loved it and he wanted me to have it for the meeting.

"Come on, Cal. You can't tell me you don't think she's beautiful."

He looks over at Lucy, who's jumping rope in her driveway while we sit on the porch sucking on homemade Kool-Aid popsicles. "She's not ugly but I wouldn't say she's beautiful."

"I want a dress like that. Maybe then I'll look pretty, too." I look at Cal's purple popsicle and my, almost gone, red one. "Trade?"

We switch popsicles, but I don't stop looking at Lucy.

"Bella, she might not be ugly, but she'll never be as pretty as you."

I look over and smile at Cal. "You're just being nice because you want your popsicle back."

"If I wanted it back, I'd take it. I happen to like red better, anyways."

Lucy stumbles a bit but gets back on track with her jumping. "Do you think they won't choose me because I don't have nice clothes like her?"

"No," he laughs, "people don't choose family because of their clothes. But, if it makes you feel better, I'll ask Lucy if you can borrow a dress."

"No!" I spit out, "that's so embarrassing. She'll know I'm poor."

"Bella." Cal levels with me. "We're orphans who live in a group home. She knows we're all poor."

"Please don't ask her. I'll just wear the dress I always wear. Maybe I can sew the hole in the armpit."

"I like that old dress better anyways. It's unique."

"Unique," I chuckle, "more like an antique."

Cal snatches back his popsicle and takes the last bite. "You know, maybe purple is better."

Hugging the dress tightly to my chest, all my emotions spill onto it. My eyes swell from crying so hard, and my throat aches. I have to find him. I have to tell him thank you. He lost out on the life he wanted because he was trying to make me happy. Trent and Mark set him up and he took the fall. Then I left and he was sentenced to misery.

With the dress in hand, I leave the box and the room, searching high and low, but Cal's nowhere to be found.

I go to the sixth floor to Peter's room, and when he doesn't answer, I use the key to go inside.

It's at this moment the world stands still. My heart stops beating, the tears stop falling, and I hold my breath before screaming at the top of my lungs, "Nooooo!"

Still clutching the dress, I snap out of the state of shock I'm in and hurry over to Peter's lifeless body, lying in a puddle of blood on the floor.

Maybe it's not too late. Maybe I can save him.

"Oh, Peter," I choke out as I reach down and place my fingers on his cold wrist. It's no use. He has no pulse.

Peter is dead.

I sit there next to him, crying for minutes before I finally get up to try and call for help, then it hits me. Someone did this. Peter didn't die of natural causes. The puddle of blood is enough proof that he was murdered. Whoever did it could still be here.

He was such a good man with such a big heart. Who would do this to him?

Pulling open the drawer to his nightstand, I get out the diary and go to his page of passcodes, hoping like hell the password for the Wi-Fi is there. I'm pretty sure I'm the only one left here and making a call to the water transport company is the only way I'm getting off this island.

"Dammit!" I slam the diary shut and go to put it back but stop. Instead, I lay it on top of Peter. "You're dancing with your Carolina now." I smile through the tears, then hurry out of the room to try and find someone to help me.

An hour later, I've searched every part of the castle and no one is here. I'm completely alone.

Somehow I have to get off this island.

If anything happened to Cal...no, I can't think like that. He's somewhere safe. He has to be.

My only option is to walk the property and try to somehow find cell phone service. It's a hopeless option because I tried for weeks to get service to no avail.

I go out back to the courtyard and hope washes over me when I hear someone talking. "Hello," I call out, "Cal, is that you?" Keeping on the path I'm on, I follow the sound of the voice I heard.

"Byron?" I say his name in question. "Why are you still here?"

He ends a call on his phone and sticks it into his pocket. "Hi, Bella. I wasn't expecting to see you." He seems calm, which leads me to believe he has no idea that Peter is dead in his room. "What's wrong? Why are you crying?"

"I need to use your phone. Peter...Peter is in his room. He's dead."

Byron's jaw drops. "What?"

"I said Peter is dead. Someone murdered him."

Byron retrieves his phone from his pocket and begins tapping into it. "That's ridiculous. I'm the only one here."

He's right. I've searched everywhere. Byron is the only person I've found. Paulina is gone. The guards are gone. Cal is gone.

But if he's here and Peter is dead...

I backstep a few times until I bump into the glass table on the patio. It tips over and the sound of the metal hitting the cement startles me. I don't take my eyes off Byron.

"Bella," he says, closing the space between us, "I didn't...you don't think it was me?"

I steady myself and take a step back for every step he comes forward. "How long have you been here? Where's Cal?"

His eyes widen and he suddenly wears a look of displeasure. "I just got here. I've been searching everywhere for Callum. He's missing, Bella."

My heart drops into my stomach. *No. He can't be.* "What do you mean he's missing?"

"No one has been able to reach him since yesterday morning when he left the island for a meeting. Peter got a call to send you away, so you were safe, but we've got no idea what's going on."

"Have you talked to the people he had a meeting with? Maybe he's still there?"

Byron shakes his head no. "That's the thing. We don't know who he met up with. I came in on my private boat to see if maybe he came back. Bella, if someone killed Peter, that means we need to leave, like right now." Byron wraps an arm around my shoulder and leads my hesitant body toward the entrance of the castle.

I shake uncontrollably as we walk to the front doors. "We have to find him, Byron. What if—"

Byron's phone buzzes in his pocket and he holds up a finger to me then pulls it out. I stop, listening intently as he takes the call.

"What? When? Where?" Byron looks at me as he speaks into the phone. "Shit." He rubs his hand over his forehead. "All right, keep me updated."

"We've gotta go." He steers me quickly down the path to the dock.

"Who was that? What happened?"

Byron swallows hard and there's a look of fear in his eyes. "They found a body. Apparently, it washed up at a public beach on Bradburn Isle."

"No!" I gasp, slapping a hand to my chest, "please tell me it wasn't him. Dammit, Byron. Tell me." I choke out the words that are barely audible.

"They haven't identified the body yet, which means you need to go home to your family where it's safe, and I'll call you if I hear anything."

I HAVEN'T STOPPED CRYING. Can't catch my breath. I can't even think as I ride in the back seat of my parents' car. They picked me up at the ferry docks after Byron had his captain give me a ride. We exchanged numbers and he promised he'd keep me updated if he hears anything.

So far, I haven't heard anything, but I haven't stopped staring at my phone, waiting for it to ring. I've even searched the news for reports on the body found, but so far, it's all hush-hush.

I refuse to believe it was Cal. He's out there some-where, and I will find him. I'll do whatever it takes because, as Peter once said, the heart wants what the heart wants. And my heart wants him.

Together.

Forever.

Until kingdom come.

EPILOGUE

ONE MONTH LATER

Bella

"DARLING," Mom says, peeking her head in my bedroom. "We're heading to Luciano's for pizza, would you like to join us?"

I close the book I was reading and set it down beside me. "No, thanks. You all enjoy."

Mom steps into the room, drawing closer to the bed. Each step has me wishing she'd turn around and walk out. I know she's worried about me, but nothing has changed. I'm still here, and he's still missing.

"Mark is only home for the holidays for a few more days. You already missed Christmas dinner. It would really be nice for us to all have dinner together before he goes back to New York." She sits on the edge of the bed and begins tracing her fingers over the cover of my book.

"I'm really not up for it. I'll try to see him before he leaves." It's a lie. The truth is, I'm still angry with Mark.

"Have you heard from Trent at all?"

I shake my head no. "Nope. And I hope I never do again."

"Mark said he's living in New York now, apparently your friend threatened his career if he ever came back to this state again."

"Good. And if I know that friend of mine, he'll hold true to his threat."

"Bella, honey," Mom says in an attempt to swaddle me like a baby. "It's time to let go. If he was out there somewhere and wanted to be with you, he would find a way."

Pinching my eyebrows together in frustration, I speak loud and clear, "He is out there, Mom! And we will find a way to be together."

I didn't tell my parents everything, but Trent told Mark about his visit to Cori Cove and everything that happened, then of course, Mark told our parents. I told them about Cal and our past and how we reconnected before he went missing.

They were anything but receptive after hearing what Cal did to Trent. In fact, they insisted I fix things with Trent. I know they just want to try and help and I love them for that, but sometimes, I wish they'd let me make my own choices.

She places a calming hand on my arm, but it does anything but soothe me. "Did you make it to therapy this morning?"

I shake my head and press my chin to my chest, fighting back the tears. "It doesn't help, so I'm not going anymore."

"I wish you'd give it more time. I think it could help."

Mark comes into the room, interrupting us and, for

once, I'm happy to see him just so this conversation with my mom can end.

"Hey, Ma. Do you mind if I talk to Bella for a minute?"

She nods, then presses a kiss to my forehead. "I love you, honey, and I'm always here for you." With that, she leaves Mark and me alone.

Mark presses his lips together and rubs his fists as he walks over, avoiding eye contact. "Look. I know you're pissed about the whole Callum thing from twelve years ago, but we were kids and made a stupid mistake."

"If that's your apology, then you can shove it up your ass and leave my room."

His eyebrows hit his forehead, probably surprised that I grew a bit of a backbone while I've been gone.

"He didn't suffer. He's a billionaire who has everything anyone could possibly want."

"Everything except for a family," I snarl at him in disgust. He doesn't know Cal. No one does. "Cal was severely abused, Mark. His mind was tortured and he's been through things he can never come back from. If you and Trent would have just left everything alone…"

"Then he'd be here and I'd be the one missing."

I never thought of it that way. If Cal would have gotten adopted with me, then Mark would have likely ended up with the Ellis family.

"That's not what I meant."

"We can't change the past. All we can do is try to make better choices in the future. I'm sorry I fucked things up for you two. But I'm not sorry I got you as a sister."

He's got a point. We can't change the past. Not mine, not his, not Cal's. All we can do is move forward.

"Tell Mom I'll meet you guys at Luciano's for dinner."

Mark smiles and I do the same.

I smile while I internally cry. My heart screams for Cal. No matter how much time passes, I will never get over him. Even if he's never found, I will die loving him.

I reach under my bed and pull out the box of letters I wrote him during all the years we were apart. Inside is the dress he stole for me. On top is the master key to the castle.

Byron never called me to give me an update on the body, and when I went to call him, the line was disconnected. There was never a news report done about the body being found, but I tried like hell to get answers. In fact, I lost sleep and ten pounds because I tried so hard. I called the number to his assistant who set me up with the job and left dozens of messages with no return call. I went to the police on the main island, the mortician, watched the obituaries, and did countless searches. In the end, I never got answers, but I still don't believe it was Cal. I can feel him. He's out there, and he's alive. My heart would know if he was gone.

I look down at the priceless items and draw in a deep breath. "I'll find you. One day, I will find you."

Pulling myself together, I throw on a pair of jeans and a tee shirt and head downstairs. Everyone has left, so I take my time getting out the door.

When I go into the kitchen, I notice a stack of my mail sitting on the counter.

The first couple aren't of any importance. One from a local college, the other an unpaid credit card bill. It's the third one that catches my eye. It's from Carnegie Hall.

The odd thing is, it's not addressed to Isabella Jenkins; it's addressed to Bella Jenkins.

Wasting no time, I tear the top of the envelope off and pull out the letter.

Dear Bella Jenkins,

Thank you for your interest in performing at Carnegie Hall. We've received a sample of the song you sent in two weeks ago and we'd love to invite you to perform on Saturday, January 1st, 2022, in a solo symphony, performing *Our Song*.

I don't even continue reading at this point.

I never sent them a sample. I've never even recorded "Our Song." In fact, I've never even told anyone about it. Cal is the only one who knows the title.

The letter says they received the sample two weeks ago.

Cal did this.

This means...Cal is alive.

Read book two, Her Broken Pieces!

PART II

HER BROKEN PIECES

PROLOGUE

FOURTEEN YEARS OLD

FROM THE MOMENT I was born, I was destined to be alone. Found behind a dumpster in an alley at the backside of a bar. My birth mom left me there only hours after having me. From what I've heard, the owner of the bar found me wrapped in a dingy towel covered in blood, with my umbilical cord still intact.

I was told I didn't even cry. Just looked up at the bearded fella and stared at him as if I knew my battle against the world had begun. At least, that's what I took from the story.

I was a loner through and through. Didn't care to please anyone. Never tried.

Until I met her.

Isabella, or Bella as we all call her. She's the only reason I ever smile unless I'm getting kicks for screwing with someone. That can be pretty fun. More so than not, my smiles are accredited to her.

She's my best friend, my only friend. The only one I need or even want.

Which is exactly why I need to repay her for all the smiles she's given me. Tomorrow we're getting adopted together and our lives are about to begin. Public schools, dances, sports—we're doing it all—together.

Layla, one of the foster girls here, pops her head in the door of my bedroom as I slip on my hoodie. "Where ya going?"

I grab my coat off my bed pole and throw it on. "Gotta take care of something. Cover for me if the old hag comes looking for me?" I give her a pat on the back and leave my room before she even has a chance to respond.

Looking right then left, I make sure the coast is clear before jogging down the staircase and out the front door. The sun hasn't risen, but the streetlamps give enough light for me to see where I'm going.

There's about a foot of snow and my sneakers sink right into it, filling my socks with the cold shit. I don't stop hurdling over the mounds until my back is pressed against the siding of the Beckhams' house. They should all be at evening mass, but regardless, I hold my breath to make sure I don't hear anyone walking around inside.

When I'm sure it's safe to enter, I go to pull open the door beside me to the garage, but it's locked.

A locked door isn't stopping me from getting inside. I round the house and try to push up the living room window. It sticks from the ice building around it, but eventually budges and slides up.

I punch out the screen, fling my legs over the frame

and climb in, poking my head out to look around the yard. Coast is still clear.

Once I'm inside, I stomp my feet on the clean white carpet to get the excess snow off, not caring that I left footprints on my way. It'll snow more and cover them up —I hope.

The house smells like fresh baked banana bread. I draw in a deep breath letting the scent linger. The Beckhams' house always smells like sweet treats and home. Anyone would kill to have what Trent and Lucy have. A mom and a dad who love you. Separate bedrooms, and television whenever you want it.

I've only been in this house a couple times, and it was never because I was invited. One night when the family was on vacation, I came here after Mrs. Webster, my foster parent, had gone to bed, and I ate all the Beckhams' snacks and watched three episodes of *Dexter*.

The next night, I brought Bella with me, and she played dress-up in Lucy's closet.

That's how I know which one I need to get. I'll never forget the sparkle in her eyes when she put on that pink dress. It's like she escaped to another world in just those few short minutes. Staring at herself in the mirror and pretending that this was her life. She was happy, and I swore I'd do anything to make that smile permanent.

I find myself grinning at the memory as I go into Lucy's bedroom. Trent's little sister really does have it all. Probably even more than Trent. She's spoiled, and I wish I could say she wasn't a brat, but she definitely is. Bella doesn't see that side of her, though. All she sees is everything she wants that Lucy has—mainly the family and love.

Shuffling through all the dresses, I find the pink one and pluck it off the hanger. When I hear footsteps coming from somewhere in the house, I immediately ball it up and stuff it under my coat then zip it up.

I'm not sure who it could be, but I need to get the hell out of here before I'm caught. The last thing I need is for a member of this family to contact Mrs. Webster and tell her I broke into their house—again.

With my head poked out the door, I listen intently, looking both ways. When I don't see or hear anything, I head back the way I came.

As soon as I reach the staircase, I realize I'm screwed. Though, I'm actually sort of relieved it's not Mr. or Mrs. Beckham.

"Well, well, well. What do we have here?" Trent asks, alongside Mark.

"Look, guys," I begin my descent down the stairs, brushing this off like it's no big deal, "just forget you ever saw me and I'll owe you both one."

Trent shares a look with Mark. "Oh yeah? One what? From what I hear, you might be getting outta that orphanage soon. Not that I believe anyone would want a loser like you."

"It's not an orphanage," I spit out defensively. I hate when anyone calls it that. It makes feeling like an orphan all the more real. I reach the bottom of the stairs, standing beside them. "I'll tell ya what. Twenty years from now when you losers need an alibi, give me a call. I've got you covered." I push past them, hoping they'll let this go.

Mark grabs ahold of my arm, ruffling my jacket. "What'd ya got under there?" His eyes wear his surprise. "Are you stealing something from the Beckhams?"

"No!" I huff. "It's just…none of your damn business." I jerk away from him.

Trent crosses his arms over his chest, puffing it out like some sort of superhero who has all the power. "Tell us what it is and maybe, just maybe, we'll let you live to see another day."

I don't dare tell them what it is. They'll ridicule me to no end. Call me pussy-whipped. Claim I'm in love with the girl, but it's also my best shot. "It's just something for Bella. She needed it."

Trent, being the asshole that he is, begins laughing. "What? Did she start her period or something?"

Fucking moron.

Mark just stands by idly, allowing Trent to do all the bashing. Mark is a follower, through and through.

"No. Gross," I snarl. "Don't worry about what it is."

They share another look, and Mark nods in agreement. "All right. We can let this go, but like you said, you owe us one."

I don't even say another word. I just haul ass out while I've got the chance. I'm not sure if I can trust those guys, but right now, I have no choice. I've gotta go wake Bella up before our future parents arrive. I swear, the girl would sleep all day if she could.

Once I'm back at the house, it's like I never left: still quiet, and Mrs. Webster is nowhere to be seen.

I go straight to the attic and pull the dress out of my jacket and stuff it in the box where I keep all my prized possessions—not that I have many. There are a couple things I'd like to keep with me no matter where I go. I shuffle through a few of my belongings. One in particular —a picture of all the neighborhood kids at the annual block party the Beckhams have. I could cut everyone else out and not miss them one bit. I keep it because it's the only picture I have of Bella and me.

"Callum!" I hear Mrs. Webster shout. The tone in her voice is enough to alert me that she's not happy. Not that she is often, but she sounds pretty fired up.

I close the box back up and kick it under the old armoire closet, unsure how long I was staring into the black hole of memories.

I slip off my jacket and toss it aside. It lands among some dirty books, and I head out of the room. Don't want to keep the queen waiting. God knows she already hates me enough.

I'm tucking my shirt in when I spot her walking out of my room. She closes the door with a loud thud and strolls toward where I stand at the opposite end of the hall.

"You just couldn't help yourself, could you?" Her jaw clenches, and she reaches out, grabbing my ear and pulling. "Breaking into the Beckhams' house and stealing. Don't you know this behavior will keep you here until you're eighteen years old?"

"Son of a bitch!" I spit out, immediately regretting my choice of words.

Mrs. Webster drags me to my room, by the ear, and opens the door then shoves me inside. "You've just lost your chance at getting a family today. Do not exit this room until you're called for breakfast."

"Wait. No!" I shout as the door slams shut.

Disregarding my punishment, I open it back up. "Mrs. Webster, I didn't steal anything." It's a lie, but it was only a dress. Who cares about a measly old dress?

"That's not what Trent Beckham says. Claims you stole money from Mr. Beckham's safe. Don't try to deny it, Callum. I saw the picture as proof that you were in that house minutes ago."

She stomps off in a fit of rage and I'm almost thankful because I don't like dealing with the old hag when she's acting like a royal bitch.

One thing is for certain, if I lose my place in this adoption, those boys will live to regret what they did to me. It's like I've always said, "Trust is priceless, but once you lose it, you are useless."

1

MY NERVES ARE OFFICIALLY SHOT. I'm holding the weight of a thousand bricks on my chest, and my heels feel like they are on the verge of snapping in half. It would be just my luck. They break and send me crashing down on the stage before I can even perform.

I grip the banister beside me, squeezing it so tight that the braided embellishment imprints on my skin.

I'm not sure if I'm losing my mind in the process of trying to find Cal, but I've noticed things lately. Or a person, rather. One man in particular that I'm almost positive has been following me since I arrived in the city this morning. The first time I saw him was when I checked in to my hotel. He stood back idly watching me over his phone. If he was trying to be inconspicuous, he failed.

The second time was when I arrived here at the hall. He was walking casually with his head held low, failing to be discreet once again.

It doesn't scare me, though; I'm almost positive Cal has sent him, or them, if there are more.

And now, I've managed to spot him in the crowd. Out of hundreds of people, there he is. Same guy with the same *Men in Black* suit. Slicked-back, black hair and dark eyes.

I'll know who he is soon enough.

There are so many people out there. At least two hundred, all expecting me to perform like it's the most natural thing in the world.

I pinch my eyes shut, thinking that maybe if I do it long enough, the entire crowd will be gone when I open them.

Nope. Still there.

It's been years since I've played the piano for an audience—well, aside from the time Cal requested I play for him nude. But it was only him and, oddly enough, I felt at ease.

This is by far the largest audience I've ever faced and I'm not exactly thrilled to perform. Playing the piano is a passion I have behind closed doors. During high school, I dabbled in some musicals, but it wasn't the same as playing from my heart. I'm not sure that I'll be able to give this crowd what they want.

Nonetheless, I'm here. The only reason because I know damn well Cal sent my audition tape of *Our Song* to Carnegie Hall. It wasn't actually an audition. In fact, he must've recorded me playing for him during my stay at Cori Cove. There is no other way that anyone would know about this piece, unless it came from him.

Now I'm standing behind this cracked door, ready to

make my way across the stage, wearing a teal gown similar to the one I wore that night I played for Cal. My caramel-colored hair in tiny little ringlets bounce off my shoulders as I take my first ungraceful step. Palms sweating, thighs sticking together, and breath being held as everyone watches me.

There are rows of people. Some on the ground level, some on the second floor, and more on the upper tier. The lighting dims over the crowd, and all that's left is a white beam following me as I make my way to the piano.

Another step. And another.

God, please don't let me fall.

My heels clank against the hardwood floor, the echo reverberating through my entire body.

Everyone begins clapping, and it's during that melancholic sound that I'm offered a sense of peace. A smile tugs at my lips, and before I know it, I'm at the piano. I place one hand on the hood and tuck the other around my waist as I bow before them.

The clapping subsides and I take a seat at the stool, sliding it in until my elbows are bent at a ninety-degree angle. My trembling fingers hover over the keys and I fill my lungs before beginning.

As soon as the first note fills the empty space around me on the stage, Cal enters my mind.

That first smile when I saw him at the top of the stairs at The Webster House. It was a cheesy grin and I knew at that moment that boy was nothing but trouble. Once my social worker left and I witnessed him filling his pockets with snacks, when he didn't think anyone was watching, I knew I wanted to be part of that mischief.

My heart cries for him. My soul bleeds for him. Each night apart has been an agony worse than the years we spent apart the first time I left him. There are times I cry myself to sleep, wishing I'd never known him at all, because then I wouldn't know what missing him feels like.

In a fluid motion, I hit the chorus. Pounding away at the keys, pouring my heart into the piece I wrote for him.

When I wrote it, it was meant to radiate positive energy. Now when I play, it's heartbreaking. I see two soulmates living a life where they are unwanted by others. Brought together during hard times and torn apart just to test the depths of their love. Only to be reunited and tested again because life is cruel like that. So very cruel.

It's like the crowd has disappeared, and it's just me. Back at The Webster House. An eleven-year-old orphan, gyrating my fingers across the keys as I search for myself in each note I hit.

Tears prick the corners of my eyes. It's impossible not to get emotional. Something this deep is meant to make you feel. As much as I don't want to, it's necessary to convey the passion as I play.

Near the end of the song, my heart gallops in my chest in anticipation of the crowd's reaction.

Seconds later, I end it on the final note and rest my hands in my lap. My eyes close briefly before I slide the stool back. To my surprise, the crowd erupts in a burst of applause. A smile grows on my face. I'm not sure if I'm humbled or surprised.

I feel empowered. Overjoyed and proud. Really

fucking proud. I did it. I am the reason for the chants and whistles.

I take a bow, and as I come up, I skim the crowd. I'm not sure anything could bring me down from this high. What's even better is that I can feel him watching me. He's here. I just know it.

Now, I have to find him.

I'm heading back to the door of the sound room where I entered the stage from, but my movements stop before I reach it. I'm frozen in place—stunned at the familiar face before me.

"Byron?" I mutter, feeling the prominent crease in my forehead. Why is he here?

Once my head unfogs slightly, I continue to cross the stage in his direction. "What...what are you doing here? Did Cal send you?"

Byron places a hand on the small of my back, motioning me inside the room. "That was amazing, Bella. Even better than the recording I heard."

"Cut the bullshit, Byron. What's going on? Where's Cal?"

"Cal?" He laughs. "What makes you think Cal is here?"

My heart sinks into my stomach, deeply and painfully. "You mean, he's not? Then—"

"Cal's gone, Bella. On the verge of being presumed dead. Why the hell would you think he was here?"

My brows perk, and a moment of hope washes through me. I'm confident Byron will feel the same way, once he hears what I'm about to say. "No. He's here some-where. He's not dead, Byron."

His puzzled look leads me to believe he's skeptical, so I

continue, "Cal is the only one who knew about that song. He had to have recorded me playing it for him during my stay at Cori Cove. He's the one who sent the tape. He's alive."

"Great performance, Isabella," Paul, the booking manager, says. "Your unease was for nothing." He smiles kindly, and while I know I should thank him for everything—the pep talk an hour ago, the opportunity—all I can focus on is Cal.

"Thank you, Paul. It was a pleasure to have had this opportunity." I grab Byron by the arm and pull him away, probably a little too rudely, so we're able to talk in private.

Once we're away from all the backstage people, I look up at him. "Please Byron, tell me you don't really think he's dead? How can you?" I wave my arms around. "I'm here because he brought me here."

It's the only reason I came. Sure, playing at this place is a dream, but I would have likely torn up the invitation and never given it a second thought had it not been for the song chosen.

Byron scrunches his shoulders, his expression loaded with sorrow that I have the urge to smack away as I scream that he's wrong! "Sorry, Bella. No one has seen or heard from Callum since he went missing. If he were alive, I have no doubt that you'd be the first to know. He loved you."

Tears prick the corners of my eyes, but I ward them off. "Then who would have…" I take a few steps back, bumping into some control panels. "It was you, wasn't it? You sent the audition?"

"It was a beautiful piece. I thought you deserved recognition for your talent."

No! "No! It couldn't have been. How...how did you get it? Why would you..."

I can't even speak, unable to form a coherent sentence. For the last week, I've had hope. Celebrating the holidays, knowing I was going to see Cal soon.

My legs feel weak. There's a chair to my left, so I grab it and pull it over, then sit down.

"I went back to Cori Cove to search for answers as to where Callum might be. While I was going through some of his belongings—"

My eyes snap to him. "You went through his things?"

"I'm his attorney, Bella, and also his friend. Yes, I went through his things...to try and help him. I found a recorder and hit Play. It was the same song I heard playing the night I escorted you to the ballroom to meet him."

"And you just took it upon yourself to interfere with my life and send in *my* recording?"

"Well," Byron chuckles unnervingly, "if we're being technical here, it was Callum's, which, in turn, makes it mine, considering I am the rightful beneficiary of his estate."

Chewing on my bottom lip, I glower at him. His stance over me feels domineering, and I'm not in the mood for it. "Well, Byron," I emphasize as I stand up, "you being the beneficiary to his estate does not mean you get to control me or my life. In fact, no one does. Not even Callum. So thanks for setting all this up. But it's over now and you can go home."

Disappointed doesn't even begin to explain how I feel. I'm gutted. Downright heartbroken.

It was him all this time. It was never Cal.

Spinning on my heels, I begin unstrapping the left one as I walk, yanking it off my foot. Then the other, until I'm padding barefoot to the dressing room.

Fortunately, Byron doesn't follow me in, so I close the door and chuck my shoes in a corner, having no interest in bringing those damn things home with me. I can't believe I ever wanted to own all the dresses and shoes in the world. I had princess dreams as a child, but as I get older, dreams fade and reality slaps you in the face.

As I'm getting dressed, there's a knock at the door. I quickly finish by stepping into a pair of gray sweats and throwing on a black crewneck sweatshirt, then step into my, already laced-up, tennis shoes.

It's probably Byron. I can't imagine he brought me all this way just so I could play a song and leave. I don't like the guy much. Not only did Cal warn me before he went missing that Byron was up to no good, I'm also pretty sure he was only Cal's friend for his money. I shouldn't speculate, because I don't know much about their working relationship or friendship, but I took notice of the small things he did to piss Cal off.

"One moment, please," I holler as I roll up my dress and stuff it into a duffle bag.

With my bag and purse flung over my shoulder, I open the door, and sure enough, there he is. One arm pressed to the frame, a smirk on his face.

"I'm sorry," he says with remorse in his tone. "We got off on the wrong foot. Can we start again?"

"There's nothing to start, or finish, Byron. Please move. I have a warm bed at a nice hotel waiting for me." When he just stands there, gawking, I tip my head to his arm. "Do you mind?"

"Oh, right." He drops his arm and steps aside.

I go out and begin down the hall as he walks at my side, so I say, "I know he's alive. You can believe whatever you want, but he's out there, and I will find him."

"I've got no doubt that you will." I catch his glance in my peripheral. "Assuming he is alive and all."

My palms press to the exit door and I step into the darkness of the parking lot. Snow falls softly to the ground but melts before accumulating. It's cold here in New York City, but it's no different from home in Rhode Island.

I click the remote start on my car, but something stops me from walking. None of this makes any sense to me. I look at him, shivering under the lamppost as people pass by in the parking lot. "Why did you come here, Byron?"

Byron stuffs his hands in the pocket of his black trench coat, snow sprinkling on his sandy blond hair. "Came to watch you play."

"But why? We're not friends. Hell, we barely even know one another. Why would you go through all this trouble?"

"I made him a promise, Bella. A promise to make sure you are happy and safe, if anything should ever happen to him. I'm a man of my word, so here I am."

"Cal was never confirmed dead. A body wasn't found. As far as legalities go, he's still alive. Meaning, you're furloughed from your promise to him. I can take care of myself." I keep walking to my car, and of course, he's still here.

All I want is to go back to my hotel, get a good night's sleep, and go home tomorrow and continue my quest to find Cal. I don't give a damn what Byron or anyone says, he's alive. I can feel it. Cal and I are soulmates, and I'd know if he were gone.

"One drink," Byron says as I pull open my car door.

"Excuse me?"

"It's New Year's Day. Have a drink with me. We can talk about your theories on where he might be. I can't shake the feeling that someone put a hit on him. Especially after that body was pulled from the bay and the identity was never shared."

"It wasn't him," I spit out on impulse. I just know it wasn't.

This might be a good chance to find out if Byron has been searching for Cal. It is New Year's Day and there's no harm in one drink. Even if Cal's warning is true—that Byron can't be trusted—it's a public place. He can't hurt me.

I toss my bag inside, keeping my purse on my shoulder, then close my door. "One drink."

2

WE END up in a hole-in-the-wall bar about a block from the hall. Driving in the city is a bitch and I have no intention of doing so when I don't have to, so we walked. A very awkward, quiet walk. Now that we're inside, I almost think I'd prefer that over the blaring music and loud chatter of the drunks.

It is a holiday, so I should have expected it. This isn't my scene, though. Not anymore. I prefer to live under the radar in my own little bubble. For a while, I floated outside of it, and it was freeing and eye-opening, but in the end, I crawled back in with a broken heart. Now I never want to leave it again. *It* being home. My hometown, my family. Should've never left in the first place. If I could go back and live my life with just the childhood memories of Cal, instead of adding the ones we made during my stay at Cori Cove, I would. Maybe then it wouldn't hurt so badly.

Byron manages to find us a small, empty, round table

at the back of the bar. It's covered in a sticky liquid and breadcrumbs, so I avoid touching anything but the chair.

Byron places a hand over mine, and I take a step back, letting it fall to his side. "I'll get the waitress to clean this up and get us some drinks at the bar." He must've noticed my turned-up nose at the grotesque table. "What'll you be having?"

"Dry martini, please." I sit down and take my phone out of the front pocket of my purse and begin scrolling through it like I actually have anything to read.

A few minutes later, Byron returns, and I put my phone away and take my drink from him. The first sip feels nice. I relish in the burn as it slides down my throat, already relieving some of my stress.

With a draft beer in hand, Byron sits down across from me. He takes a sip, then licks the foam from his lips. "So, Bella. Tell me what makes you think Callum is alive."

"No, Byron. How about you tell me why you think he's not?"

"Easy. If he were, he'd have come for you. Callum spent most of his life pining over you. Exacting his revenge and planning your," he points a sharp finger," future. There's no way he'd just let you go after everything he did to get you back."

"Or maybe this was part of his plan all along. Capture me, keep me long enough to make me fall in love with him, then push me away. It's actually a solid act of revenge, if you ask me." I take another drink as the words I just said replay in my mind. I never even thought of that until now. Talking about it has me considering different scenarios and what I just said is very possible. I tip my glass back, taking down half the contents.

No. He wouldn't do that. Would he?

"Doubtful. Callum doesn't play games like that. He wanted you, therefore, if he's alive, he will be coming for you. Watch and see."

My brows rise. "I guess I will." I finish off my drink, already thirsty for another. My fingers dig into the bottom of the glass and I pull out the toothpick and take the olive off with my teeth.

Byron searches the crowded space. "Where the hell is that waitress?"

"I don't know, but when you find her, tell her I need another one of these." I hold up my glass, then set it on the table, already feeling a little woozy from drinking it so quickly.

Byron finishes off his beer in one big gulp. "The service here is fucking ridiculous. I'll be right back."

I nod, bored and ready to drink away my sorrows before passing out in my hotel bed.

Once again, I pull my phone out and look at nothing as I wait for him to return.

A guy passes by the table, gives me a double take while I resume doing nothing on my phone. When I glance up, I see that he's standing right in front of me. I'm not really in the mood for small talk, but I'm also not a total bitch, so I say, "Hi."

He leans forward, hands pressing into the goo on the table. I don't even tell him because he's going to figure it out in two seconds when I shoot him down and send him on his way. "Sorry, I just had to ask why a pretty girl like you is sitting here all by herself?"

"Actually, I'm not alone."

"Hmm," the guy looks around, "I don't see anyone coming for you. Maybe you should let me buy you a drink."

I avoid eye contact and look down at my phone in my hand. "I'm good. Thanks."

"Oh, come on. No one should be alone on New Year's."

Getting frustrated, I shut my phone off and drop it into my purse. "Listen, asshole, I told you I'm here with someone, so if you wouldn't mind backing up and leaving me alone, I'd appreciate it."

"Wow. Someone's a feisty thing. I happen to like feistiness."

I reach into my purse, clenching my pepper spray, ready to use it if need be. "Get lost, creep."

His lip tugs up in a cocky grin and he leans in, invading my personal space. I crane my neck at the repulsive smell of ash and stale beer rolling out of his wretched mouth. When he wraps an arm around my neck, I lift my arms up between us; I'm able to shove him back and he stumbles into a table, knocking down another guy's drink.

"You bitch!" he howls. He comes charging toward me, but I'm ready for him. Another guy comes into view and tries to pull him back while shouting profanities, but I cock my fist back and lay it right on his nose. Except, it's not him. I accidentally punch the guy trying to help. The familiarity throws me off guard. I've seen him before.

"I'm…I'm so sorry," I say. Blood streams down his face, and I give my hand a shake, working out the kink in my knuckles.

Byron comes out of nowhere, grabbing me by the hand and pulling me away. "Come on," he says, "let's get out of here before you get your ass arrested."

"That poor guy. He was trying to help and I punched him by accident." I look over my shoulder, realizing it's the same guy who's been watching me.

"He'll be fine. Pick up your pace." Byron begins walking faster, as if he really believes I'll get arrested.

Once we're away from the crowd, he lets go and holds the door open for me. The cool, fresh air hits my face, and I take a deep breath before I burst out laughing. "I can't believe I just did that." I'm still shaking my hand. There's a bite of pain, but my adrenaline is pumping.

"Damn, girl. That was quite the punch. Maybe you should take up boxing."

"Yeah. Maybe it would help to alleviate some of this stress." I look over my shoulder, though we are already halfway back to the performance hall. "Who was that guy?"

Byron glances over his shoulder. "What guy?"

"The one I hit. I've seen him before."

He shrugs his shoulders, without a clue as to what I'm talking about. "No idea."

We walk down the snow-dusted sidewalk, passing by the same stores we did only thirty minutes ago. Though, they look different—blurry almost. I find myself staggering, and Byron places an arm around my waist. "You okay?" he asks.

I look down at the space between us, hoping he drops his hand before I have to move it for him. When I look back up and he catches the scowl on my face, he lets go.

"Hey. If he is out there, we'll get him back. Don't worry."

Just hearing him say that offers me a sense of calm. Byron was so skeptical at the hall and I was sure he was going to try and convince me that Cal is dead. Now, my hope is slowly returning.

"He is. And we will."

We reach my car and I struggle to get my keys out of my purse. My head feels like it's spinning, and I can't focus my eyes. "Sorry the night was cut short, but I really should get back to my hotel. I'm not feeling so good."

"You okay? Maybe you should let me drive your car to your hotel. I took an Uber anyway."

I grab my stomach, suddenly feeling nauseous. My head feels like it holds the weight of a bowling ball and it's a struggle to balance it on my neck. "Umm. Yeah. That might be a good idea. I'm at The Veranda. Up on Seventh Street."

"Really?" he says, surprised. "That's where I'm staying. How bizarre." His hands fly up. "It's fate."

Fate. It's the word Callum used when we reunited. He said it was fate, but I soon learned it was orchestrated.

Much like then, I highly doubt fate has anything to do with this encounter with Byron or the fact that he's staying at the same hotel I am.

I'VE BEEN SO closed off the past few weeks, and it was nice to get out after my performance. Even if it was just for a half hour that ended with swollen knuckles.

"Penny for your thoughts?" Byron says from the driver's seat.

My fingertips dig into my temples, massaging them and trying to alleviate this strange feeling in my head. "Save your penny. I wanna know about you and Cal. How did this whole working relationship turn into a friendship?"

Byron glances at me, one hand on the steering wheel and the other in his lap. "Well, let's see. I worked for the former Mr. Ellis as his attorney. He and I put our heads together and came up with some ideas that would really make Ellis Empire stand out against our competitors."

I look over at him and notice the cheeky grin on his face. My eyes sway from him to the road. "Wait. Are you talking about the sex club? Were you part of that addition to the hotels?"

Byron shrugs sheepishly. "I might've had a thing or two to do with it. The club was already established at one of Ellis Empire's biggest resorts in Europe. It was doing exceptionally well, so Vincent and I decided to expand to the U.S. resorts. We had a partnership that continued even after his death. Only now, that partnership is with Callum." I nod, listening intently and watching the road as he continues, "Callum was never a big fan of the clubs. Thought the resorts would do fine without them. I beg to differ. We draw in men from all over the world who have an insatiable need for…"

"Sex," I spit out. "You can say it. I'm not a child, Byron. I know exactly what happens in those clubs."

"Oh yeah? Callum filled you in, did he?"

"He didn't have to. I snuck down there one night and saw it with my own two eyes. Actually, I saw you." I look over at him, expecting him to look humiliated, but instead, he smirks.

"Did you like what you saw?"

"What?" I gasp, picking my jaw up from my lap. Is he serious right now?

"It's a simple question. Did you like what you saw?"

"No! Absolutely not. I was…disgusted." It's partially a lie. I was intrigued. Okay, I was highly turned on, but not by Byron. I find him to be a good-looking guy, but he's also somewhat of a creep to me.

Byron chuckles. "It's nothing to be ashamed of if you did like watching. You'd be surprised at how many people enjoy that sort of thing."

There is no way in hell I'm admitting to Byron, of all people, that part of me did enjoy watching. We're way off topic here, though. "Back to our original conversation. Yes, I know all about the clubs."

"Right. So the clubs are part of my partnership with Callum."

"And the fact that you know he killed Mr. Ellis?" I look to my left and notice the stunned look on Byron's face.

"Wow. Is there anything he didn't tell you?"

Byron pulls into an empty parking space, and suddenly I'm feeling worse. Barely able to keep my eyes open, they slowly close as my head sways back and forth.

Byron reaches over and grips my chin, forcing me to

look at him. I don't even have the strength to ask what he's doing. "You know, Bella, too much knowledge can get a pretty girl like you in trouble."

My heart drops into my stomach, pulse racing as Byron's expression shifts to one of mischief. The look on his face is formidable. "What?" I managed to choke out.

His hand reaches out like a claw, fingers spread wide as he grabs me by the throat. I squirm, trying to free myself from his clutches, but he only tightens his hold as his fingertips dig into the thin flesh of my neck.

I'm not able to do a damn thing to stop him. I feel so weak. I'm so tired. So helpless.

"By...Byron," I sputter as he chokes the life out of me.

This is it.

This is how I die.

3

CUFFED. Tied. Shackled. My entire body is bound to this bed. Sprawled out like an X, with each bedpost holding one of my limbs.

This has to be a nightmare.

I close my eyes, only to open them again, finding myself in the same position, wearing the same clothes I put on when I left the hall last night.

My head lifts, trying to get a look at my surroundings.

I've been here before.

I'm in the basement on Cori Cove. The island where it all began. And Byron brought me here. But why?

"Help! Somebody, help me!" The words scratch at my throat like a sharp razor blade.

I'm thirsty. So damn thirsty. My entire neck feels swollen and these thick metal cuffs are digging into my wrists. I wriggle, trying to loosen something, anything, but it's no use. He did this with the intention of keeping me in place.

I rest my head back, tears sliding down my cheeks and falling onto the red satin pillowcase.

I'm at The Grotto, but this time, I'm not watching anyone. I have no doubt someone is watching me, and that someone is most definitely Byron. There's a camera on the ceiling pointed directly at me.

"I hate you." I clench my teeth and hiss the words knowing he hears me. "When I get off this bed, I will kill you."

My body jolts when a door opens then closes. Footsteps drudge in my direction, coming closer and closer as my heart beats faster and faster with each step.

Byron comes into view, wearing different clothes than when I last saw him. He's got on a pair of gray slacks and a white dress shirt. He adjusts the buttons on one of the sleeves and rolls it up, then does the same to the other. "Good morning, Bella. Welcome back to Cori Cove."

"You tricked me, you son of a bitch." I was feeling sick last night. Far too woozy for one drink. "You drugged me, didn't you?" He drugged me, then choked me out to finish me off so I was lifeless for the trip here.

"In my defense, you made it quite easy. After Callum lured you here the first time, I figured you'd be a little more vigilant. You ate right out of my hand, though." Byron presses his hands to the mattress between my widespread legs. "Maybe you're just hungrier than I thought you were." He moves one hand up, then the other, crawling up the open space.

"Byron," I say his name as a warning. "What are you doing?" I pull my hands, trying like hell to free them, even though I know I'm stuck. "Stop!" I'm not sure what he has planned, but that devilish smirk on his face says it can't be anything good.

How could I have been so trusting? I talked to him like he was an old friend, even though I knew something felt off. You'd think I would have learned my lesson after Cal coaxed me here two months ago and wouldn't let me leave.

Cal could be here. He could be tied up, too. Or worse, he could be part of this.

No. He wouldn't allow this to happen. There is no way in hell he's working with Byron this time. If Cal is here, then he's likely restrained the same way I am.

I glower at him as his face lingers over mine. "Where is he?"

The deceiving, sweet scent of cinnamon rolls off his vile tongue. "Who?"

"Don't play dumb with me. I know you did something to him. It all makes sense now. This was never about a partnership. You want Cal's money and the only way to get it is to kill him. Something tells me you didn't because, otherwise, you wouldn't have me here."

"You know what I don't like about you, Bella?" He enunciates my name in a way that sends chills down my sweaty spine. "You're too perceptive. You have all these pieces scattered all over and you observe each one until you find out where it fits."

Byron sits up, straightens his back, and digs a knee into my crotch. I make a mental note to shatter that kneecap once I'm free from this bed. "However, this time, you're wrong and all your little pieces are floating in the bay with your boyfriend's dead corpse."

His words are like a knife to the heart. More tears fall, but I don't stop thrashing, trying to get one of my limbs free. I grit my teeth, glaring at him. "You won't get away with this."

"Oh, I will. I always get what I want, sweet Bella." He presses a disgusting kiss to my forehead and slides down the bed the same way he came up.

"Why are you doing this?"

Byron pulls out his phone and begins tapping into it as he speaks. "Because I deserve it. All of this should be mine. It almost was. I got rid of the one person standing in my way. Now I have the final piece to my own little puzzle," he smiles cruelly, "you."

My eyes pinch shut, pushing out more tears. "Did you...kill Peter?" It hurts to even say the words. I'm still not over Peter's death. I go to sleep at night, and I still see his cold, blue face. He didn't deserve to die, especially not like that.

I go to the sixth floor, to Peter's room, and when he doesn't answer, I use the key to go inside.

It's at this moment, the world stands still. My heart stops beating, the tears stop falling, and I hold my breath before screaming at the top of my lungs, "Nooooo!"

Still clutching the dress, I snap out of the state of shock I'm in and hurry over to Peter's lifeless body, lying in a puddle of blood on the floor.

Maybe it's not too late. Maybe I can save him.

"Oh, Peter," I choke out as I reach down and place my fingers on his cold wrist. It's no use. He has no pulse.

Peter is dead.

I sit there next to him, crying for minutes before I finally get up to try and call for help, then it hits me. Someone did this. Peter didn't die of natural causes. The puddle of blood is enough proof that he was murdered. Whoever did it could still be here.

I knew I should have fought harder to find out what happened to Peter. I never should have believed Byron when I saw him right after finding Peter's body. I'm not sure if it was because I was in shock, or because I was desperate for help. Regardless, I was a fool.

"And another piece fits," Byron says, all too cheery.

He's referencing my puzzle pieces that he claimed were scattered in the bay with Cal's body. It's an admission without saying the words. He did kill Peter.

There's a pang in my chest. But I use my heartache to fuel the fire inside me. It's another reason for me to torture this man and make him pay miserably.

I don't take Byron to be a complete idiot, but he seems to be ignoring one big possibility. "You know if Cal is alive, he could easily hire a new attorney and change his will."

It's actually ridiculous to me that Cal didn't do that a long time ago. We never really talked much about the will, but I do know that they can easily be changed.

"Ah, but you're wrong. Callum and I have a written contract that his will cannot be revoked. Therefore, I'd have to die before him for that to happen." His hands rest on his chest, head tilted to the side condescendingly. "And here I am. While he is…well, dead."

"You did something to him. I know you did."

"Enough of this senseless conversation," Byron continues, stuffing his phone in the front of his pants pocket.

"We have company joining us and I'm going to need you to be a good girl."

"Company? Here on the island?"

"Here, as in, this club. I'm running a business, Bella. My business."

Is he insinuating that this hotel is up and running and there are guests? "What kind of business?" Byron disappears from view, so I shout. "What kind of business, Byron?"

He returns seconds later, and I immediately notice the collar-looking thing in his hand. "What is that?"

Coming closer, he never loses that sinister grin he's been wearing. He looks completely deranged. Like he's manic and lost his damn mind.

Fear washes over me, once again. Byron is a fucking psycho and he has access to do whatever he wants with me and to me.

"This will ensure that you don't get out of hand. I wouldn't want to have to hurt you, Bella."

I'm able to get a better view of the collar as he unfastens it. There's a black ball on the end with a...

He shoves the ball in my mouth so hard, it hits my top and bottom teeth. A mask-like shield presses to my face, covering my entire mouth. I try like hell to spit it out. Pressing my tongue forcibly against it, hoping it will budge, but he has the upper hand and fastens the clasp around my head, setting it in place.

My heart is beating so rapidly that it's rattling my rib cage. I'm suffocating. My entire body is filled with heat while feeling like I'm getting poked continuously with pins and needles. Anxiety is kicking into high gear because, no matter how hard I try, I can't get a grip on it.

I've never been so scared in my life. I think I'd rather die than face what Byron has in store for me.

Please. Please get me out of this, Cal.

Byron reaches into his pocket and pulls something out.

A needle.

He presses his index finger to the end, pushing up some of the liquid inside. It squirts out before he grabs my arm.

I flail through my restraints, crying out around the gag in my mouth.

It's no use, though. The needle pierces my skin, and he pushes down, watching me with menacing eyes as he pumps me full of whatever drug he's feeding me.

My arm goes limp. Hot and cold collide inside me. My thoughts shut down, and I just lie there, slowly drifting to sleep.

4

I SEE A GIRL.

No. Two girls.

Maybe three. And a guy. He's big. Really muscular and tan with black stubble coating his sharp jawline. He's not wearing a shirt. My eyes skate down his body. He's not wearing anything.

I'm hardly fazed. Even the fact that there's a girl on her knees sucking his dick doesn't fully register. My mind and body are so relaxed that nothing seems out of the ordinary. Or maybe I'm just too high to care.

I'm too high to even care that I'm high.

She's a pretty girl. Long, blonde hair that dips below her perky breasts. Nipples puckered around her golden locks. Her mouth forms the perfect O around his cock. Sliding back and forth, taking him so far that I can see the bulge in her throat.

Does anyone even care that I'm lying here shackled without a voice?

No one seems to mind.

My heart gallops when the muscular guy's eyes land on mine. He tips his head, smirks, then returns to fisting the girl's hair. His slow and steady movements quicken as he begins fucking her mouth so hard that she can barely keep up with his thrusts.

Why am I here? What is the point of all this?

Another girl joins. This one's a short brunette, wearing a black, leather bustier with chains on the front. She looks familiar. When she catches my gaze, she licks her bottom lip in a seductive manner, and I remember where I've seen her before. The waitress from the yacht. I think her name is Serena.

I'm not even sure she recognizes me. Our first encounter wasn't a pleasant one and Cal fired her that night. It seems Byron has rehired her, or he's just fucking her still. I watched them once. Watched him ram his dick in another girl while she feasted on Serena.

The image in my head is oddly satisfying.

Serena steps behind the blonde on her knees, gives her hair a jerk and pulls her mouth from the guy's cock. She leans forward and kisses her. Hard. So hard that the blonde loses her footing and drops back. Being the bitch that she is, Serena pushes her to the side and steps up to the muscular guy. Her hands shimmy down his arms, and she licks the side of his face. "I thought you were waiting for me," she says to him before getting a firm grip on his cock.

I'm deranged for enjoying this so much. It's like watching dramatic porn.

I close my eyes. This is too much of a distraction, and I

need to think about how the hell I'm supposed to get out of this mess I'm in.

Where is Byron? And what the hell did he inject me with?

The three shadows in front of me become blurry, and I find myself fighting to keep my eyes open again.

I'm not sure how long I dozed off this time, but I'm woken up when the mattress presses down at my side. My eyes open, and I blink a few times before I realize that it's Byron. I'm grateful to see that he's dressed, unlike the other people I see. There are at least six of them now. Two guys and four girls, not counting Byron.

Byron crawls toward me, straddling my lower half. My stomach clenches, and I gasp behind the ball in my mouth. I gurgle and choke, trying to get words out, but it's pointless.

"Time to get you up, pretty girl." He reaches over me and unclasps the cuff on my left arm. It falls weightlessly. If I had the strength, I'd try to fight him off with just my one free hand, but I'd fail miserably.

He undoes my other hand, then moves to my feet. He knows whatever he gave me has made me weak and incoherent enough to let him do whatever he wants to me. I can think logically, but my body fails to react the way I'd like it to.

"Come on, let her join in," I hear a guy say. "We won't hurt her...much." He chuckles, and it's unnerving.

"Not yet," Byron says as he scoops me in his arms like a baby. He carries me through The Grotto, passing everyone who is still chasing an orgasm even as a prisoner is being carried away with a gag in her mouth.

They must all work for Byron. At one time, they worked for Cal. Byron must've taken over Cal's place in the business. He must have inherited it all, just like he wanted.

But why does he need me?

"Time to get you cleaned up and ready for the ball, pretty girl."

We go out the door that leads to the main entrance, and I remember it all so clearly.

The backside of the castle that was once open is now closed with a pair of wooden double doors, ones that resemble the doors to a barn, only with gray-weathered wood instead of the common red barnwood.

A beam of light shines through, which tells me that it's either early morning or late afternoon. I must have been out all night.

Byron flips me over his shoulder and takes the elevator up. It stops on the eighth floor—the floor I stayed on.

He doesn't stop until we get to my old room. The memories hit me like a tidal wave. From that first day to the last night. So much happened in those short weeks, and while it was only a month ago, it feels like an eternity.

I'm dropped onto the bed like a sack of potatoes. Byron reaches around my head and unclasps the collar. I immediately spit out the ball in my mouth, then wipe the excess saliva from my face with the back of my hand. I'm half tempted to rub it all over his face, but I refrain.

My entire jaw aches. My teeth chatter from the

constant pressure against them, and my tongue is just happy to be able to move around.

Byron goes into my closet, returning with a dress.

"Please, just let me go." I whimper through clipped breaths. I'm thirsty as hell, my heart feels weak, and I'm almost positive Byron injected me with some sort of sedative.

I slide down until I'm sitting on the end of the bed with my feet on the floor. I could try and run, but I wouldn't get far. I have to save my strength to use it at precisely the right time.

"This one should do." He holds up a red, satin gown.

My head lifts, slowly. Staggering breaths escape through my gritted teeth. "Fuck you."

Byron laughs in a mocking tone. "Eventually."

Fuck saving my strength. I should jump on this bastard right now and dig my dirty nails into his perfectly-sculpted cheeks.

"Callum was obsessed with finding you, Bella. I've never seen a man so hell-bent on capturing a woman in my entire life—even as an attorney for psychos and stalkers. For years, he planned for you." Byron slouches down in front of me, slipping off my shoes. "The thing is, I'm not sure if he loved you more than he loved his empire. He planned on marrying and impregnating you just so that I could be taken off his will," he laughs. "Who fucking does that?"

Impregnating me? Cal mentioned marriage, but he never mentioned a baby.

Why am I even listening to this asshole?

My eyes roll, looking away from him. "Quit speaking

of him in the past tense. *Loves* me." I raise my voice. "Not loved. Besides, you're lying. Cal had me take birth control just because he *didn't* want a baby."

That laugh again. I never imagined a simple sound could infuriate me so much. "Shows how gullible you are. Don't feel bad, I fell for his games, too. He swore he'd never get married or have kids, and I'm the dumbass who believed him while thinking my place in his will was secure." Byron begins pulling at the straps of the gown like a demented maniac. "That fucker doesn't give a damn about you. You're his escape clause—the future wife he never wanted. All he cared about was getting me out."

The threading of one of the straps comes undone, and he holds it up with an ominous grin. "Looks like we need to find you a new dress."

God, Cal. Please come save me from this lunatic. There is no saying what lengths Byron will go to at this point.

I'll deal with Cal's lies later. If there even are lies. I'm not sure why Byron would insinuate that I was gullible when it comes to taking birth control, but the guy talks in circles and I'm having a hard time believing anything he says right now.

Byron returns from the closet with another dress. This one is form-fitting and black velvet. "I've always liked black more than red. How about you?"

I just sit there, looking at him and waiting for his next volatile move.

He tosses the dress at me. "Put it on."

My eyes wander to the dress. Gaping at it like it's coated in anthrax.

"Now!" Byron snaps. "Or else I'll put it on you myself. I've been wanting to get under those clothes, ever since I watched Callum fuck you on that piano. "

"How do you know about that?"

"Because I was watching. I heard every moan, saw every kiss, and watched every thrust as he pounded your pussy that night. I won't lie and say I wasn't jealous that it was him getting all the action."

I stand up, grab the dress and throw it at him. "You're the one who recorded me playing, aren't you? You said it was Cal, but it was you."

A smirk parts his lips. "It was a beautiful song."

"How long have you had this planned out?"

He doesn't answer, just throws the dress at me again. "Put the fucking dress on, Bella. Don't make me take what I want because you want to behave like a stubborn little cunt."

His words should cut deep, but they don't. They only make my impending victory that much sweeter. Byron will not get away with this.

In the end, he will lose, even if I pretend.

"Fine," I snatch up the dress. "I'll put it on. *If* you promise me a dance." The thought makes my skin crawl, but I'm willing to do whatever it takes. It's time to repay Byron for knocking me out and holding me against my will. We'll see how he likes it.

Byron's eyes dance across my body, his mouth drawn up in a smile. "A dance?"

Gripping the ends of my sweatshirt, I lift up and peel it off, exposing my bra to him. I feel sick for what I'm about to do. "Mmmhmm. In the ballroom. Just like my dance with Cal. I've always loved dancing."

Cal used to say that without trust you are useless. If I gain Byron's trust, then maybe I'll be of use to him, maybe even sway his plans. At the very least, distract him when and if Cal arrives.

His eyes never leave my peeping cleavage. My fingers trail downward, painting the way to the cup of my bra. I bite the corner of my lip. "What do you say?" Bypassing my breasts, I keep going until I'm at the waistband of my pants. I push them down, stepping out one leg at a time until I'm standing there in nothing but my bra and panties, feeling more exposed than I ever have in my life.

"Umm. Yeah. I guess a dance wouldn't hurt."

Hook. Line. Sinker.

"Great. Now if you don't mind, I need to get changed."

Byron clears his throat. "I'll just…" His thumb shoots over his shoulder. "I'll just be outside the door. No funny business."

"Byron," "I chuckle, "I'm not Rapunzel. I can't escape from this tower. I'll be out in a minute. Promise."

"Wouldn't matter if you were. You should know by now, you can't escape the island." He heads for the door, but stops midway in the room. "And don't think I'm falling for your little reverse psychology tactic. I know you hate me. But one day, we will learn to tolerate one another."

Tolerate him? Never! I'm not sure why it's even necessary, but I'm beginning to feel like this is a permanent placement and not a temporary stay. Just like last time I was here. Only, this is different—I hate Byron with every fiber of my being, whereas Cal held a piece of my heart.

This could be harder than I thought. Byron isn't going to be an easy one to crack, but I have to gain his trust somehow. I still feel pretty out of it, but I'm coherent enough to make rational decisions. At least, I hope I am.

I just know Byron did something to Cal. Even if I don't believe he's dead, I know he was behind his disappearance.

Byron chews on his bottom lip, glaring at me, before he turns and leaves. The door closes behind him, and my smile instantly drops. I mutter under my breath, "Asshole."

5

Bella

I STEP into the black gown and slide my arms beneath the thin spaghetti straps. Reaching back, I zip it up as far as I can reach, knowing that I'll need to ask for help to get it all the way up.

An eerie feeling washes over me. It wasn't long ago that I was in this room and Peter was waiting outside the door to zip me up. He was such a gentleman. This time, Byron is out there and the thought of his filthy fingers grazing my skin is as appealing as getting my fingers chopped off. For what it's worth, I prefer the latter.

In the closet, I pull down a pair of flat sandals and put them on. Screw heels. I'm done with them.

Without even bothering to look in the mirror, I walk to the door. It doesn't matter that my makeup from last night is probably smeared all over my face. My fingers rake through the matted mess of my hair, and I don't care about that either. I have zero interest in looking presentable for this asshole, so he can take it or leave it.

As he said he would be, Byron is waiting on the other

side of the door. At first sight, I'd probably fall for a guy like him. On the outside, he's so put together. On the inside, I'm pretty sure he's dead.

Byron's eyes rake over my body a few times before landing on mine. "You look lovely. Would have been nice if you'd run a brush through your hair, but this'll do."

Such a fucking asshole. I snarl before turning my frown into a smile. "Didn't want to keep you waiting." I turn around, giving him my back. "Would you mind?"

Byron's cold, calloused fingers scratch against my skin as he zips me up. Once he's finished, he ushers his arm out, and I hook mine around it, hesitantly. "I'm sure you're starving, though the sleeping medication may have curved your appetite."

"Sleeping medication?" I ask, playing dumb, though I assumed it was some sort of drug he injected me with.

"It's very safe. No need to worry. It was the same medicine used to comatose patients when they have an operation. The last thing I want to do is hurt you, Bella."

I blow out a sarcastic chuckle. "Right? So kidnapping me and bringing me to this island is for what...my protection?"

"If I remember right, Callum did the same thing, and by the time he left you, you were head over heels in love. Who's to say it can't happen again?"

We reach the elevator, and the doors open. As soon as we're inside, I slither out of his hold. "Cal and I have history. He was never a stranger, and he didn't kidnap or drug me."

"Oh, but he did lie to you. And if he were alive, he'd

still be lying to you. There's so much you don't know. Don't fret, I'll fill you in eventually."

The elevator comes to a stop, and Byron offers his arm again, but I snuff my nose at him and walk on my own. I know exactly where the ballroom is and I don't need his assistance this time.

Last time he ushered me to Cal, I tripped and fell and threw a shoe at him. If I had heels on this time, I might hammer it into his thick skull.

It won't be necessary, though. Somehow, I'm going to steal Byron's phone. There might not be any boats for me to escape on, but if I can reach Mark or Dad, they'll send for help. Until then, I just have to bide my time.

When I enter the ballroom, I'm taken aback by the changes. The piano is now in the far corner, and there's a large, white screen hanging on the back wall with a projector pointed at it.

"What's this?" I ask Byron when he enters behind me.

"Tonight's entertainment." Music begins playing and it's "Für Elise," just like my dance with Cal. "But first, we dance." Byron takes my hand and I follow his lead as we chassé across the dance floor.

Each step pools more nausea in my stomach until acid starts creeping up my throat, readying to spill out all over Byron's white shirt.

Every now and then I look up and see him peering down at me like I'm some prize he won at a fair, by cheating his way to the win.

He will not win. Not me. Not Cal's empire. In the end, I'll make damn sure that Byron has nothing. Even if Cal is never found, I will fight for what belongs to him.

I decide to break the silence with a simple question. "So, how'd you manage to take over if Cal isn't even presumed dead?"

Byron extends his arm with my hand in his and twirls me around before pulling me snug to his chest. "It's easy to take over when there is no one to stop you. Ellis Empire might not be legally mine...yet," he snickers, "but as far as all the staff go, I am in control now. Out with the old and in with the new. It's only a matter of time before his body is found and the estate is settled."

Byron missteps, causing me to step on his shoe, and I grumble under my breath. He's a terrible dancer.

The music comes to a stop and Byron takes a step back, still gripping my left hand in his. "You must be tired after the events of the last twenty-four hours. I have one more surprise before you can settle into your room with dinner. I expect you to get a good night's sleep, because we have a busy day tomorrow."

"Can't wait to see what my next surprise is." My words are laced with sarcasm, and I'm beginning to realize that even pretending with this guy is damn near impossible. "I'm feeling pretty thirsty, though. Would you mind getting us something to drink? Wine, perhaps?"

Byron's expression shifts unceremoniously to one of anger. His voice rises. "You can't wait two damn minutes, so I can show you my surprise?"

My eyes shoot wide at his outburst. He's completely unhinged. "Okay," I say quietly, "show me your surprise."

Byron's scowl turns into a beaming smile. Almost too excitedly, he pulls out his phone and begins tapping into it. A sinister glance at me and he walks over to the projector and grabs the remote.

The white screen fills immediately.

I gasp at the sight in front of me. My knees buckle, and I stumble, trying to catch my fall.

"What the hell is this?" I sputter, now looking at Byron who's on one knee with an open jewelry box held out. My voice rises to a scream. "What the fuck did you do to my brother?" Air gets lodged in my throat, and I feel like I'm slowly suffocating.

"Save him and marry me. It's the only way."

I walk steadfast toward Byron, who's still crouched in a proposal stance. My arm extends, and I slap the box out of his hand, sending it flying across the floor. "Marry you? Have you lost your damn mind?"

Byron stands up, grabs my shoulders, and grinds his molars. "Marry me or Mark dies."

I'm speechless. At a loss for words. My head is spinning so fast that I don't even know what is real anymore. This has to be a nightmare. I convulse in hysterics and my mind escapes me as my hands begin flailing at Byron. I smack him, punch him, knee him, all while screaming profanities and vile words of hate. I could kill him. I *am* going to kill him.

A swift slap across my face halts my movements. Byron grabs my wrists, restraining me. "Listen here, you fucking cunt. You will marry me or I'll kill your goddamn brother. In fact, I'll kill your entire family. Everything you love will be gone."

Tears fall recklessly down my cheeks while my already broken heart shatters into tiny pieces. "Why are you doing this? Why me?"

I don't understand any of this. Byron has Cal's fortune like he always wanted. He has it all. Why me?

"Because I lied to you. Callum did love you. More than anything in this world. His empire included. I vowed to myself long ago that I would take everything he loved and make it mine." His cold lips press to mine. I'm too stunned to move or care or react. "You included, Bella. Callum is gone and he's never coming back; I can promise you that. No one else wants you but me. You have nothing to lose."

My eyes find the screen once more. Mark is bound and gagged. His head hangs unconsciously with his chin pressed to his chest. I see blood. Lots of blood. He's really hurt and if I don't do what Byron wants, I don't doubt for a second that he will kill my brother.

My face falls into my hands, unable to look at Byron or that screen any longer. What is this life anymore? All I want is normalcy, but I don't even know what that is. I never have. An orphan at the age of four, who never knew what love truly was until I was eleven years old. All my life, I've searched for happiness as if I'd find it behind a closed door. Then I did. I found it when I wasn't even looking and it took me by storm. Then in the blink of an eye, it was gone. Just like everything that made me feel whole, as temporary as it is, it just vanished. *He* vanished.

"Okay," I finally say, my voice almost a whisper, "let him go and I'll marry you."

Byron squeezes my wrists harder, his blue eyes wide and full of anger. "Stop treating me like a fool. You will marry me, *then* I will let him go."

I clench my jaw, attempt to jerk my wrists away to no

avail, and hiss, "And you stop treating me like a damn fool. How do I know you won't kill him anyway?"

"Your brother doesn't know who has him or why. He has not seen any of my men's faces; therefore, I can safely free him without implication."

I'm trying so hard to piece together the events of the last twenty-four hours and come to terms with my reality, but it all feels too unreal. Like a horror movie playing out before me.

When I don't respond, Byron tosses my wrists away and stops the livestream on the screen. "It's been a long day. Get some rest and we will talk tomorrow. Before the ceremony."

"Tomorrow?" I spit out in one breath. "You can't be serious."

"Oh, I am serious. This time tomorrow, you will be Mrs. Byron Davis."

My eyes pinch shut as tears still manage to find their way out. I open them abruptly. "Like hell I will."

I storm out of the room, my feet never stopping until I make it to the elevator. I hit the button and take it up, then go straight to my room.

My door slams shut, and I curse Cal for never putting a lock on this door.

I'm hungry, exhausted, and feel like I'm on the verge of vomiting, but sleep is the last thing I plan to get. I have to devise a plan to either escape this island, or kill Byron.

One way or another, I'm saving Mark, and it will not be by me taking Byron's hand in marriage.

6

I've paced the length of this room at least a dozen times. I've even gone as far as throwing a leg over the banister on the balcony, thinking I'd attempt to escape even if it meant falling to my death. Death actually sounds more appealing than marrying that scumbag.

I don't have a clock, so I'm not sure on the time, but I'd say it's somewhere around midnight. For all I know, Byron could be a night owl. I'm also certain that there are eyes on me at all times, but I have to try something. I can't just sit in this room while Mark is being held prisoner and Cal is still missing.

Barefoot, in a pair of black, silk pajamas, I creep down the hall, glancing at all the cameras I pass by. I see them, but most importantly, they see me.

Screw it. I've got fight left in me and it's time to prove it.

I stroll down the hall, casually, as if I'm up for a midnight snack. Heading for the elevator, I pass by Cal's old room. My heart twinges, and I find myself backstepping. One hand reaches out, presses to the door, and my eyes close.

God, I miss him.

We spent so many years apart, and I really wasn't sure I'd ever see Cal again. Our reunification was not as sweet as I would have wanted it to be; in fact, it was torturous at best. But the more time we spent together, the louder his heart sang to mine. I wanted to fill that empty void inside him and repair all his broken pieces. In the end, I'm the one who paid the price. I paid with my heart shattering and now Byron expects me to pay him with my soul.

Fuck that.

I drop my hand and continue to the elevator, but stop abruptly, when I hear footsteps coming down the hall. My heart jumps and, on impulse, I go back to Cal's door and take the risk of it being locked.

To my surprise, it opens. I go inside, closing the door quietly behind me.

With my breath held, I tiptoe over to the closet, hoping like hell I don't have to go inside. But when the bedroom door creaks open, I go in as fast as I can.

I don't let go of the handle as I close the closet door behind me. I grip it tightly, afraid that if I let go, it will latch and Byron will hear it.

I hear a switch flip, likely the light. "They're still here," Byron says, angrily. "I told you I want these fucking snakes gone or else I'll chop their damn heads off myself."

Oh my God, the snakes. I forgot all about them. I hope someone has been feeding them and giving them care. I don't even like snakes, but the thought of them being harmed while Cal's been missing breaks my heart.

"I don't give a shit who takes them. Call a fucking reptile shelter, for all I care."

There's a long beat of silence before I hear the shuffle of feet through the room.

My abdominal muscles pull in as I hold my breath. He comes closer. And Closer.

I'm a millisecond away from being caught and a sense of horror ripples through my bones.

My body jolts when Byron's phone begins ringing. I blow out a pent-up breath as the sound continues.

"It's about damn time you called back. How are our guests?"

Guests? As in hotel guests?

I can't imagine anyone else staying here. Especially since I have the freedom to roam. Byron knows I can't leave, but he wouldn't risk me alerting guests of my kidnapping.

No. It's only me and the staff that he's paying. He has to be talking about another hotel.

"Keep the brother bloody. I need her to see how far I go to get what I want. As for the other one, bring him to the brink of death, for all I care. Just make sure he's able to view the livestream of the wedding. I want him alive when I take everything he loves."

I gasp, clapping a hand over my mouth as the sounds continue to ride up my throat.

He has to be talking about Cal. He has him held captive somewhere with Mark and plans to livestream the wedding, just so he can watch before he kills them.

But the wedding is supposed to be tomorrow, or

today, since it's past midnight. There's no way I can save them both. I only have one choice. I have to—

The door to the closet flies open, and I lose all train of thought.

I stumble back, tripping over a box and falling into the hanging suits.

"Aren't you just a sneaky little bitch?"

My hands move backward, attempting to crawl to get away from him. I reach back, touching the wall in search of the opening where the door to the basement is.

"Get out of the fucking closet, Bella."

I keep searching for the door, finally finding it, but I'm too late. Byron grabs my foot and begins pulling me. Slapping my hand around on the floor, I look for something to hold on to or to grab to use as a weapon against him, but all I find is a metal hanger.

Byron keeps pulling until I'm flat on my back and he's standing over me.

He crouches down, looking into my eyes with a heinous scowl. "Looks like we have to do this the hard way."

Gripping the hanger, I bring it up quickly, shoving the hook right into his eye. Well, at least that's what I tried to do. Instead, I missed and got the side of his face. Blood runs down his cheek, falling onto my chin.

"You're gonna pay for that. Oh, are you gonna pay."

Cold hands wrap around my throat, and it's a feeling I'm not foreign to. It was only yesterday Byron choked me from the driver's side of my car.

With his hands still around my neck, he lifts me up,

and I press my hands against the floor to gain momentum as I'm pulled to a standing position.

I gasp, and fight, and try to get out of his clutches, but once again, I'm too weak.

Byron pulls me out of the closet and tosses me onto the floor of the bedroom. Coming out after me with thunderous steps, he begins unfastening his belt. I crawl backward again, trying to get away from him, while knowing that there is nowhere to run.

"You know," he begins, "I wanted to wait until we were married to consummate our wedding vows, but you've proven to be unworthy of my patience. Therefore, I should fuck you now. It's also never too soon to try for a baby, *baby*."

"No!" I screech. "Get away from me!"

He doesn't.

He comes closer and closer, his feet touching mine. Reaching down, he grabs me by the arm and pulls me up, then pushes me back until I'm lying on Cal's bed.

A lump lodges in my throat, and I swallow it down, tasting my tears on my tongue.

Fight, Bella.

Each movement he makes has me slithering farther up the bed until I hit the headboard. When there's nowhere else to go, Byron blankets my body with his. I snarl in disgust as he begins kissing my neck.

Crying and writhing beneath him, I try to fend him off, but it's no use. He's made it clear that he gets what he wants.

With my head turned to the side, I see a lamp on the end table.

Byron reaches down between us and cups my crotch while I reach my arm out to grab the lamp, but it's too far.

I reach farther, hoping he doesn't notice, and when he begins kissing my neck again, I know he doesn't.

Just a little...bit...farther.

In one swift motion, I pull the lamp, unplugging it and taking the cord along as I bash Byron over the head with it.

His body goes limp, and I shove him off me. Another shove sends him falling to the floor and I jump off the bed. Instead of leaving immediately, I grab the base of the lamp, go over to where he lies, and hit him in the head again to make sure he's knocked out cold.

I reach into Byron's pocket and take his phone.

Then I run like hell.

Tearing open the door, I go straight for the elevator in a panic. My pulse never slows as I tap the elevator button over and over and over again until the doors finally open. Once I'm inside and riding down to the main floor, I swipe the screen on Byron's phone. My hands shake uncontrollably, forcing me to grip it harder out of worry I'll drop it and never have the chance to pick it back up.

"No!"

Stupid fucking passcode.

Wait. There should be a way to call for help from the lock screen.

I try everything. Pressing buttons at the same time, swiping up and down. Nothing works.

I feel defeated as the elevator comes to a stop. I slam

the phone down on the ground, ready to stomp on it, when I pause, my foot in midair.

I just have to wait for a call to come in. Once it does, I'll be able to answer and hang up right away, which will leave me on the home screen and able to call for help.

I'll just hide somewhere until that happens.

I go out the main doors and the light snowfall has turned heavy and blustery. A gust of wind has me hugging my chest as my bare feet sink into the accumulating fluff.

The cold snow doesn't even faze me as I make my way to the side of the castle, leaving a fresh trail of footprints. Fortunately, the snow is falling heavy enough that they should be hidden before the sun rises.

Without stopping, I keep going, until I'm hidden among untended bushes and weeds that have overgrown. Then I crouch down and I wait.

Someone will call soon. Hopefully long before frost-bite takes hold.

7

WITH MY PHONE held out and a picture of Byron pulled up, I ask the nitwit for the umpteenth time, "You're sure this was him?"

"Yes, sir. That's definitely the guy she was with."

I continue to rummage through the hotel room, looking for something. Anything. "Fuck!" I shout, tossing the comforter to the floor. "Nothing. There's not a damn clue as to where she might've gone."

"Look. I'm sorry, Boss. After the girl broke my nose, I lost her."

I feel my jaw clench as I spin around and grab the imbecile I hired by the collar of his pretty-boy shirt. "You had one fucking job! One job and you screwed it up."

His cigar-infused breath hits my senses and I toss him back, allowing him to crash onto the bed.

"She's a feisty bitch. I'm telling ya—"

My fist meets his jaw, hoping I broke it to match his nose. "You ever call her that again and I'll shatter every bone in your goddamn face. You're fired. Now get the hell outta here." His eyes widen with surprise, and he just lies there propped up on his elbows. I point at the door. "Now!"

Crawling off the bed like the lowlife he is, he walks out with his tail between his legs. I slam the door shut behind him and immediately pull my phone out of the pocket of my pants to call my other, recently hired, man, hoping like hell he has more brain cells than this guy.

"Any word?"

"Nothing, sir. We've scoured every street she might've crossed, and there's not a single breadcrumb."

"I'm searching her car. Keep looking and call me the minute you find something."

I end the call and slam my phone down on the bed. "Dammit, Bella. Where the hell are you?"

I kept my distance for her protection. Watched from afar to make sure she was safe. I've had eyes on her ever since I gave Peter the orders to get her home. I didn't want to let her go. I can barely fucking breathe without her, but I had no choice.

Bella's life is more important than my own.

Byron took everything from me. Made my men believe I was dead and showed them that he was now in charge of Ellis Empire. The bastard is even spending my money already.

Fortunately, I had an offshore account and was able to tap into it to hire my own temporary crew. I've also made contact with Anders, my original head of security. The search for Bella is now underway. *Unfortunately*, these new guys are all amateur ass-kissers and I can't tell if they're keeping their eyes on my girl for the money or because she makes their dicks hard.

I snatch my phone off the bed and leave the room. It's been three hours since he lost her. Three fucking hours that she could have wandered to God knows where. Or worse, been taken.

I swear on everything worth a damn, if anyone touches a hair on her head, I will murder them in their sleep. Or maybe while they're awake, so I can look into their sorry eyes as I do it.

My thunderous steps take me down the hall, knocking into a housekeeper's cart and sending a tray of food to the floor, but I don't stop.

"Excuse you." The lady growls as I punch the down arrow for the elevator.

Once I'm in the main lobby, I stop at the front desk and slide the clerk my business card with a hundred-dollar bill beneath it. "If the guest in Room 280 returns, you call me immediately."

He picks up the card and money, taking a look at it before nodding. "Yeah. Sure thing, Mr. Ellis."

I tap the counter, then head out the revolving door into the parking lot.

There's a chill in the air that has me slipping on my black, leather gloves. The entire city is lit up in an array of red, green, and white lights. It's a miserable reminder that it's New Year's. I'll be thankful once this day is over and the holidays have passed.

Another one alone. It was supposed to be different this year. We should have been together—married, perhaps. Instead, my fortune and identity were stolen from me and

I have to fight tooth and nail for what's mine, once again —her and my legacy.

Dragging my feet through the light blanket of snow covering the pavement, I go straight to her car. One good thing about the asshole I just hired is that he was able to attach a tracking device to her car. Little good it does when she leaves without it.

My eyes skim the parking lot before I take my elbow to the driver's side window, busting out the glass. A couple walking by hand in hand gives me an apprehensive look, before picking up their pace and walking off.

I reach in the open window to unlock the door, and dammit, it was never even locked. That's what I get for being presumptuous. I'll buy her a new window. Hell, when I find her and get my money back, I'll buy her a brand-new car.

With the door open, I lean inside and begin searching for anything—her phone, an airline ticket, her luggage. That's when I spot a bag. I pull it out and rifle through it. There's a dress and some makeup, but nothing helpful.

I toss the bag back inside and open the glove box. Nothing.

Damn.

Just as I go to stand up outside the car, something catches my eye on the driver's side floor.

Slouching down, with my gloves still on, I pick up an empty needle syringe. Upon closer inspection, I notice a smear of clear liquid trickling down the inside.

Dread washes over me. Gut-punching, rage-infusing dread.

I can feel it in my bones. He took her and it won't be

long until he knows I've escaped. Once he does, there's no saying what he'll do.

He doesn't just want my empire.

He wants the only thing I love in this world.

Her.

Thirty-Six Hours Earlier

Blood pools in my mouth from the last blow, and I spit a mouthful on the man in front of me. I can already feel my eye swelling shut, and I'm almost positive I was knocked unconscious more than once. I'm not even sure how long I've been here or what day it is.

I knew he was coming for me.

Fuck! I should've been more prepared. Thought I had more time to get ahead of him while getting Bella to safety. She is safe, though. At least, she was the last time I talked to Peter. He had put her on a boat back to the main island, and she was going home. My only hope is that she never comes looking for me. I couldn't live knowing that she was hurt in a quest to save me.

It wasn't five minutes after I ended that last call with Peter that a bag was thrown over my head. I woke up in a cement block cell in a basement with my hands and feet tied up. At least the gag was removed, so I could spit at this guy a few times.

"Got anything more to say because this game of cat and mouse is pretty entertaining."

"Cat and mouse?" I chuckle sarcastically. "Who's hunting who? Seems I'm right where you want me. The question is, why?"

"That you are. Now, why don't you sit back and relax until you're needed."

My wrists lift, pressing against the metal cuffs they're

restrained with, and I shout, "How the fuck am I supposed to relax?"

The asshole takes a sip of his crisp water from the bottle in his hand and screws the top back on with a shit-eating grin on his face. "Not my problem. I'm paid to watch you. Don't give a fuck if you're tense or relaxed."

"Paid, huh? By who? That fucker Byron Davis?"

He shrugs an unknowing shoulder. "Name doesn't ring a bell."

"Like hell it doesn't." I spit again, this time the blood splatters in a clot on the dirty cement floor. "How much is he paying you?"

"Not enough to deal with your chattering ass."

"Do you have any idea who I am? I'll double it. Hell, I'll fucking triple it."

"Don't know and really don't care. All I see is a bum who got himself in some deep shit with the wrong guy."

The only bum in this room is this jackass, and I'm almost positive he'd do just about anything for a buck. Obviously. He's here babysitting me.

"Give me a number. Whatever you want, it's yours."

"No amount of money you could pay me would be worth a bullet in my head. It's a hard pass but nice try. Now, if you'll excuse me, I'm gonna go fetch you a nice bologna sandwich so you don't wither away before my boss gets what he wants from you."

"Wait," I say, but he doesn't listen. Just tosses his empty bottle in the corner, on top of a pile of trash, then walks to the door. "Wait a damn minute," I shout louder. He clicks the lock on the metal door and leaves. "Fuck!"

My hands skew under the cuffs. I stretch my feet, trying to

get something to snap or break that will free me.

He's a dead man. Byron and the assholes keeping me here. Once I'm out of this damn place, I will kill them all with my bare hands.

My chin tucks to my chest, and I close my eyes, still feeling the sting from the last punch.

A few minutes later, the guard returns, and my head slowly rises at the sound of the door opening. Sure enough, he's got a sandwich on a paper plate in one hand and a dirty glass of water in the other.

He comes closer, raising the sandwich pinched between his grubby fingers. "Open up."

"Get that thing out of my fucking face."

The sandwich flies across the room, hitting the cement wall and sliding down. "Fine. Starve, for all I care."

"Fifty thousand."

His brows hit his forehead, and it seems I've piqued his interest. "Come again."

"Fifty thousand in your account in minutes. You let me out of here and give me a head start, before alerting Mr. Davis that I've escaped."

"Mr. Davis, eh. Who?"

"Quit playing dumb with me."

The guy ponders for a minute, likely considering my offer.

"Sixty thousand," *I say, upping the ante.*

He turns away, pacing the floor while stroking his coarse, salt-and-pepper beard. "A buck fifty or no deal."

"Deal," *I say in one breath. I'm surprised he's settling so quickly. I was prepared to go higher.* "You let me out and I'll have it delivered on your doorstep tomorrow morning. But I need at least forty-eight hours before Mr. Davis knows a thing."

It'll take me some time to track Byron down and I need the element of surprise.

He laughs. "You think I'm fucking stupid." *Grabbing his phone, he begins tapping on the screen.* "A wire transfer before I let you go. And when I do, you walk out of this room and I'll give you thirty-six hours before I tell my boss you broke free."

"Fine. Gimme the damn phone."

He puts it in my restrained right hand, and I go into the browser to get to my online banking.

Seconds later, I'm cursing internally when I see that my password has changed.

I try another account.

Same fucking thing.

"That measly son of a bitch," *I mutter.* "Well, this might take a minute. Seems your boss is a fucking snake and a lousy thief."

I've got an offshore account with at least a half-mil in it. It was there for emergencies, and this is exactly that.

The guard gives me his bank info and the transfer is seconds away from being complete. Well, half of it. I'm not a complete fucking idiot.

All I have to do is hit Send.

"Now," *I begin, gripping the phone in my hand.* "To ensure your compliance, you get half now and half will be automatically deposited after thirty-six hours. You rat me out like the dirty crook you are and you're out 75K. Got it?"

"Look. A deal's a deal. You're good for thirty-six hours."

I scoff. "I highly doubt that."

He pulls out a key and doesn't hesitate to click the lock on the first cuff, freeing my right hand. I roll my wrist, working out the kinks, and breathe a slight sigh of relief. "And the other?"

"Make the transfer first."

I could probably manage to fight this guy with one hand. He'd come for his phone; I'd shatter it, then I'd shatter every bone in his face. He's not that big, just smells really fucking bad. I'm at more of a risk of throwing up than losing a fight to him.

I hit Send and the guard is seventy-five thousand dollars richer.

"Done," I tell him. "You fuck this up and not only will you lose the second half, I'll hunt you down and Byron Davis will be the least of your worries."

He uncuffs my other hand, then my ankles. It takes me a minute to stand up, but once I'm steady on my feet, I hand him his phone. Just as he reaches for it, I grab his head and ram my forehead against his. Stumbling back a few feet, he crashes into the door.

"That's for the fucking black eye. Thirty-six hours or I'll thank you for the bloody lip with a broken jaw."

I snatch the keys from his hand and toss his phone at him.

It takes me three tries to get the right one, but when I do, I leave the room and don't look back.

I'm not sure if there are other guards, but the place is pretty quiet, and I make no attempt to silence my steps.

As I'm making my way out, I notice a few more doors similar to the one I was behind. The possibility that Bella is behind one of them occurs to me, but it quickly diminishes when I remember that she's safe in Rhode Island.

I've got no idea where I am or how I'm leaving, but somehow, I'll find a way.

I have to get to Bella. Then I have to kill my fucking attorney.

8

BYRON'S PHONE DIED. There was a sliver of battery life left, and my continuous attempts at unlocking the screen must have drained it completely.

No one has come to look for me.

Not Byron, or his men.

I'm curled in a ball beneath the sloping branches of a tree with bare feet, wearing thin fabric. It's eerily quiet aside from the chatter of my teeth.

The temperatures are frigid, and the snow continues to blanket the tree that I'm using as a fort to hide out.

It's been two hours. Two long and treacherous hours, and I'm not sure I can make it much longer.

Byron knows I'm here. He has the safety net of my inability to escape, ensuring that I am somewhere on this island. It's only a matter of time before I'm found, and I'm wondering if I might as well face him before I die of hypothermia or lose any limbs from extreme frostbite.

Shifting my legs, I tuck my feet over them to keep them out of the snow. My fingers rub aggressively at my blue-colored toes, trying to warm them, but I can't even feel them anymore to know if it's helping.

My entire body shivers, and I can't take it any longer.

Leaving Byron's phone behind, I crawl out from under the tree and stand up. The moon shines brightly over the bay, offering me a source of light as I walk back toward the castle. I have to go inside and hide somewhere warm before I freeze to death.

Only, my plan is derailed when I go to open the main door and notice it's locked. Hugging my chest tightly, I go around the side and try another door. Then another. And another.

All the doors are locked.

I find myself at the back of the castle, where the new doors were installed, but no luck there either.

He locked me out.

Byron wants to marry me to hurt Cal but killing me might be the next best thing.

My back presses to the wooden door and I slide down. At least there is a lip on the roof that stops the snow from falling here. It's still cold as hell, but it's dry.

I close my eyes and wait. That's all I can do at this point.

"I FOUND her and she's alive."

That voice. It's so familiar.

"Bella. Bella, wake up."

My dry lips smack together. I dart my tongue out to

wet them, feeling the rigid cracks and tasting a hint of metal.

"Come on. Let's get you inside."

Someone begins pulling me up until I'm standing, but it's a dream. No one is coming to save me.

I've only got myself.

The weight of my body leaves my feet, and I'm cradled like a baby.

"Shit. You're cold as ice."

It's a dream, Bella. Don't wake up. Just go with it.

I swallow, and it feels like razor blades sliding down my throat.

God, he's so warm—whoever *he* is. Pulling me tighter, I rest my head on his chest and smile.

If only he were real.

Warmth. I can feel it. There's no longer a cold breeze scratching at my skin. There's a fire. I smell wood burning and I can feel the heat of the blaze kiss my cheeks. It feels nice.

We sit down, me still in his arms. A warm blanket wraps around me with strong hands holding me tight. "Bella, wake up."

Don't do it. Don't wake up. You'll find yourself out in the snow again. Just enjoy the dream, even if it's not real, it's safe.

"Bella," he says again. My eyes open, and I immediately push myself off his lap.

"Trent?" I take a step back, making sure my eyes aren't deceiving me. "What the hell are you doing here?" The feeling returns to my feet, and it's a sharp, tingling pain. I sit down in the chair behind me as I try to wrap my head around Trent's arrival. I squeeze my toes, rubbing them and trying to get the blood flowing.

This has to be a dream. Or maybe even a nightmare. There is no way that Trent would be back on the island. He shouldn't even know I'm here.

"I came looking for you. Your parents said they haven't been able to reach you or Mark, and I was worried. She mentioned how you've been obsessed with finding Callum Ellis and I had to at least check this place. Why the hell were you out in the cold like that?" Trent jumps up, blanket in hand. "Did that bastard lock you out? I'll fucking kill him."

I spring up and grab him by the arm, attempting to pull him toward the door so we can leave, but his feet stay planted. "We have to go. Like right fucking now."

He doesn't move, just looks at me like I've lost my mind.

"Trent, I'm not kidding. We *have* to go!"

His arms extend and he sweeps the blanket out and wraps it around me. "You need to rest. Don't worry. I'll handle Callum. He'll never be able to hurt you again. I promise you, Bella."

My head shakes, and I try to speak, but the words don't come out.

"Just calm down—"

"No! Don't tell me to calm down, Trent. It's not Cal. It's Byron. His attorney. Or friend or whatever he is." I look over my shoulder, feeling like Byron is going to walk in here any minute. "He kidnapped me and we need to go right now." I pull him again, my hands shaking frantically, and the perplexed look on his face is unnerving. "Why aren't you listening to me?"

"You seem disoriented. Let me see if I can find someone to get you some water."

"I don't want water! I want to leave." I drop my hand from his bicep and hold it out. "Give me your phone."

"My phone? Why?"

"Have you not heard anything I'm saying to you? Give me your damn phone, Trent. We need to call for help."

He's acting weird. Looking at me like I'm a stranger who's lost her mind. Why is he just standing there staring at me like that?

"Phone!" I snap my fingers. "Now, dammit."

Trent reaches in his pocket, his eyes never leaving mine. He retrieves his phone and places it in the palm of my hand. "Won't do any good. I have no service out here."

"But you were just talking to someone outside. I heard you," I choke out before my tears thaw and fall again. I drop down into the chair, still unable to control my shakes. Was it part of the dream? Was he really talking to someone on the phone?

Wait a damn minute!

My back straightens against the chair. "How did you get here? Do you have a boat waiting?"

"It's returning in one hour. But here's the thing, Bella…" His words trail off, eyes shooting behind me, wide and cautious.

I look behind me to see what stole his words, and my heart stills.

Jumping to my feet, I hurry to Trent's side, grabbing

his arm and showing Byron that his game is over. Trent will never let him hurt me.

"Get away from me!" I screech at Byron.

Slow and steady steps bring us face to face. He looks at Trent, then me, with a spine-chilling grin.

I take notice of the huge gash on his forehead, blood trickling down from the wound and coating the left side of his face.

"It's over, Byron. We're leaving and there isn't anything you can do to stop us." I squeeze Trent's arm tighter, but he moves it, loosening my grip. I look up at him and notice he's staring down at me. The look on his face alarms every cell in my body.

"Trent," I say softly.

He moves his arm again and I completely lose my hold on him.

"Trent. What are you doing?" I look from him to Byron, and it's like four walls closing in on me, only it's two men. "No." I shake my head. "Please tell me you're not on his side?"

I take a step back, tripping over the curled rug, but I manage to catch myself before backsliding into the fireplace.

Byron walks toward me, reaches out and grabs me firmly by the wrist, digging so deep I can feel my pulse pound against his fingertips.

"Money is a beautiful thing, Bella. And you should be thankful that my new employee found you out there or you'd have frozen to death." He shoves me until I fall back into the chair.

Employee?

"Sorry, Bella," Trent says with no empathy in his words. "When an old law school buddy reaches out and offers you a partnership at one of the biggest firms in the nation, you have to accept."

"Old law school buddy?" I mumble. How did I not see this? Mark and Trent went to law school together. That is, until Mark dropped out. That's how he got Mark. They all know each other and he lured him in with Trent's help. "Mark is your friend," I say to Trent. "How could you do this? Not just to me, but to him?"

My stomach churns. I grab it, feeling the rise of bile up my throat.

"What is a friend, anyways?" Trent continues, "Someone who takes his whore of a sister's side when she fucks her boss? Or how about a person who calls one time in the past eight weeks after you're brutally beaten to a near-death state? Mark's not my fucking friend." He comes toward me, crouches down to where I sit in the chair, and places his hands on my legs. "And neither are you."

9

Callum

A GUN, a phone, and list of every fucker who will pay for turning their backs on me. That's what I've accumulated since realizing Byron kidnapped Bella.

Now I'm on a call with my pilot, trying to fix the mess Byron has made. I can't even bring out one of my own jets because that asshole will be hot on my tail. "I don't give a flying fuck what he made everyone believe. I want a jet on the ground at LGA in twenty fucking minutes, without his knowledge, or you'll never fly again." I end the call, trying to calm the raging storm brewing inside me.

Fucking New York City. That's where this asshole held me captive. This whole ploy has Byron's name written all over it. Not only is he a native to New York City, but he also attended law school at Columbia and his largest firm is in the Big Apple.

I fucking hate the city. I hate crowds and I hate people. It's why eighty percent of my hotels are on private islands, with the exception of one that is actually here…in the city.

It's on a smaller scale and doesn't have all the same luxuries as the other resorts, but it brings in good revenue, so I keep it open.

A call from my head of security, Anders, comes through, and I take it immediately. "Anything?"

"Actually, Boss. We've got reason to believe he's taken her back to Cori Cove. Jeffery confirmed the coming and going of a few different watercrafts over the last forty-eight hours."

"All right," I grumble. "I'm headed to the main island. I've got a crew waiting to be transported. We have to do this right. There's no room for fuck-ups."

"You've got it. We'll get her back, Boss."

"Damn straight we will." I look up at the gray skies, feeling the snow fall on my face. "Any word from Peter yet?"

"Nothing. I can only assume he's there with them."

"Keep me updated on any changes. Otherwise, I'll see you within the hour."

Byron's gone too fucking far this time. It seems the entire world believes I'm dead, and he's out there living my life with my girl.

"Stop here," I tell the driver. He slams on the brakes, likely out of fear of pissing me off further by going a foot too far. I've had a few choice words with everyone I've encountered today. It seems that coming back from the dead isn't an easy stint.

I get out, button my suit jacket, and knock knuckles to the driver's window while taking in my surroundings at the airfield.

His window comes down and I lean forward, invading his personal space. "You didn't give me a ride. In fact, you didn't even see me. Got it?"

His response is a coy, "Yes, sir."

The last thing I need is Byron catching wind of my escape and doing something to harm Bella out of spite.

After standing around wasting time I don't have, the private jet finally arrives.

I get in, get comfortable, and begin making calls to the men I know will have my back. Loyalty and trust have nothing to do with it; it's because I pay them and I pay them well.

Deep down, I know I can't trust anyone. Never have, never will. Every single person in the world is out for themselves, no matter what bullshit lies they tell you. My past is proof of that. My future, on the other hand, will ensure that those who deemed themselves untrustworthy suffer the most extreme consequences. If they've placed themselves in my life, they should know better than to double-cross me because payback will be had. It seems there are more than a few that do not.

I'd like to think I can trust Peter, but you can never tell. The guy's been with me since the beginning, and he's never betrayed me, but he's no spring chicken and he needs the comfort of food and a roof over his head. If he had to take Byron's side, while assuming I was dead, he's the one person I'd consider forgiving. My only hope is that Byron has treated him well.

When the pilot announces we're clear to land, I stick my phone in my pocket, check my gun in the holster around my waist, and mentally prepare for any possible outcome.

I'm coming for you, Bella.

10

NOTHING MATTERS ANYMORE. Another person who I thought I could trust has turned on me. This time, it's Trent. The man I spent two years of my life with and considered marrying at one point.

Now he's forcing me into a wedding gown, so I can marry someone else.

"Put your fucking foot in, Bella."

I don't. I just stand there in the laced bodice he managed to get on me. After quite the quarrel on the floor, I lost. My strength is no match for his.

One thing he should know by now is that I do not go down without a fight.

Trent kneels at my feet, trying to get me into a wedding gown, because that's what Byron told him to do.

"All this for money. You're despicable, you know that?" I begin unstrapping the ties of the bodice, undoing all the work he just did. It doesn't matter that I'll be standing completely naked in front of him.

As I said, nothing matters anymore.

"It's not about money. Consider it helping an old friend."

"Old friend?" I laugh. "Because you went to law school together? That hardly makes him your friend. He's using you, Trent, and the sooner you realize that, the better off you'll be." I scoff. "Wouldn't surprise me if he kills you when he's done with you."

"Byron contacted me once he put two and two together and realized you were my girlfriend, or ex-girl-friend. He made me an offer I couldn't refuse. An act of revenge, per se. Look," he drops his hands, peering up at me, "I've worked my ass off to get where I'm at and I've got nothing to show for it. A partnership with Davis & Davis law firm would be a dream come true. It's not like I've got anything to lose here. You made it clear where we stand."

I could kick him in the face right now. I really could. Just one lift of the leg and he'd be eating my toes. Then I could run. But running has proven to be a waste of time because I have nowhere to fucking go.

"Cal can help you. If you just stop all this and take my side, he will help you."

Trent stands up, nostrils flared and chest puffed out. "Fuck Callum Ellis." He leans closer. "And fuck you for fucking him."

Running might not be an option, but nothing stops me from raising my hand and slapping him across the face. "No, Trent. Fuck you!" The sting on my palm is actually gratifying. That was the best decision I've made all day.

Standing here arguing is getting me nowhere so I do

what's asked of me in hopes that I'll find a way out of this mess.

I reach down and pull up the dress that's pooled around me. It's actually a beautiful dress. Off-white— because Byron said whores don't get to wear white—with an impressive floral, lace overlay. It's much too poufy on the bottom and nothing like I planned to wear on my wedding day. Not the wedding I dreamt of, anyway.

"Zip it up." I give Trent my back, and he does as I say without a word.

Not even looking back at him, I walk out the door, barefoot. The dress is the only beautiful thing about me right now. I didn't even brush my hair again because I have no interest in looking acceptable for my soon-to-be husband.

I also have no plans to actually marry him.

Instead of taking the elevator to the ballroom, where the ceremony is being held, I go straight to the kitchen.

I'm not sure why I didn't think of this before, but a butcher knife straight to his heart should do the trick.

"Good morning," I say to the cook. It's not the same one who was working here during my last stay on the island. In fact, Byron has taken on all new staff. Peter has been replaced with an uptight doorman who smells like green beans and farts and never smiles. The position might have been filled by someone else, but Peter himself is irreplaceable.

"You shouldn't be in here, ma'am."

I spot a knife block and walk straight to it. Reaching down, I pull out the biggest one. It illuminates under the dome light hanging from the ceiling, and it's so big I can see my reflection in it. "And you shouldn't be working for a criminal who kidnaps women and forces them into marriage."

His eyes widen, darting from me to the pointed blade. I wink back at him before leaving with the knife in one hand, and my dress balled in the other to stop me from tripping over it. That would be just my luck—fall and stab myself in the gut. That's one way to end this madness.

No. I prefer to die while trying to live. At least then I know I gave it my damnedest.

I go up to the seventh floor, where the ballroom is, and I'm prepared for what I have to do. Actually, I'm not, but it's best this way. If I think too much about it, I'll cower.

The elevator doors slide open and I'm greeted with a very angry Byron, dressed in a black tuxedo with a cream-colored bow tie to match my dress. He shoots daggers at me before dropping his gaze to the knife at my side.

"Clever, Bella. If only you had the guts to use it."

"You'd be surprised how gutsy I am, Byron." I hold the knife out and walk forward. Each step has him walking backward. "Tell me why I shouldn't slit your throat right now."

Trent comes walking toward us, spots the knife, and throws his hands up, halting his movements.

Two more men follow behind him—men I've never seen before.

"Restrain her," Byron orders the men.

I look at the guys, waiting for them to do as they're told, but no one moves.

"Now!" Byron barks the order.

The smaller of the guys, who's actually shorter than I

am, starts my way. I hold out the knife, testing him. "Stay the fuck away from me." I choke on my words. "I'll do it."

"Bella," Byron says in a high-pitched voice, "think of Mark."

My attention snaps to him, the knife swinging with me. "I am thinking of Mark. And the rest of the world who I'd be doing a favor by taking you out. I will not marry you, Byron. Not today, not ever. I'll die first." I hold out my wrist, resting the knife against it.

Would I do it? Would I really die before marrying this guy? He'd end up killing Mark, probably Cal, too. I know he has him somewhere. I heard the conversation. He wants Cal to watch us get married, then he will probably kill them both.

"Go ahead," he nods toward the knife pressed to my wrist, "do it and save me the trouble of having to marry you. With you gone, I get everything I want."

"How?" I huff. "How am I standing in your way? What the hell do I have that you want?"

"Sir," the taller of the guys cuts in. "Sir, we have a problem."

Byron looks at me, the knife, then the guy. "What the hell is it now?"

The guy tips his head, calling Byron over.

With his back to me, I eyeball Trent, challenging him to stop me before I hit the button on the elevator.

Byron and the guy exchange some heated words and I tap my foot anxiously waiting for the doors to open. When they do, all eyes shoot in my direction. "Get her!" Byron shouts.

I step into the elevator and hit the button to close the

door repeatedly. They begin to close, but a hand slaps between them, causing the doors to open back up. It's the smaller one of Byron's goons. I swing the knife at his hand, slashing it. His howls echo through my head and I turn away so I don't see the deep wounds pouring blood onto the doors and the floor of the elevator.

With my head turned, I begin vomiting. It all just comes out with no chance of holding it back.

The next thing I know, arms wrap around me and the knife is taken from my hands. "The boat is coming. We need to get the hell out of here now. Give me your fucking phone," Byron snaps at Trent.

Still holding me, Trent reaches into his pocket and pulls his phone out. Asshole told me he didn't have any service. How did I not see what a snake he is?

Vomit hangs from my mouth, and I'm unable to wipe it away as my arms press tightly to my chest in Trent's hold. Byron and the other guys ride the elevator down with us.

My mouth tastes like ass and I'm on the verge of emptying the rest of whatever is in my stomach. "We're leaving the island?"

Byron taps into Trent's phone and doesn't even look at me when he speaks. "Seems we're getting some unexpected guests."

The elevator stops, and he slaps the phone in Trent's hand. "I'll take her from here. Go wait for the boat."

Trent shoves me into Byron's arms in the corridor of the main entrance. Everyone leaves, so it's just us. Byron holds me from behind and I can feel the tiny hairs on my arms standing up when his hot breath rolls down my neck.

"Seems I've got a decision to make, Bella. I can bring you with me and keep you, even though I don't need or want you. Or I can kill you and leave your body right here on this floor for my good friend and former client, Callum, to find."

"I thought…I thought you planned to marry me?"

Something happened. For some reason, everything has changed.

"You know, the first time I saw you, I knew you were trouble. I fought like hell to get you out of Callum's mind, but he fought me harder. I used to watch you for him. I saw you sleeping peacefully in your bed at night, not a care in the world. I jerked my cock while you were showering once. That was a good time. Then there was the time I saw you fingering yourself on your bedroom floor while your parents watched the evening news. Talk about rebelliousness."

My heart kicks into high gear because what I'm hearing is sickening. All those days that I went on with my life as a normal person, and I was completely oblivious to being watched.

"Each day Callum got closer and closer to getting you, until finally, you came, just like he knew you would. You fought him hard for a while, but eventually, you caved and fell under the spell of the infamous Callum Ellis. Such a fucking fool you are. You see, Bella, you can call me a crook and a liar, but you fell in love with a monster. What I could do to you wouldn't touch the betrayal he bestowed upon you."

"I don't believe anything you say. So shut the hell up!"

"Is that so? What if I told you that you were never protected when you had sex with him? What if I told you that instead of taking birth control, you were taking fertility pills because Callum was trying to impregnate you? Still want me to shut up, Bella?"

"I'd say I don't believe a word that comes out of your disgusting mouth." My head tilts down, and I bite into the flesh of his arm. My teeth sink deep, piercing his skin, and the bitter taste of salt and blood seeps into my mouth.

"You fucking bitch." Byron tries to shove me away, but my mouth is latched so tightly that he'd risk losing a chunk of his skin.

When he grabs me by the hair and jerks my head back so hard I get whiplash, I finally release my bite. My head swings and thrashes as he pulls and the next thing I know, my head is crashing into the wall. My body slides down slowly as everything blurs around me.

"Hurry your ass up. We gotta go," someone says, though I can't make out the face or the voice. "There's a lot of them, Byron. We gotta go, right fucking now!"

I can feel him lift me up, but I'm unable to fight him off.

My eyes close, and I allow myself to drift away to a time I was happy.

"Come on," Cal says, taking my hand and leading me out the back door of the church.

I laugh as he pulls me, though my resistance tells him I'm not so sure about this. "Cal, we can't. If Mrs. Webster finds out, she's sure to kill us."

"Nah. She won't even know we're gone. No one will."

When the door closes behind us, I drop my head back, letting the warmth of the sun kiss my cheeks. It's a beautiful day without a cloud in sight.

"Still wanna go inside for youth group?" he asks, his hand still holding mine.

My head comes forward, and I look at him, our smiles matching. "No way."

Cal leads me over to the side of the church. Not a person, car, or house to be seen. We sit down in unison, backs pressed against the building, legs bent at the knees.

Once a week, we take a bus to youth group. Now that I'm eleven, I've been moved up to the same class Cal is in. It's a two-hour break for Mrs. Webster and a chance for us to get right with the Lord—aside from our regular Sunday morning service.

"Is this where you disappeared to the last couple classes?"

Cal smirks. "Maybe."

"And why wasn't I invited then?"

He grabs my hand, flips it over, and begins tracing the lines on my palm. Something happens inside me. My stomach does this weird flip-flop thing and my heart begins beating superfast.

"Didn't know you'd wanna hang out with me outside of the home."

"Cal," I blow out his name in one breath, "I always want to hang out with you. You've been my best friend since I got here. Why would you say that?"

He doesn't look at me, just keeps drawing on my hand and causing goosebumps to ride up my arm. "Saw you with Mark and Trent a couple weeks ago. They were poking fun at my pants being too short and you laughed with them."

The flip-flop of my stomach stops when my heart settles inside it. "I'm sorry, Cal. You never should've heard that."

"You never should've let 'em get away with saying it."

"You must've missed the part where I told them to both eat a bag of dicks."

Cal's eyes widen, finding mine. "You didn't?"

"Oh yes I did." I laugh. "And I'd do it again, even if it meant getting my mouth washed out with the nasty dollar-store soap."

Cal's expression gets serious, though I find it hard to take him seriously at all. "Always go for the blue bar if it's available. The green one tastes like perfume-infused ass."

We both burst out laughing.

"Really, though, Cal. I'm so tired of trying to fit in with these kids. Me and you. It's me and you. Ride or die."

Cal holds out his pinky. "Promise?"

I wrap my pinky around his and give it a shake. "Forever and ever, until kingdom come."

11

"GET HIM!" I shout through gusts of wind as pelts of ice lash at my face. I'm running as fast as I can, unable to see a damn thing. But I won't stop. I will not stop until I have her.

I watch in slow motion as Anders takes Byron down to the ground, Bella's body falls weightlessly from his arms, and she topples face-first into the snow.

The two of them begin a wrestling match, rolling, punching, kicking, but I offer no help to my guard as I go straight for Bella.

My eyes skim over her body. Bruised, cold, and bloody.

"Jesus Christ, Bella. What did he do to you?"

Her eyes flutter open, lips smacking, and as much as I want to warm them with my mouth, I have to make sure she's okay first.

"Am I dreaming?" she asks through parted, cracked lips.

I breathe a sigh of relief at the sound of her beautiful voice. "No, baby. You're not dreaming."

Scooping her into my arms, I head for the castle. Looking over my shoulder, I shout to my men. "Rough him up. But keep him alive."

I don't even look back. I may have lost some men when the world assumed I was dead, but the ones still standing by my side are an army of soldiers. They have what it takes to restrain Byron and they'll be on guard until I'm one hundred percent certain Bella is safe. Not that I plan to take my eyes off her.

Her lashes bat snowflakes off them as I carry her in my arms like a small child. "Cal. Is it really you?"

"It's really me. You're safe now."

A sigh of relief escapes her, followed by a gasp. "Oh my God, Cal. Your face. What happened to you?"

She's taken notice of my swollen eye and bruised cheek. That son of a bitch holding me captive thinks he's got away with what he did because I paid him a measly seventy-five grand. He also expects the rest by this evening. Joke's on him. "It's nothing. Don't worry about me."

Bella locks her arms around my neck, peppering my face with kisses through cries of happiness, while sharing my breath to fill her lungs.

"You're alive and you're here."

I look down on her, smiling, though my insides are screaming for what she's endured. "I'm here and I'm never letting you go."

"Mark," she whispers through parted lips. "Byron has Mark."

"Don't worry. We'll find him."

This day has been like a repetitive kick in the gut. I'm not sure I'll ever stop blaming myself for what has happened to Bella. She's in a wedding gown. *Why the fuck is she in a wedding gown?* I can't even think about what would have happened to her had I not made a deal with the prison guard.

Once we're inside, I go straight up the elevator to the sitting room. Every few steps, I peer down at Bella and see her soft, green eyes staring back at me, trying to figure out if this is real or not.

We reach the sitting room and I take her straight over to the fireplace. It's like a moment of déjà vu, only this time, I'm not the monster she took me for that night. At least, not to her. Everyone else in this world? Well, they are about to see just how much of a villain I really am.

I lower her down to the ground and reach over, grabbing a throw blanket off the chair. My legs straddle her from behind. I quickly wrap the blanket around her cold body and squeeze her tightly in my arms.

My chin rests on her shoulder, and I inhale the scent of her damp hair. "Tell me everything."

"I...I don't even know where to start." She turns to the side, legs draped over mine. I press a chaste kiss to her cheek, still reeling from this unexpected reunion with her. "I've missed you so much, Cal." Tears slide down her cheeks and I use my thumb to sweep them away.

"I've missed you, too. But we're together now and nothing is going to tear us apart."

She begins sobbing, head resting on my chest, and I

stroke her hair in an attempt to calm her. "Is Byron really gone?"

"He's gone, baby. I swear over everything, that guy will never touch you again. *No* guy will ever touch you again."

Fuck. The thought of him putting his grubby hands on her makes me fucking crazy. Like boiling water coming to the surface, ready to implode all over anything and anyone who comes near me.

"Bella," I tip her chin with my thumb, looking into her eyes and searching for the courage to ask what I'm about to, "did he...did he touch you?"

If she says yes, so help me God, I will go out there and dismember that son of a bitch before I'm able to get any answers. I will chop his body up into tiny pieces and use it as bait.

"No. Not like that."

A heavy breath of relief parts her hair and I pull her head against my chest. "You have no idea how happy I am to hear that."

We sit quietly for what feels like hours. Warming by the fire, just breathing and holding one another when the sound of heavy footsteps grabs our attention.

I look back first and see Anders, holding up another one of my men. He's severely injured and in dire need of medical assistance.

I tuck the blanket around Bella and scoot out from beneath her. She grabs my leg. "Don't leave me."

"I'm just going over there. I'm not leaving."

Once I'm on my feet, I walk steadfast to Anders. "What the hell happened?" I whisper, trying not to alarm Bella.

"He got away. Greg and Nico are dead. Ben, here, was shot in the abdomen."

I look at Ben, who begins coughing, spewing blood from his mouth. My eyes wander down to his stomach, where Anders has his hand pressed firmly. Blood oozes from his wound, dripping onto the hardwood floor. "Lay him down," I tell Anders.

He helps him down to the ground and I kneel over him, until the coughs and groans subside, then I sweep his eyes shut.

One glance over my shoulder and I see Bella coming toward us. I hold up my hand. "Stop. Don't come over here." Her movements halt, but it's too late, she sees him.

Her hands clap over her mouth, and she points her finger at Ben. "Who did that?"

I get to my feet, hurry over to her, and lead her toward the door. "Call for another boat for me and Bella. You guys go with Leo to the main island. I'll meet you at the docks." I keep walking, then shoot Anders one last look. "And get rid of all the bodies."

Anders nods and I take Bella out of the room.

"It's okay. I promise. We're going somewhere safe. We just have to get Peter first."

Bella bows her head, breaking eye contact. "Cal," she begins.

Something isn't right. I can feel it in my bones. I tip her head up, forcing her to look at me. "What is it? What happened?"

"Peter died over a month ago. Byron all but admitted to killing him."

"What did you just say?" It doesn't need repeating. I

heard her loud and clear. I'm just having a hard time processing the words that just came out of her mouth.

"Peter is dead, Cal."

It feels like the world has stopped spinning. My hollow heart cracks beneath the surface, unable to feel it beating. All the blood drains from my face and it's also in this moment that I realize how human I really am. I've never felt loss. Never knew what it was like to feel that sort of pain.

No. It's not true. It can't be.

Peter was like a father to me. He was a mentor, a friend, a confidant. Aside from Bella, he is the only person in the entire world I ever gave a damn about.

"He's gone?" I ask, unable to believe it, even though the words were clear as day.

Bella nods before throwing herself into my arms and holding on to me like our lives depend on it.

Peter is dead, but I push the pain aside as something awakens inside me. I pull myself together and prepare for war.

12

NOTHING I SAY or do will ease his pain. He won't even admit that he feels any, but I can see it in his eyes. Those wide, dark orbs roaming around the abyss. Lost in his thoughts, while I'm curled against his chest.

I want to ask him if he's okay, but I know the answer. He'll lie and say he is. Put on a front because that's what Cal does. He wears this rock-hard exterior, even though he's crumbling beneath the surface.

Instead of saying anything at all, I just sit here quietly and savor this moment. We're finally together. After weeks of sheer torture, while everyone told me he was dead, he's here.

The boat slows, and I straighten my back on Cal's lap. My hand rests on his cheek, and I turn his face toward mine. "I'm here for you," I whisper, before pressing my mouth to his. It's a soft kiss, with no effort on his part. I can feel his sadness bleeding into my mouth, so I pull away. Looking into his eyes, he looks past me.

My hand drops and I put little thought into the

distance he's putting between us. He's been through a lot and needs time to process everything. Peter was the closest thing he ever had to family, to a father. He was so much more than just a butler, and I know this because I felt it in my own friendship with Peter.

There is a lot we need to talk about. So many unanswered questions that are gnawing on my insides, tugging at my heart and begging to be asked. And I will, in time.

We come to a stop at the dock, and Cal pats my thigh, telling me to get up. I do, and as I go to reach for his hand, I stop myself. His attention isn't on me. It's on the men waiting at the end of the dock.

Right now, Cal has a one-track mind. I'm not upset about it. He saved me, and now he will work tirelessly to ensure my safety, while also avenging Peter's death. I know Cal will keep me safe, even if it won't be an easy task. Byron is smart—though a menace to society—and he will not make the hunt for him an easy one. I just hope in the process, we do not become the prey. For whatever reason, Byron is hell-bent on taking over Cal's empire. He could go out and steal from anyone, but he's after Cal. There has to be a reason for it.

Cal surprises me by taking my hand in his and leading me off the boat. The sun has dipped behind the clouds, making for a gloomy setting. A group of men await us. Some wearing suits, some looking like they just rolled out of bed. My bet on the most badass are the grunge-looking dudes. They look like they're ready to take care of business, scowls and all. One in particular catches my eye.

I squeeze Cal's hand, and he looks down at me. "Hey," I

tip my head toward one of the familiar faces, "that guy with the bruised eyes and swollen nose. Who is he?"

"Ah, you remember?"

I snort. "Yeah. Actually, I think I'm the one who did that to his face."

Cal laughs, and it's a sound I've missed. "Yeah, babe. Yeah, you did. He was hired to watch you, and he failed. In fact, he shouldn't even be here." Cal picks up his pace, taking me with him. "Ludwig," he shouts, "I thought I fired your ass."

We approach the guy and Cal drops my hand before stepping up to him. "What the fuck are you doing here?"

"I called him," Anders chimes in. "Look, we need all the help we can get and regardless of a little mishap, he's a good one to have on our side."

Ludwig—I assume is his last name because it's a ridiculous first name—watches me as I join Cal's side. "Hey, sorry about your nose," I say to him, and he completely ignores me. *Jerk.*

Cal nods to the left, looking at Anders, and he takes me with them as they leave the group. "I'm taking Bella to the Manhattan resort. I want you to work with these guys and find that son of a bitch. Once you've got him, call me. But keep him alive. I wanna be the one he's looking at when he takes his last breath."

"You got it, Boss."

Cal wraps an arm around my waist and takes a step to leave, but stops. "Oh, and Anders, find out what happened to Peter's body. He deserves a proper burial."

Anders gives a sympathetic nod with his lips pressed together firmly.

We leave the docks, and the army of men Cal has rallied together. A shiny black car awaits us, and Cal opens the back passenger door. I slide in, and he joins my side.

For the first time in days, I feel safe as he wraps his arm around my shoulders. My head nuzzles into the pit of his arm as he says, "Tell me everything you know about Peter's death."

So, I do. I tell him how I found him on his bedroom floor. How Byron showed up on the island right after and told me about a body that was pulled from the bay.

"It was a former guard. Anders's brother. He was a fuck-up, and I won't deny I had him killed. I'm a monster, Bella. No matter how hard I try to be good, it's what I am."

I go on to tell him how Byron escorted me off the island and promised to keep me updated and that I didn't hear a word from him until two days ago at the performance hall.

Cursing and fuming, he listens to it all.

Cal decided it was best to drive to the hotel we're staying versus taking the private jet. He thinks Byron has access to the pilot logbook and will be able to find out where we're going if we use one of his. Fortunately, it's only a three-hour drive, and we drove past a fast-food restaurant and got greasy burgers, fries, and shakes for the ride.

I swallow down my last fry and place my hands on my bloated stomach. "I'm stuffed."

"I bet you are. You scarfed that food down like you haven't eaten in days." Cal takes a drink of his shake. I watch as his mouth wraps around the straw and then his tongue licks the excess liquid from his lips.

Food isn't the only thing I'm starving for. I've almost forgotten what it feels like to be with him intimately. He was my first, and naturally, he was my last. Once I got a taste of what sex was like, I've craved it ever since.

Cal catches me looking at him and smirks. "Why are you looking at me like that?"

My hand rests on his lap, climbing up until it's sitting on his crotch. "I've missed you."

He places a hand on mine, squeezing it until I'm squeezing him. His erection grows little by little, until he's rock-hard beneath my hand. He leans over and whispers, "Have you now?" Warm breath hits the nape of my neck, sending chills down my spine.

"Mmmhmm," I hum, rubbing his cock through his pants.

His eyes burn into mine, biting at his bottom lip. "Well, I'm here now. What are you gonna do about it?"

I look past him at the driver's rearview mirror and catch him watching us. He immediately returns his focus to the road. I move my hand to my lap and sulk. "Absolutely nothing because we have company."

Cal shoots a look at the front seat. "Who? Him?" He says in a breathy voice, "Fuck that guy. I'll fire him when we're finished to remove all awkwardness." Strong hands grab my waist, and he lifts me up until I'm straddling his lap. "There, now he can't even see you."

I chuckle. "He can see me. I just can't see him."

His mouth finds my neck, and I welcome it by tilting my head. "Same thing."

When his hand slides up the sweatshirt I changed into before we left the island, I give in to the desire. Reaching under my bra, he pinches the bud of my nipple and a whimper of pleasure climbs up my throat.

Cal moves his hand back down, trailing his fingers delicately across my stomach and beneath the waistband of my sweatpants.

"Maybe you're right. Maybe we shouldn't do this," Cal says, taking me by surprise.

"What? Of course we should. I need this. I need you."

"You've been through a lot today. You sure?" he asks, eyes wide and full of mischief. I think part of him likes that we have an audience, and part of me is also turned on by that fact.

I lick my lips and nod. "Positive."

His hand slides down, thumb grazing my sensitive nub. My heart picks up speed and I pull his face to mine, cupping his cheeks in my hands. Our mouths collide recklessly. My back arches as I roll my hips, forcing pressure on his hand down my pants.

Curled fingers dip inside me and I lift up just a bit, giving him better access. I can already feel my desire for him pooling around his touch. I shouldn't want this right now. But after all I've been through, I just want to feel something other than terror and torment.

Before long, I'm riding his hand, and we're full-blown making out like two teenagers in the back seat of the car. There's no hiding how much I want this, how much I've missed this. Cal and his magical fingers continue to work me, bringing me to the brink of orgasm.

His hand grips my hip, teeth dragging across my lower

lip and sucking it in his mouth before releasing it like a rubber band. We resume tangling our tongues and stealing each other's breaths.

"Fuck, Cal," I cry out as he pushes harder and deeper. I bounce up and down on his hand, driving his fingers farther inside me.

"That's right, baby. Show me how much you've missed me. Come around my fingers."

His words turn me on even more. Pushing me over the edge as I come undone. I don't even try to muffle my cries of pleasure. My thighs tighten, walls clenched as my orgasm spills into his hand.

When I come down, I smile through the aftershock rippling through me. His fingers leave me and I miss them already.

Cal slides his fingers in my mouth, feeding me my arousal. My lips close around them, tongue swirling, licking my own juices while gazing into his molten eyes.

He pops them out of my mouth, then kisses me. "You taste so good, baby."

I purr into his mouth, our chests heaving together.

In one swift motion, Cal undoes his pants and his cock springs free. Hungry and ready to reclaim what's his. "Take these off," he commands, pulling on my sweatpants.

I look over my shoulder, catching the driver's eyes again, but smirk inwardly. He's a driver for the rich and reckless, I'm sure this isn't the first time someone has fucked in the back seat of his car.

Cal grabs my face and presses his lips firmly against mine, teeth colliding and lips swelling. He mutters into my mouth, "Let him watch."

I'm not sure why that thought is satisfying, but it is. I'm learning a lot about what I find to be sexually satisfying. Like watching those people in The Grotto. I was highly aroused by it.

I lift up and tug my sweatpants and panties off, letting them fall to the floor. Cal pushes his pants all the way down, then pulls me onto his lap. His cock sinks inside me, wasting no time. Completely filling me up, I take all of him.

"God, I've missed you." His fingers sweep beneath my shirt, then pull my bra down, freeing one of my breasts. Leaning forward, he takes my nipple between his teeth. Biting, tugging, and sucking.

I kiss his swollen eye, down to his bruised cheek. "Not as much as I've missed you." My fingers dig into his hair, hugging his face to my chest. He moves to the next breast, sucking with so much tenacity that pain quickly becomes pleasure.

I ride him harder, faster. My tits bouncing with me. One hand pinches my waist as Cal holds me tightly, as if he fears I'll escape him. Our bodies meld together, a sheen of sweat coating both our foreheads.

"Holy shit, Bella," Cal grumbles, dropping his head back and watching me as I fuck him. His eyes burn into mine, while every inch of him consumes me.

I grip his shoulders, using them to balance myself as I move faster. I don't muffle my sounds, knowing full well that the driver hears me, sees us, and is likely jerking his cock as he takes us down the highway.

Cal's head comes back up; he plants both hands on my

waist and squeezes as his breath holds and he grunts through his release.

We're both breathless, sweaty, and trying to calm our racing hearts.

My head rests on his shoulder, and he strokes his fingers through my hair.

As I'm sitting here, coming down from my high, I remember something Byron said.

What if I told you that you were never protected when you had sex with him? What if I told you that instead of taking birth control, you were taking fertility pills because Callum was trying to impregnate you?

I sit up, adjust my shirt, and broach the topic casually as I reach for my pants. "Hey, Cal. Remember those birth control pills you had Peter give me?"

He quirks a brow. "Yeah, what about them?"

I raise my shoulder nonchalantly and continue to fumble with my pants. "They were birth control pills, right?"

Cal goes quiet for a minute and I feel like he's sucked the air right out of my lungs. His silence is alarming. The tiny hairs on my arms stand up as I press for an answer. "Right?"

Cal lifts his waist and pulls his pants up, avoiding eye contact. "Why are you even asking about those pills?"

Once we're both wiped up and dressed, I curl one leg under the other and face him as he stares straight ahead.

Agitation takes hold of me and I'm not in the mood for this beating around the bush shit. "Just answer the damn question, Cal."

He finally looks at me, sorrow in his expression. He

takes my hand in his. "No, babe. They weren't birth control pills. But let me—"

I jerk my hand away, cutting him off. "Don't!"

"Bella," he begins, though doesn't finish. Likely because he sees how upset I am.

I can't even look at him. All the words I want to say escape me.

It wasn't enough that I agreed to be his wife, because of some stupid will, but he intended to go one step further and trick me into getting pregnant.

13

THE REST of the ride is quiet. There's so much I want to tell her, but I use this time to let her collect her thoughts and calm down.

Yeah. I fucked up. What's new? I always fuck up. In a desperate attempt to keep her forever, at the possibility of her not agreeing to marry me, I made her think we were having protected sex, when really I was giving her medication to stimulate her ovaries. It's a safe medicine and has been known to aid in conception.

It was an asshole move, but at the time, I didn't care. Before Bella came to the island, I had the perfect plan laid out. I never intended to fall for her as hard as I did. If I'd known then that we could have a relationship built on trust instead of lies, I would have never done half the shit I did.

With the extra time, I was able to make a call to my new attorney, who's getting a new will drawn up for me as we speak. After reviewing my former will and testament, along with the contract Byron and I both signed, he's made it clear I'll be paying Byron a nice chunk of change for breaching the contract. I've agreed to the terms, but I also know that Byron won't be getting shit from me.

My accounts are in the process of transferring back to me, and I relinquished my rights to press charges against Byron. He'll get what's coming to him, and it won't involve any law enforcement.

We arrive at the hotel and it's past midnight. I fully expected Bella to fall asleep, but I don't think she's even blinked since I was truthful with her about the pills. Well, somewhat truthful. I'm not sure if she knows what they really were, but she does know that they weren't birth control pills.

I place a hand on her leg. She doesn't even flinch. "The driver will get our bags. Let me take you up to our room."

She scoffs, slides across the seat and exits the door opposite me.

My head drops, a pang burning in my chest and a sigh slipping through my lips. "Okay, then," I mumble. It seems she's going to make this harder than I expected.

"Eighth floor suite," I tell Gustav, the driver, who's lugging our bags onto a cart. "Oh, and I hope you enjoyed the show. You're fired." I don't even wait for a bitter expression or angry reply. I walk in through the automatic double doors, past the front desk, where a short brunette is biting into a crumbly muffin.

She has no idea who I am and I don't make my identity known. Right now, it's best to keep things under wraps. Bella and I both need to lay low until Byron is found.

I find Bella sitting on a beige sofa in the common

room across from the elevators. Her arms are crossed over her chest, legs crossed at the knee, and the wry look on her face has creased her forehead.

I stick my hand out to her, though she's at least ten feet away. "Come on."

Blowing out a breath of annoyance, she gets up and walks toward me, bypassing my hand and standing directly in front of the elevator.

"Do you plan on being this much of a grump ass our entire stay?"

She huffs. "A grump ass? Why not use the word on the tip of your tongue—a bitch?"

I bite back a smile. "Okay. Do you plan on being this much of a bitch our entire stay?"

Her nostrils flare and she stomps a foot. "Did you just call me a bitch?"

Is she serious right now? "Yeah. Because you told me to."

"No. I was implying that you shouldn't lie."

I'm suddenly reminded why I've never had a relationship, or wanted one.

We take the elevator up and Bella walks slowly behind, following me to our suite. The entire eighth floor is ours. We have everything we need up here. Six of the eleven hotels I own have one floor specifically for me. All being the eighth floor. There's no rhyme or reason for it; I've just always liked the number eight.

Okay. I guess there is a reason.

I moved to The Webster House on the eighth day of the month. Bella was adopted on the eighth. I moved in with the Ellis family on the eighth. I killed my adopted father on the eighth. Some would say those are reasons to hate that number, but I use those incidents as a reminder of why I keep my walls up.

Slowing my steps, I wait for Bella to catch up. When she does, I place my hand on the small of her back. She grumbles under her breath but makes no attempt to remove it. "I'm sorry," I finally say, hating the way those words sound coming from me. I don't apologize often and when I do, it's because I truly mean it.

Her eyes roll but no nasty comment follows. We're making progress.

I use my master key to unlock the door. It's one key used to enter all the rooms. I have one for each resort—Cori Cove being the exception, since it's not finished, and we're still using skeleton keys.

I'm not sure what I'll do with that place now. Not even sure I want to open it up to the public. I bought it because it had special meaning to Peter. The entire process was planned with Bella in mind. I'd bring her there. Force her into marriage. Keep her there. I'm not sure when shit went awry, but plans changed fast when I fell in love with her. Then she reciprocated that love and days later, she was ripped out of my arms.

And here we are. Back together but miles apart.

We walk into the suite. It's the size of an apartment, with all the furnishings. A living room, full-size kitchen with all stainless-steel appliances, one bedroom, and two bathrooms. The best thing about this hotel is the view overlooking the city. I'm not a fan of the hustle and bustle of city life, but I can handle looking at the glowing lights atop the buildings from this viewpoint.

Bella must've caught a glimpse because she walks over to the patio doors and stretches the blinds open.

I come up behind her, arms wrapping around her waist, chin pressed to her shoulder. "What do you think?"

There's a beat of silence before she turns around. My chin lifts, but my hands never leave her waist.

Her tear-soaked eyes speak volumes about how she's feeling. My heart stings at the sight. "Why'd you do it?"

My thumb sweeps under her eyelid, catching a tear before it falls. "I was scared of losing you again." It's the truth, as painful as it is to admit.

"But you had me. I was there."

I give her more truth, and it hurts like hell. "We once made a pack and a promise of forever, and you left me. How was I supposed to know you wouldn't leave me again?"

"I was a kid!"

"You made a choice." My hands drop from her waist. I run my fingers through my hair. "Dammit, Bella. You were given two choices: stay or leave, and you left."

This is not going the direction I intended it to. I turn away from her and cross the room to the minibar between the kitchen and living room. I had the staff stock it with my favorite bourbon, and red wine for Bella.

I take the top off the decanter and pour myself a shot. Tipping it back, I take the contents down in one swallow.

"Is this what you're going to do every time you screw up? Turn everything around on me and throw it in my face how I left you behind when I was eleven years old?"

I pour another shot, taking that one down just as fast. My eyes close and I allow myself to feel the burn riding down my throat and settling in my stomach. Once it does, I set the top back on the bottle and turn around. My palms press to the bar behind me and my head tilts slightly. "You know, you're cute when you're mad."

"Fuck you."

"You're even cuter when you curse."

Bella spins on her heels, pouting as she looks out at the city beneath us. "In case you were even wondering, I'm not pregnant. I had my period two weeks ago."

I come up behind her, inhaling her hair and wrapping my arms around her tense body in the same manner I did minutes ago. "Good. That means you're ovulating. Maybe I should plant my seed in you right now."

Shoulders drawn back, she turns around to face me. "You already did it in the car, you idiot."

"Oh, so now we're name-calling?" It's a bad time for jokes, but I'm having a hard time taking her seriously when she looks this cute. It's also been over a month since I've had a drink, and those two shots have me feeling pretty good right about now.

She pushes past me, making a beeline for the minibar. "How do you even know about ovulation and cycles? That's sort of creepy, Cal."

"I read books. I'm full of useful and useless information."

Bella opens up the wine cooler and pulls out a bottle of Cabernet Sauvignon. She begins fidgeting with the top, peeling off the foil, so I walk toward her to offer a helping hand.

"Corkscrew should be in one of the drawers." I rifle through a few until I find it. Hesitantly, she hands me the bottle. I grin in response because I know allowing me to help is torture for her right now.

A twist and a pull and the cork pops off. Bella startles at the sound, and I chuckle at her timidness, though she's not timid at all. She's fierce and a force to be reckoned with.

She goes to grab the bottle, but I hold it up, out of her reach. "Forgive me?"

She shakes her head no.

"Will you *ever* forgive me?"

Her shoulders shrug.

"I don't wanna fight with you, Bella." I lower the bottle, but she doesn't take it from me.

"I don't either. I'm just wondering how we're supposed to have a future together that's built on nothing but lies."

I set the bottle down on the counter, grab her by the waist, and pull her flush to my chest. "We start over and we build something better." My lips press to hers, but I can still feel resistance on her end. "Can we do that?"

Bella pulls away and my shoulders slouch when she leaves my arms. "So much has happened, Cal. So many bad things, and I hate to say it, but it's all because of…"

Reality slaps me in the face, and it fucking hurts. "Because of what? Me?"

She doesn't have to say it. I know what she means. Bringing her to the island was the start of a series of unfortunate events. Bella has been emotionally beaten and had her heart shattered into tiny pieces. It is all because of me. I've hurt the only person left in this world that I give a damn about. And now, I don't think she can ever fully forgive me.

14

THE DAYS that follow are quiet. Me, lost in my thoughts; Cal, busy with his search for Byron. We haven't left this suite and it feels like the walls are beginning to close in around me.

Cal made some headway in finding Mark. It seems Cal was held in the basement of some building in the city, and he has a swarm of men heading there, because he's almost positive there were other prisoners.

I've been on pins and needles waiting to hear if Mark's been found. It's eleven o'clock at night and there hasn't been any word on him yet.

"Why don't you come to bed?" Cal pats the mattress beside him. We've slept in the same bed since the first night here, but Cal has never felt like more of a stranger than he has these past three days. Not even when I arrived at Cori Cove and saw him for the first time in twelve years. At least then I had hope. Right now, I feel like all hope is lost.

Regardless, I still slip my robe off and climb into bed,

wearing the baby pink nightgown Cal bought me. He had bags upon bags of clothes delivered, and it was an assurance that we're going to be here awhile.

"Please just talk to me," Cal says with that same sadness in his voice he's had all day.

"I'm not really sure there's anything to say right now." Of all the things he has done that hurt me, giving me false hope of protection while trying to 'stimulate my ovaries' has been the one that hurts the most. Maybe I'm overreacting, but the way I see it, he tricked me. He stole the fight in me, and I feel breathless, without a voice. I trusted what he was having me take and he was using my body to try and create a baby that would be used as a pawn in this sick game he and Byron are playing.

I still love Cal. Don't get me wrong, I'm not throwing in the towel or giving up on him. I'm just stuck in this headspace of 'what-ifs' and 'what-now?' What does any of this mean for our future? Am I subjecting myself to a life in hiding because Cal has so many enemies? What other secrets don't I know?

Cal rolls onto his side, fingertips floating down my arms, leaving a wake of goosebumps in their path. "Can we please move on from this?"

He's been so sweet. So attentive and kind. I know he's hurting, but I am, too.

"It's late," I tell him. "Can we talk tomorrow?"

He blows out a heavy breath, drops his arm then rolls onto his other side, facing the wall. "You said the same fucking thing last night, Bella."

I don't react. Don't respond. Instead, I tug the blankets over my shoulder, turn away from him and lie there, replaying the events of the last couple months. Just like I do every night.

I'VE BEEN LYING in this bed still and quiet for two hours. Cal hasn't said a word and his heavy breathing leads me to believe he's asleep. Slowly, I sit up with my back pressed to the headboard. He's on his side, still facing the wall. I watch the rise and fall of his chest and my heart warms at the sight. There's something about watching him sleep. Being in a vulnerable state when he puts on such a badass front for the world.

I wrap my arm around him softly, nuzzling my face into his back. I'm so full of love for this man that sometimes I feel like I will burst at the seams. I know I'm being stubborn. I was born with the dastardly trait. I'm just not sure I'm cut out for the life he has planned for us. Half of my life was spent fighting against the world. I don't want that for my future. I don't want that for my kids.

Unable to sleep, I move my arm and crawl out of bed, taking care not to wake him up. Cal hasn't been sleeping the best either, and he could really use a good night's sleep.

I step into my slippers and wrap my black, silk robe around me, tying it at the waist. It's been made clear that I am not allowed to leave this room because someone could see me and alert Byron. However, I'm restless and I'm suffocating.

Leaving the bedroom, I close the door gently behind me. We're staying at one of Ellis Empire's infamous hotels; however, this one is much different than what we were planning for Cori Cove. Instead of being secluded, it's in the city. There isn't a Gothic, kingdom-like appeal as I've seen in pictures of the other resorts. But there is one thing that has curiosity gnawing at me. The Grotto. Cal said every hotel has one. They are strictly for VIP members, but with Cal's master key card that has The Grotto logo on it, I'm just that—VIP. I pick it up off the kitchen counter and drum my fingers on it. *What the hell, why not?*

I sneak back into the bedroom and pull on a pair of sweatpants underneath my nightgown, then leave again. This time, leaving the suite. I walk casually down the hallway to the elevator and take it to the lowest level of the hotel.

The scent of chlorine floods my senses as the elevator descends, telling me that this one has an indoor pool.

When the doors open, I step out into the hall of the basement. I was expecting it to be empty, but instead, there are a handful of people. One couple holding hands and a girl in a bright red costume made of feathers and black fishnet stockings. People pass by and walk away, not even giving me a second look, although it's apparent I just rolled out of bed, because I did.

The decor is similar to Cori Cove. Lit lanterns spaced out perfectly: a dimness that offers a sensual vibe.

Keeping my distance, I follow behind a younger couple, who are flirting and can't seem to keep their hands off one another.

My feet stop moving when I see a guard outside the door they stand in front of. The guy holds something up

—a badge, maybe? A key card? The guard opens the door, granting them access.

I reach into the pocket of my robe and pull out the key card. It has the logo on it, so I'm hoping this is all I need to get in.

Approaching the guard, my nerves get the best of me. My hands tremble as I hold out the card from six feet away. He waves me closer, agitated at my pokiness. With it held out, I walk toward him.

"Nice outfit." He snorts before opening the door for me.

As soon as I step inside, my eyes shoot wide open.

Okay. I've seen The Grotto on Cori Cove. It was… interesting, to say the least. But this place, I never would have expected the scene in front of me.

People. So many people. Prancing around in barely anything. Disco lights, music, a dance floor, even a hot tub. There's a long red leather couch that extends the entire length of one wall. There are doors that lead to God only knows where. There are beds—some empty, some occupied. There are couples, trios, quads. My hand claps over my mouth when I see a guy wearing a thong with a leash attached to it and what appears to be a harness. The girl walking him seems very proud of her obedient pet.

I shouldn't be here. This is not my sort of thing. I'm more out of place in this room than I would be in a church completely naked.

"Mojito?" someone asks, snapping my attention away from the human dog.

A petite waitress, who looks younger than I am, stands

beside me. Long, tight blonde curls, full lips with cheek-bones that could chisel glass. She's wearing a black leather bralette, a pair of leather boy shorts, and five-inch heels. Extending a tray, holding three glasses with cute umbrellas and a cherry on top, she offers me a drink. "Umm, sure. Thanks."

I take a glass, bring the straw to my lips, and sip on my drink as I take in my surroundings.

"First time?" the waitress asks.

The straw leaves my lips, settling back into the glass. "That obvious?"

"Well," her eyes roam my attire, "you are hiding a nightgown and sweatpants under that robe. And don't get me started on those slippers."

"Hey. I happen to like these slippers." I stick one out, looking at the gray furry thing before laughing. "Okay. They're hideous."

"Cherry," she extends her hand, balancing the tray on the other.

"Cherry? That's a pretty name."

"It is. Unfortunately, it's not my real name. But it's what everyone knows me as."

With the straw parting my lips, I speak around it. "It's nice to meet you, Cherry. I'm B...Brooke." Fortunately, those few sips of alcohol haven't gone to my head yet; otherwise, I'd be spilling all my tea.

"You, too. Enjoy the festivities and holler if you need anything."

"Thank you."

Cherry walks off and I can't help but notice the confidence she ensues. Just the way she walks with her back straight, chest puffed out. It's an assurance I wish I had.

I walk farther into the room, sucking down my drink and trying to blend in as much as possible, for someone dressed to stand out. Even the girl in the business suit is getting attention, while no one even notices I'm here. I'm not sure if I should feel insulted or thankful. When the business girl turns around, I see exactly why the attention of three men is laser-focused on her. Beneath her open blazer is a pair of perky breasts with two hoops hanging from her nipples.

"Okay, then," I whisper under my breath.

I'm walking through the spacious room when a door opens just as I pass it. One glance inside turns into gawking on my end. It's a swimming pool. A very large pool full of naked guests. That explains the chlorine smell in the elevator.

"Going in?" a guy asks. He's tall. Bright blue eyes that are more blinding than the sun. Gorgeous shoulder-length blond hair and a rigid six-pack."

"Umm. No thanks."

Blue eyes pats a towel at his dampened locks. "You sure? It's pretty refreshing."

"Nah. I'm good. Need to work up a sweat first, if you know what I mean?" I snort and immediately wish I could take it back.

The guy gives me a heated look, then closes the door, only to disappear into the crowd.

Yeah. I don't fit in here.

I keep sucking on my straw, until nothing comes back up. Another waitress walks by and I grab a drink off her tray. She doesn't even acknowledge me, just keeps walking by.

Somehow, I find myself sitting on the wall-length couch beside a couple making out. At least they're dressed, so I don't feel too uncomfortable. Suddenly, it feels like I'm back in high school at my freshman homecoming dance. The odd one out. The girl who always watched the fun instead of partaking.

Another door opens, this one straight across from me, and I see Cherry. She's serving up drinks to a few guys, one of which is getting a blow job. A hand lands on her ass, squeezing the tanned flesh of her cheek. She squeals in excitement and leans forward, whispering something in his ear. He gives her ass a slap, making it jiggle, and something ignites inside of me.

I'm not sure what it is or why. I'm not into girls, but just watching the action taking place inside that room, and all around me, is fascinating.

Cherry comes out of the room and her eyes immediately land on mine. "Now, what are you doing sitting there all by yourself?" She eats up the space between us, takes my hand, and pulls me up. "Since you're new here, I'll let you in on a little secret. But first, are you a voyeur or do you like to get in on the action?"

I clear my throat, unsure what she's even talking about. "A what?"

She giggles. "Do you like to watch or participate?"

"Umm…" I'm not really sure how to answer this. I could tell her that I'm a nosey shit and just want to see what happens in places like this because I'm tired of being stuck in my room with my boyfriend/former boss/childhood friend/criminal who is hiding me, so I don't get us both killed. Instead, I opt for the easy response. "I like to watch, I guess."

Her brows dance across her forehead and she smacks her lips. "Perfect. Come with me."

"I, ugh… Look, I'm not really—"

"Have a little fun, Brooke. That's what this place is all about."

She's right. It's about damn time I have a little fun. Even if I have zero interest in joining in on any of this, there is no harm in watching and letting loose for a little bit.

A minute later, Cherry is taking me into a room. Not just any room, though. It's a dark room with dim red lighting. There is one ginormous bed in the center and a swing hanging from the ceiling. On top of the bed are at least six people having a full-on orgy. There's a girl in a swing, sucking on a lollipop and watching the action. Two guys in a corner are getting blow jobs from one girl. She literally has two cocks in her mouth. My tongue pushes against my cheeks just watching it. Then there's a girl fingering herself at the end of the bed. She's all by her lonesome. Just her and her own fingers, giving herself pleasure.

"Grab a seat. Grab a swing. Take your clothes off, or don't. Just enjoy the show. You'll thank me later." Cherry flashes me a wink before leaving the room. My heart jumps when the door latches closed and I expect everyone to look at me—but they don't. They don't even care that I'm here.

I decide to take a seat on a barstool that sits all by itself in a corner. With the glass clenched firmly in my hand, I take a small sip, uneager to finish the drink off because I need something to do with my hands.

On the bed, there are three guys and three girls. The guys and two of the girls are stark naked, while one girl wears a sexy lingerie getup. A blonde girl lies flat on the bed, sucking a big cock; her legs are spread as a brunette girl sweeps her tongue up and down her pussy. The girl eating pussy is getting fucked in the ass by a slender guy with glasses. Each pounce has him pushing the glasses back up on his nose while sweat dribbles onto the frames. He's also got an entire hand in his ass by a girl who's getting fucked three ways from Sunday. Okay, I've lost track of body parts. All I can focus on is the way that girl is sucking dick like it's her favorite meal. It glides into her mouth so effortlessly and she doesn't even gag, taking all eight, girthy inches down her throat.

My eyes skate up from the cock to the body of the man who owns it and I immediately jerk my attention away when I see him watching me. Staring at the wall beside me, I take a long sip of my drink, then slowly look back—and he winks.

My stomach somersaults and I begin watching the girl who's getting pounded from behind. The guy with glasses digs his fingertips into the meaty flesh of her hips. Rolling his hips and sliding his cock in and out of her. He grunts, taking her faster and filling her up completely. His pelvic bone crushing against her ass. His mouth falls agape and lust is written all over his face as he comes.

When their motions stop, I take a deep breath, feeling like I was on the verge of climaxing myself. I cross my legs, feeling the dampness pooling in my panties, tingles riding through my entire body. My nipples pucker against the thin fabric of my sheer nightgown and holy shit, I wanna get fucked. Like right now.

I finish off my drink, set the glass on a table, and leave the room without a word. I'm not sure what the etiquette is here, but I seriously feel like I should tip them for the show.

My feet don't stop moving as I tuck my hands in the pockets of my robe and walk toward the door I entered.

"Brooke," someone calls out behind me. It takes a second for the name to register when she hollers again, "Hey, Brooke. Wait up."

I spin around and see Cherry walking briskly toward me. "Well, how was it?"

There's no fighting the smile on my face. "Amazing. Thank you."

"You're welcome. Come back Friday. It's ladies' night and we've got a wet tee shirt contest in the pool room. It's always a good time."

"I wish I could, but I'm sort of…in a weird place right now."

Her expression shifts to one of concern. "Are you okay, babe? Is someone hurting you?"

"Oh no." I laugh. "Not like that. It's just my boyfriend. He wouldn't be too happy if he knew I was coming down here."

"Girrrrl," she drags out, "never let a man tell you what to do." She checks me with a wink. "See you Friday?"

I smile back at her. "I'll try."

This wasn't what I expected; it was so much more. I've never felt so enlightened and free and so fucking horny.

I hurry back up to the room only to find Cal sleeping away. That doesn't stop me from crawling under the blankets and waking him up with my mouth around his cock.

15

I'M NOT sure if this is a dream or reality, but if I am dreaming, I have no intention of waking up. My cock twitches between the warm lips wrapped around it. Twitching and growing with each flick of her tongue. I know that tongue; I know that mouth. "Bella," I groan, my hand beneath the blanket, fingers wrapped in her hair as her head bobs up and down.

Warmth surrounds my balls, squeezing ever so gently. Nope. Not a dream.

I rip the blanket off of us, only to see her doe eyes peering up at me in the glistening beam of moonlight.

She smiles around my cock, sliding her beautiful lips up and down. Her nightgown dips in the front, giving me a peek of her tits. "Baby?" I moan out through my dry mouth and cracked lips. "Come here."

Her head shakes no as she continues to suck, and if she keeps it up, I'll be coming before I get a chance to get her off.

My cock pops out of her mouth and she slides her

tongue up and down my length, hitting every nerve before taking me back in. I can feel my head reach her tonsils and I fist her hair tighter, rocking my hips with her motions.

One hand slides up my chest, running over my rigid abs, then sliding back down again and returning its attention to my balls.

"Fuck." I shiver when she rolls her tongue around my head and shoves my cock back down her throat. So warm, wet, and seductive. "I've missed the way that dirty mouth feels around my cock."

She looks up at me, and I point a finger, curling it and calling her to me. She shakes her head again and smirks like a devious child.

"Now!" I demand.

She finally does as she's told and climbs up my body on all fours. Once her bare pussy is straddling my chest, she peels her nightgown over her head. She must've taken off her panties before removing my boxers while I was sleeping. "Turn around," I tell her.

Doing as she's told, she twists until her ass is in my view. Both hands plant on her cheeks and I squeeze them in my palms before lowering her down until she's sitting on my face.

"Keep sucking."

Her mouth finds my cock again and my tongue sweeps up her slit. She tastes better than I remember. Sweet and salty. Her arousal drips into my mouth and I'm not sure what got her so turned on, but I want it to happen again and again. Every fucking night.

My tongue flicks against her swollen clit before I suck

it between my teeth. Her body jolts, so I do it again, causing her to cry out in pleasure. Her head bobs up and down, mouth wrapped around my dick as she sucks it like it's her favorite flavor.

"God, your mouth feels so good, baby."

I part her ass cheeks with my fingers and swirl my tongue around her asshole. I'm not sure if she likes it, but she doesn't stop me, so I keep going.

"Cal," she whimpers.

"Want me to stop?"

"Hell no." She moans, lathering my cock with her saliva then sucking it off.

With my tongue still circling her hole, I slide two fingers in her pussy, feeling her walls clench around them. "So fucking tight and wet."

She moans, telling me she likes when I talk dirty like that.

"Do you like sucking cock, Bella?" My voice comes out cracked and gravelly.

"I like sucking *your* cock."

That's what I like to hear. Only me. Only mine. "This pussy is mine, Bella. Only I make you come. Do you understand?"

She nods through sucks and blows on my dick. Her hips flex and her ass shifts upward as I curl my fingers, pressing them as far as they'll go and tapping against her G-spot.

More moans around my dick and the vibration rides through me like a tidal wave. Hitting me head-on and sending me soaring. My tongue sweeps across my wet lips, watching her ass bounce in front of me as she fucks my fingers.

I slap a hand to her ass, squeezing as her skin separates my fingers and leaves a handprint behind, claiming her—owning her.

"Mine," I growl, before flexing the muscle of my tongue and licking her up and down.

"Oh God," she cries out. Squeezing my fingers and unleashing her orgasm.

At the same time, I warn her, "I'm gonna come." Thinking she'll pull out and let my jizz shoot all over her neck. Instead, she keeps going, taking me all the way in her mouth and opening her throat as she swallows my cum.

My cock twitches as it leaves her mouth, missing the warmth already.

Bella turns around, wiping her hand across her parted lips. She settles on my chest, blanketing my body with hers.

I stroke her hair, wondering where this sudden sexual desire came from, but I don't overthink it. She's here, and she's mine. That's enough for me.

16

I WAKE up to Cal standing over me, hair glistening from his recent shower and only a towel wrapped around his waist. He's got a steaming mug of coffee in his hand. "Good morning." He hands me the cup with a cheeky grin.

Smiling back at him, I scoot myself up and take the cup.

His lips press to my forehead and the scent of his cologne surrounds me. "Last night was amazing. I'm glad you've finally came to your senses."

I scoff. "Came to my senses? You sure do have a way with words, Callum Ellis." I take a sip of the coffee, black and hot. It burns my top lip a tad, but it's too good not to keep sipping.

He takes a seat on the edge of the bed. Beads of water rolling down his abdominal muscles. "I assume last night means you forgive me?"

"Cal," I say softly. "Last night was incredible but nothing has changed. I'm not mad at you. Not really. I'm just…stuck." I'm hurt by what Cal did to me. No amount of apologies can change the fact that he took advantage of my body as a woman and tried to get me pregnant without my knowledge. However, I'd be a hypocrite to keep battling this out with him, considering we've been having unprotected sex. The difference is, it was my choice—or lack of restraint—and not his.

"Stuck?" He laughs, though it's void of any humor. "Bella, I have offered you anything you could possibly want. A kingdom, protection, all the money in the world. Most of all, I've offered you my heart, and now you're going to tell me you're stuck because I made one lousy mistake?"

It's too early for this. I take another sip, collecting my composure before I totally lose my shit on him. Then I set the glass on the nightstand and toss the blankets off me. "I'm going to take a shower."

Cal blows out an exaggerated breath but doesn't stop me.

This isn't how I wanted our reunion to go and now that it is going this way, it has me wondering how many days will be spent like this. Distant and bickering with a lack of trust.

As I'm lathering up my hair with the shampoo Cal had delivered for me, I think back to last night. How I snuck out of the room while Cal was sleeping and went to The Grotto. Here I am preaching about honesty and I'm pocketing secrets on night four of being back together.

Are we back together, though? I mean, he's here and so am I. After weeks apart, this is what I wanted. It doesn't feel like the relationship I expected. It's more like two people in hiding who are trying not to kill each other—while also sleeping together.

"Ugh." I breathe out a heavy sigh. How did everything get so messy?

Knuckles knock on the bathroom door, snapping me out of my thoughts. "Yeah?"

"Everything okay? It's been almost an hour."

Wow. An hour already. Feels like I just got in here. "Be out in a minute."

The next thing I know, the shower curtain is parting and Cal's standing there. He flicks the towel around his waist and it falls to the floor. "Want company?"

My eyes skate down his perfect body, stopping at his erection. "Umm sure. But didn't you just take a shower?"

He steps in, one foot at a time. "I did, but I'm not here for myself. Turn around," he demands, and I do.

I hear the sound of liquid squirting from a bottle. Standing under the stream of water, Cal begins rubbing his hands on my shoulders in a deep massage. My head tilts to the side, eyes closed, as I relax under his touch.

Smooth hands glide over my skin as goosebumps spill down my arms. "Cal," I say breathlessly.

He turns me around, eyes burning into mine. Hungry, yet vulnerable. As if he senses I'll push him away when all I want to do is pull him close.

"Baby," he whispers. "Don't do this to us."

A lump lodges in my throat and I swallow it down. Tears prick the corners of my eyes, but I fight them off. "I don't want to." My body connects with his, my head resting against his chest as the hot water pelts my skin.

Cal pulls my head away, cupping my cheeks in his hands. "Don't you love me anymore, Bella?"

My heart pangs with remorse. How could he even ask that? "Of course I do, Cal. I love you so much that it feels like my heart could explode at any given moment. That's what scares me."

His eyes dance across my lips, then back to my eyes, burning into them with so much desire that my soul catches fire. "Don't be scared, Bella. I'll never hurt you."

"But you do hurt me, Cal."

Saying the words hurts almost as much as the realization that I'm madly in love with this man.

Sadness sweeps across his eyes and the guilt of being so honest gnaws on my insides. "I know I have and I'm going to spend the rest of my life making it up to you. If you'll let me."

It wasn't a question, but it felt like one. *If I'll let him.* Imagining a life without Cal in it is damn near impossible, but when I try to picture our future together now, all I see is darkness. I look down, watching the beads of water spill down my legs, to my feet, then slowly disappearing.

"Ever since I was a kid, I could look ahead and picture everything I wanted. Before my mom died, I imagined a dad. When she was gone, and I met you, I saw us as best friends in high school together. Going off to college and going to parties. I could even picture my wedding day. One night I was lying in bed after we had just finished an entire blueberry pie in the attic, and I saw us." My eyes skate up his body, finding him staring back at me. "We were holding hands and even though it was a daydream, I felt butterflies in my stomach. A few days later, I left and you stayed behind and I couldn't see you anymore. You weren't at school, or the parties, and we never held hands again."

"What are you saying, Bella? You don't want a future with me?"

"Let me finish. That's not what I'm saying at all. It wasn't until the dance in the ballroom, the night you took my virginity on that piano, that I was able to see you in my future again." A smile spreads across my face. "It was perfect. I imagined us living at Cori Cove and going to see my family for the holidays. I pictured kids and tubing behind a boat on the bay. I saw it all."

"And now?"

"Now I see a life on the run. Hiding out and looking over my shoulder because you have so much money and power that someone out there is always going to try and take it, the same way you took it from your adopted dad. I see our kids living in fear. Never seeing my parents because it's not safe to go home. I see loneliness. And that's exactly what I don't want in a marriage."

Cal shakes his head, disagreeing with me. I'm not surprised he doesn't see what I see. He's lived in the darkness since he was adopted as a teenager.

"You're wrong." He laughs. "You are so wrong. You wanna know what I see?"

I nod in response.

"I see breakfast in the courtyard. Dinners on the yacht. Flower gardens and sandboxes. Midnight swims when the kids are asleep. Smiles, laughter, and memories. Most importantly, love. I see all the things we wanted as kids that we never got. I don't see a second of my future without you in it. You think too much, Bella. For once, stop planning and just live."

I bite back a smile, my heart feeling all warm and fuzzy. "You really see all that?"

"I really see all that. Now kiss me and tell me you forgive me before all the hot water runs out."

I'm not sure forgiveness was ever a question. It was more about moving on from it all. Maybe Cal is right. It's time to stop trying to plan my entire life out. "Okay. I forgive you under one condition."

"A condition, huh?" He pulls me so close that I'm forced to tip my head back to look at him.

"And what's that?"

"Once this is all done. We go back to Cori Cove and finish the renovations."

"Actually. I was thinking about keeping that one for ourselves."

"No hotel?"

"Do we really want guests in our home twenty-four seven?"

I actually like the idea of running a hotel together. "How about we keep this conversation open for discussion."

His lips press softly to mine. "Deal."

Cal's attention is pulled away, lips leaving mine when his phone begins ringing from the sink vanity. Tugging me closer, his words whisper across my lips, "It can wait."

"It could be about Mark. You should get it."

Cal growls into my neck, resting his chin on my shoulder. "What about makeup sex?"

"Oh, that will happen. After you take the call." I push

his shoulders back, forcing him off my body. The phone stops ringing but a voice message pings. "Please."

He kisses me once more, before opening the shower curtain. "Fine. But I'll be back. Wait for me."

Once he's out, I finish washing up. He must be listening to the voice message. "Who was it?"

Seconds later, the shower curtain parts, and he pops his head in. Wide eyes and water dripping down his forehead. He sweeps his tongue across his lips, catching a drop.

"You might wanna get out of the shower."

"No," I drag. "Please, Cal. Tell me he's not…" I can't say the words. I tear the curtain open and get out, immediately grabbing a towel from the hook and wrapping it around me. "What happened?"

"They found Mark. He's gonna be all right."

I blow out a heavy breath of relief. "Thank God. But what—"

"It's Trent." There's concern on his face that is surprising. He hates Trent as much as I do. Even if Cal doesn't know how much I've grown to hate him over the past week.

"He's dead, baby."

"Dead?" That's all I can say. I'm not sure how I feel. Trent was awful to me and I hoped I'd never see him again, but I'm not heartless. I didn't want him or anyone else to die. It's still a life and he has a family who loves him.

"Hey," Cal wraps his arms around my body, pulling me in for a hug, "you okay?"

"How?"

"From what my liaison said, it was Byron. Apparently, he went nuts and shot up an entire room of people."

I pull back and look at him. "But Mark got away?"

"Barely. But, yeah. Anders and a few others were able to make it in time and get him. We had an insider distracting Byron, and when he found out, he lost it."

I begin drying myself off quickly. "I need to see him. I have to go to my parents and tell them what happened."

"I can't let you do that, baby."

"Can't or won't?" I toss the towel on the floor at my feet, my hand lingering on the door handle.

"Both. I swore I'd never let anything bad happen to you again and I meant it. It's too risky to leave this place right now. It'll all be over soon, though, I promise."

"Will it, though? Will it ever really be over?" I tear open the door and go straight to the bedroom. My bag sits open on the floor and I shuffle through it and grab some clothes.

"What are you doing?" Cal asks, standing in the doorway with just the towel around his waist.

I clasp my bra behind my back and pull a black sweatshirt over my head. "I have to go, Cal."

Cal slams the door closed and closes the space between us. The towel dropped somewhere in between. "Dammit. Don't do this."

"Please don't try to stop me. I have to go to them. Mark is hurt and it's all my fault. All of this is my fault. Trent's dead and his parents are likely mourning their loss as we speak. Everything that happened is all my fault." Somewhere between shouts and cries, I fall apart in Cal's arms. Sobbing hysterically into the nape of his neck.

It is all my fault. If I'd never taken that stupid job offer then none of this would have happened. None of it. Not even us.

"It's not your fault, Bella. It's mine."

I don't say anything. I don't agree, and I don't disagree because, deep down, part of me knows that to be true. Cal started all this. He dragged me into his world, and in the process, it turned upside down. Now I have to decide if it's all worth it.

17

SHE DIDN'T LEAVE. Thank fuck I was able to calm her down and convince her it was a bad idea. Byron's out there watching and waiting for his opportunity to take something else from me—namely her. I'll die before he lays a single finger on her delicate skin again.

I'll die fighting for her, so she can live. Bella deserves it all. A life full of happiness without worry. The kids, the yard, the white picket fence. She deserves everything I don't. But I have the power to give it all to her. Even if I don't deserve her.

I'm despicable compared to this goddess. She's vibrant and full of life and here I am sucking it right out of her because I can't live without her in my life. How selfish is that?

I'm lying on my side, watching her sleep. Each breath flares her nostrils and every once in a while, her lips part, cracking a smile, and I find myself smiling in response. She's perfection personified. The most beautiful art piece imaginable—a Mona Lisa.

Most people don't believe in soulmates and maybe I've read too many novels, but I'm a firm believer that I was left in that alley as a newborn for Bella. So that one day, we would meet and our lives would be forever changed. She's the only person in the world who's ever given a damn about me and I'm not about to let some money hungry bastard take away everything I've fought my entire life for.

I haven't told Bella yet, but I'm thinking about changing my last name as well as the name of the company. I never wanted to be an Ellis. In fact, I hate the fucking name and everything it stands for. I'm not even sure what last name I was born with. Hell, I don't even know what time I was born. No clue if it was a hard labor or a C-section. Don't know my birth weight or how long I was. I could probably pick any name in the world and go with it. Blake, perhaps? It's Peter's last name and he was the closest thing I ever had to a family.

My head rests on the pillow right next to Bella's, and I watch her until my eyes don't allow me to any longer. Slowly, I drift into a deep sleep. And when I do, I instantly regret it.

"Mr. Ellis," I say, my voice soft and almost a whisper.

He doesn't even look at me, just keeps his eyes on the spread newspaper in his hands. "What the hell do you want?"

"I was thinking maybe we could talk about school. Ya know? Me, attending."

Mr. Ellis folds the newspaper in half as laughter climbs up his throat. "First of all, Caden," he enunciates the name he's plagued me with. "In this house, you call me Dad. Second of all," he stands, pressing his hands firmly to the desk in front of him, "you will never attend public school. Now get your ass back in your room and do your schoolwork before dinner. Mom's cooking tonight and I expect your compliance."

I go to walk out, tail between my legs and head hung low, but instead of pulling the door open, I shove it, so that it latches closed.

Slowly, I turn around and meet his gaze.

With drawn shoulders, he steps around the desk and pins me with a hard stare. "You got a problem, boy?"

"Actually. I do." My feet stay planted, fists balled at my side. His eyes wander to them, then back to my face, before erupting in full-blown laughter.

Heavy steps bring him closer. "Unclench your fists and walk your ass out of here before you make a big mistake."

My heart is going a million miles a minute, sweat dripping down my forehead. I'm gonna do it. I'm gonna punch this fucker right in the face. I've been doing lifts with my bed every day. It might not give me the brawn needed to lay him out, but I've got the mindset.

One more step and he's in arm's reach.

I'm gonna do it.

His hand extends, fingers spread as he goes straight for my throat. Before he can make contact, I cock my fist and aim right for his nose. Somehow, it lands, and I'm as surprised as he is as he cups his face.

Only, I didn't think ahead, and I'm not sure what to do now. So I go in for another, ready to pound my knuckles into his wrinkly flesh.

This time, he stops me. Catching my fist and squeezing before twisting my arm in a full three-sixty. Cries of misery fill the room, echoing in my own ears. But, I don't even feel the pain, all I can focus on is the sound of my bone snapping.

The look on his face is malevolent. This is no man; this is the devil incarnate. Inflicting pain on others is his favorite pastime. My punch to his nose didn't even draw blood. I'm almost positive he's not human. He doesn't have a heart, that's for sure.

Tears prick the corners of my eyes, but I use them as fuel as I jerk my hand away, now able to feel the pain shooting up my entire arm. My hand hangs freely, but I don't dare look at it out of fear of passing out. If he sees my weakness, he'll use it to his advantage.

"Maybe you'll think twice before you try that shit again. Now wrap that hand up and do your schoolwork." He turns around and walks back to his desk. "Dinner is in an hour and if your mom asks, you fell."

I hug my hand to my chest, the pain almost unbearable. It's like my hand doesn't even belong to me anymore. It just hangs by a thread of bone on my wrist and I can already feel the swelling around it.

Without a word, I turn and leave quickly. Once I'm out of his sight, I scream at the top of my lungs and fall to the floor in the hall outside his office.

"Cal. Wake up." Bella shakes me, pulling me out of my dreadful nightmare. "Hey," she peers over me, beautiful green eyes looking into mine, "I'm here. It was just a dream."

I sit up, wiping the sheen of sweat from my forehead and rubbing my wrist. I look down and see the scar from the surgery. It's another reminder of how hard I had to fight for what I've earned. I grab my bottled water from the nightstand. "If only it were a dream," I tell her between sips.

I've been cursed with nightmares and rarely dream at all.

Bella places a calming hand on my arm. "You wanna talk about it?"

"Nah. It's nothing. Go back to sleep, baby." I kiss her forehead, hoping she doesn't drag this out.

The only thing worse than a nightmare is having to relive it once you're awake.

CRAZY HOW A NIGHT full of monsters in your head can turn into the best night's sleep you've had in months. It's all because of the girl by my side. I smile, eyes still closed, and wrap my arm around her. Only, my arm sinks into the down comforter.

I open my eyes to see that Bella is not there. My mind immediately goes to the worst possible scenario, and I shoot up to a sitting position. That's when I see her. Sitting at a desk in the corner of the room, blinds still closed and barely a wink of light.

"Whatcha doing over there?"

She spins around in the chair, my phone in her hand. "Trying to get into this thing. What's the passcode?"

I tear the blanket off me and walk toward her, my morning wood greeting her through the fabric of my boxers.

"That depends on what you need it for." I press my

palms to the desk, caging her between my arms, and I kiss the top of her head.

Worried eyes look up at me. "Cal, please just let me call my parents."

"We've been over this, Bella. It's not safe."

I can feel the tension building between us, and I'm trying really hard to avoid another argument. But she can't make contact with anyone. Not yet.

"Dammit, Cal!" She pushes me back and gets up. "I want to know that Mark is safe." She's full-on yelling, hands shaking and tears welling in her eyes. "I want to see how Lucy is doing after the news of Trent's death. I want to talk to my fucking family!"

I take a deep breath, contemplating the best approach here.

"Give me my phone," I finally say, holding my hand out.

She slaps it in my palm, curses, and storms out of the room.

A quick call to Anders, and hopefully, we can come to an agreement that works for both of us.

"Hey," I say when he picks up on the first ring, "I need you to do something for me."

"Anything, Boss. What is it?"

"Go to the brother's hospital room and call me when you get there."

Anders laughs, though there is nothing comical about this situation. "He's at NYC General. I'm back at Cori Cove."

My teeth grind. "Did I ask where the fuck you were? Do it. Now."

I end the call and slam my phone down on the desk. There is nothing I hate more than an employee who questions a job I give. I pay Anders damn good money, and I do it because he's the best.

The sound of a door slamming has me hauling ass out of the bedroom. "Bella," I holler, searching the suite frantically. "This isn't funny, Bella. Where the hell are you?" I open and close closets, the bathroom door. "Fuck!"

She's gone.

And she took my damn key card with her.

18

"Can't even make a damn phone call. What is this? Prison?" I'm halfway down the hall in the basement when I realize I'm talking to myself and getting strange looks from passersby.

Cal could be hot on my tail, for all I care, and that's the thing—I don't care. I'm twenty-three years old and if I want to leave that suite and go watch people prance around naked while getting groped, fucked, or both, then I have every right to do that. If I want to make a phone call to my mom to make sure she's okay, I can do that, too.

I quickly hold up the card to the guard, and he gives me access to The Grotto.

I'm so sick and tired of everyone trying to tell me how to live my life. Foster parents, foster siblings, case workers —I've dealt with authoritative people my entire life. I'm an adult and I'm free to make my own choices. I'll be damned if someone is going to tell me otherwise. Let alone impregnate me because it fits *his* plan.

No. Not anymore.

"Brooke." Cherry beams with too much excitement. Her bright red lips match the nickname she's presumed. "You came back. And you're not in pajamas this time."

I snatch a drink from her tray and tip it back, gulping down the entire contents before setting it back on the tray, empty. "Sure did."

"Well, someone was asking about you after you left the other night. Maybe you could...give him a show." She angles her head toward the guy who winked at me mid blow job the last time I was here.

"Oh, no. It's not like that, Cherry. Actually, I'm in a relationship. I just...like the thrill, I guess."

"No worries. I totally get it. Trust me, babe. You're not the only one." She nods toward a lady wearing a leopard suit, only it's missing the crotch and the breast coverage. "Lady Leopard over there. Married to a state senator. Doesn't even know she frequents this place."

My eyes widen. "Really? That's crazy." I take a more serious note. "Cherry, can I ask you a question?"

She adjusts the tray on her hand, moving glasses around to balance it out. "Of course. Ask away."

"Is this..." I'm not sure how to word what I want to ask. "Is this considered cheating? Ya know, coming here without the knowledge of your significant other."

Cherry draws in a deep breath. "Well, that depends on how your significant other would feel if he found out. If he'd get mad, then yeah. Probably. But if he wanted to join in on the entertainment, then I'd say no."

"He has definitely done his fair share of joining in."

Her hand sets on my shoulder and she grins widely.

"Then don't sweat it, babe. He'd be a hypocrite to judge you."

I nod. She's right. Cal has been part of this club for years. Hell, he owns the damn place.

"Listen," she continues, "if you're worried about upsetting your boyfriend or getting caught, just disguise yourself. There is nothing wrong with watching. It's porn, only live."

"Thanks, Cherry. You've been extremely helpful." I point to a full glass of mojito, lime this time. "Mind if I have another?"

"Have all you want. You pay your dues and we supply the drinks." She picks one off the tray and hands it to me. "Holler if you need anything else."

"I will. Thanks, again."

With my drink in hand, I mingle through the crowd. I end up at the far side of the basement at a round table with two stools. There's a small stage with three poles, running from the ceiling to the hardwood platform. Two girls dance around in sexy lingerie while men gawk, and a few even jerk their cocks. One is in the midst of fucking a girl from behind. Though, his eyes are not on his counterpart, they're on the dark-haired stripper holding eye contact with him.

I wonder if he's fucking his wife and the dancer is his mistress. Maybe he's not married at all and doesn't even know the girl whose pussy his cock is stuffed in.

Then there's the beefy biker dude who's stroking his three-inch penis. I'd never guess a man of that stature was that small.

One of the things I like about this place is trying to

guess the story behind each person. It's sort of fun and exciting. I wonder if anyone is watching me and trying to guess my story.

Girl is hiding out because some deranged man wants to kill her and her boyfriend, so he can take all his money. She gets pissy and wanders here out of vengeance while searching for a thrill.

If only I could predict my outcome in this messed-up situation. Will Byron win and kill me eventually? Will someone kill him first? Will Cal and I end up married? Most importantly, now that I've found this place, will I ever want to give it up?

"Ready for another?" Cherry asks, coming out of nowhere. Before I even respond, she sets a full drink on the table and takes my empty one. I didn't even realize I'd finished it off.

"Don't mind if I do." I smack my lips before wrapping them around the straw.

Cherry leans in, her lips practically brushing my ear. "See that dark-haired girl on the stage? That's his wife." She tips her head toward the guy who's pounding his cock in another girl.

"Really?" I drag. "I knew there was some sort of connection there."

Interesting. This *is* fun.

"Bella!" someone yells. Only, it's not just someone, it's Cal. I turn around and see him walking steadfast toward me. I look at Cherry, who's glancing back and forth from me to Cal.

"I thought you said your name was Brooke?"

"And yours is Cherry, right?" There's a sliver of sarcasm, but I think she gets the point.

"How do you know Callum Ellis?"

Before I can even answer her, Cal stops me from talking by throwing me over his shoulder.

"Put me down," I curse, slapping my hands to his back, and déjà vu hits me full force. I've done this a couple times.

"If you wanna act like a child, then you'll get treated like one."

He carries me across the room, grabbing the attention of everyone in our path. I look up and see Cherry watching us in shock. My shoulders shrug, and I mouth the words, "I'm sorry."

"Give me the card, Bella." Cal holds his hand up, expecting me to give it to him.

"I don't know what you're talking about."

"Oh. So it's gonna be like that." He slaps a hand to my ass. I shrill at the pain but crack a smile at his tenacity.

"Didn't you learn your lesson about sneaking around during your stay at Cori Cove?"

"And didn't you learn that I don't take orders from anyone?"

"Like I said, Bella. You act like a child, you'll get treated like one."

"This is absurd. I'm fully capable of walking." I'm no longer fighting to get down. The humiliation has passed and I know Cal, he won't free me until I'm holed up in the suite again.

Cal slams his thumb into the elevator button and the doors open, letting a trio of men out. They stop, looking at me with questioning eyes, likely wondering if I'm okay. It has to be due to the pinched eyebrows and furious expression on Cal's face.

"Mind your fucking business," Cal barks at them, then steps into the elevator. "Let me ask you something, Bella. Do you have a death wish?"

"I mean, we're all going to die sometime. Why not have it be in a place with live porn?" It's what Cherry called it, after all.

"You think this is funny?"

"Yeah, Cal. I think it is. For the past couple months, everything has been so serious. Maybe I just wanted to have a little fun for a change?"

We reach the eighth floor and he still doesn't set me down. For being hauled away over someone's shoulder, I should be angrier, but I'm actually feeling pretty good right now. I'd say it's attributed to the drinks I sucked down in a matter of minutes. I'm not a heavy drinker, and it doesn't take long for the effects to go to my head.

"You want fun? I can give you fun. In the safety of our suite where you're supposed to stay until we catch that son of a bitch."

"Oh yeah? What kind of fun, Cal? You wanna play checkers, maybe some Go Fish?"

We're halfway down the hall when my feet finally hit the ground. "Are you drunk?" Cal asks, eyebrows perched on his forehead and back stiff as a board.

"Maybe? Why? Will I get in trouble for that, too?"

He takes my hand, leading me to our suite, and I stumble over my feet with the first couple steps. "You shouldn't be drinking. We've had unprotected sex and you could be carrying my baby."

"Oh," I blow out a heavy breath, "is that so? Is that part of your devious plan, Callum? Are you still trying to get me pregnant?"

He shrugs his shoulders. "Not trying, but anything is possible when you're not protected."

"Yeah." I jerk my hand away from his. "Anything is possible because I probably still have those damn fertility pills circulating through my bloodstream and," I quote, "stimulating my ovaries."

Cal stops walking and I do the same. He looks me dead in the eye. "He told you about that, too?"

"Yeah. He did. At least someone is honest with me." My feet start moving again, getting a few steps ahead of him. I still have the key card, so I pull it out of my pocket and swipe it through the pad.

I don't bother holding the door for him, but he catches it before it latches. "Is this your new thing, Bella? Sneaking off to go to The Grotto?" My response is a smug grin as I drop down on the couch. "How often have you gone?"

He eats up the space between us, crouching down in front of me. "How often, Bella?"

Why does he keep saying my name like I don't know it? Normally, I like the way it rolls off his tongue. Right now, it's downright annoying.

"Twice, Callum." I emphasize his name. "I've gone twice."

"And...do you like it?"

I shrug my shoulders, almost embarrassed to admit that I do. "A little bit."

To my surprise, a smile spreads across his face, though it feels condescending. "Why didn't you just tell me?"

My hands fly up. "Because of this. Look at how you're reacting."

"It's okay to enjoy that sort of thing. For a while, I did, too. Eventually it gets old, though."

He's piqued my curiosity, so I lean into the space between us, hands resting on my knees. "How often did you go?"

"For a while, every night. It sizzled down to a couple nights a week or check-ins with the staff. Once you came back into my life, never."

"Are you mad that I…like it?"

His hands rest over mine, reassuringly. "I'd never judge you for your sexual fantasies. All I ask is that you let me be a part of them. Now," he drawls, "if I find out one of those men touched you, then we have a problem."

"No," I spit out, "No one's touched me and I'd never… I'd never do that to you. Or to us."

"Good." He pushes himself up, pressing his lips to mine and speaking into my mouth. "Now that that's settled. It's time for your punishment."

My heart skips a beat, excitement pooling in my stomach. I must be out of my mind for wanting this. "Take it easy on me. 'Kay?"

His hands slap to my waist and he lifts me up, tossing me over his shoulder again. "Don't count on it."

My smile never leaves my face as he hauls me off to the bedroom, slamming the door closed behind us.

He tosses me onto the bed and we begin tearing each other's clothes off like animals in heat. "Fuck me, Cal." I moan into his mouth.

"I'm gonna fuck you when I'm good and ready. You just lie back and take whatever I give you."

I'm not sure when I crossed the line from being vanilla to wanting all the dirty talk, while fulfilling sexual desires, I didn't even know I had, but now that I have, I'm never going back. Cal is so aggressive in bed, in such a way that has my body sweltering. Any time we've had sex, he's taken control. He's punished me, degraded me, and called all the shots. Feeling pretty brave, thanks to the alcohol I've had, I think it's time I turn that around.

My hands meet his chest, pushing him off me, lip curled and eyes burning into his. "Or, you take whatever I give to you."

Once he's on his back, I jump on top of him, straddling his chest and locking his hands over his head.

Too stunned to speak, he just lies there.

"You can move when I tell you to move, Mr. Ellis. Until then, lie down and keep your dirty mouth shut."

When his eyebrows hit his forehead and a smirk draws on his face, I know he's loving this. Even if he won't admit it. Even if he'll probably put up a fight for control.

"You're asking for it, baby."

In a knee-jerk reaction, I raise my hand and slap him across the face. My hand immediately claps over my mouth. "Oh, shit. I'm so sorry! I was trying to be...kinky."

His laughter eases my embarrassment, and when his fingertips pinch my waist, I'm completely over it.

"You don't have to pretend with me. We both know who's in control in the bedroom."

I feel like he's testing me. Trying to see how far I'll take this.

"Is that so?" I bite my bottom lip, observing the cock-sure expression on his face. "Sounds like a challenge." He goes to sit up, trying to move me, being the control freak that he is. I push him back down. "Whoever comes first loses. If I win, you forgive me for running out and going to The Grotto."

He quirks a brow. "And if I win?"

I tap my finger to my chin, thinking. *I've got it.* "If you win, I'll let go of all the asshole things you've done to me."

"Including the birth control?"

"That's a big one. But, sure. Why not? I plan on winning anyways."

Cal laughs. "Oh, it's on, baby." He holds out his hand, ready to shake on the deal.

Even though it was my challenge, I'm hesitant. Mostly because I've always been one to hold on to grudges. I have a problem with throwing mistakes in people's faces, even when I've made my own fair share of them. Maybe it's time to change that.

I place my hand in his and give it a jerk, sealing the deal. Before I can even pull away, Cal is flipping me over until he's the one on top. I let out a squeal as his naked body cloaks mine.

Our mouths crash together. Hard and forceful, teeth clanking, lips bruising. When my tongue invades his mouth, he sucks the tip of it then moves to my bottom lip, sucking so hard that the taste of copper seeps into my mouth.

My hands coast down his back, nails digging into the skin as I roll my hips, trying to gain friction. Then I remember this is a challenge, not a quest. Sliding my hand between our bodies, I get a firm grip on his erection. He presses down, stopping me from stroking, while breathing heavily into my mouth.

In a swift motion, he pulls my hand out from between us and pins it over my head.

"Oh, this is war," I seethe into his mouth.

He grabs my other wrist, restraining it in the same manner. "Bring it on."

He devours every inch of my neck—nipping, biting, sucking—then moves to my ear. Tingles shoot through my entire body, and I'm half tempted to throw in the towel.

My need for him overpowers my desire to win. I can move on from everything he's done. I pretty much already have. What started as one thing, grew to something so much more with us. He couldn't have predicted that.

"Crumble, baby. You know you want to." His words sweep across my mouth in a gruff whisper.

Nope. I will not crumble.

Using all my strength, I push my hands to his chest. To him, it's laughable, but I manage to get a firm grip on his erection between our smoldering bodies. Cal works up a sweat, trying to gain the upper hand, but when I squirm out from beneath him and he flips on his back, I know that I've got this in the bag.

He tries to stop me when my lips wrap around his girth, tongue flicking against his under shaft.

"I was born with restraint, Bella. Suck my dick all you want...holy fuck!"

I smirk around him while I slide him in and out of my mouth.

His fingers wrap around the ponytail on my head and he tugs forcefully. So much that it feels like my follicles are on fire, though it only arouses me further.

I pop him out of my mouth, then lick my way down to his balls, sucking one in my mouth and humming.

"God, baby. Don't stop."

I question him with raised eyebrows as I suck his other ball into my mouth. It seems he's forgotten this is a challenge. My mouth presses to his pelvic bone, and I kiss my way up to his stomach. "Giving up already?"

I'm desperate for him to be inside me. So desperate I'd give up the win.

Once I'm straddling his thighs and his dick is lined up with my entrance, he lets out a gravelly breath and grabs me by the waist, lowering me onto his cock.

It slides in with ease, filling me completely as I begin bouncing on him. Two hands pinch my hips, gliding me up and down.

My nails rake against his chest, clawing their way down.

Cal presses his thumb to my clit as I ride him, rubbing in vicious circles that instantaneously bring me to the brink of orgasming. If I don't stop him now, he'll win.

His tenacity doesn't falter. He pushes hard, rubbing

faster. Lust-filled eyes meet mine, the rise and fall of his chest mimicking my own unfulfilled breaths.

My head falls back, eyes closed as I give in. Climbing higher and higher. Electricity riding through my veins and hitting every nerve in my body.

I hold my breath, squeezing his cock as my walls close tightly around him. I'm not even sure how I stand a chance at winning now and I don't even care.

"I'm gonna lose," I cry out, bringing my head forward. My mouth falls open, and I'd swear my eyes roll into the back of my head.

"Give me your hand," Cal says, not waiting for me to offer it to him. He picks it up off his chest, takes two of my fingers and closes the others. Pressing my own fingers against my clit, he grumbles, "Rub it."

I do as I'm told. Rubbing slow circles with little pressure. I've never done anything like this with an audience. It's exciting and new and the way his eyes watch my movements as I take control of my own pleasure turns me on. Each passing second gives me a new sense of comfort and before I know it, I'm vibrating against the pads of my fingers and screaming as I ride his dick.

Grinding against him, rolling his cock inside of me, I keep rubbing myself—watching him, waiting for him to explode inside me.

My orgasm hits me full force as I spill around his cock that's still engulfed in me.

Without warning, Cal grabs my waist and lifts me up, a stream of his cum shoots upward, hitting my fingers as I continue to rub myself, using his arousal as lube for my pleasure.

It's probably the sexiest thing I've ever seen—even more than watching the couples at The Grotto because I get to experience it.

When I become sensitive to my own touch, I stop rubbing and collapse on top of Cal. Our sticky bodies come together and he wraps his arms around my head, holding me close.

"Well, who won?" I ask breathlessly.

"Let's call it a tie. We both won."

I lift my head to look at him. "Or we both lost and we stick to our end of the deal."

"I like that idea." His hands grab my cheeks and he pulls me in for a kiss.

Looks like it's time for us both to forget the past and start planning for our future—together.

19

"It's about time," I say to Anders through the phone, my eyes wandering to Bella, who's spreading cream cheese on a bagel, while sitting on the bed and watching *Friends*. "Give him the phone."

I walk over to Bella, grabbing her attention as she bites into her bagel.

"Everything okay?" she asks around a mouthful.

"What the hell do you want?" Mark growls.

I put the call on speaker phone, so I'm able to hear the conversation.

"Mark?" Bella tosses her bagel on the plate on the bed and jumps up, causing it to flip over onto the, was-clean, comforter.

She grabs the phone from my hand and I let her. Holding it up to her face, she talks into the speaker. "Mark, is it you?"

"Bella. You gotta run. You gotta do whatever it takes. Get away from that Ellis guy or you'll end up dead. I mean it—"

Bella looks at me as she tries to calm her brother down. "Mark, I'm okay. I promise Cal would never hurt me."

"That's what he wants you to believe. Listen, that Byron guy and Trent, I heard them talking and Ellis is bad news. Lures young girls to work at some club and promises them the world only to—"

I cut him off by snatching the phone away and shutting the speaker off. "Listen here, you nitwit. Did it ever occur to you that those guys let you hear what they wanted you to hear?"

His response is just heavy breaths.

"That's what I thought. I'd never hurt Bella. In fact, I can ensure your safety, too, if you'd quit being a jackass and listen to what I have to say."

"Give me the phone back, Cal. I wanna hear what he has to say."

Ignoring her pleas, I finish up the call with Mark. "A guard will be outside your hospital room. Seems you're gonna be there for a while."

I tap End and stick my phone in my pocket, preparing for the wrath of Bella.

She looks past me, lost in thought. When she speaks, it's like she's talking to thin air. "I'm glad to hear he's going to be okay. Thank you for setting that call up for me."

"Of course. Everything is going to be okay, baby. I promise you."

Bella laughs condescendingly. "Okay? Everything is not okay, Cal. Everything is a mess."

I position myself on the end of the bed where she's

kneeling. Bagel crumbs coat the white comforter and cream cheese has smeared on the pillowcase. "Eventually, it *will* be okay."

She drops onto her back, staring up at the ceiling. "What did Mark mean when he was talking about young girls working for you?"

"Bella, I swear he's lying. It wasn't me, it was—"

Her head shoots up. "I believe you."

I give her a sideways glance, finding it hard to believe that I don't have to go to great depths to explain myself. "You do?"

Bella sits up, crawls across the bed until her arms are around me. "Of course, I do. I wish I could believe that everything is going to be okay, but when you tell me you didn't do something, I believe you now."

I pull her onto my lap, burying my face in her hair. "Byron has pretty much always run things at the clubs. I'm still in charge, but I let him do his thing, thinking he was doing a good job. A few years ago, during the recession, we had a hard time finding girls to work at the club. He said he had it under control and I assumed he did. It wasn't until shortly before you arrived that I did some research on the employees and realized they were young girls. All of consensual age, but eighteen, nineteen-year-old girls straight outta high school. Do you remember me telling you that he was doing some shady business?"

"Yeah. I think so. It was the night you told me about the contract and how I'd basically agreed to marrying you without my knowledge."

One of my many fuck-ups with Bella. "Yeah. Yeah, I did do that," I admit.

"Hey," she turns my face toward hers, "in the past, remember?"

"Yeah. In the past." For now. "Anyways, he basically had men go out and find these girls who were living in poverty or needed some extra cash. Lured them in and promised them the world. Once they were in, he gave them no choice but to stay."

"I mean, if they agreed to it and they were old enough to make the decision, I don't see how it's that bad."

"It's the way he treats them that's wrong. A couple nights after you arrived at Cori Cove, I found him slapping a girl around and belittling her. A minute later, he was consoling her and apologizing, behaving like the sociopath that he is. He uses his narcissistic behavior to manipulate these women. Makes them think they need him and the job."

"So, what are you gonna do about it?"

"Well," I drawl, rubbing my thumb across my chin. "Once Byron is no longer a problem, I'm hoping to find someone to help these girls. Rehabilitate them and find them jobs that will help them in the long run, maybe even help them with schooling."

Bella's eyes light up as if she's had an epiphany. "Let me help. Please, Cal. If these girls are in trouble, then I want to help them."

"I think we could work something out. I think I'm shutting the clubs down, so a lot of employees are going to be out on their asses. I might offer a small severance, but I'm not sure what more I can do."

She looks surprised. "You're shutting the clubs down?"

"It was never my thing. It was always Vincent's and Byron's. Sure, I enjoyed them from time to time, but it's no loss to the company if I close up shop."

Bella doesn't say anything, just gives me that voided look as if her wheels are spinning. "What if I help run the clubs? If the girls choose to stay, then I can be their boss."

That warrants a laugh on my part. "Not a chance. Those men have grubby hands that like to touch every ass that walks by. I'd have to sit in a corner with brass knuckles and a shotgun in my hand." I crane my neck to get a better look at her. "Why is it so important to you?"

"It's not...important to me. I just kind of like the environment and I can tell others do, too."

"Of course they do. It's sex. Everyone loves sex."

Bella shakes her head. "No, it's more than that. For the employees, it's a job. For the members, it's an escape. A chance to be more than a spouse or a parent or a businessman. It's a place where you can be and do whatever you want without judgment."

"All right. I'll put this on the list of things to revisit once we're out of this damn suite."

Bella grins, then softly kisses my lips. "Deal."

20

I can't stop thinking about Cherry. She doesn't look a day over twenty. I get the feeling that Byron is using manipulation tactics and abuse to keep her there, the same way Cal said he was doing to the other girls.

I have to talk to her. I know we're not friends, but she's such a sweet girl, and if there is anything I can do to help her, I have to at least try.

"Do you trust me, Cal?"

Concern sweeps across his face. "Of course I do. Why do you ask?"

"Just making sure." I kiss his lips, knowing that I'll be asking for forgiveness later.

Cal falls asleep only minutes later with me in his arms. I close my eyes, trying like hell to do the same, but my mind keeps wandering back to Cherry and all the girls who were victimized by Byron.

Peering up, I look at Cal's face. His nostrils flare with each breath, and I smile at his vulnerable state. These past couple months have been tainted with bad luck and bad experiences, but Cal is right, eventually, this will all be over and we'll be able to start our lives together. For the first time in a long time, that glimmer of hope has returned.

Part of putting all the bad behind us includes making sure Cal's company is running smoothly. He's been so caught up on protecting me and the search for Byron that I'm worried his employees are suffering—particularly the young females who were brainwashed. Possibly Cherry.

I lift Cal's arm slowly and rest it on his chest. He squirms a bit but falls back into a deep sleep. In just his tee shirt, I climb out from under the comforter and get out of bed.

One last look at him and I'm grabbing some clothes from my bag on the floor. Cal has told me many times that I should unpack, but unpacking means accepting that we'll be here awhile, and I refuse to do that.

I tiptoe out of the room, leaving the door slightly ajar to keep from waking him when I return. Instead of using the bathroom in our room, I go to the extra bathroom and change out of my clothes.

Fuck. I forgot my bra, and it just so happens that I grabbed a white tee shirt from the pile and Cherry had mentioned it was ladies' night, complete with a wet tee shirt contest—not that I'll be participating.

My fingers run through my hair and I wipe my thumb under my eyes to try and force the bags away. It doesn't work, though. Those bags are a sign that I need to start getting more sleep. Maybe tomorrow I'll try. Tonight, I have something to take care of.

Quietly, I grab the key card, from the drawer I stuck it

in yesterday, and my black zip-up hoodie that's lying on the barstool, so I can cover up my breasts showing through my top.

I go out the door to the hall, and a few minutes later, I'm flashing the card at the guard. He gives it a double take, looking from me to the card, then holds up a hand. "Wait a damn minute. You're the girl Mr. Ellis escorted out of here the other night. Are you sure you're supposed to be here?" His hand rests on a walkie-talkie attached to his jacket, like he's about to rat me out.

Think fast, Bella. "Mr. Ellis happens to be my fiancé and if you know what's good for you, you might not wanna piss me off."

My heart is racing so fast, but I think I handled it well.

He sighs heavily, before opening the door and letting me inside.

I smirk, rolling my eyes like a bitch, though I feel really bad for threatening the poor guy.

Ignoring all the action going on around me, I skim the open room for Cherry.

This place is completely packed. Way more than it was the last couple times I was here, and it's mostly all men. I'm pushing through crowds of people who are standing around talking—likely waiting for the contest to begin.

I walk straight toward the pool room, remembering where it is from the time I was invited in. As I reach for the door, the crowd behind me begins shouting profanities. I turn around, catching the stare of a grouchy man. "Hey, lady. You can wait in line like the rest of us."

Stretching my neck, I look down the line of men and

woman, and it extends all the way to the door I just entered.

I look down at my zipped hoodie, bite my bottom lip, and go for it. In a swift motion, I jerk the zipper down, exposing not only a white tee shirt, but also my puckered nipples that peek through the see-through fabric. "Actually, I'm part of the show tonight." I smile, hoping they all bought it.

No one says a word, so I open the door and step inside. Standing around the pool are about two dozen girls, all in white shirts. Some tank tops, some swim tops, and some tee shirts like my own. I seem to be the only one wearing jeans and a pair of flip-flops, though. But at least I've got half the outfit right.

The oval-shaped underground pool isn't huge, but I'd say it could hold at least one hundred people, assuming they want to touch body-to-body. The entire wrap-around area is furnished with lounge chairs, some round tables with stools, and even a tiki bar in the far corner.

"Brooke," Cherry hollers, and I catch her making her way toward me from the other side of the pool. "Or should I say, Bella?" Her arms cross over her chest, pushing her cleavage up through her V-neck bralette.

"Look, Cherry. I'm really sorry about that. It was a nickname, much like yours."

With a scornful look, she plants a hand on her hip. "It's not the name I'm upset about. It's the fact that you're one of them."

I have no idea what she's talking about. "One of who?"

She shakes a finger, pointing around the entire space.

"Them. The owners. The assholes. The ones who treat us like dirt."

"No. I'm really not. Cal...err, Mr. Ellis and I are together, but I promise he's not like Byron and the other guys who run the clubs."

"Uh-huh. Sure. It's your word, baby girl. But I don't trust ya." She checks me with an eye roll and spins around, strutting back to her girl gang.

I jog after her, grabbing her by the arm. "Cherry, wait."

Sneering, she snaps back around and pulls her arm away. "Do you have a death wish, Bella?" She emphasizes my name for added effect.

"I know what Byron, or Mr. Davis, or whatever the hell you call him, does to you all and I want to help you."

"Help me?" She laughs, the sound mocking, but fully loaded with sarcasm. "Help me, what? Make more than minimum wage? Work less than seventy hours a week? Or are you referring to my cracked and bloody feet because I'm forced to wear high heels with no breaks?"

"I...I had no idea it was that bad."

"Of course you didn't. Because you're living up in your ivory tower with the riches, while we're all down here in rags," she snaps the waistband of her black miniskirt, "literally."

I look around at the girls who are all watching us, some looking like they're ready to attack if I so much as make the wrong move. "Can we talk somewhere more private?"

Cherry looks over her shoulder then back at me. "Fine," she breathes heavily, "but make it quick. In about two minutes, those doors open, and men will be swarming."

I follow behind Cherry, and she opens up a door to leave the pool room. Inside is a long hallway, with more rooms that section off.

We walk into a large room that's decked out with vanities covered in makeup, racks upon racks of costumes, and open boxes scattered all over.

I reach down into one and pick up a platinum blonde wig, wanting to try it on for good measure. I've always wondered what I'd look like as a blonde.

Cherry clears her throat, grabbing my attention. "You wanted to talk?"

"Yes," I clutch the wig, running my fingers through the golden locks, "listen, I know this all seems very odd to you and I'm not even sure why I'm about to fill you in on what's going on, but I like you, Cherry, and I'm also worried about you."

An annoyed smirk replaces her indignant look. "Worried about me? You hardly know me."

"I know enough. You were kind to me and made me feel welcome."

She waves her hand through the air, trying to move this conversation along.

"Anyways, my name is Bella, and I've known Mr. Ellis since I was a child. He's a bit rough around the edges, I know. At the end of last year, I fell in love with him, but it didn't come without a cost. You see, Byron is after me... well, Mr. Ellis. He wants his money and he's hell-bent on killing one or both of us to get it. I've been hiding out here until Byron is found so that—"

"So that Mr. Ellis can kill him first?" She's not as taken aback as I thought she'd be. In fact, she's abnormally calm after everything I just told her.

"Yeah. Pretty much. I know it all sounds crazy."

"Girl, you don't know crazy until you've lived my life."

I blow out a breath. "You'd be surprised."

"So, what does this all have to do with me?"

"Last night, Callum told me he was recently made aware of how Byron's been treating the female staff. He had no idea and I swear if he did, he would have stopped it sooner."

"Yeah," Cherry sighs, "it's quite a nightmare working for that asshole, but it's a job and most of us can't afford to quit it, not that he'd let us." She drops down into a swivel chair in front of a vanity and begins dabbing some blush on her cheeks. "Mr. Byron Davis has made it very clear that if we want out, we will pay the ultimate price."

My eyebrows rise, hoping she doesn't mean what I think she does. "What price is that?"

"Our bodies, our livelihood. He's threatened to go as far as shipping us off to Mexico and selling us to the cartel. I think he's probably talking out of his ass and he's just desperate to keep the place staffed, but there was one girl who quit six months ago, and she's been missing ever since."

"Oh my God," I gasp. "Look, Cherry, Callum and I are going to help you all. Soon, Byron will be out of the picture and some big changes are coming to these clubs."

Cherry drops a lipstick back on the vanity and smacks her lips while looking at me through the mirror. "From your mouth to God's ears." She spins back around and stands up. "I gotta get back out there, but thanks, Bella. And I hope you're right about the changes. We sure as hell could use them." Cherry takes the wig from my hand and flips it until it's placed on top of my head. Her fingers comb through the stray strands, and she smiles at me. "It suits you." Then she heads out the door while I'm still standing here.

My eyes dart over to the vanity. My cheeks could use a little color. Going with a shimmery rose color, I run the brush up and down, highlighting my cheekbones.

I stare into the mirror, appreciating the girl looking back at me. She's full of mischief and capable of raising hell, given the right opportunity. My palms press to the makeup-stained vanity and I look closer. "Hello, Brooke."

Feeling carefree, I go out the way I came in, still wearing the wig. I'm already here, might as well see what this event is all about. Nothing wrong with sitting back on the sidelines and watching the action.

Cherry wasn't kidding when she said the place would be swarming. Men flock over every foot of space in the pool room. There are girls jumping around in the pool, tits bouncing through the wet fabric of their white shirts. Some have even removed their tops altogether.

In a matter of minutes, the place went from radio silent to sex-party central.

There are a couple waitresses walking around with drinks, Cherry included, though she's on the far side of the room. I opt out of drinking tonight, knowing that I can't stay here long.

Before Cal fell asleep, I asked him if he trusted me. I knew exactly what I intended to do tonight, but I also knew he'd stop me. I had to talk to Cherry. Now that I have, I'm surer than ever that I was brought here for a reason. I have this aching desire to help these girls and show them that they are more than just a body to be slapped around and mishandled. If they want to work here, then more power to them, but they don't deserve the disrespect they've had to endure.

I'm walking around, trying to find a corner to tuck myself in, so I don't stand out in the crowd, when my eyes meet Cherry's wide ones. Red flags immediately rise when I see the expression of dread on her face.

Her head shakes no, but I have no idea what she's referring to.

"Well, well, well. I can't say I've seen that ass around here before." That voice. I'd know it anywhere. His hands get a firm grip on my ass as he pulls me down until I'm sitting right on his lap.

My heart gallops in my chest, hands trembling and lip quivering as I try to come up with a plan of escape.

Eyes deadlocked on Cherry's, I mouth, 'help me.'

"I must say, you fit pretty well on my lap, little girl. Why don't you turn around, so you can shove those tits in my face?"

My entire body shivers, chills skating down my spine. I hold my breath, afraid to breathe, afraid to move.

His hands come around, squeezing my thighs. Fingers begin riding up, pressing into my crotch through my jeans. "I bet you've got a nice, tight pussy on ya, too."

I have to get up. I have to get out of here before Byron realizes it's me.

Cherry struts over with her tray balanced on one hand

and a fake smile plastered on her face. "Hey there, Mr. Davis. I wasn't expecting you tonight. Can't say I'm disappointed." She forces out a bout of fake laughter, and I'm officially indebted to her, assuming she can get me out of this.

Byron leans forward, me still in his lap. "And I wasn't expecting you to stand around doing nothing. Get to work."

Asshole.

While I want to scream it from the rooftop, so everyone knows what scum this man is, Cherry takes it with stride. "See my hand? It's a tray holding drinks." She grabs one off and hands it to him. "Would you like one, Mr. Davis?" She smirks.

He scoffs a bit, then takes the drink from her hand. "One for my new friend here, too."

Cherry looks at me, bewilderment in her eyes. I nod, accepting the offer, and she hands me a glass, too.

"Actually, Mr. Davis," Cherry begins, "there's someone I wanted you to meet. A potential new hire who I think would do a damn good job."

"If I wanted to know what you think, Blueberry, I'd ask."

Cherry grimaces, and I can tell she's offended. "It's Cherry." She grabs a toothpick stuck in one of the full drinks and pops the cherry on the end into her mouth. "And you'd be a fool to let this girl go. She's got a way with the gentlemen."

Byron squeezes my thigh tightly. "What about you, little girl? Are you in need of a job? I'm sure the men would love to get a look at that tight ass while you serve them drinks…and maybe more."

My stomach twists in knots, bile rising up my throat. I don't say a word out of fear he'll know who I am.

His hand moves to my cheek and he tries to get me to look at him. "Turn around. Let me see that pretty face."

I have to get out of here. I feel faint and my rapidly beating heart feels like it's going to explode from overexertion.

In a swift movement, I push myself off his lap and walk steadfast to the doors out of the pool room.

"Hey!" Byron hollers. "Where ya going?"

I reach the doors, and in a knee-jerk reaction, I look back, instantly regretting it when our eyes meet. Byron's blue orbs stay affixed on me, and his mouth drops open.

Shit.

I pull open the doors and run across the club toward the exit. There are so many people shuffling in and out that I'm forced to push my way through the crowd, knocking down a petite, young woman who spews profanities at me while I keep moving.

There are more people in the hall, lined up and waiting to get in. I pay them no attention as I hustle to the elevator. There's a line and it's taking forever. My foot taps impatiently when I finally give up, knowing that Byron is likely on his way to find me.

I keep going down the hall to the door that has a sign above it that says 'Stairs.' I push it open and go up them as fast as I can, tripping over my own feet a few times. As I'm hurrying up, I tear the wig off my head and toss it behind me.

I'm out of breath and my anxiety is so high that I fear I'll pass out and topple down the staircase along with the blonde wig.

When the sound of a door below me opens and closes, I stop momentarily and look down the winding staircase. As soon as I hear footsteps thudding up the stairs, I move faster.

He's going to catch me. He's going to grab me and take me away again. This time, he'll make sure I'm not found. This time, he might even kill me.

"Bella," Byron singsongs, sending shivers through my entire body.

There is no way I can keep going to the eighth floor. He'll catch up before I make it and then he'll know exactly what floor we're staying on. Though, I'm sure he already does. He's well aware of Cal's private space at the hotels.

I reach another level and the door has the number five on it. Hoping like hell that it opens, I give the handle a turn and internally scream with excitement when it does.

As I run down the hall, I'm well aware that this feat is far from over.

I'm mid-panic, practically hyperventilating and ready to curl over and give up, as the elevator takes its precious time to come up.

It's likely from the event downstairs. All the people going in and out are holding it up, and I'm expecting the doors to open to a full crowd.

I look over my shoulder as the bell dings and the doors slide open. Still no sign of him.

There are two people—a man and a woman—looking

back at me, waiting for me to get on, and they have picked up on my unease.

"You okay, hun?" the lady asks, stepping aside and making room for me.

Just as I step on, the door to the staircase flies open, and Byron comes running down the hall.

"Yeah," I tell her in a panic. "Just go. Make the elevator go. Eighth floor." I'm almost crying at this point. On pins and needles, hoping the doors close in time.

"Hold the—" I hear Byron shout, just before the doors seal and his voice becomes a whisper that quickly fades.

I curl over, grabbing my stomach as I catch my breath.

I made it.

"Was someone chasing you?" the sweet lady asks.

"No." I shake my head. "No, I'm fine."

The truth is, I'm far from fine. I'm watching and hoping we're not stopping at any other floors on my way up because there's a good chance Byron will be waiting outside the door for me. He's no idiot, and he knows this place like the back of his hand.

Dread washes over me when we stop on the seventh floor.

He's going to be there. I know it. I can feel it.

The doors open, and I'm half tempted to grab the burly man and ask him to save me.

But, Byron isn't there.

"Take care, hun," the lady says with concern written all over her face.

I force a smile and thank her before she disappears, and I'm pounding on the button to close the doors.

One more level. I'm almost there.

Seconds later, I'm getting off on the eighth floor, and I still don't see Byron. I run as fast as I can down the hall to the suite with my key card ready in my hand.

As soon as I swipe it and the door opens, I go inside, slam it shut, and slide down the door onto my ass.

"Cal," I scream at the top of my lungs between breaths. "Cal!"

My head rests between my shaking knees. My entire body trembles and my lungs still fail to fully inflate.

Cal comes hurrying out of the bedroom, rubbing his eyes in a pair of black briefs. He drops down at my side. "Baby, what's wrong? What happened?"

"Byron," I choke out. "He's here and he saw me."

21

Callum

"WHAT DO you mean he saw you?" I'm half asleep, and I've got no idea what the fuck is going on. All I know is Bella is sobbing and shaking uncontrollably on the floor in front of me.

"He saw me," she says again, her lip quivering and eyes pooling with tears.

"Saw you where?" I shout, not at her, but out of frustration. "Where the hell were you?"

She lifts her head slowly and looks at me. "I went back. I'm sorry, Cal. You said you trusted me, and I had to go see her. You shouldn't have. You shouldn't have trusted me because I screwed everything up."

"You're not making any sense, Bella. Went where? Seen who?"

"Cherry. A girl I met at The Grotto."

My face drops into my hands, massaging my temples as she continues, "She works there and I wanted to make sure she was okay, after everything you told me about

Byron and the way he treats the female employees. Byron was there. He didn't see me at first—"

"Byron was at The Grotto?"

"Mhmm. He was being the total douchebag he was. Before he even saw my face, he pulled me on his lap and was—"

Rage builds inside me, unleashing in a shout, "He pulled you on his fucking lap?" She nods. "Aside from pulling you on his lap, did he touch you, Bella?" God, please tell me he didn't touch her. I can already feel the heat rushing to my head, my fists clenching, veins bulging.

"He was very touchy-feely. Grabbed my ass, rubbed my thighs, and cupped my crotch. I tried to get up, but I was so scared he'd know who I was." I feel gross just talking about it. Like tiny spiders are crawling all over my skin.

I don't even hear anything except the sound of my knuckles crashing into the wall beside the door. I bust through the drywall. Blood streaming down my hand and dripping onto the hardwood floor.

"Cal! What the hell?" Bella grabs my hand, looking at the cuts.

I pull my hand away and get up, ready to run out that door, to find him and kill him. "Give me the key card." I hold out my bloody hand, waiting for her to give it to me.

"Why? Where are you going?"

My fingers roll against my palm, hand still extended as I wait impatiently. "Give me the damn key card, Bella. He must've been out searching all the resorts, knowing we're at one, and now, he's found us."

"Please don't go out there. I'm scared, Cal. Don't leave me. Don't do anything stupid."

"Stupid?" I laugh. "There will be nothing stupid about me slitting that bastard's throat."

Bella throws herself into my arms. "Don't leave me."

The fire inside me slowly begins to subside from a boiling point to a slow simmer. That's all it takes to calm me down. Her touch, her scent, her soft voice. I kiss her head, stroking her hair as she presses her face to my chest. "I won't leave you."

I hold her for what feels like minutes, knowing that he's out there somewhere—either trying to find us or trying to escape. Once I've got her calmed down and I'm ready to think clearly, I step away to make a call in the bedroom.

I'm standing in front of the window, looking out at the city, as I tap Anders's name. He picks up on the first ring and I cut right to the chase. "He's here at the Manhattan resort. Bella blew our cover tonight by sneaking down to The Grotto." Sensing her presence, I turn around and see Bella standing there. Her hip pressed to the doorframe and a look of remorse on her face.

"Baby, I didn't mean—"

She holds up a hand, stopping me. "It's okay. It's the truth." She turns and walks away and as much as I'd like to chase after her and apologize while explaining myself, I have to get things rolling.

My attention returns to the call. "I need all of our top men here. Put this place on lockdown. Contact Edward, Jason, Pedro, and all the head guards at the other locations and alert them of what's going on. If Byron shows his face anywhere, they are to detain him and contact me immediately."

"I'm on it, Boss. You want me there, too?"

"Yes, I want you here. You're my head of security and I need you to fucking catch this guy." I end the call before I blow up and say shit I'll regret. It seems I've already put my foot in my mouth enough tonight.

With my phone still in my hand, as I anticipate a call back from Anders once he's made contact with everyone, I leave the room. "Bella," I holler out. She shouldn't have heard that. Hell, I shouldn't have said it. I was trying to get as much information out as I could, as fast as I could. "Baby, I didn't mean it like that. Don't be mad."

Noticing the light on in the bathroom, I go toward it. "Bella?" I push open the door, but she's not there. All I see is the pajamas she had on when she went to bed. She must've changed here before going to The Grotto.

I scoop up her pajamas and let them fall back to the floor, wondering where the hell she's at. Something doesn't feel right.

"Bella," I holler again, now frantically searching the entire suite. When she doesn't turn up, I scream. "Fuck!"

Why the hell does this girl keep sneaking off? Since the minute she came back into my life, she's constantly disappearing and getting herself into trouble.

I hurry into the bedroom, pull on a pair of dress pants that were lying on the floor and fasten my belt. Skimming the room for a shirt as I try to hurry, I don't see one. I rifle through the drawer I unpacked in. I go for the first white undershirt I find and slip it on, along with a pair of socks.

Once I'm in my shoes and ready to search this entire

fucking property, I go to the door—without my key card, because she still has it.

What a fucking mess.

Just as I open the door, I hear her sniffling. My head snaps around and I see that the balcony door is open a tad.

Relief washes over me. I kick my shoes off and cross the room.

Sliding the door open, I see her leaning over the railing, looking down. She flinches; I know she's aware that I'm here. I come up behind her, pressing my arms to the railing on either side of her.

"I'm sorry," she says as I go to speak, "I didn't mean to blow our cover."

"That's not what I meant. I had so many thoughts running through my head, and I was trying to tell Anders what went down and it came out wrong."

Bella turns around. Her eyes are swollen and it's obvious she's been crying. "No. You were right. I've been careless. Hell, I'm always careless. I should have never left this suite to begin with."

I sweep my thumb under her eye, then the other, before resting my hand on her cheek. "I love the careless side of you. The carefree, vibrant, 'never giving a shit' side. When you get something in your head, there's no stopping you."

She looks down at the space between us. "Yeah, I'm a royal pain in your ass."

I tip her chin up, feeling the warmth swimming through my chest like it does each time I look at her.

"That you are. But you make life interesting. Did you know that before you came back in my life, I did the same thing every single day? Wake up, drink coffee and have breakfast—alone—make a shit-ton of business calls, feed Amara, have lunch—alone—handle more business, have dinner—alone—and I'd attempt to sleep only to be haunted by my nightmares. You've shaken things up in the best way possible. I'd hide away with you forever if it meant being with you forever."

Finally, a smile. It's just a little one, but it's something.

She raises a brow, chewing on her bottom lip and driving me wild like she always does. "You mean that?"

"I absolutely mean that." I kiss her lips, tasting a hint of saltiness from her tears. "Without you, I'm nothing."

Her hint of a smile grows to one that pushes her cheekbones up, showing her pearly white teeth. "I feel the same way."

"Good." I tuck a stray strand of hair behind her ear. "Now that we have that settled, I need you to promise you'll quit sneaking off all the time. I'm not even thirty years old and you're giving me gray hair."

She laughs. It's a beautiful sound that I want to hear every day for the rest of my life. Bella has given me life. She's made me feel things that I swore I'd never allow myself to feel. My heart is no longer empty, it's so full of love for this girl.

"I promise I'll try to run things by you first."

"Okay. That's a start." I kiss her again, and when I go to pull away, thinking she needs some sleep while I handle this business with Byron, she pulls me back in. Hands wrapped around my head, fingers intertwined in my hair. She kisses me hard and every emotion spills into my mouth. I feel it all. I feel her, the woman of my dreams, in my arms, and a permanent fixture in my life.

22

"CAL," I grumble, rolling over to my side. I watch him in a pair of gray joggers as he paces the bedroom with his face in his phone. "It's two in the morning. Come to bed."

He holds up a finger, eyebrows dipped in a deep V as he finishes reading whatever is on his phone.

It was after midnight before I finally fell asleep, even then it was broken chunks. All I could think about was Byron's dirty hands all over me in the pool room. The look on his face when he realized it was me is etched in my mind and will likely haunt me in my dreams.

Cal finally lifts his head and cracks a smile. "Anders has a lead. He'll be updating me as soon as he has more information."

"That's great." I pat the mattress beside me. "Now come and sleep while you can." I've gotten used to having Cal by my side every night, and I sleep so much better when I'm in his arms.

Giving in, he drops his joggers to his ankles and kicks them off.

I lift the blanket, inviting him in, and he slides beneath the covers. His warm body engulfs me, arm wrapped around my waist as he pulls me close.

My head nuzzles up to his scruffy chest and everything is perfect.

I'M WOKEN up to the slamming of drawers. When I spring up on the bed, I find Cal pulling on clothes like he's in a hurry.

Hugging the blanket to my chest, I watch him, blinking a few times to adjust to the light shining in the room from the open door. "What are you doing?"

"I have to go, baby," he says, his words as rushed as his movements.

I throw the blanket off me and get out of bed. "What do you mean you have to go?" I walk over to him, putting my hands on his shoulders to stop him from moving like a crackhead in need of a fix.

"Anders called. They found him." For a brief moment, he looks into my eyes before he begins hustling again.

"Found him? Is he dead or something?"

He pauses, stares at the window, then resumes slipping his socks on. "If only." He reaches for his dress coat that sits on the dresser beside me, and I grab it before he does.

"Would you just stop and tell me what the hell is going on?"

"I have to make a little trip. I shouldn't be gone long. There will be a guard outside the door twenty-four seven."

"Twenty-four seven?" I spit out. "I thought you said you wouldn't be gone long?"

He takes the jacket from my hand and slides one arm in, before pressing his lips to mine in a hurried kiss. "A day, maybe two." He puts the other arm in, zips his long black coat, and walks past me.

I follow behind him, not letting him get away with only the few details he's sprinkled on me. "Where is this trip taking you?"

He stops. Turns slowly with a shoe in his hand. There's a beat of silence that has my heart pounding in my chest. He finally says, "Rhode Island," before putting on his shoes.

"Rhode Island? But, what the hell would Byron…" My hand claps over my mouth, and I shake my head.

"He's got your parents, Bella."

"Oh my God," I cry out. "What do you mean he's got my parents? Please stop with all these one-liners and tell me what the fuck is going on?"

Cal closes the space between us, places one hand on my waist, and looks deep into my eyes with a serious and concerned expression. "I didn't wanna tell you. I know how you are. You can't go and try to play the hero, Bella. Do you understand? Let me handle this."

Tears stream down my cheeks as I think of every possible scenario. Did he kill them? Is he going to kill them?

"What did he do?" I choke out, my words muffled with my cries. "Did he hurt them?"

"No. At least, not yet. He's two steps ahead of us and baiting us to him. I got a cryptic text and a picture—"

"Show me."

He stands idly, not wanting to show me the image he was sent.

"Show me the damn picture and text, Cal!"

Dropping his hand from my waist, he reaches into his pants pocket and pulls out his phone. A second later, he's holding it up, and on the screen is a picture of my mom, my dad, and Mark—all gagged and tied up in our dining room. I gasp, feeling like the air has been sucked right out of my lungs.

"And the text?"

He swipes up, showing me the words on his screen.

Unknown: These should have been your parents. You seem to have forgotten that bitch left you. She's the only one to blame.

"Did you respond?" I grab the phone from his hand, scrolling down and reading the exchange of messages.

You son of a bitch! Touch them and I'll be sure to cut off your nutsack and use it as bait on my next fishing trip.

Unknown: I'd like to see you try. You've got until noon, or they all die. Come alone or they die anyways.

I toss the phone back at him and he catches it in midair. I spin around, burying my face in my hands as I break down.

Cal comes up behind me, turns me around, and lets me fall apart in his arms. "You see why I have to go."

I nod through sniffles and tears. "Okay." I look up at him, seeing the worry in his eyes. He's putting his life on the line to save my parents—parents he thought would be his, too. "Be careful." I don't want to let him go. I want him to stay here where he's safe, but I know that no matter what I do or say, he'll go anyway. We're alike in that way.

His lips press to my forehead, then he takes a few steps back and pulls his phone out of his pocket, though it's different. It's not his phone at all. He hands it to me. "What's this?" I ask.

"A temporary phone, so I can reach you. Under no circumstances do you leave this room. I mean it, Bella."

I nod in agreement, clutching the phone in my hand. "Call me as soon as you're all safe."

"I will. I promise."

"Don't get yourself killed, Cal. I can't live in this world without you."

The corners of his lips tug up. "I love you, baby."

I throw myself into his arms one last time before I let him go. "I love you, too."

Cal opens the door and I see the guard. As soon as I lay eyes on him, I know I'll be safe here. He's about seven feet tall and at least three hundred and fifty pounds of solid muscle. His tattooed arms are folded in front of him and he tips his head to Cal.

"That's my whole world in that room," Cal says. "Don't let anything happen to her."

"You got it, Boss. She's in good hands."

Cal gives me one last look before he pulls the door shut. The latching sound mimics a prison cell being closed. Only, I'm not in prison; I'm in hell. With Cal out there and me in here.

He's going to be fine. He'll save them, and everyone will be okay.

It's the only ending I'll accept.

23

It's a quick flight to Rhode Island. We touch down at a private airfield, about twenty minutes from Bella's house. As we're bussing through the space, I send Bella a quick message to check in, just to make sure she hasn't knocked out Stanley, the guard, and hopped on a commercial flight to try and save the day. I can't help but smile, knowing it's totally something she would do.

She responds right away with a picture of her sitting on the couch in our suite. She's wearing one of my black tee shirts, her legs crossed like a pretzel and her eyes swollen from crying so much. Fuck, I miss her. It's only been two hours, but I'm ready to be back by her side. I long to dry her tears and sweep her hair out of her face while kissing her until our lips bruise.

Me: Good girl. I'll be in touch. Love you.

I put my phone back in the front pocket of my coat and unbuckle my seat belt as soon as I'm given the green light to get off the jet.

Lloyd, the pilot, bids me farewell with a handshake.

I go down the short staircase and my car is waiting about three yards from the jet. The driver exits, pulling the back door open for me. Inside, I see Anders waiting.

He's got a scowl and he's shaking his head, and I know this isn't good.

I pick up my pace and slide in the back seat. "What's with the pissed-off look?"

"I got a call from one of my new guys. It seems Byron has the entire Jenkins house surrounded. He wants you alone, and I worry he'll go to extremes if we carry out the plan and have an army of men showing up."

"What do you suggest?" It's not often that I take advice —I prefer to give it—but in this case, it's necessary. Anders is highly trained, and he's handled situations much worse than this.

"We'll have the driver drop me off somewhere near the Jenkins' house. I'll have everyone gather there." He hands me a small object that looks like a black thumbtack. He reaches over and drops it in my front pocket. "We'll be listening the entire time. The minute we think you need backup, we'll be there."

I should be scared. Should fear for my life. Going up against Byron is one thing, but a flock of men who are likely trained assassins, members of the militia, and mafia partners is risky business. But, I'm not. Growing up, I had so much fear inside me. Fear of ending up alone, fear of failure, fear of living. I'm not sure I'm even able to encompass those feelings anymore. Now, I thrive when danger lies ahead. I seek out a challenge, and I fight like hell for what's mine.

"Fine. Let's just get this shit done. I've got better things to do with my time."

Anders makes a call and relays the plan on an untraceable phone. A few minutes later, we parallel park on the side of the street in front of a quaint little bed and breakfast that looks like something straight out of a country magazine. It looks like a house that was built in the early 1900s. All white siding, a white picket fence, and what I imagine is a well-cared-for lawn, though it's covered in snow. In the summer, there's probably flower gardens surrounding the place. A sign hanging in front of the house reads, 'Betsy's Bed and Breakfast'.

"Looks cozy." Anders laughs. It's a far cry from what we're used to, but I actually kinda like it. It does look cozy, mostly because it's quiet. There aren't dozens of people lurking around. No clubs, no bars, no noise.

"Yeah. Now get your ass out and round up the troops."

Anders's hand lingers on the handle. "Code word: Nuggets."

"Nuggets? What the fuck kind of code word is nuggets?"

He shrugs a shoulder, a smirk on his face. "One that works." The door opens, and he gets out. He taps the hood as he walks by and the driver pulls back out onto the street.

As we travel down the road, I slide on my black, leather gloves and double check the microphone in my pocket. Still there, let's just hope the damn thing works.

I contemplate texting Bella one last time before going in, but when the driver slows the car, I realize there is no time. We pull up in front of the house, parking on the side of the road instead of using the driveway.

At first glance, I don't see anything that appears to be out of the ordinary. No men, no fresh tracks. In fact, it looks as if the last car in the driveway was before the heavy snowfall began.

The driver looks at me in the rearview mirror and says, "I'll be waiting, Mr. Ellis."

I nod, then open the door and put one foot on the ground. The packed snow on the road makes for a slippery step, so I'm cautious as I get to my feet.

Closing the door behind me, I look at the house. It's just as I remember it all those times I checked in on Bella, without her knowledge.

I've never been inside, and I'm curious to see what the house she spent her teenage years in looks like. I imagine it smells like freshly baked cookies with family pictures covering the walls. Nothing like the home I had at the Ellis mansion.

There's a sheet of ice on the road so I take care as I walk toward the driveway. Once I make it down without falling on my ass, I pull one hand out of my coat pocket and knock on the screen door. It rattles against the frame a bit, and when no one answers, I knock again.

"Doesn't look like anyone's here," I say in a whisper, yet loud enough for Anders to hear me through the mic.

This time, I open the screen door and knock harder on the main door. Stretching my neck, I look over the railing on the small cement slab and try to get a peek in the window to the living room.

It's eerily quiet, and my gut tells me to just go inside. I

knock a couple more times before I turn the handle, but it's locked.

"Door is locked. No answer."

I go back down the stairs and step beside a big bush in front of the picture window, trying to get a look inside.

There's a haze on it, or maybe it's fog from the cold temperatures. I move even closer, shielding my eyes and getting a better look.

Then I see them.

"Fucking Christ!"

Three chairs, holding three people. Tied with their hands behind their backs, ankles restrained, and duct tape across their mouths.

Duct tape, Byron? Really?

Just proves he's as classless as I thought he was.

Trudging through the snow, as it seeps into my socks, I hurry back up the stairs and tear open the screen door. With it wide open, I stretch my leg out and kick, hoping to knock the main door open. I try a few more times, before giving up and running around the side of the house to try and get in through a back door.

There's a sliding glass door on the deck. With the snow now soaking my feet. I run up the deck, knowing this door is likely locked, too.

And it is. *Dammit.*

"I need backup. I can't get in this damn house and Bella's parents are tied up. I've got no tools on me to pick the lock."

I pull my phone out of my pocket, wondering if Byron's attempted to call. I'm not sure what his endgame is here, but he's definitely got a plan.

Bella.

What if this was a decoy? A distraction so I'd leave her. He would have known I'd come to try and rescue Bella's parents if they were in harm's way.

I pull the mic out of my pocket, speaking directly into it. "Hurry the fuck up."

When Anders and the guys are still a no-show, I give him a call.

He picks up immediately. "We're thirty seconds away. Listen, Boss, it could be a trap. Don't enter until we get there."

"Just hurry your ass up." I end the call and stick my phone back in my coat pocket. As soon as it drops down, it begins vibrating against my side.

Retrieving it, I look at the screen and see it's Bella calling from her dummy phone. I tap End, knowing that if I take this call before I have answers, she'll panic.

I leave the deck and go back around to the front of the house; Anders is already here, along with a train of six or seven, matching black cars lined up in front of the house.

"'Bout fucking time."

"Came as soon as we could, Boss." He's got a pick in his hand and he wastes no time picking the lock.

Simultaneously, the car doors all open and out steps a dozen men who are armed and ready. Anders gives them a quizzical look before picking at the lock again.

This is why he's head of security and the reason I pay him so well. Anders is the best of the best, and the only person I know who could throw together a team like this at the last minute.

A minute later, he looks over his shoulder at me as I

stand in the snowy yard at the bottom of the porch steps. He tips his head at the door, asking if I'm ready to go in, and I nod in response.

We move silently as Anders retrieves his gun from the holster then opens the door. The army of men scurry across the yard, ready to take action.

Following behind Anders, we enter the house and the men follow behind me.

Anders waves his arm around the room. "Search it top to bottom," he tells them. "Even if you come up empty-handed, search it again."

I go straight into the living room. My eyes land on Bella's mom first, then to her dad. Lastly, Mark. Anders begins helping Bella's parents, so I pull the duct tape off Mark's mouth. They shrill and immediately begin flooding our ears with what happened. I can't make out a word they're saying because they're talking so damn fast.

I hold up a hand, hoping to shut them up. When they continue to speak at the same time, I shout, "Shut the hell up."

Bella's mom and dad appear stunned at my outburst, but Mark just grits his teeth, staring me dead in the eye. "If anything happens to my sister, I'll kill you, you son of a bitch!"

Ignoring him, since he's obviously got a stick up his ass, I start with Bella's dad. Crouching down, I level with him. I've learned to never untie someone you need answers from. It's the one useful bit of information I learned from Vincent.

I reach into my pocket and pull out my phone, bringing up a picture of Byron. "Was this guy here?"

His eyes squint as he tries to get a better look, so I bring it closer to his face. "Ugh, no. Doesn't look familiar. The guys that were here were heavyset with leather jackets and combat boots."

I look over my shoulder at Anders and we speak without words. He taps into his phone and makes a call as I continue my questioning.

Just as I go to speak, I catch a glimpse of Mrs. Jenkins, Bella's mom. Something jabs inside my chest, and it's a strange feeling, knowing that she was supposed to be my mom. Short brown hair, glasses, dressed like a librarian. She looks sweet. Like someone who would listen when you've had a bad day and hug you when you're hurting. It's a surreal moment that I quickly snap myself out of because I can't handle any more what-ifs.

I push myself up and turn my back to Bella's family. "Were you able to track him?"

Anders shakes his head no, still holding the phone to his ear. He walks away, into another room, and I return my attention to Bella's dad.

"Bella is safe. I can promise you that."

"Liar!" Mark shouts. "None of this would have happened if it weren't for you. Why couldn't you just stay dead like we all thought you were?" He squirms and curses, trying to free himself.

"I'll admit, much of this is my fault. But," I pause for a moment, looking Mark dead in the eye, "one could say it's your fault, too. After all, I should have had your place with this family."

He doesn't say a word, just continues to wriggle against the ropes on his wrist.

"Cat got your tongue, Marky? Don't your *parents* know what you did all those years ago? Lying and setting me up so I'd miss out on the adoption?"

"Mr. Ellis," Bella's mom begins. Her voice is just like I imagined it: soft, sweet, compassionate. "We all make mistakes, myself included. But we can't change the past. Everything worked out the way it was meant to."

I turn around, unable to look at them any longer. They'll always take Mark's side. He's their son, after all. My fingers run through my hair, dampened by the snow. "Yeah. The way it was meant to."

I'm not here to make friends with this family. Sure, they'll be my in-laws one day, but I don't fit in here. I'm too broken while they're all so well put together.

Putting the past where it belongs, I focus on the future. "How'd he get you, Mark?" I spin around, looking at him as he sits there with a fat lip and a scorned look on his face. "Was it through Trent?"

"Fuck Trent and fuck you!"

Seems we're not getting anywhere by playing nice. I eat up the foot of space between us and press my hands to the arm of his chair. "Answer the fucking question if you ever want to be untied."

"Yes. Okay? Trent invited me over to his place to play poker, and as soon as I walked in the door, I was knocked over the head. It was the last time I saw him before he was found dead on the Elizabeth Islands. I'd just heard of his death when I returned after being tied up for a fucking month! Don't even try to pretend that you had nothing to do with that or Trent's murder."

I blow out a heavy breath of laughter. "I don't pretend.

But I didn't kidnap you. In fact, I was held in a room in the same building. Had no idea you were there. And I didn't kill Trent. He's lucky Byron got to him first because I would have tortured the fuck out of that piece of shit for what he did to Bella."

Mark's eyes widen. Now I've got his attention. "What the hell did he do to Bella?"

"Lied to her. Tricked her into believing he was a good person."

"Oh, you mean pretty much what you did to her?"

He's got a point, so I don't argue it, even if my motives were different.

Anders returns and grabs my attention. There's panic in his eyes. "We gotta go."

My heart jumps into my throat. Fear consuming every inch of my body. "Where is he?"

The men all begin hustling out the door, except for two, who enter the living room and begin untying the Jenkins family. "These two will be guarding the house until we know it's safe," Anders assures the family as he moves quickly to the door. "In the car, now!"

I don't even say anything to Bella's family before hauling ass out the door. As we're hurrying to the car, I press for more information. "Tell me what the hell is going on!"

"He's at the Manhattan resort. He's going for her, Boss."

24

"DON'T PANIC, BABY," Cal says through the speaker before I can even get a word out. Him telling me not to panic has me jumping off the couch.

"What's going on? How are my parents?" The blanket that was wrapped around me drops to the floor, and I walk over to the balcony doors, looking out into the night, fearing someone is going to bust through the glass at any given moment.

"They're fine. I'll fill you in later, but they're safe."

There's a knock at the door that has me spinning around. "Someone's knocking, Cal. Should I answer it?"

"No!" he blurts out without a second thought. "Do not go near the door, Bella."

I grip the phone tighter, chills running down my spine. "You're scaring me."

"Go in the bedroom and lock the door."

"What if it's the guard?" Regardless, I do as I'm told and head for the bedroom.

"It very well could be, but we can't take any chances."

There's a worry in his voice that tells me there's no way it's the guard.

"Please tell me what's going on. Why did you tell me not to panic?"

He takes an audible breath and exhales slowly. "We lost Byron."

My heart jumps into my throat, my pulse throbbing in my neck, and it only gets worse when the knocking on the door becomes erratic. "They're not going away, Cal." My voice cracks, hands trembling. "What do I do?"

"We've got more men on the way. Just stay put and do not leave that room."

My entire back vibrates off the bedroom door from a loud bang outside the room. "Cal," I whisper, frantically, "I think someone's inside."

"Baby, stay on the phone. Anders has men on their way up. Do not leave the room!" His voice is as panicked as mine, and it does nothing to calm me. Not that he could at this point.

"Come out, come out, wherever you are."

Every alarm in my body is set off by the sound of Byron's voice. My heart is beating so fast that I fear it will jump right out of my chest. "It's Byron," I manage to choke out.

I step away from the door, not taking my eyes off it as the handle begins shaking. "Open the door, Bella."

"Leave me the hell alone!"

Cal is still on the phone, mumbling words I can't comprehend when the bedroom door flies open. I walk backward until I hit the bed and the phone slips out of my hand, crashing onto the bedroom floor.

Byron wears a devious grin on his face as he walks toward me. The closer he gets, the more I try to get away, but I'm cornered.

I fall back onto the bed, immediately trying to roll to get off, so I can run, but his hand grabs my ankle.

"Ya know, I'm getting really tired of having to chase you down, Bella." He yanks my ankle, pulling me back down the bed. My nails claw into the blankets, trying to climb my way back up, but he takes back each inch I gain.

Once Byron has me right where he wants me, he presses a firm hand on my stomach, holding me in place. I can hear Cal shouting through the speaker of the phone on the floor and it grabs Byron's attention. He bends down, picks it up, and brings it to his ear.

"Hello, old friend." He smirks, eyes still pinned on me.

I snarl, raising my knee and kicking him in the gut. It hardly fazes him as he squeezes my stomach with all his strength, fingertips digging into my skin. "You're gonna pay for that, you little bitch."

Cal's voice raises through the phone and Byron releases a menacing laugh. "She's mine now, fucker. I've been wanting to taste this pussy for a long time."

Dread swarms in my belly. I have to get out of here. My eyes scan the room, taking in objects I could potentially use as a weapon. Damn you, Cal, for not leaving me a gun.

Byron ends the call and whips the phone over my head. It crashes into the wall behind me.

"Now, let's have a little fun, shall we?"

In one swift motion, he tugs my satin pajama pants down until they're lingering beneath my ass. My legs flail, trying to kick as I scream at the top of my lungs. "Someone help me!"

The sound of the button popping on his pants is deafening. It's nothing compared to the sound of his zipper sliding down. He pushes his pants, letting them drop to his ankles as his belt clanks together.

"You should have been mine, Bella. And now you will be."

"Byron, please. Please just stop this."

"I can't stop now."

His cock springs free from his boxers, and he begins stroking it over the top of me. "I'm gonna fuck you, Bella. Then I'm gonna kill you and fuck you again."

I'm past the point of tears as anger ripples through me. He can try, but he won't take me without a fight.

"Fuck you!" I shout in his ear as he begins slobbering kisses all over my neck.

He fidgets with his cock, and when he raises his hips, lining his dick up with my entrance, I squeeze my legs together and lift my knees to my chest. My feet press into his abdomen and I use all my strength to kick him back. With the upper hand, I shove him hard until he flies off the end of the bed.

In one fluid motion, I roll off the mattress and drop to the floor.

Byron gets up quickly and stands over me with a clenched jaw, "You little whore!"

I scream again, fearing no one can hear my cries. As Byron stoops down, I notice a figure behind him and relief sweeps through me.

Cherry.

Byron catches my gaze and spins around, but before he can react, Cherry smashes him over the head with a lamp. His body goes slack and tumbles on top of me, and I immediately shove him off.

The base of the lamp drops to the floor before Cherry kneels beside me. "Are you okay?"

Blood rolls down the side of Byron's face and I've seen enough horror movies to know that he will wake up in about thirty seconds. I grab the base of the lamp, push myself up and smack him in the face with it. His head moves a bit, eyes still closed. "I am now." I grab my sweatpants off the floor and pull them on before throwing myself into her arms like she's an old friend. "Thank you. How the hell did you get in here?"

Cherry pulls out of the embrace and sets her hands on my shoulders. "I came to make sure you were okay. I saw him chasing after you. It took me a minute to find you, but when I saw the dead man outside your open door, I knew exactly where you were." Her tone shifts quickly as she grabs my hand. "Come on, we need to get out of here."

I look from her to Byron, still in shock about what just happened. "No," I blurt out.

Cherry gives me a puzzled look and stands up. "No?"

"If we leave him here, he'll escape, then he'll come after me and Cal again."

Cherry raises an eyebrow. "Do you suggest we kill him?" The casual tone of her voice is astounding. She asks the question in the same manner one might ask someone if they want crackers with their soup.

"I'm...I'm not sure. Do I want him dead? Yes. Do I

want to be the one to do it? No." I'm not a killer, but if I had to be to save mine and Cal's lives, I think I could do it.

"Then don't. It will stay on your conscience forever, and you don't want that burden." She bends down and grabs one of Byron's limp feet. "Help me get him in the kitchen. We'll tie him up until someone who will feel no remorse can do the job."

Byron's pants are still hovering around his ankles. "Ugh," I cringe. "Can we cover up his penis? I'm gonna be sick."

Cherry laughs and grabs a sheet from the bed and tosses it on him. "Better?"

"Much." I grab his other foot, and we pull him across the room. He's heavier than I expected.

A trail of blood streaks across the hardwood floor as we drag him. His jacket ruffles up around his head and the sheet begins to slide off, but it's still covering enough of him to appease my stomach.

We're pulling him out the door, trying to maneuver him to fit through the doorway, and his hand bangs against the frame. "Oops," I say, sort of hoping it happens again.

We finally make it to the kitchen and drop his feet to the floor. "What are we gonna use to tie him up?" I look around the room, as if something will just pop out that we can use.

"Look in the drawers and cupboards."

I highly doubt we have anything, but I begin searching. As I'm opening and shutting cupboards and drawers,

Byron lets out some muffled sounds, and I move quicker. "I'm not finding anything."

"Wait," Cherry says, holding up a finger. "The guard outside. He has to have something. A gun at the very least."

"Yes!" I cross the room to the open door. I look out and see the guard lying there, dead. Cherry's standing behind me and I'm thinking she'll have to take on this task.

"What are you waiting for?" she asks. "Search him."

I'm looking at a guy with a bullet in his head. "I...I don't think I can do it."

She huffs, brushing past me. "Move. I'll look."

I step aside and watch as she digs into his many pockets and retrieves a gun, a baton, some pepper spray, and a ball of twine.

"That should work, right?"

"It'll keep him restrained temporarily, but we need backup to hurry their ass up, because it won't hold him long."

Cherry carries everything she took from the guy back in the suite and drops them on the counter, except the twine, which she begins unraveling. "All right, let's get to work. Grab his hands."

I'm reaching down, ready to grab Byron by the wrist, when his head begins moving around. I look at Cherry who waves her hand, rushing me along with the twine spread in her hands.

I take one wrist, then the other, and just as I'm bringing them together on his chest, Byron's eyes shoot open and he grabs my arm. "Ahhh," I scream, trying to pull away, but he overpowers me.

Out of nowhere, Cherry kicks him square in the temple, knocking him out again. I look up at her, stunned. "Damn, girl."

Her shoulders shrug. "What can I say, I've had to fight off my fair share of men."

With both hands together on his chest, Cherry wraps the twine around them so tightly that it digs into his skin.

Once we're sure it's secure, we move to his ankles. "Ya know," Cherry begins, "we could just wrap this around his throat and end him now." There's a glint of humor in her eyes, and I can't tell if she's serious, or joking.

"I think Cal will appreciate us leaving him alive, so he can get the answers he needs."

"You really like that guy? Mr. Ellis?" She seems surprised, as if he's unlikable. I suppose to many people, he is.

"Yeah. Yeah, I like him a lot. The Mr. Ellis you all see isn't the one I get. He's had a rough life, but he's a good man."

"If you say so." Cherry ties off the twine on Byron's ankles, then drops her butt to the floor.

I know that most people won't understand my relationship with Cal—my family included—but that's the beauty of it being *our relationship*, it doesn't matter what they think. It's ours and ours alone.

"What now?" Cherry asks, getting to her feet. "Should we call someone?"

"Oh shit!" I get up quickly and hurry into the bedroom

to find my phone. Cal is probably a mess with worry right now.

I find it lying on the floor, screen shattered, as suspected. Fortunately, it seems to still work. I tap the button on the side to open the home screen then hit the phone icon. A piece of glass sticks into my finger, and I shriek, pulling the glass out then sucking my finger into my mouth.

There are like fifty missed calls and messages from Cal, and when I go to call him again, it rings before I have a chance.

"Cal," I say into the speaker.

"Thank God, Bella. I've been worried sick. Listen, I'm here. I'll be in the room in a minute. Are you okay? I swear if that son of a—"

"Babe, I'm fine. He didn't hurt me."

Cal breathes out an audible sigh of relief. "All right. I'm coming down the hall."

I run out of the bedroom, stopping in front of where Byron lies on the floor. Cherry gives me a weird look, and I return the gesture when I see that she's eating a handful of pretzels while standing over a passed-out body. Girl's got a strong stomach, I'll give her that.

"Help is here," I tell her, before stepping over Byron and going out the open door.

Cal's walking steadfast down the hall with his phone still pressed to his ear. A smile draws on my face and I toss my phone onto the floor as I run to him. Tears of happiness stream down my cheeks. I wasn't sure I'd ever see him again, but here he is.

I throw myself into his arms, jumping up and wrapping my legs around his waist. "I'm so happy to see you."

"You have no idea how fucking worried I was, baby. I had men on their way, but they were delayed, and I thought for sure…it doesn't matter. I'm here. Fuck! The thought of him touching you, hurting you." His head shakes, eyes closing momentarily. "I can't even comprehend what I'd do if I lost you."

"I'm here. I'm okay." I kiss his lips over and over again as he carries me into the suite.

As we approach the room, I figure I should probably give him a warning about what he's walking in on. "I had help," I tell him. "It's the girl I was telling you about. She saved my life, Cal."

Cal sets me down on my feet. "The waitress from The Grotto?"

I nod, my words scratching at my throat. "Byron was planning to rape me and she came just in time and knocked him out." Cal pushes past me to go into the suite as I keep talking. "So, we tied him up." I wave my hands over Byron, who is now wide-eyed and alert.

Cherry points at Byron with a pretzel rod in her hand, then takes a bite. "Shithead woke up."

I can't help but laugh at this very non-humorous situation.

"Well," Cherry continues, "I'm gonna let you two deal with that, so I can get back to work." She brushes off her hands and swallows down the last bite. "It's Gentlemen's Night tonight, and I've got some waiting for me." She goes to leave the room, but I stop her.

"Thank you, Cherry. You saved me, and I'm forever in your debt."

Cherry looks from me to Cal. "Giving me a new boss is a good start. Mr. Davis was a fucking prick."

Cal extends his hand to Cherry, and she looks down at it like it's tainted. "Callum Ellis. It's a pleasure to meet you, Cherry. You'll be compensated fully for your help tonight. And I can promise, you'll never see this son of a bitch again."

She nods, half-smiling, and shakes his hand. "You've got a tough girl, here. Don't fuck it up."

Cal looks into my eyes. "Wouldn't dream of it."

Once Cherry's gone, Cal practically begs me to wait in the bedroom. Says I don't wanna see or hear what's about to go down. There are a dozen men outside our room, Byron's tied up, Cal's here—I'm safe now. So I do as he asked.

25

PACING UP and down where Byron lies on the floor, speechless and staring back at me, I grind my molars and restrain from stomping his face in. My fists clench so tightly, I can feel the blood draining from my hands.

I'm tempted to lift the sheet to see why his lower half is covered, but I know it'll only infuriate me more. There's a good chance he's pantless, which means he had intentions that I can't fathom at this moment.

"You've done a lot of things to piss me off," I begin, slouching down and putting my knee to his chest. He blows out a heavy breath as I deflate his lungs. "You tried to steal my empire, stabbed me in the back, and took the life of my good friend, Peter." I press harder as I try to pull out the words while leaving my emotions behind. "But nothing you've done has pissed me off more than you hurting my girl." I cock my fist and release it right on his nose.

"She's mine," I scream. "She will never be yours. Yet, you tried to force her to marry you and…"

Fuck! I can't even say the words, but it's necessary to get this out before I kill him. "You fucking touched her. What gives you the right?" It's a closed question and I want no response. No bullshit excuses or creative lies.

Now that I got that out, it's time to ask the questions I *do* want answers to. "Why the fuck did you do it? I know damn well it's not because you caught feelings for her?"

A smirk tugs at the corner of his lip, and my blood hits a boiling point. "You think this is fucking funny?" I punch him again, this time, hard enough to crack his nose. He shrills as blood spills down the side of his face. His legs begin kicking, trying to free himself from whatever the hell he's tied up with.

"You son of a bitch!" Byron shouts. "If you don't kill me, I will kill you. So you might as well end this shit right now."

"No! Not until you answer the damn question."

"And why the hell should I answer questions that will give you peace of mind? If you must live, I want you to live a miserable life, wondering why I tried to destroy your life."

I scream so loudly that my words echo off the walls surrounding us. "Whyyyy?"

It's obvious that there is nothing but hatred between this asshole and me. It wasn't always like this, though. It's like one day, something snapped inside of him and he thought it would be fun to try and wreck my life.

"You were my fucking friend, Byron. My attorney. My business partner. What the fuck happened to make you do a complete one-eighty. To go as far as kidnapping me, killing Peter, and trying to take over my men, my money, and my company. Not to mention, the woman I love. It's like you wanted to be me."

Byron pushes his hands against my leg, trying to get me off him, but it only makes me push down more. Putting my full weight on him, I guarantee he's not going anywhere. "Answer me, dammit!"

He inhales a deep breath, as deep as he can with the little air that can get through, and he stares back at me. "Because it should have been me." His voice is tranquil with little to no fight in him.

"It should have all been mine."

"You really are a delusional motherfucker." I'm not sure why my father's attorney—one who helped change his will, stating that I was the sole beneficiary—thinks he should have gotten everything I have.

Byron groans, squirms, and finally gives up again. "You call it delusional and I call it the truth."

Getting bored with this conversation, I'm ready to get it over with. "All right. I'll bite. Why should it all have been yours?"

"Lift your fucking leg off my chest, so I can breathe, and maybe I'll tell you."

"Ah. There it is. You just want me to move, so you can try and overpower me. Not happening. Now, if you've got nothing left to say..." I pull my knife out of the holder clipped to my pocket and flip the blade open. "Let's get this over with."

Byron's eyes shoot wide open. It seems I've got his attention now. He had to know how this would end. Bella and I will never be free until he's done. He'll never stop.

I press the tip of the blade to his throat, and he sucks

in a breath, trying to escape what's inevitably coming. "Wai…wait. Okay. I'll tell ya."

"You've got ten seconds. Nine…eight…seven…"

"Because I'm Vincent's son!"

This time, I laugh. He's really pulling out all the stops. I press the knife deeper, piercing his skin and drawing blood that trickles down his neck.

"It's true. That love child I told you about, it was me. He wasn't planning to leave everything to a son he'd had out of wedlock. His beneficiary on the will was some distant cousin of Delilah's, before we changed it. He barely even knew the kid. He just wanted to be a dick and leave us nothing."

I don't believe a word he says. Why the hell should I? Byron has proven to be a loose cannon. "So that's your lie. That's the story you're going to tell me to try and escape death." I breathe out a laugh, though it's empty of humor. "You're gonna have to try harder."

"I swear to you, Callum. It's the truth. Believe me or not, but I am Vincent's son." My leg lifts a tad, giving him a little more breathing room. He takes advantage of the extra breath in his lungs and keeps on with his story. "Vincent had an affair with my mom. It wasn't until I was going through some of my mom's things, when she passed away, that I found out who my dad was. A DNA test confirmed it. I was only eighteen years old, never had much of anything, not to mention a backbone. I cowered to the man. He asked me to keep his secret and promised to be part of my life, while helping me financially. He put me through law school and eventually hired me. It was all for show, though. He didn't give a damn about me. He just didn't want his wife to know, so I went along with it and milked him for everything he'd give me."

I'm trying really hard not to buy into this story, but his details are astounding. Even if it were true, there are still some things that don't add up. "Why not just change his entire will over to you. Why use me as a middleman and allow me to have all the control?"

"Undue influence. As the attorney in charge of his estate, it was impossible."

"Impossible and illegal are two different things, and I don't think you care much about the latter. Besides, you were the executor of my will and you were fully prepared to have me killed so you could take it all."

"I knew you'd be a pain in the ass. Eventually, you would have looked into it all and I'd be investigated. It was a risk I wasn't willing to take. You were the last person alive who had any interest in his money. So, the easiest thing for me to do was get rid of the one thing standing in my way. It was a solid plan—until she fucked it up."

There's a good possibility he's telling me the truth, but it doesn't change anything. "Well, old friend, I guess we'll never know how things could have panned out, had you told me the truth from the start. Instead, the empire is mine, the kingdom is still standing," I lean forward and whisper into his ear, hoping to hit a nerve, "and I got the girl."

When he begins trying to fight me off again, the blade returns to his throat, and he settles back down.

"I didn't want that washed-up bitch anyways. She's a headache and a pain in the ass."

That she is. All the more reason I love her.

"I just wanted to see your face when I told you I took everything from you. I wanted to look you in the eye and see that pain before I killed you."

"Well, it looks like the roles have reversed." I press the blade deep into his neck and drag it across, slitting it wide open.

There was nothing left for me to say and nothing he could do to prevent what was coming. He double-crossed me, and for that, I could never let him live.

I drop the knife to the floor and climb to my feet. Once I've scrubbed the mess from my hands in the kitchen sink, I go into the hall and call in the men to get him out of here.

It's finally over.

26

Bella

It's been almost a week since Byron died. I've talked to my parents, who are hell-bent on me coming home and leaving this life behind me. I tried to make them understand, but I don't think they ever will. My life is with Cal now.

After staying in a separate hotel, one not connected with the Ellis name, Cal is taking me on a little trip. He won't tell me where we're going or for how long, so I'm just sitting back and enjoying the ride, or flight, rather. He's assured me we'll be there within the hour, which leads me to believe we're going back to the place where it all began. It's the one little hint he dropped that sort of spoiled the surprise.

I'd love to return to Cori Cove. It's become one of my favorite places. It might have a lot of bad memories, but it's got some pretty great ones, too. Regardless, I'm happy to go anywhere with Cal, as long as we're together.

He squeezes my leg, winking at me and sending a swarm of butterflies through my stomach. He's on the phone, talking business, and his serious voice is sexy as hell. What's even more sexy is when he drops the tough guy facade and shares a glimpse of his humanity with me. It makes me feel pretty special—knowing that everyone else gets his ruthlessness and I get the sweet stuff.

"All right, Anders, I'll be unavailable for the next thirty-six hours, so if you need anything, it'll have to wait." Cal looks at me again, biting his bottom lip as his hand slides up my thigh.

I put mine over it, pushing it up farther and curling his fingers with my own until they're pressing against my sex.

"Yeah. Yeah. Yeah. Gotta go." Cal ends the call and sets it on the rooted round table in front of us. He hums, leaning into my space and tickling my neck with his breath, causing the tiny hairs on my arms to stand up.

Cal's mouth finds mine and he pulls me in by placing a hand on the back of my head while his other rubs my crotch through my leggings.

There is nothing gentle about the way his lips devour mine. It's unruly and fervent. Raw and profound. My hand wraps around his head, weaving through his hair that's in desperate need of a cut. I get a firm grip, shoving his face closer to mine, feeling as if I can't get enough of him. I rest my other hand on his cheek, fingers grazing his short stubble.

We tear into each other like wild animals, not giving a care that the members in the cockpit could see us. Cal lifts up my shirt, our mouths parting momentarily, and I miss his taste already. They reunite as his hand sweeps around my back and unclasps my bra.

"I want you, Cal." I hum into his mouth, sharing his breaths.

My bra drops to my waist, exposing my breasts. My back arches, legs spread wider to give him better access. "Now," I beg in desperation.

Pulling out of the kiss, he looks lustfully at my breasts. "You've always been such an impatient little thing."

It's true. Patience is not my strong suit. And right now, it's downright torturous.

I reach over and grab his cock through his pants, giving him a taste of his own medicine as I rub my hand up and down his length. "That's because you like toying with me."

"Hmm. Seems you're picking up on that. I might need to up my game."

I squeeze him harder, smirking against his lips. "Bring it on."

My need for him to do something, anything, is agonizing. My insides are practically quivering. I'm not above begging at this point. "Please, baby."

It seems my pleas are working. Cal grabs my waist in a viselike grip and pulls me on his lap effortlessly, as if I'm as light as a feather in his hands.

My legs straddle his lap and his hand drags down my leggings, finding my want for him pooling in my panties. "You probably should've taken these off." He hints at my leggings, knowing I'm about to soak them.

I look over his head at the front of the plane. It's a small jet and there's only three seats and a curtain separating us from the cockpit.

The old me would never. The new me says *screw it.*

I lift up and let Cal strip me out of my clothes. Once I'm fully undressed, I tap my chin with my index finger. "Your turn."

He wastes no time ridding himself of his pants and boxers, letting them drape around his ankles. His cock springs free and my eyes land on his smooth pink head. Legs spread, balls resting against the seat while the tiny black hairs on his legs stand tall. He strokes himself a few times, giving me a show. "You want this?"

My tongue sweeps across my lips as I slouch down between his legs and take the shallow end of him in my mouth.

He rubs my head like I'm a pet. "That's my good girl."

I take more of him, feeling his head hit the back of my throat while I swirl my tongue around the bulging veins of his length.

An airy moan escapes him and it's an assurance that what I'm doing feels good. It's a satisfying feeling, knowing I'm the one bringing him this pleasure. That I'm able to make my man feel good.

Cal taps my shoulder. "Come here, baby," he says in a raspy voice.

I peer up at him with questioning eyes, wondering why he wants me to stop. "I wanna come with you." His voice is a low growl, one that sends waves of shivers down my spine. "On my lap. Now."

Pushing myself up, I climb on his lap, knees locked on either side of his torso. Fortunately, the seats on this private jet are good-sized or this wouldn't work so well.

Cal leans forward, cupping my left breast, massaging as he sucks my nipple into his mouth, and my stomach pools with hot desire. His lips glide upward, hitting my neck, and I tilt my head instinctively, savoring the tingling sensation that rides down my body from his touch.

His warm fingers sweep across my lower abdomen, and when he begins pressing them against my sensitive nub, I raise my hips to give him better access. Bridging my back, I roll into his touch. Electricity ripples through. I need more, my body aches for him.

Cal pushes his fingers inside me, and I begin riding his hand. I cry out in pleasure, not caring who might hear us. These men are on Cal's payroll; I'm sure what they're hearing is expected from a man of Cal's stature.

Curling his fingers, he presses deeper, hitting the spot that has me screaming. Our mouths collide, masking my whimpers, and I kiss him hard. So hard my lips swell and bruise and bust, metallic liquid seeping onto my tongue as I share the taste with Cal. "Ugh. Fuck me, Cal." I want him so damn bad. I also don't want him to stop what he's doing. I shut off all thoughts, falling into his touch and the way his fingers work their magic on my pussy. My man makes me feel so fucking good.

Moving faster, he digs his fingers in so deep that I'm on the brink of explosion. I clench my walls, squeezing him, as I reach the height of my orgasm.

"Did that feel good, baby?"

I lock my lips, grinning. "Mmhmm." Just as I kiss his mouth, Cal shoves his cock inside me. Filling me and gliding me up and down with his hands gripping my waist.

"That's right. Fuck me like you love me."

I moan in a high-pitched voice. "I do love you."

"Tell me you love fucking me."

I feed him the words he wants to hear, giving him the truth. "I love fucking you."

A raspy groan climbs up his throat as he meets me thrust for thrust. His hands move from my hips to my breasts, squeezing and using them as friction as he pounds me from the bottom.

My head rolls back, eyes closed, while I grip his shoulders and bounce on his cock.

"Fuck, Bella. You're so damn sexy." Soft lips find my collarbone, peppering kisses all the way up to my ear. He sucks my earlobe in his mouth, teeth grazing the sensitive skin, and I whimper in delight. Chills shimmy down my body as I chase my second orgasm of the night.

"I'm gonna come," I cry out. My mouth falls open, and I don't even recognize the sounds that escape me.

"Come for me, baby. Soak my cock."

And I do. I completely come undone, and he fills me up at the same time.

Our motions slow until we're completely still. My head rests on Cal's shoulder while we both steady our breathing.

We stay there quietly, holding one another for a few minutes before I finally climb off him. Proof of our orgasms spill down my legs. "I need to clean up before I get dressed."

"No one can see you. Just carry your clothes to the bathroom."

I'm hesitant to walk through this jet nude, but it's not like I didn't just ride my boyfriend completely naked, while I'm sure everyone in the cockpit was listening.

I really don't want to soil my clothes with our bodily fluids, so I ball them up in my arms and walk hurriedly to the lavatory. As I reach the door, the pilot announces that we're preparing to land. I clean up quickly, wiping myself down and washing my hands before getting dressed and heading back to the seat next to Cal to buckle my seat belt.

"I'm anxious to see where we're going," I tell Cal as I snap the buckle. He's already cleaned up and dressed with no evidence of our rendezvous.

His hand rests on my leg, and he smiles. "Don't get too excited. You might not like this place as much as I do."

"As long as I'm with you, I'll go anywhere you take me." I rest my head on his shoulder, closing my eyes as the wheels touch down on the runway. I could peek out the window and try to make a guess, but I'll let him keep his surprise a little longer.

We're told we can exit the jet, and Cal takes my hand as I walk behind him down the aisle. He thanks the pilot, and we walk down the steep staircase out into the fresh, night air. There's a running car not far away with its lights on. All the cars that we get in and out of are the same—sleek and black.

I can tell just by the moisture in the air that we're near water. It's crisp, clean, and cold. There's snow on the ground, but only a light dusting.

I know exactly where we are.

Squeezing Cal's hand with both of mine, I nuzzle against him as we walk to the car. "We came back."

He looks down at me, a glint of a smile along with a sliver of disappointment. "You know?"

I shrug my shoulders. "I can feel it. We're going back to Cori Cove, aren't we?" I squeal a little bit, excited to return to the place where we fell in love.

Cal stops walking, reading my expression. "Are you okay with that? I know there are some bad memories there."

On my tiptoes, I kiss his cheek. "I'm more than okay with that. The good memories override the bad ones. I fell in love with that castle the moment I fell in love with you."

THERE'S STILL daylight left when our boat arrives at Cori Cove. We took the small charter over, so we could haul all our luggage. We're only staying for a weekend, but it looks like I packed for the rest of winter.

Cal steps off first, offers me his hand, and ushers me down the dock. I look up at the stone structure and smile. So many memories hit me at once, but I only let the good ones infiltrate my thoughts. Like my conversation with Peter on the turret when he told me about the love of his life, Carolina. How this castle was special to them both. It's ironic that his life was taken at such a monumental place. My heart should ache for the loss of him, but it actually squeezes when I think about him and his Carolina being reunited.

As we walk toward the main entrance, I think of seeing Cal for the first time in his study. I knew there was something familiar about him, but I didn't put my finger on it until he spoke of my eyes. "Your eyes. They once spoke to me. I could read your thoughts with just a look," he said. The weeks that followed were brutal. I felt like a prisoner by a stranger and I mourned the loss of my friend. Slowly, I started to see fragments of the boy I once knew. Before long, he held the key to my heart. Now, I can't imagine life without him.

I look over at him and he catches my stare. Squeezing my hand, the corner of his lip lifts. "What?"

I smile back at him. "Nothing. Just thinking."

"About?"

"Us. Our past. Our future."

"Oh yeah? What do you see in the future?"

My lips press together, biting back a smile before I finally say, "you."

We walk hand in hand through the main doors and I'm stunned when we step inside. "Wow, Cal. Who did this?"

The patched-up hole in the ceiling that once leaked is now unrecognizable. The cement floor is now a sleek gray that's so glossy it looks like marble. A large chandelier hangs overhead from the finished ceiling, and the doors that were put up on the back wall are now gone. I'm grateful for that. I didn't like those doors. There's something comforting about the opening to the back yard. But, Cal didn't know I felt that way.

Ignoring Jeffery, who is carting our luggage to the elevator, I glance up, down, and around the entire space. "How did you have time to do all this?"

"Time isn't an issue when you have money. I made some orders and told them to finish by the time we arrived."

It's perfect. Everything I would have done if I had

designed it myself. "This is why you wanted to stay in a hotel for a week. You were having the entrance renovated."

"Maybe," he raises a shoulder, smirking in delight, "or maybe I had it all renovated."

"You didn't?" My eyes widen, excitement taking over. "The guest rooms? The design ideas I had?"

"No," he deadpans, crushing my spirits.

My shoulders go slack. "Oh."

"Not at this place, anyways. Your designs are great and they'll be used, but this one's just for us." He pulls me toward the elevator. "Come on. I'll show you."

Just for us. I'm okay with that. "Wait," I say, stopping him before he presses the elevator button. "Does that mean—"

"This is our home. Yes. That's exactly what it means."

"Ahh," I squeal, clapping my hands together before throwing myself into his arms. "We're going to live here?" I pull back, looking up at him. "You're serious? You better be serious."

"Would I lie to you?" He stops me before I can speak. "Don't answer that. Would I lie to you…again?"

Cal has lied to me. The job I was supposed to have when I came here the first time and countless other white lies. It didn't ruin my trust in him, though. Not once I broke through those barriers he put up. "No, you wouldn't."

He stands there, staring at me. "Hey, what's wrong?" I give his hand a squeeze. It's not the fact that he's staring at me that has me perplexed. It's the look in his eyes. They're almost…sad. As if he just had a self-realization—a moment of truth. My heart twinges at the realness in him that I've been seeing more often. Like he's ripping off old Band-Aids and letting emotion spill from his scars.

"Nothing. I just…thank you." His forehead crinkles and I place a hand on his cheek.

"For what?"

He doesn't shy away. Doesn't look down at his feet or brush this away because vulnerability is a weakness to him. Instead, his brown eyes bore into mine. "Not giving up on me. For staying and not leaving. For just…being you."

I can't explain what my heart does next. It's a feeling so new and raw and stronger than any sensation I've ever felt. To the point that tears prick at the corners of my eyes. "You never have to thank me for loving you. It comes naturally and it's infinite. You are worthy of love and I'm not going anywhere."

"*We* are worthy of love."

Those words speak a thousand volumes. Born into madness, passed around like we were bags of old toys, surviving the loneliness. Yet, somehow, we found our way back to one another.

We are worthy of love.

I press my lips to his in a soft, subtle kiss. One that I can feel in my bones. "I love you so much."

"I love you more," Cal breathes into my mouth. "Now, let's get on that elevator, so I can show you the rest of your home." He smacks a hand to my ass and I yelp before jumping back and tapping the elevator button.

As the doors open, Jeffery steps off the elevator, and Cal and I both thank him before he leaves.

I'm so anxious to see what he's done with the place. I wonder if my room is the same. Or if I have a room. We didn't talk about the living arrangements, but I'd assume we'd probably share a room now. Or maybe Cal wants his own space, which is understandable...for now. I mean, eventually, when we get married, we'll share a bed, but we're not even officially engaged yet.

My hand hovers on the panel, waiting to hit the button. "Which floor first?"

"Lucky number eight."

"Eight it is." I tap the button and curl up to his side, wrapping my arms around him. "So, what do we do now? We have this entire island to ourselves."

"Now," he kisses my head. "We relax like we're on a honeymoon. I don't know about you, but I've had a stressful couple months and I could use a little R and R."

"You," I chuckle. "Relax? I don't see it happening."

"Oh, it's happening. No business, only pleasure for the next couple days." He snatches me up, hands gripping my ass. "You've got me all to yourself. So, tell me what you like. Chick flicks? Walks along the waterfront?"

"Foot massages," I blurt out. "Yep, I love foot massages while watching chick flicks."

He scoffs teasingly, reaching into his pocket and pulling out his phone. "Oh damn, looks like I do have work to do."

I grab his phone from his hand and stuff it in the pocket of my zip-up hoodie. "Nope. A promise is a promise."

"Never promised," he teases again.

"Ohhh, but you never lie to me."

"I did say that, didn't I? All right. I guess I'll rub those things."

I stretch up on my tiptoes and lay a gentle kiss on his lips. "I know you will."

The elevator stops on the eighth floor, and we get out. Our luggage is all placed on the floor, right in front of Cal's room. Hand in hand, we walk down the hall and I ask the question burning on my mind. "So, I assume I'll be in my old room."

Cal stops unlocking his door, jerks his head around, and gives me the stink eye. "What? No. You're in my room, baby. Or should I say, *our* room."

I smile inwardly, biting my bottom lip. "Okay."

Guess I got my answer.

27

WE'RE FINALLY SETTLING BACK into life. Bella seems to be happy we're back on the island. I'm thrilled to be with her, no matter where we are. For the first time...ever, I think I'm finally getting the happiness I so desperately wanted all my life.

I watched her sleep for a good thirty minutes before peeling myself away to go down to the dining hall. Everything has to be perfect and the only way to ensure it is, is by doing everything myself. Well, almost everything. Some of the staff returned last night. I've hired more live-in guards for the time being. Byron had a lot of enemies, but I'm sure somewhere out there he had a friend or family member who would want to avenge his death. Or not. I just can't be too sure. My personal chef has returned, as well as the housekeeper. Peter's position has yet to be replaced, and I'm not sure I'm ready for that.

For breakfast, we're having Bella's favorite—blueberry pancakes, greasy bacon that she loves so much, and lemonade.

I've got some instrumental music playing through the speakers that are perched in every corner of the room. Four vases holding white roses are placed up and down the length of the dining room table. Then, there's the box. It's safely placed under the lid of a platter.

I rub my sweaty hands together, making sure everything is in place. I suppose there isn't much that could be out of place, considering it's just a breakfast setup.

Albert, the chef, is in control of the music, and he's been instructed to begin a special song at exactly eight o'clock. I glance down at my wristwatch. It's seven-fifteen now, which means I need to get Bella up and get her fed before it begins.

Leaving the dining room, I run my hands down my pants. Didn't think I'd be this nervous. She's already agreed to marry me. She was under pressure then, though, since I had coerced her with a contract. Agreeing and wanting are two different things.

There's no doubt in my mind that Bella loves me. I'm not just some egotistical man with a big head—I can feel it. The connection we share is extraordinary.

Once I'm in the bedroom, I close the door and walk over to the bed where she's still sleeping. Only, she's not there. Panic ensues. It's a feeling of dread I've experienced with this girl one too many times. Seems like every time I turn around, she goes missing. "Bella," I shout, looking around the room. "Bella. This isn't funny."

"Good morning," she finally says, stepping out of the bathroom with a toothbrush in her mouth.

I immediately grab my chest in relief. "Don't ever do that to me again." I cross the room and squeeze her waist.

She giggles and continues to brush her teeth, speaking with foam on her lips. "I'm sorry. You were gone, and I was ready to get up." Going back into the bathroom, she leans over the sink and spits, then rinses her mouth out before turning back to me. "You have to stop worrying so much." She pats a towel to her mouth and sets it back on the sink.

"Eventually I might. Right now, I'm still on high alert. It's only been a week. Be patient with me."

On her tiptoes, she presses her lips to mine, and I can taste the sweet mint from the toothpaste. "And you need to trust me. I think I've proven I can take care of myself, if worse comes to worst. Cherry and I did manage to restrain Byron."

"Oh, I know you're tough. But I also know you seek out trouble."

"Mr. Ellis," she smirks, "are you calling me a troublemaker?"

I grab her ass cheeks, peering down at her. "That's exactly what I'm calling you."

Her hands rest on my chest, and she kisses me again. "Then you'd be correct. And I'm about to show you just how much trouble I can cause." She begins walking me backward toward the bed. My body rushes with heat, wanting her so fucking bad right now, but I have to be the asshole who turns her down.

"Later, baby. Breakfast is waiting." I instantly regret the words. Fuck breakfast. All I wanna do is fuck her.

Her head twists, and she grins. "Wait. Are you seriously rejecting me to go eat breakfast?"

I exhale profoundly. "Yes." Dammit. I hate that I'm

such a stickler when it comes to plans. I've got everything set and ready.

Bella takes a step back, still questioning me with squinted eyes. "Who are you and where is my dangerous boyfriend?"

"It'll be worth it. I promise." I take her hand and begin leading her out of the room, hoping she doesn't drag this out. As we're walking, I adjust my erection in my pants nonchalantly, but she takes notice.

"I'm glad to see it wasn't an issue of impotence."

I let out a roaring laugh. "You never have to worry about that. All I have to do is look at you and my dick twitches."

We make it to the dining room with twenty minutes to go. I pull out a chair for Bella, and she takes a seat, inhaling a deep breath as she lifts the lid on the pancakes. "Blueberry? My favorite!"

"Everything blueberry is your favorite."

"And lemonade? What's the special occasion?"

I take a seat right beside her, adjusting my napkin in my lap. "Didn't know we needed a special occasion to have lemonade."

"Well, usually it's orange juice. I'm just surprised." She takes a bite of bacon and points to the lidded platter holding the box, speaking as she chews. "What's that?"

She knows. Dammit, she fucking knows. I can't put anything past this girl. "Dessert. Just eat your breakfast, Sherlock."

I can't even look at her because I know she's observing me as I poke my fork around at my food, not even taking a bite. My appetite is nonexistent. My hands are shaking; my heart is racing. I need to just get this over with.

"Are you done?" I ask her, my eyes still on my plate.

"Cal," she chuckles, "what the hell is going on with you? I've never in my life seen you nervous, and you're acting like you're about to propose or something."

Yep. She knows.

"No." I finally take a bite, a big-ass bite that fills my entire mouth.

Bella drops it and continues eating. "What's the plan for the day?"

"I thought maybe we'd tour the castle. I could show you some of the finished rooms. Maybe have lunch in the courtyard."

"Sounds nice."

Why does it suddenly feel like we're a fifty-year-old married couple who has nothing to talk about? Is this what marriage will be like? What if she gets bored with me—with us? What if, suddenly, I'm not enough, and she wants more? She'll leave me eventually. I know she will.

Maybe this is a bad idea.

I'm not sure where all this self-doubt is coming from. *What am I thinking?* Bella has always been mine, and she always will be.

Bella sets her fork beside her plate, turns her entire body toward me, and places a hand on my lap. "Then maybe we could take a nice hot shower together." She waggles her eyebrows, and it's cute as hell, because she has a smear of syrup on her chin.

I set my fork down and run my thumb over it, then lick off the sweet maple. "I could use another shower."

"Maybe we could talk about some ideas I had for the clubs."

"You've really taken a liking to the clubs, haven't you?"

Her cheeks tinge pink. Also cute as hell.

"Don't be embarrassed." I chuckle. "I'm excited to hear your ideas because I seriously think we should just shut them down. I hope you're not expecting one here, though, because the only show you'll get at this castle is from me."

She leans in, the scent of pancakes and syrup spilling from her breath. "I only need you." Her lips press to mine.

Okay. I can do this. We're good. No matter what obstacles we face, we'll face them together. She's not going anywhere.

I lift the napkin from my lap and pat my mouth before dropping it on my plate. A glance at my watch tells me it's time.

My chair pushes out and I stand between *it* and the table. Reaching over, I pull the platter toward us, without lifting the lid.

Bella sinks back in the chair, her hands resting on her stomach. "I'm so stuffed. I'm not sure I've got room for dessert."

My lip twitches with humor. Maybe she doesn't have any idea.

My entire body is trembling. Pretty sure my face is pale, too.

I turn toward Bella, still standing, and take both of her hands in mine. "Do you remember the day we made the pact, Bella?"

She nods, looking at me like I've lost my mind. "Of course I do. We were in the attic and you were upset about breaking the Beckhams' window with that baseball. Mark and Layla had just ratted you out and you thought for sure Mrs. Webster was going to send you away."

"That's exactly right. You told me, in no exact terms, soulmates come in different shapes and sizes. That best friends can be soulmates, even if they don't love each other."

Her lips tug up in a smile and my heart skips a beat. "That was before I knew what love even was."

"But you weren't wrong. You said we were soulmates and that nothing could tear us apart. I think we've proven that to be true. Bella," I drop to my knee, "you are my soulmate. You are my best friend."

"Cal?"

The music begins, soft, but audible. It's *Our Song*. The one Bella composed.

"Oh my gosh." She gets choked up. "This is our song."

"Let me finish," I press as she claps one hand over her mouth. "Against all odds we found our way back to each other. Through oceans and mountains. Downpours and blizzards. Our hearts cried for one another and we followed the sound. I can't promise it will be easy. But I can promise to smile with you when you want to cry, hold you when you want to run, and love you when you don't feel strong enough to love yourself. I can give you that same promise I made all those years ago—a promise to never part. Until kingdom come."

Tears fall from the corners of her eyes. Tears of happiness that clench my heart. Her hand drops, and I see the smile on her face.

"Will you marry me, Isabella Jenkins?"

She squeals, throwing herself into my arms, and shouts, "Yes! Hell yes, I will marry you."

I lift the lid on the platter and reveal an ivory box with gold-encrusted embroidery. Picking it up, I take her hand in mine, then flip the top. Inside is a custom-made, ten-carat ring. Engraved on the inside, it reads, *until kingdom come.*

Her eyes light up, and she gasps at the beauty of it. "Oh my God, Cal. It's exquisite."

I take her left hand and slide the ring on her finger. It fits perfectly. Just like us.

Bella looks from the ring to me with puffy eyes and a red nose. "I love you so much."

"I love you more."

AFTER BREAKFAST AND THE PROPOSAL, Bella and I decided that it was a good day to just lie in bed. It's exactly what we've done for the past week, but it doesn't matter. I could do this with her every day, and it would never get old.

I was an idiot for questioning things. What we have is solid and real. Bella is never going anywhere, and neither am I.

My phone buzzes on the nightstand, but I ignore it.

Bella lifts her head from my chest. "Should you get that?"

"Nah. If it's important, they'll leave a message."

It buzzes again, and again. And when it stops, it starts right back up.

I huff, leaning forward and reaching for it. "Unknown caller." I glance at Bella before finally accepting the call.

"This is Mr. Ellis." Bella lays her head back on my chest, fingers floating over my stomach.

"Yes, Mr. Ellis. This is Jim from Water Express Delivery. We've got a package for you from Gunders Cremation Services. We're docked at Cori Cove, but the guards won't let us up to deliver the package, and we need your signature."

"I'll be down shortly."

I end the call abruptly and go to get up. Bella lifts her head, tugging the sheet over her chest. "What is it?"

"Peter's remains are here."

My feet hit the ground, and I snatch my clothes off the floor.

"Do you want me to come with you?" Bella asks, still lying in bed, looking so inviting.

"No. You stay here where it's warm. I won't be long."

Ten minutes later, I'm at the dock, wearing nothing but a tee shirt, joggers, and a pair of boots as the snow falls from the sky.

I greet the delivery guy, and he hands me a rectangular box. "Sign here," he says, holding out an electronic keypad with a pen attached.

I scribble my name, thank him, and head back to the castle with Peter.

So many emotions take over as I make the trek. There is so much I want to say but talking to a box seems ridiculous, so I think the thoughts instead.

I never got to say goodbye. I never got to thank you for picking me up from The Webster House that day. You were there for me when no one else was. Cleaned my wounds when Vincent got out of control, adjusted the thermostat when he'd crank it up and try to roast me in my bedroom. You taught me how to ride a bike when I was fifteen years old, when Vincent took Delilah to a clinic out of state. I was embarrassed as hell that I was a teenager and didn't know how to ride one, but you never once judged me. And you never gave up when it took all day. You were a good friend. The father I wish I'd had. I won't let you down, Peter. Bella and I will live out the dreams you and Carolina had—right on this island. It'll be a home full of laughter.

Before I know it, I'm standing in the sitting room on the staff floor where Peter would often have his nighttime tea.

His chair is still there, weathered and used. It was his favorite chair. He didn't care what it looked like. Always said it was the comfort that mattered.

He was right. What we see is not always what we get.

I sit down on the chair and begin peeling away at the packaging tape on the box. Inside is a heavy-duty, wooden box. I pull it out, letting the shipping box fall to the floor. Holding it up, I read the engraving on the front.

Peter Blake

February 8, 1948 - December 8, 2021

"Happy Birthday, Peter."

28

STANDING in the doorway of the sitting room, I just watch him. It didn't take me long to find where he'd gone. When I rang the guard and he said Cal had picked up the delivery twenty minutes ago, I knew he just needed some time.

Ten minutes later, I checked the cameras.

Slow, soft steps lead me over to him. I wrap my arms around him from behind as he sits in Peter's chair. "Hey. You okay?"

He runs his fingers over the top of the box. "Yeah. Just wish I could've been there for him. I let him down."

His words are like a knife to my heart. "Babe, no." I round the chair, keeping one hand on his neck as I slouch beside him. "Don't think like that. There was nothing you could do."

"I should have acted faster when I knew what Byron was up to. I should've never left the island that day."

"You had business to tend to. Peter would never want you to blame yourself."

"There was no business."

I tilt my head. "What do you mean?"

"I said I had business to take care of on the note I left you, but I lied." He turns to look at me, and I can see the sorrow in his eyes. "I went to the main island to get you this. While I was at the jeweler's, I got a tip-off that Byron was rallying men for some big scheme he'd been planning that involved you. That's when I called Peter to get you out of here. I left the purchased ring with the jeweler, with plans to return and pick it up. As I was heading back to you, someone stuck a bag over my head and knocked me out. Anyways," he lifts my finger that has my engagement ring on it, "I knew this one was perfect for you."

I had no idea Cal was going to buy me a ring. Sure, I told him I'd marry him the night before that day, but at the time, it was all because he needed me to. "I can't believe you went and bought me this."

"It was never about the contract or my will. It was always because I loved you so much that I couldn't imagine spending another day without you."

My fingers graze his as the glow of the fire in the fireplace hits my ring, illuminating the ceiling with glimmering oracles. "Well, I have a confession, too. When I agreed to marry you, it was never because I thought you needed me to be your wife. It was because I *wanted* to be your wife."

Cal flashes a half of a smile as he still looks down at the box. I can tell he's pretty down on himself still.

"Peter would be so proud of how far you've come. Don't beat yourself up over what could have been."

He nods, though I don't really think he's accepting

what I said. It'll take time, but lucky for both of us, we have all the time in the world.

"I decided on my new last name."

"Oh yeah? What's it gonna be? Stanford, Vanderbilt?"

"Blake. Callum Blake."

"I think it's absolutely perfect. Peter would be honored, and I'm honored to take the last name when we're married."

He looks at me then, light finally showing hope in his eyes and replacing the sadness I saw moments ago. "Bella Blake."

"I like the sound of that."

Cal doesn't have a middle name. He was never given one, and I'm not even sure how he got a last name to begin with. Obviously, Ellis was given to him when he was adopted, but he was never an Ellis—he's said so himself.

I'm glad he decided to take Peter's last name. It's one that he can be proud of.

"What about the company?" I ask, curious if he'll keep the Ellis name for the resorts. A cramp in my leg has me standing up, and Cal does the same, still holding the box.

"I was thinking, Blake Hotels and Resorts."

"Oh, wow. You've already figured it all out."

"It's got a nice ring to it, don't ya think?"

I wrap my arms around his neck, our noses brushing against one another. "I think it's a great name."

Cal presses a chaste kiss to my forehead. "All right, let's get back to bed. We're supposed to spend all day there."

I smile against his mouth, kissing him over and over again. "I like the way you think."

Cal sets the box down in the chair. "We'll leave him here for the night and find a good spot for him tomorrow."

"I think that's a good idea. He always liked this room."

I take Cal's hand and we head back to our room. It's obvious he's hurting and I wish there was something I could do or say to make him feel better; I just don't think there is. He needs time.

We get back to the bedroom and crawl into bed. My head rests on Cal's chest as he stares wide-eyed at the ceiling.

Before long, I'm drifting off to sleep.

29

I WOKE up before Cal for a change. He didn't sleep well last night. I felt him toss and turn for hours as we battled for the blanket. Each time he'd roll, he'd pull it off me. Each time I pulled it back, he rolled again. Finally, I took the whole damn thing and covered him with the flat sheet.

Sharing a bed will take some getting used to, but I'm sure that's the case for all newly-engaged couples.

I've already showered and have coffee in the room for us when it occurs to me that I should cook breakfast this morning. I love to cook, but I've never had the chance to cook for Cal.

I sneak out of the bedroom, closing the door gently behind me. I'm half tempted to go check out the other levels to see what changes are being made. We never did a tour last night, so I'm still not sure what his plan with all the extra space is. Cal wasn't feeling up to it and I honestly wasn't either.

Deciding against it, I go to the kitchen and find that the chef is not there, so I help myself. It's a large, commercial kitchen with anything you could ever need to make any food you want. I find a large refrigerator stocked full and decide on scrambled eggs and hash browns.

I get all the ingredients out on the counter and begin my search for utensils. A big kitchen is nice and all, but when I'm a mother and wife, I'd like to be able to cook for my family in a room that doesn't feel like I'm serving up a restaurant full of people.

My agitation gets the best of me when twenty minutes have passed, and I can't find anything I'm looking for.

That's it. We need a smaller kitchen. Cal will argue and say I don't need to cook and that we have people to do it for us. Same with the housekeeper. He'll insist that she can do all the cleaning and I never need to lift a finger. I wasn't raised that way, though, and Cal wasn't either. We know hard work and we also know that it pays off. I don't want someone else taking care of my family and I'll certainly never hire a full-time nanny to watch them while I do absolutely nothing. An occasional sitter, fine. We all need a break, but my dreams of being a mom and wife include doing all the things that moms and wives do.

I'm pulling out pans, dropping them to the floor with a thud and making an obscene amount of noise, when I hear laughter from behind me.

My head jerks around and I see Cal standing in the open doorway. "Good morning, beautiful," he says, arms crossed over his chest and humor on his lips.

I drop down on my ass, feeling defeated. "I wanted to cook you breakfast." I bury my face in my hands, on the brink of tears.

"Baby, we have a cook for that." He crouches down

beside me and rubs a hand up and down my back. "I put in an order for omelets. Come to the dining room, it will be ready shortly."

"No, Cal," I raise my voice, not meaning to, but really wanting to get my point across. "I wanted to cook for my fiancé. How can I, though, when this kitchen is the size of a house? I can't find anything."

"You really wanted to cook me breakfast?"

I look up at him, a serious expression on my face. "Yes. I want to do all of those things. But this place is... too...big."

"I thought you loved it here?"

"I do. As a vacation or even a place of work. But not as a home."

I'm being so selfish. My face drops back in my hands and I begin sobbing like a baby. "I'm sorry. I know you went through all the trouble to have these renovations done that you want to surprise me with, and here I am acting like a brat."

Cal laughs and the sound calms me slightly, knowing that he's not angry. "Stand up." He gets to his feet. I look at him, and he's holding out a hand. "I want to show you something."

I place my hand in his and he pulls me up. "What is it?" I ask, never being one to have an ounce of patience.

He leads me out of the kitchen and we begin down the hall. "I told you I had some changes done, but I never told you what they were."

"Well," I drawl, "what are they?"

"You'll see."

We end up in the elevator and back on the eighth

floor, where our room is. Cal takes me down the hall, and we stop in front of the room I stayed in when I was here. "Ready?" he asks, wide-eyed and excited.

I nod, anxious to see what's behind the door. He pushes it open, and I look inside. "Cal," I gasp. "Are you serious right now?"

I'm no longer looking into my old room. I'm now looking at a baby nursery. Gray carpet, with white walls, a white crib with matching dressers, and even a rocking chair in front of the balcony doors. "This is..." I fall into his arms, ready to cry again, "I love it so much."

"I know we're a long ways away from having a baby, but I figured we could at least be prepared. The plan was for you to decorate however you want, but now, I'm thinking we need to talk about what exactly it is you want. I'm not so sure anymore."

Our hands clasp together, bodies level, and I look up at him. "I just want something...smaller."

"So you want to leave Cori Cove?"

"No!" I blurt out, "I don't want to leave here. I absolutely love this island. It's surrounded by beauty and I love the way I feel when I'm here."

"Okay, then it's settled. We'll build our own house, just the way we want, on the backside of the property."

My eyebrows hit my forehead. "Really?"

"Sure." He shrugs causally. "Why not?"

"And what will we do with this place?"

"What do you want to do with this place?"

I grin, biting my bottom lip. He knows what I want. "How about we stick to the original plan. Open it up to guests. We have our own home separate from the resort, and I can help out here when needed."

"As in, you can work at the club? No. Not a good idea. There'd be too many bodies to get rid of, and I just don't have the time for that."

I can't help but laugh. I know he thinks I'll get hit on left and right, and he'd have to take guys out, but I also think he's letting his mind wander to the worst-case scenarios.

"I don't want to work at the club. I want to manage the waitstaff and help the girls. I've actually been thinking about it and I have a plan."

Cal walks into the nursery and takes a seat in the rocking chair. For a brief moment, I see it. Him holding a baby and being a daddy. It's a beautiful picture painted in my mind that will someday be a reality.

Cal blows out an exaggerated exhale. "All right, tell me this plan of yours."

I walk over and take a seat on the floor in front of him with my legs crossed. "First, I want to give them raises. Not much, but something to show they're appreciated. Second, we place a waitstaff manager at each location and they work with the staff on what hours they are able to work. No more eighty-hour work weeks. New work attire that they are comfortable wearing. The managers can check in with me weekly, and we can reevaluate things as needed."

"That's it?"

"I think so. For now, anyways."

"Done," Cal deadpans.

"Really?"

He leans forward in the chair, forearms resting on his legs. "Yeah. Welcome to the Blake Hotels and Resorts team."

I laugh. "You're serious? You're okay with me taking the lead with the waitstaff, without even knowing my credentials?"

"I'm serious. Whatever makes you happy, babe. I'm here to please." Cal pulls my hand until I'm on his lap in the chair. "Now, enough about work. Let's discuss our new home. If we open the resort, our private property will be gated. I'm thinking four or five bedrooms, three baths. And I happen to know an interior designer who will do a stellar job with the inside." He smirks, referring to me.

My eyes light up with excitement. "I get to design the inside?"

"Well, yeah. It's your house."

Part of me still feels guilty for changing all the plans we made. "You're sure this is okay? We can sit on it for a while before jumping in."

"I don't sit on things. It's settled. We're building a house and opening the Cori Cove resort to the public." He bops my nose before kissing me softly.

My arms envelop his neck in a hug. "How did I get so lucky?"

"Luck has nothing to do with it. It was always fate."

Cal ended up bringing breakfast to bed. An entire tray of carbs—bagels, muffins, croissants, donuts. He's currently in the shower while I go over an employee list for all the clubs at each resort. I don't see Cherry's name anywhere on the list, and I assume it's because that's not her real name. After a bit of research, I find out that her legal name is Sara Hopkins.

I'm excited to start making the changes necessary to keep the waitstaff happy. I'm even more excited to start looking at designs and layouts for our new house. Cal insists that it will be move-in ready by summer, but unless he has round-the-clock workers, I don't see how that will happen. I'm leaving all the construction to him while I stick to countertops and paint colors.

On top of a new house and managing staff, I've also got a wedding to plan. Life is going to be busy as hell, but in the best way possible.

I take another bite of my blueberry muffin, dropping crumbs on the open folder on my lap. I sweep them away and chew my food, but my stomach begins to unsettle. Suddenly, blueberries don't taste so good. In a knee-jerk reaction, I shove the folder off me, the papers scattering on the bed. I jump up and haul ass to the bathroom. Cal is in the shower and steam fills the room. Ignoring him peeking out the side of the shower curtain, I drop to my knees in front of the toilet.

"Hey, what's wrong?" he asks, right before I throw up.

All of my breakfast comes out in one hurl.

"Shit, babe. You okay?"

I didn't even notice when he got out of the shower. He's standing behind me, dripping wet and rubbing my back while the shower still runs. "Maybe we should've stuck to omelets."

I smile through the nausea. "Maybe." Grabbing a hand towel off the vanity beside me, I wipe my mouth and clench it in my hand, still feeling like my stomach needs to be emptied even more.

I sit down on the bathroom floor, feeling the water from Cal's wet body soak through my pajama pants. "I'm okay," I finally say to him.

"I'll get you some water." He goes to leave, but I grab his ankle. "It's okay. I'm good. Promise."

I flush the toilet and get off the floor.

"All right. Why don't you get in the shower with me? It might make you feel better."

I nod. That sounds nice. "Let me brush my teeth real quick and I'll join you."

Sliding the curtain back open, Cal gets in the shower as I grab my toothbrush and slop on some toothpaste.

It's so strange. I felt awful, and now it's like I was never sick. It had to have been the muffin.

Peeling my clothes off, layer by layer drops to the floor. I poke my head in the opening of the shower curtain, watching Cal as he suds up his body. God, he's so sexy, and he's all mine.

Just watching him sends my body into a frenzy of need. Tingles shoot down my chest, going straight to my sex.

I went from vomiting to wanting to fuck in less than five minutes. My hormones must really be out of whack.

Hormones. That's what Cal said I was taking in place of birth control a couple months ago. I didn't even think of that. Maybe that's why I'm feeling so strange lately.

I jerk the curtain closed when the possibility of being pregnant hits me full force.

No. I can't be.

Sure, Cal and I spent an entire week at a hotel doing nothing but reacquainting ourselves with each other's bodies, but we've only just reunited. It's too soon.

Cal pops his head out, the black tips of his hair glistening from the water. He's got a little scruff on his face from not shaving for a few days and he looks hot as hell. "Are you coming or what?"

I pull open the curtain the rest of the way and get inside. Cal wastes no time pulling my body against his. "Feeling better?"

I look up at him, blinking away the drops of water coating my lashes. "Oddly, yes."

"Hmm. Hopefully it's not a stomach bug."

I could tell him that there's a possibility I'm pregnant, or, I can waive suspicion and take a test before I even mention anything. I'm sure I'm just overthinking this. I threw up one time and my period isn't even that late. I'm not even exactly sure what day I should have started, but I'm almost positive it was only a couple days.

Maybe I could call the pharmacy on the main island and order a test. I'm sure I could get Jeffery to deliver it. I'd just have to make sure he knows it's a secret. I'd have to use the word surprise to get him to oblige—no one wants to go against the infamous Mr. Ellis, by keeping secrets from him.

"Yeah," I say. "I hope not. The last thing I want to do is be bedridden with the flu, when we just got here."

Cal chuckles. "Well, we've basically bedridden

ourselves for the last week and a half, so I'm not sure it would make much difference."

My hands rest on Cal's shoulders while his set on my waist. "That is true."

His face nuzzles into the crook of my neck, and he begins laying wet kisses down my collarbone. "Since you're feeling better..."

I bite my bottom lip, liking the way he thinks.

30

Drops of water pelt my skin as her hands glide up and down my arms. My mouth trails kisses down her neck, to her collarbone, then to her chest. My legs bend at the knee as I cup her breasts, sucking her pink bud in my mouth.

Bella takes my erect cock in her smooth hand, stroking it up and down as the water coats her hand.

I moan around her nipple. "See what you do to me, baby."

Both of her breasts fill my hands as I massage them. Thank God she's feeling better. I had every intention of fucking her once I got out of the shower, but now that she's here with me, I think I'll fuck her right here and now.

Unless… "You wanna get out of here? Have a little fun with Amara?" I know she hates the snakes, especially Amara, but there's something about making her squirm that turns me on. In fact, I think she likes the thrill as much as I do. I know Amara would never hurt her or I wouldn't dare bring her out.

"Not a chance." Her hand moves faster, sliding up and down my cock, thumb grazing my head before resuming to stroke my full length.

I'm so hungry for her. I want to devour every inch of her body. Kissing my way up her inner thigh while my tongue does laps around her clit.

Then I'll bend her over while her hands press to the wall of the shower, jerk her by the hair and fuck her from behind.

Fuck. I need her so badly.

But, first, I need to get my girl off.

My hand sweeps the crease of her leg beneath her knee, bending and lifting until her foot is sitting on the ledge of the shower. With her legs spread for me, I drop to my knees. Bella runs her fingers through my soaked hair, tugging and pulling before slamming my face into her cunt.

She's a feisty thing with zero patience when it comes to her desires. It's the innocent ones who harbor all the sexual fantasies. I plan to fulfill them all, one day at a time. If she wants me to fuck her in the club, behind a one-way glass, while she watches others go at it, I'll do it for her. I'm onto her fascination with voyeurism and I'm all for it if that's what she wants. As long as I'm the only one to touch her.

With two fingers spread against her sex, my tongue slides up and down between her folds. Stopping at her clit, I dart my tongue out in a rapid motion, and her body quivers, hands tugging tighter at my hair.

My cock twitches in delight as she cries out in pleasure.

I slide two fingers inside her, feeling the warmth and tightness of her pussy. I add in another finger, going knuckle-deep until I reach her G-spot.

Her legs spread wider as she rolls her hips, forcing my face against her. "Faster, Cal."

My fingers delve deeper, curling, and pressing, then pulling in a repetitive motion. I suck the water off her clit, grazing my teeth against her sensitive nub.

"Oh, God." She howls and rides my face like it's her own personal toy. She can use me and she can abuse me. I don't care as long as it makes her feel good.

"Come for me, baby. Come around my fingers and let me taste your orgasm."

My words hit a nerve inside her. Her walls contract, cries become high-pitched, and her nails drag down the shower wall while her other hand pulls the hair on my head.

Wetness pools around her pussy and I sweep my tongue around her sex, licking her clean and tasting the sweetness of her orgasm.

When she releases my hair and drops her foot to the shower floor, I stand up, working the kink in my leg.

Bella begins stroking my cock again, lust-filled eyes locked on mine. I kiss her lips, sliding my tongue inside her mouth, giving her a taste of herself. "See how good you taste?"

Her response is a hum against my tongue. In a swift motion, I spin her around. Her hands hit the wall of the shower, and I lift her leg again, letting it rest on the ledge.

My cock enters her pussy, like it's home and it knows exactly where to go.

Squeezing her hips, I fill her up from behind. Our bodies fit perfectly together, and I could stare at this ass all day. I slap a hand to her left cheek, pinching the skin and watching as it fills the gaps between my fingers. "All mine."

Bella moans, her hands sliding up and down the slippery shower wall. "This won't take long, baby."

I'm on the verge of combustion, so I slow down, letting the anticipation build. A second later, I'm fucking her again. Her brown hair rests against her back, and I sweep it to the side, pressing kisses on her spine.

"So fucking beautiful." She's like a dream I never want to wake up from.

My pace quickens, and I can't hold it anymore. My entire body is zapped with electricity as I release inside her.

Bella drops her hands and straightens her back, and I slowly pull out. When she turns around, I embrace her and kiss her lips. "I could get used to these morning showers after breakfast."

She smiles against my mouth while our hearts beat rapidly against one another. "I think that can be arranged."

BELLA INSISTS she's feeling better, so she's been working hard on the changes to the clubs all day. I was able to make a few business phone calls and set up an appointment with a builder as well as get the process moving with my new attorney on getting my name changed. After speaking with my business advisor, we've decided to hold off on changing the company name until I'm officially Callum Blake. I told him in that case, I'd prefer to wait until after the wedding, so all the announcements can come at once.

I'm in my study, when I see Bella scurry past the open door and down the hall, I push my chair back, get up, then go out in the hall. "Babe, where ya going?"

Bella stops, turns around with her hands folded in front of her and a perplexed look on her face. I know that look. She's up to something. I quickly eat the space between us, meeting her at the elevator doors. My head tilts, examining her. "Why do you look like you're plotting a murder?"

She swats at me playfully. "You're crazy. Or paranoid. Maybe both."

"All three. But I know that look. Where are you running off to looking sexy as hell in that jumpsuit?"

It's true. She's drop-dead gorgeous in her all-black, long-sleeved jumpsuit with a pair of matching black flats on her feet.

"I had a package delivered from the main island." She holds up a hand, averting me from asking questions. "It's a surprise, so don't ask."

I zip my fingers across my lips. "I won't say a word. It's cold out there, though. Would you like me to have the guard bring it up?"

She shakes her head no. "My boots and coat are downstairs. I'll be fine." She kisses my lips, then taps the elevator button.

"Meet me in my study in twenty minutes and we'll go get lunch."

Her eyebrows waggle. "It's a date, Mr. Blake." Her smile widens. "I like the sound of that."

"I do, too, Mrs. Blake."

I wait until the elevator doors close before taking my phone out of my pocket and dialing Anders. "Hey. Bella is on her way down there to fetch a delivery. Keep an eye on things."

"You got it."

I end the call and put my phone back in my pocket as I walk back down the hall to my study. She's got something up her sleeve. Says it's a surprise, and I didn't have the nerve to tell her I hate surprises. They make me anxious, and I don't like that feeling.

Back in my study, I go over to the wall-sized window behind my desk and look out with my hands stuffed in my pants pockets. I can't see her from this view. I begin pacing the floor, thinking about what she could be up to.

A surprise that involved a delivery from the main island? Could be something for a new position with the company. Maybe something for the new house that isn't even in the first phase of building. Wouldn't surprise me if she's already purchasing decor. Sounds exactly like something she'd do.

I could always contact her bank and see where the purchase came from.

What the hell am I thinking? I can't do that. *Let the girl have her surprise, Cal.*

It seems I have some work to do on myself, if I plan on being a good husband. Old habits die hard and all that shit. Might take some time before I stop peering over her shoulder, out of fear that she's going to run off or get taken away from me. Baby steps. That's all I can do.

I sit down, then stand back up, opening then closing my laptop. I pace the length of the room three times and check the time twice. And now a third time. It's been twenty minutes, and she's still not here.

I grab my jacket off the hook by the door and go to leave when I meet Bella face to face. "Oh hey. I was just coming to look for you. You're late."

She cranes her neck, looking at me with a crease on her forehead. "Yeah, by two minutes." Her hands run down the sleeve of my jacket. "You really need to chill out."

I blow out a heavy breath through my nose. "I'm chill."

"Come on, you. Let's go eat." Her fingers intertwine with mine, and we head down to the yacht. It'll be nice to get out of here and get some fresh air. We've both been cooped up for a while. Cori Cove is the perfect location, but winters can be a real drag.

Once we're off the elevator on the ground level, I pry, trying to figure out what she's hiding. "Did you get your package?"

"Mmhmm."

I nod in response as we approach the main doors. "Was it in good condition? I mean, if there was any damage, I can make a call."

"Cal," she drawls with a giggle behind her audible breaths, "you're not going to let this go, are you?"

"Nope."

Bella releases my hand and scours the area. "Darn it! I think I left my boots upstairs."

There's at least a foot of snow out there and her feet will be icicles if she walks outside in those shoes. I step in front of her, slouch down, and say, "Hop on."

A second later, she's jumping on my back with her legs wrapped around my torso. "It feels like it's been forever since you've given me a piggyback ride."

"It has been. At least twelve years." I didn't do it often, but there were a few times I'd give Bella piggyback rides just for fun. One time, we had a piggyback race with some of the other kids in the house. We won, of course.

I step out the door and carry her through the snow, and once we're on the dock, I let her fall to her feet.

We walk hand in hand to the cabin of the yacht. A fire is lit in the electric fireplace, the table set with our hot meal already waiting in platters.

Bella shivers, so I grab a throw blanket from the closet next to the sofa and wrap it around her shoulders before pulling out her chair for her.

"This is perfect, Cal. You really do think of everything, even when it's just a simple lunch."

"It's all for you. I plan to spend our entire lives giving you everything you deserve."

She reaches for my hand over the table, her smooth fingers grazing my scarred knuckles. "You once told me that you wanted to buy me all the dresses in the world to prove they don't hold my beauty. And now it's my turn to tell you that all the objects in the world do not hold my love for you. I only want you, Cal. Rich. Poor. It's you and me, forever."

I'm not sure how I will ever convince myself that I'm worthy of this girl, but right now, I'm definitely not. I have so much to make up for.

Bella lets go of my hand and digs her hand down into the cup of her bra. I laugh at the expression on her face. "What are you doing?" She pulls something out and slides it across the table. "What is this?" I pick it up and...I'm speechless. I know exactly what this is. I might live a life of solitude, but I know what these two lines mean. "Seriously?"

"Looks like it's you, me, and a baby, forever."

I jump up so fast that my chair tips over as I round the table and embrace her. My mind is going a million miles a minute. *Is this real? Is she pranking me? We're having a baby? I'm going to be a dad? Fuck. I'm going to be a dad.*

I pull back and look at her, frozen in place. "When? How? Is this what you had delivered?"

Her head nods up and down. "I suspected it when I got sick this morning, then I remembered the fertility pills I took. My body has been out of whack, so I did a little research and the effects of those pills can last through a couple cycles. I didn't think it was true, but I ordered a test just to find out. And...well, it's true."

I'm stunned. Trying to put together the right words, but I've got nothing.

Bella looks longingly into my eyes and there's a sliver of worry. "You're not disappointed, are you?"

"What? Hell no, I'm not disappointed. We're having a baby, baby." I've never been more excited for anything in my entire life. This is what I've always wanted. Bella—a family with her.

Then it hits me. "We have to tell your parents, and they fucking hate me."

"Hey," she lays a hand on my cheek, "you and me."

She's right. It's us against the world, and Bella and this baby are my entire world.

My lips press to hers. "Forever and always."

"Until kingdom come."

31

FIVE MONTHS LATER

Mom is shuffling around like a mad woman as we all pitch in and help set up for the Fourth of July picnic in the park. "You can just set that on the picnic table, sweetie," she says, referring to the large bowl of mixed fruit I'm holding. "Wrong table, Dave. Food goes on this one," she barks at Dad, who's carrying a plate of hot dogs.

Dad walks behind me to set the hot dogs down beside the fruit bowl. He leans close and whispers in my ear, "It's just a few hours. We can get through this if we stick together."

I laugh, knowing that we will get through it because we have every year since I joined this family. "It's all about teamwork," I tell him.

I'm wiping down an empty picnic table when I catch Cal out of the corner of my eye. He's playing catch with Benji, Mark's new girlfriend's son. I smile at the sight. It won't be long, and he'll be playing catch with our little guy.

He glances in my direction, catching my stare. His back straightens, and he winks, right before the ball smacks him in the stomach. Cal curls over, exaggerating, while Benji laughs hysterically. "Did you see that, Mark. I hit that guy with the ball."

Mark looks over his shoulder at Benji, who now has the ball back. "Aww, I missed it, bud. Why don't ya do it again so I can see?"

I swat Mark with the rag in my hand. "Be nice."

"Hey, I'm here. He's here. No one's killed anyone yet. I think it's a good start."

Dropping the rag on the counter, I place a hand on my growing bump. "Please just try."

Mark throws his hands out. "This is me trying."

"Okay. Please try harder. You've both made some mistakes. Some much bigger than others. I've forgiven you for a lot of shit, now please just forgive him."

"Forgive him for almost getting us both killed through his game of manipulation? Or forgive him for luring you into his darkness and putting a ring on your finger while knocking you up, so you're stuck forever?"

"I'm not stuck, Mark. I've loved Cal since I was a little girl, and if you can't see that, then you can turn your head and pretend we don't exist, for all care."

Maybe it's my hormones, or maybe it's because I'm being rational for once. My parents and Cal have made amends, and they've agreed to welcome him into the family with loving arms. In fact, he and my dad are talking right now.

Shit. They're talking. I toss the rag at Mark and hurry over to them, hoping I'm not too late before one of them puts a foot in their mouth and a brawl begins at our annual family picnic.

I step beside Cal, listening in on the conversation.

"Stocks are predicted to skyrocket within the next couple months. Now's a good time to hit the ground running."

I breathe a sigh of relief. Just a boring conversation about stocks.

"Hey, hun," Dad says, poking a finger at my arm. "I see you managed to escape your crazed mom."

I look over and see her piling plates, napkins, and cutlery in Mark's arms. He glances in my direction and scowls. "Yeah. I think she's got help for the time being."

"Listen, you two," Dad begins while my pulse quickens. *Here we go.* "We're really happy for you guys. Cal, I know we got off to a rocky start, but I can see the way you look at my little girl. I trust that she's in good hands."

My heart doubles in size. "Thanks, Dad. I am in good hands. Cal's the love of my life."

Dad extends a hand to Cal. "Welcome to the family, Callum."

I look up at Cal, who is just standing there, staring at my dad's hand like it's contaminated. I give him a nudge, and he snaps out of his slumber, then finally shakes my dad's hand. "Thank you, sir."

"Well, I better go check in with the old ball and chain. I'll hear about it later if I don't."

Cal and I both laugh as my dad walks away. Once we're alone, I turn to face him and take both of his hands in mine. "You okay?"

He stares past me as if he's deep in thought, then finally says, "He welcomed me into your family."

I squeeze his hands and give him a reassuring look. "This *is* your family now, Cal."

"Ironic, isn't it? Thirteen years ago, we were preparing to get adopted into this family together, and now we're both part of it."

"It's not ironic." I kiss his lips. "It's fate."

We're interrupted when Mark joins our side. I take a step back, still holding Cal's hands. Mark needs to see that this is real. That I am marrying Cal and spending the rest of my life with him. Even if I have to shove our relationship down his throat, he will see that I choose Cal. Today, tomorrow, and forever.

Mark rubs his hands together, glancing back and forth from me to Cal. "All right. I'm not good with this shit, so here goes." He inhales deeply. "Bella, I know we haven't always been close, but you're my sister, and I love you. Cal, I know we have a rocky past and we both did some stupid shit, but I love my sister. Therefore, I'm willing to let bygones be bygones, if you're cool with that."

Well, damn. I didn't think he had it in him. I know Mark loves me and the reason he's been so cold toward Cal is because he wants to protect me. It's his own fucked-up way of being a good brother.

I look at Cal, who seems hesitant. But I'm hopeful he'll swallow his pride and put the past where it belongs.

When he drops my hand and offers it to Mark, I let out, yet another, sigh of relief. "Works for me."

Mark shakes his hand, then resumes helping Mom and Nina, his girlfriend, with the canopy.

It's a step in the right direction and I'm so grateful that Mark came over here. I know it wasn't easy for either of them.

"I'm proud of you," I tell Cal. He brushes it off like it's no big deal, but it is a big deal *to me*. Cal and Mark are actually a lot alike. Stubborn as hell, protective, and terrible baseball catchers.

"Anything for you, babe," he finally says, laying one on my lips. His hands cup my belly, fingers grazing gently, when I suddenly feel the baby kick. His eyes widen and he looks at me. "Tell me that wasn't just your breakfast from this morning."

I laugh. "That wasn't my breakfast. That was our baby boy. He must know Daddy is touching his mommy."

"Well," Cal nuzzles up to me, "he better get used to it because I plan on touching Mommy a lot."

I look down at my stomach. "You hear that, Jaxon Peter Blake, Daddy's making promises he better keep." I look back up at Cal. "Because I can't get enough of you, Mr. Blake."

His lips press to my forehead, holding their place. "Good. Because you've got me for the rest of your life, soon-to-be Mrs. Blake."

EPILOGUE

NINE MONTHS LATER

"Holy shit. I didn't think it was possible to be this nervous." I'm talking to myself, adjusting my bow tie in the mirror of my bedroom. When you plan a wedding, you learn a lot about yourself. Like how many friends you *don't* have. Bella wanted to have a huge bridal party. Unfortunately, I'm a lone wolf, so I couldn't match her six bridesmaids. We settled on a maid of honor—she chose Cherry—and a best man—mine being Mark.

Mark and I aren't exactly friends, but when you lack relationships with other humans, it's damn near impossible to find someone to stand next to you on your big day. Doesn't matter anyways. I don't need anyone but Bella. It's been proven to me time and time again that friendships aren't all they're cracked out to be. Everyone I've encountered in life has betrayed me in one way or another—all except Bella. And Peter, but he's not with us any longer.

I'll stay in my bubble on my island. Occasionally

venturing out for business or whisking Bella and Jaxon away on a family vacation. Then there's the obligatory family visits on holidays. I'll likely just drink my way through those, so I don't have to remember any of it.

Life is good.

Dave, Bella's dad, pokes his head in the open door. "They're ready for ya."

I take in a deep breath; one he must have heard because he's now walking toward me. "You all right, son?"

Son? I turn and look at him, a quizzical expression on my face. No one's ever called me that. Sure, I've been called a son of a bitch countless times, but no one's ever referred to me as *son*. I'm not really sure how to react to the title.

"Ugh. Yeah." I turn back to the mirror, fluffing the tips of my black hair. "I'm fine. Why do you ask?"

"Ya know, I remember the day I got married." I can see him in the reflection of the mirror standing behind me. He's gazing up at the ceiling, as if it's playing memories of his wedding day. "Best day of my life and the worst day of my life at the same time. If you think that's impossible," he looks down, a glint of humor in his words, "you're wrong."

I humor him as I continue to straighten my tie. "Oh yeah? How so?"

Dave places a hand on my shoulder; it's an odd feeling, and to be honest, it makes me feel uncomfortable. I'm not a fan of human touch unless it's coming from Bella. "You get to marry your best friend." He checks me with a smile. "But you also get her crazy family." My lips tug up in a smile as Dave continues, "Bella told me all about what happened before we adopted her and Mark. If you took Mark's place, well...then you probably wouldn't be marrying my daughter. Things always work out the way they're meant to." He pats my shoulder and leaves the room.

All these years, I've blamed Trent and Mark. So many nights of what-ifs and what-could-have-beens invaded my mind to the point of insanity. I spent my life plotting revenge against them, and Bella. I wanted to make them pay, while making her mine, whether she wanted me or not. Never once did I consider the outcome had I been adopted. She would have been my sister. Bella and I were never meant to be siblings; we were meant for so much more.

Chills skate down my entire body as the realization hits me—it has been fate all along.

"Ready, man?" Mark asks, poking his head in the door.

I really need to get used to other people being around. For a man who likes his privacy, it's definitely different.

I step away from the mirror, almost positive my tie is still crooked after messing with it for twenty damn minutes. "Yeah. All set."

"Wait until you see her. She's stunning."

My palms begin sweating profusely. Pretty sure this tie is trying to choke me. I loosen it a tad, then rub my hands together. "I'm sure she is." We leave the room and walk to the elevator.

I'm not good with words. Now I'm expected to stand in front of a crowd and speak from my heart, and I'm not so sure I can do it. If I had my way, we'd elope. No guests, just us. But Bella has always dreamed of a big wedding with a gown and family in attendance. We compromised on a small wedding with close friends and family in the courtyard here at Cori Cove.

"Hey. I'm not sure I ever told you...congrats, on the little man. Jaxon is adorable."

"Yeah. He's a keeper."

The day Jaxon was born was one of the best of my life. It'll be hard to beat, but today might be a close second. Bella decided on a home birth. It was just me, her, and the midwife. Everything was perfect and the minute I laid eyes on my baby boy, I couldn't imagine life without him. Bella did so good and I now have a new appreciation for women, particularly her. She's simply amazing.

We step into the elevator and the tension is thick as we make our way down. I should say something. Mark's been trying, and it's time I give a little on my end.

"I appreciate you standing up with me. I know we're not exactly friends."

"You're right, we're not." I can't tell if that's sarcasm or seriousness in his tone. "We're brothers now." He cracks a smile, and I do the same.

"Yeah. Yeah. I guess we are."

Walking out the back door, it's like my nerves have suddenly settled. It's a perfect day on the island. The sun is shining, it's not hot, but not cold. The flowers have bloomed, the trees have grown over. The entire area decorated in white gardenias. The fountain is running and it's the only sound present, aside from the small chatter of guests. Bella wanted to invite all the staff. Aside from them, it's just her family. She reached out to Bibs, an old friend from The Webster House, but she wasn't able to attend. It's a shame; it would have been nice to see Bibs all grown up. We did make plans to meet up in the city someday soon.

I hear Jaxon fussing with Linda, his grandma, so I put my hands out to take him for a minute before the ceremony begins.

"I thought we talked about this, buddy. You can't fuss on Mama's big day." He looks up at me with a cheeky grin, his two bottom teeth sticking up. "Can I count on you today?" He giggles and I kiss his forehead. "I thought so."

I hand him back to Linda, and she begins bouncing him again as he fusses for me. "You better get up front. She's coming," Linda says.

I glance over my shoulder, thinking I'll catch a glimpse, but Bella is nowhere in sight.

Mark and I make our way to the front, where Cherry is standing in a mint green gown with a bouquet of white gardenias.

With my hand held in front of me, I steal a glance at Peter's urn on a stand next to a vase of flowers. I thought it was insane, but Bella insisted he be here.

I take a deep breath as the music begins. We decided on the traditional wedding march because Bella said that's what she'd imagined when she pictured her future wedding.

I'm staring straight ahead when she steps out of the back doors of the castle. I can't even explain what overcomes me when I see her. Like Mark said, she's stunning. It's possible my heart has stopped beating altogether.

She takes slow, graceful steps toward me. Walking into our future together.

Her green eyes are wide and beautiful and outlined with makeup. Her brown hair is all up in some fancy updo with a see-through lace veil hanging over her face. An all-white dress that hugs tight to her frame and flows out into a train at the bottom. It's simple, yet elegant. Floral embroidery covers the full length, and that top. Fuck, that top. It dips down in a V, exposing her full cleavage.

With one arm wrapped around Dave's, she clenches the bouquet that matches Cherry's, and I can tell she's a ball of nerves.

I need her to hurry and get to me, so I can calm her. I want to take her hands and squeeze them, letting her know I'm always here when she's nervous or scared.

Just a few more steps. She's almost here. My heart begins racing, ready to do this. To make her my wife and begin our lives together.

She's here. And she takes my breath away.

"Hi," she whispers. Cherry steps out and takes her bouquet. I can't help but smile at her nervousness, it's cute as hell.

The officiant begins by asking, "Who gives this woman to be married today?"

"I do," Dave says before kissing Bella's cheek.

He steps back, then takes a seat in the front next to Linda, who is holding a bouncy Jaxon.

I reach out and take Bella's hand, walking her in front of the officiant. She's trembling, so I place my other hand overtop our clasped ones.

Our eyes lock as we seek stability in each other. My legs feel like they could give out at any moment.

The officiant rambles off some shit that I don't even

hear as I'm lost in her eyes. It's not until she squeezes my hand and nods toward the officiant that I realize it's my turn to speak.

"As I said, the bride and groom have decided to write their own vows. You may begin, Callum."

Shit. I had it all memorized. Replayed it in my head a thousand times, and now I'm drawing a complete blank.

I stutter, choke, and nothing comes out.

Mark leans over and whispers, "Just speak from the heart, man"

Speak from the heart. Okay. I can do this.

"Bella," I begin, still not sure what I'm going to say, "you came into my life when I least expected you. I was sure that I was meant to spend all my years alone. I'm not talking about the day you arrived here at Cori Cove. I'm going way back to The Webster House." I glance over my shoulder to where Mark stands, though I don't catch sight of him. Then I return my eyes to my bride. "You were my best friend. On the days I didn't get to see you, because I was in trouble, I counted the hours until I could be near you again. When you left, you took a piece of my heart with you, but I always knew, deep down, that we'd be together again. Whether it was orchestrated or simply fate. Regardless, we found our way. You complete me, Bella. You are the beauty I see in the world, the light in the darkness. You are the air I breathe. I promise to spend my entire life showing you how much I love you."

Tears fall from the corners of her eyes, and I can feel the sting in my own as they threaten to break free. I swallow hard, feeling a lump in my throat. I'm not sure what it is, but it's an odd sensation.

"Bella, you may begin."

"I wrote everything down, but of course, I lost it. That's me. Always misplacing things and ending up in places I don't belong." *She's not lying.* "So I'm winging this and I hope I get it right." Her throat clears. "When I was a little girl, I used to dream of my wedding day. I envisioned everything I wanted. I watched myself walk down the aisle to marry the love of my life. I have a confession," she smiles, "it was you I saw. When I was a kid, I pictured fourteen-year-old Cal. When I was a teenager, I tried to imagine what you looked like, and it was still you. There is no one in the entire world I would rather have as my husband and the father to my children. You love me in a way that makes me feel worthy. The safety of your arms is my favorite place to be. I love you more than all the castles, islands, and empires, Cal. It was always you."

I pull her to my chest, not sure if it's allowed, but hell if I care. I make my own rules. Bella begins sobbing softly against me, and I just hold her through it, even though I know they're happy tears. My heart squeezes, and at the same time, Jaxon squeals. We both laugh and look over at him.

Bella extends her hands to her mom, asking for our son.

Linda gets up and brings him over and we finish the wedding with the three of us becoming one happy family.

"You may kiss the bride."

And I do. I lift her veil, and I kiss her beautiful lips, over and over and over again.

"I'm pleased to introduce to you, Mr. and Mrs. Callum Blake."

We raise our held hands while everyone claps.
I did it. I got the girl.
The end.

If you liked this duet, check out the Redwood Rebels
Series. These boys will take you on a winding road of
suspense!
Read the full series here!

ALSO BY RACHEL LEIGH

Redwood Rebels Series

Book One: Striker Book Two: Heathen

Book Three: Vandal Book Four: Reaper

Redwood High Series

(All books can be read as a stand-alone)

Book One: Like Gravity

Book Two: Like You

Book Three: Like Hate

Fallen Kingdom Duet

His Hollow Heart & Her Broken Pieces

Black Heart Duet

Four & Five

Standalones

Devil Heir

Guarded

Claim your FREE copy of Her Undoing

ABOUT THE AUTHOR

Rachel Leigh is a USA Today bestselling author of new adult and contemporary romance with a twist. You can expect bad boys, strong heroines, and an HEA.

Rachel lives in leggings, overuses emojis, and survives on books and coffee. Writing is her passion. Her goal is to take readers on an adventure with her words, while showing them that even on the darkest days, love conquers all.

www.rachelleighauthor.com
Rachel's Ramblers Readers Group

facebook.com/rachelleighauthor
instagram.com/rachelleighauthor
goodreads.com/rachelleigh
amazon.com/author/rachelleighauthor

Made in the USA
Monee, IL
03 March 2022

92212519R00347